FARR NORTH
UNDERWORLD
NORTHERN SEA
ASHLANDS
CROWFOOT
SULNIK
BERGISH
SILVERFALL
QUARANTINE ZONE
GRAY SEA
KING'S CANYON
NENTUCK
IRONWOOD MOUNTAINS
URSANDOR
JERIKHAL
FARR EAST
EASTON
RODRICK'S WALL
THE BEARDS
TAYNE
BAY OF KNIVES
DASKEN
CODSWALLOW
TAEL
THE PHANTOM ISLES
FARR SOUTH

# THE RUINS BENEATH US

# The Ruins Beneath Us

SASHA E. SLOAN

HYPERION
Los Angeles New York

First Edition, March 2026
10 9 8 7 6 5 4 3 2 1
FAC-004510-25345
Printed in the United States of America

This book is set in Italian Old Style MT Pro/Monotype
Designed by Zareen Johnson
Stock image: morning glory 1772098355/Shutterstock
Map illustration by Virginia Allyn © 2026 by Disney Enterprises, Inc.

Library of Congress Control Number: 2025946655
ISBN 978-1-368-11751-7
Reinforced binding

The authorized representative in the EU for product safety and compliance is Disney Trading B.V., Asterweg 15S, 1031 HL, Amsterdam, The Netherlands
email: DCP.DL-EU.bookscontact@disney.com

Visit www.HyperionTeens.com

Logo Applies to Text Stock Only

*For Grammy,*

*who always believed in my Talent*

Alas, that love, whose view is muffled still,
Should, without eyes, see pathways to his will!
—William Shakespeare, *Romeo & Juliet*

# 1

ne door, two locks, and a gate. That's all that stands between me and freedom.

I find myself gazing out the window of my attic in the hour after waking. It's just before dawn, and I can hear Mother downstairs in the kitchen. She always cooks a big meal before a trip. The commotion is comforting, so I listen for a while: cracking eggs, a whirring whisk, sizzling butter. I'll take all the comfort I can get.

My night was nearly sleepless. I spent it rehearsing the same speech I've been prepping for weeks, awaiting a morning like this one.

This time will be different.

I eventually rise and tug on a linen work dress. My wardrobe is simple, far from the luxurious gowns I've read about in books. Mother values practicality over everything, and it's not like I have anyone to impress out here in the Ironwoods. I glance in the mirror and fold a silken kerchief in a triangle before fastening it over my long hair, making sure the sides of the fabric cover the tips of my ears—a habit I've had since I was little. Touching my earlobes, I murmur an incantation I've been practicing for concealment. Then I fasten my apron and slip on boots before checking under my bed for the satchel I packed the night prior. It contains gloves, snowshoes, extra woolen socks, and a two-week supply of dried meat—everything I'll need for the journey north.

Mother is a Healer, and one of the best in the world at her craft. Her work often demands long journeys to procure rare ingredients or tend to her patients. We make our living brewing potions for markets across the Midlands. Today, she's leaving for Sulnik, the icy kingdom to our north. The road is dangerous—slick in the colder months and a bandit's paradise in the thaw, or so I've been told. But I don't worry too much about Mother. She can handle herself.

She wouldn't say the same about me.

I tiptoe downstairs and find her tying her bootlaces by the door. In a hurry, apparently. There's a plate for me on the table, but hers is already in the washbasin. I sit and tuck in cautiously, tracking her expression like a weather vane.

Mother's face is beautiful, lightly lined and highly expressive. She tells me she's over three hundred years old, but to any human she would look middle-aged at most. Thick dark hair sits atop her head in a heap of braids. Her eyebrows pinch when she's nervous, and this morning, they've formed a jagged peak.

"There's plenty of food in the pantry," she says by way of hello. "Everything's labeled. You'll have to finish the everhart while I'm gone."

"No problem," I say, sighing. I can always expect instructions on her way out the door.

"I was also thinking you could start on the all's-cure," she continues, casting me an uncertain look. "There's a full moon next week, and the meadowblood is coming to seed. You'll have to ensure the cauldron is clean before you start."

I fight the urge to roll my eyes. I've trained as her apprentice since I could talk, and all's-cure is one of dozens of recipes I have memorized. But nothing escapes her scrutiny. Mother has a potioneer's mind: detail-oriented to a fault. She's always criticizing my work or warning me to slow down.

"And we could use another batch of silvertongue."

"I'm on it." I fiddle with my fork, strategizing my moment of opportunity. "Do you need help loading the cart?"

"No, thank you," she says. "I'm not taking much to trade."

There goes my speech. Half my argument was that I could help her peddle her wares. "Why not?"

"This is more of an investigatory trip," she says, fastening a cloak around her shoulders.

"What does that mean?"

"Nothing you need to worry about."

I swallow my irritation. Before I turned eighteen, I hoped adulthood would mean she'd stop treating me like a child in need of sheltering. But Mother's been protecting me for so long, I'm not sure she knows how to stop.

"So, you're not going to Sulnik?" I ask, trying to sound casual.

She sighs. "I'm going to a village near the border to investigate some rumblings about a plague. There's no proof, just rumors. But I figured it's worth a visit, to see if I can help."

Her tone tells me I'll get no further details. I frown, skewering an egg yolk. Rumor of a plague explains her apprehension but doesn't bode well for my plans. I recalibrate my argument while she checks her bags.

I've never seen Mother in anything except her work clothes: a no-frills tunic, skirts with numerous pockets, and a belt for her personal quiver of potions. The belt is notched with six hooks, strung with six finger-length bottles. Labels aren't necessary. We know the color and shape of each by heart. After running her fingers over the set, Mother scoops up her apothecary bag by the door and steps out into the cold.

Normally that might suffice for goodbye. Mother isn't sentimental, and she travels too often for either of us to get gooey about it. But I'm determined to say my piece—investigatory trip or not—so I grab my cloak and follow her outside.

She brushes snow off the wagon while I stroll to the paddock. Our horse, Tucker, trots over and presses his big head against my chest. I tickle his velvet nose while Mother circles our yard, mumbling.

Mother is a creature of routine. Setting the wards that protect our cottage is an important piece of our parting ritual. The spells will conceal the cottage, sight and sound, so long as one of us stays inside the boundaries. I've never been good at spellwork. That's just one of the many ways I fall short in her eyes.

As she makes her laps, I catch myself staring at her ears. The surgeon's handiwork is commendable. If I didn't know what to look for, I couldn't pick out the scars where the long, tapered tips were docked into humanoid stubs. She cut her ears around the time the Verdish Empire seized control, a common practice for Elves seeking anonymity.

When Mother was growing up in these mountains, they were still part of Evermore, the ancient kingdom of Elves that once controlled the heart of the Midlands. But that was three hundred years ago, before the Long War, when a human tyrant waged a bloody campaign to steal the land for himself.

His name was King Verdin. History knows him as Verdin the Vanquisher. Originally, he ruled over a small coastal kingdom called Dornak in the north, but Verdin wanted more. Hungry for expansion, he set his sights on neighboring Evermore and determined the best way to reach his goal was by seeding division.

Humans have long mistrusted magic, which is intertwined with Elven culture and religion. Verdin leveraged that fear, propagating the lie that Evermoreans secretly aspired to use magic to gain dominion over humankind. He proclaimed that runic spellcraft was evil, and that those born with magical abilities should be hunted to ensure peace throughout the land. The Midlands have long been plagued by magical daemons from the realm of the dead, so Verdin blamed the Elves for their existence, falsely casting these daemons as Evermorean servants.

He spread his hatred far and wide, rallying an army intent on destroying the Elven kingdom. A century of senseless bloodshed ensued. Verdin ordered Evermore's capital razed by dragonfyre, an act of cruelty that brought the Elves to their knees. He died smiling.

His son and grandson continued his violent legacy, forcing our people into further and further retreat. The Elven leader, King Amos, last of the great Aldain dynasty, died of a broken heart after seeing what was left of his subjects. His wife, Queen Soleste, surrendered their home to Verdin's kin.

Evermore became part of the new empire, renamed Verdinae in honor of the Vanquisher—a new kingdom in which all magic was outlawed and the land claimed by humans.

Under the new world order, speaking the old Elven language and worshipping our Gods are punishable by death, making it almost impossible for Elves to exist peacefully in Verdinae without giving up our core beliefs. After the collapse, my mother and the few surviving Evermoreans faced dismal choices: flee, die, or learn to live in the shadows. The smart ones got out early and found refuge in friendlier kingdoms like Sontaag or Ursandor. The lucky ones died quickly. But Elves like Mother, who couldn't bear to abandon her homeland, learned how to hide.

Despite years of begging, she has refused to clip my ears like hers. I always argue rationally that I'd be safer without them. She always counters with a rousing speech about my beautiful Elven heritage and the indomitable spirit of Evermore. Sometimes I'm tempted to hack them off myself. But that's just one of plenty of ways we don't see eye to eye. For example, she still believes that Evermore will one day be restored to its former glory. I've never told her just how far-fetched I find that idea. In the centuries since the Long War, Verdin's descendants have only continued his legacy of hatred. The Verdish Church and their anti-magic philosophies are stronger than ever. Almost no Elves remain in our homeland. And if anyone knew that *I* was born with magic, I'd be executed on sight.

A fact Mother has never let me forget.

After lapping three times, Mother seems satisfied with her spellwork. I put a halter on Tucker and lead him to the cart, and she fastens his harness while I scratch his head.

This is my moment. I won't get another chance. With Mother's back to me, and with the big horse for assurance, I find the courage to finally say, "Mother, I have a proposition. Before you say no, please hear me out."

Her hands freeze over the buckles. When she turns, her sunken expression is an answer in itself. "Lyria, not now."

Pain lances my chest, and I look away so she doesn't see my chin wobble. This is the answer I'm used to—the same one I'd get as a little girl, when I'd beg and sob for her to not leave me alone again. I got so used to her refusal that I stopped asking.

But I'm not a little girl anymore.

And I'm no longer scared.

I'm angry.

"I've given it a lot of thought," I say carefully, tempering my rising frustration. "I figured out a delayed irrigation system so the garden is taken care of while we're gone. And I'm getting *loads* better at handling my Talent. I could help with the plague—"

She cuts me off. "We're not having this conversation."

*NO!* I bite down a scream. "Why not?"

"Because."

In her eyes, this answer has always been enough. But it's never been enough for me.

"I-I've already packed a bag." My voice finally breaks, and now my carefully worded speech comes barreling out too quickly. "I won't make any trouble. I'll do everything exactly as you say. I can even use a concealment charm to hide my ears. See?"

I pull off my kerchief to show her, but Mother looks far from impressed. Confused, I flinch a hand up to feel the tips and realize they're still pointed. *No, no, no! I practiced this!*

Mother just shakes her head. "Not today, Lyria."

"Then when?"

"When it's safe," she says.

"It's never going to be safe!"

I can't count how many times we've cycled through this. She claims to be worried about safety, but I know what she's *really* afraid of.

As if proving her point, heat starts to simmer under my skin. I look away and force a long, deep breath, clamping down on my inner cheek until the pain centers me.

*Calm down, Lyria.*

I stare out toward the distant tree line and quivering aspens. This forest raised and sheltered me. But it has imprisoned me, too. "I can't stay locked up forever," I finally mumble, and I hate how childish it sounds.

A rare flash of sympathy softens her eyes. It's almost worse than her anger. Mother draws toward me, offering a stiff hand on my shoulder, and I breathe in her familiar scent: cinnamon and soil and fresh bread. "I know that it's hard, and I know that it's not fair," she says gently. "But it's my job to put your safety first. Even before your happiness. Do you understand?"

I've run out of arguments, so I nod my defeat. "I understand."

"When you're older and have full control of your magic, we can talk about going out together," she says. "But while your power is unpredictable—"

"I said *I get it.*"

*If they catch you, they will kill you.* That's the foremost rule of my existence.

They call it a *Talent,* with a capital *T.* While our Elven heritage makes living in Verdinae dangerous, my Talent is the reason we're on the run. It's the thing they'd kill me for regardless of whether we followed their laws. They say Verdin feared nothing more than bloodborne Talents, the magical gifts that some Elves are born with. Anyone can cast spells with runes like Mother does. A Talent is different. It's magic woven into my very soul.

I'm speaking of us like I've met another Talent. I haven't. I'm just hoping I'm not the last one.

I never knew my father, but I can only assume he was a powerful wielder, since it's his power that flows through my veins. Talents used to be as common as freckles among Elves. We can trace their inception back to our first Gods, the Three Sisters, who gifted a portion of their power to the founders of Evermore. In the old days, Mother tells me, Faeries used to attend Elven name day ceremonies, to bestow gifts upon Elven newborns and predict their Talents in honor of the Gods. Mother knew Elves with Talents to control the elements, predict futures, or even read minds. But when the Verdish Empire took over after the Long War, the Faeries vanished so completely that some claim they never existed, and Elves with bloodborne Talents were systematically hunted and slaughtered until entire magical bloodlines were snuffed out.

To protect me from that fate, Mother took me into hiding after my abilities manifested. Our sanctuary is the Ironwoods, the same mountain range where she grew up back when this land knew peace. The Ironwoods are famously inhospitable and plagued by monsters, but that inhospitality has sheltered us for nearly two decades. She planned to raise me in seclusion just until I gained control of my power, something that typically comes as easy as breathing for Elves. But my Talent is different. It's never fully yielded to my will. Our books say it's supposed to feel pleasantly warm and tingly when stress causes magic to flare, but in my case, I get more *searing agony* than *pleasant tingle.* There's something wrong with it . . . or maybe just something wrong with *me.*

Mother leans in to kiss my forehead. "I'll be gone for three weeks. Practice your spells and keep the hearth fire burning. And *don't cross the wardlines.*"

I don't ask again.

---

Routine is one of the few methods of making isolation bearable. In the wake of Mother's departure, I cling to it like a drowning person.

First, I tidy the cottage. One by one, I check the objects populating our home. I say good morning to the teakettle, good morning to my favorite chipped cup, good morning to my sewing kit, good morning to my books and chalk and painting set.

Once everything's in order, I venture outside. Our cottage sits near a glassy lake in a secluded valley. We've stayed here longer than anywhere else I can remember—six months, give or take. Typically, we "travel with the bloom," pursuing the rare medicinal flowers she uses in potions. The meadowblood in this particular valley only has weeks before it'll disappear again for years. In our garden, we grow a host of other plants commonly used in our potions. I can greet each blossom like old friends: *nettlewood, grizzlefoot, nocturn, dillfeather.* . . .

I love the Ironwoods almost as much as I long to escape them. There's usually plenty to do, like exploring the cliffs or swimming in the lake, but I'm only allowed out under Mother's supervision. Her absence constrains me within the wardlines encircling our property: the yard, the paddock, the outhouse, and the shed. I can talk to the chickens or weave daisy chains, but that's about it. If it's not too cold, I'll throw knives at a target board to blow off steam. I got good at it a few summers back. My most prized possession is a dagger with runes carved into the handle. It rarely leaves the sheath strapped to my belt, and I sleep with it under my pillow. The blade belonged to my father, who died not long after I was born.

Odds are, he was murdered for possessing the same power they'd kill me for. Mother won't talk about him. She's never even told me his name. I instinctively reach toward my belt to trace the grooves on the handle, which are worn smooth. My father's always been my favorite daydream. I used to imagine he'd show up at our doorstep and we'd start living as a happy family.

Now I just dream that he'll come to take me away.

By late morning, the sun has melted any trace of snow. It's a beautiful spring day, and the mountains are humming with their familiar music. I love the babble of the stream and singing cicadas and know every songbird's call by heart. As I wander toward the fence, I tip my face to the sun and inhale, savoring the complex perfume. My Elven senses can mark every earthly and living thing in this valley: the watercress, pines, peonies, forget-me-nots, salt and honey, a nearby beehive, a distant skunk, and something else, something warmer . . .

Every muscle in my body goes still.

Something *human*.

My head snaps toward the forest, and my eyes lock onto the figure barely a stone's throw away, partially concealed by the trees.

A boy.

A *human* boy.

For an instant, I'm petrified with all-consuming panic. Then I remember *he can't see me*. Ward spells conceal our cottage, so if Mother's spellwork is sound (and it's *always* sound), I'm invisible.

Still, I'm frozen. Transfixed.

I've seen glimpses of humans before—the rare traveler or occasional unlucky corpse—but I've never seen a boy like *this*. Close enough to count his chestnut-colored curls. He's tall and broad-shouldered, wearing a fine green tunic with a sword sheathed at his hip. When he turns, I'm given a complete view of his entire face, all sharp lines and soaring cheekbones. Every feature is balanced and symmetrical, from his full, slightly parted lips to the faint shadows under his eyes. The set of his brow is boyish but not naive. Earnest but not haughty. He's absurdly handsome—a potential lead in one of the dog-eared romance sagas Mother hides under her pillow. He could have been carved by Aurelis herself: a testament to the Goddess of Beauty. A hero from my daydreams.

It occurs to me he might be the most gorgeous creature I've ever seen.

His eyes flicker, and our gazes seem to lock. For a moment, I wonder against possibility if he can see me somehow....

Then, without warning, he turns and vanishes back into the trees.

*"Wait!"* I cry out before I can stop myself.

Not that it matters. The wardlines are sound. I'm inaudible.

I'm left with a racing heart and an unbearable lightheadedness, staring at the spot where he stood. The trees look just as they did, rustling in the gentle breeze.

I'm alone.

I will always be alone.

---

It's a long time before I can force myself to trudge back inside.

Clicking the door shut behind me might as well be slamming the bars of my cell. I can't remember feeling more trapped or hopeless.

Rising underneath those emotions is an existential rage so potent it wrenches my guts.

I think I hate Mother. I know I hate *myself.* I hate the Verdish Empire for its tyranny. I hate King Amos and Queen Soleste for yielding Evermore all those years ago. I hate the Gods for allowing it. Most of all, I hate the Talent swelling under my skin.

By twilight, I've retreated deep inside myself. There's a dark place that I sink to in my lowest moments—a place where I'm nothing, and no one at all. I'm alone like this, near-catatonic and pondering my existence, when I hear it.

It's a boy's voice, rising from the distant forest.

*"HELP!"*

I stand, then immediately sit. There's no doubt he's far past the wardlines, but to my Elven ears, he might as well be standing beside me.

He cries again, louder this time—*"HELP!"*—before the word contorts into a shriek. I'm seized by the memory of the stranger I saw earlier, imagining his handsome face twisted in terror.

I can't say exactly *why* I do what I do next.

Maybe it's brave. Heroic, even. Maybe I'm being noble. But maybe it's something else, more impulsive and selfish. Maybe it's eighteen years of resentment that launches me onto my feet. Maybe I've simply had enough of doors and locks and waiting.

It doesn't matter.

What matters is that I *run.* Out the door, past the wardlines, through the garden gate . . .

And into the beckoning world beyond.

# 2

I haul myself through the underbrush at top speed, vaulting boulders and snapping branches.

The boy's screams grow louder with each step. I pump my arms to gain speed until I hurtle over a ridgetop, then skid to a stop and try to make sense of what I see.

A swamp lies before me, murky violet in the fading sun. Two figures grapple in the shallows, engaged in what can only be described as a death match. The smaller, muck-covered one is the handsome boy I saw earlier. He's got his sword raised to face off with a much larger monster.

Terror curls in my stomach as I think, *He has no idea what he's facing.*

I'm familiar with the Moragorion, though only from descriptions in books. This one is fearsome: tall as a bear, with a gaping jaw like a crocodile. Legends call the Moragorion the Lord of the Swamp, the most dominant of all amphibious killers. An apex predator.

Everything about the Moragorion speaks of death, from the dark scales rippling over his barrel chest to his hunched posture, like a coiling snake about to strike. He's got a wide flat head like a hornet, with bulging eyes so large there's barely any space between them on his skull. Those jaws? They're for dragging prey into a death roll. Those claws? They're for gutting.

The Moragorion is one of many daemons that roam the wastelands near the Demeridian, the river that marks the border between our world and the realm of the dead. He's exactly the type of fearsome creature that drove most people out of the Ironwoods. In recent years, daemon attacks have become troublingly common, forcing most to migrate into the protected Hartlands, though I've never heard of one roaming beyond Sulnik. How he got this far south is a mystery.

I watch, horror-stricken, as the boy swings at the monster's head, missing by an inch.

*I should run*. My mother's voice and every shred of training shrieks to do so.

But something else screams louder.

*I cannot let him die.*

So, at the top of my lungs, I bellow, "*HEY!* OVER HERE!"

The distraction works. As the Moragorion turns, the boy seizes the opportunity to swing at the monster's exposed neck. But the blow glances off the rippling scales, and the Moragorion shrieks. Before I can think, he smashes a mighty paw into the human's chest.

I hear the distinct *crunch* of bone and tearing flesh, and then the boy slams into the mud. I might have *felt* his lung puncture. Something in me uproots, and I charge, roaring as I ram the Moragorion at top speed. I lean to absorb the impact with my shoulder, but it's like running into a wall.

I crumple with an embarrassing huff. Taking note, the monster emits a guttural croak in a low pitch so awful and ancient, I want to cover my ears. I want to *hide*. The Moragorion's jagged teeth snap at me in warning, but it turns back to advance on the boy, who has managed to crawl a short distance away.

This is going to be a massacre.

I fumble in the mud for something, *anything*. My fingers close on a rock, and I draw back my fist, hurling it toward the Moragorion with all my strength. It hits the beast's temple with a pitiful crack.

Then it turns its big, ugly head toward me.

I curse and scramble back, skittering like a crawdad.

*Run, run, run!* I think desperately. But I can't get my footing. I thrash in the mud as the monster slinks toward me. I can see its face clearly now: dark, gleaming eyes and a great hinged maw covered in muck.

There doesn't seem to be anything to its face but eyes and jaws. *Where the hell is its brain?*

I don't have time to consider before the Moragorion swipes. I soar through the air, smashing face-first into the shallow water so hard my teeth split my lip. I taste blood and foul water. Everything hurts. I roll over and blink at the sky, fighting for air.

That inner voice shouts, *Get up and fight!*

My legs wobble as I push myself up. My ankle is shot. But the Moragorion has turned back toward his human prey. *What next? What can I try?* As he winds up for another swipe, I sense a death blow, and I howl uselessly, *"DON'T—"*

One hit sends the boy careening, and my guts roll along with him.

He crashes into the shallow water, and this time, he does not rise. Jaws widening, the Moragorion slinks closer, perhaps aiming to swallow him whole. And the realization seizes me once again: *I cannot let him die.*

So I do something I will inevitably regret.

I reach for my Talent.

The power sits at the base of my spine, white-hot and iridescent, like a coil of lightning spiraling into a bottomless well. Drawing on it feels like tugging on a spool of invisible thread. One sharp pull, and when the bobbin starts spinning . . .

Magic surges through my skin, pooling at my palms. Every hair stands on end as I train the energy on the hulking figure. Then, with a tug of the thread . . .

I bid his organs to grow three times their size.

The Moragorion freezes, his shrieks cut off with a guttural *glug*. His eyes roll, flashing white, and he wobbles.

I pull harder. I will his guts to grow, to swell, to *explode* . . .

Until he collapses, destroyed from the inside out.

I run straight toward the boy. I don't want to see what I've done. Worse, I don't want to think about how disgustingly *good* I feel. Unleashing the magic I usually fight to suppress is pure relief. Every limb tingles like I'm suddenly intoxicated. I feel euphoric, teeming with energy, like I could sprint a hundred miles *and* fight off a dozen mountain lions.

But death is my current enemy. Reaching the boy, I seize him beneath the shoulders and lift him from the water, thanking the Gods for my Elven strength as I carry him to the bank. To my relief, he chokes and gags as swampy water pours out of his mouth. His face is ruined and bloodied, his skull cracked, and he's gushing blood above his left eye, but he's *breathing.*

Shaking, I anchor my senses. He's alive, but just barely. His mortality might be measured in minutes or seconds. In our training, Mother taught me the fundamentals of trauma medicine—when and how to react, in theory. But theory isn't life.

My hands tremble as my will cleaves in two. *I've done too much already*. But I'm overwhelmed with empathy for this human, who I know with mounting certainty is about to bleed out in front of me.

For one willful moment, I reach out and touch his face. My fingers find the line between his jaw and ear, coarse with stubble and warm with blood. The contact lights every fiber of my being, and it's like the whole world narrows to this moment . . . this beautiful creature. It's wrong, touching him like this, but it feels *right*, somehow, like my very soul is singing. Everything and nothing. An end before a beginning. I never even got to meet him.

He struggles in my arms, straining for air. I wipe spittle from the edge of his mouth, wondering how many breaths he has left.

*If they catch you, they will kill you.*

*But if I leave him, he will die.*

So, with his broken body in my hands, I make a split-second decision.

I throw him over my shoulder and trudge off toward home.

I put him up in my mother's bed, since the prospect of him sleeping in mine is, of course, unfathomable. After checking his airways, I administer nocturn to keep him sedated. Then I assess his injuries. It's even worse than it looks. He has a skull fracture, a slew of broken bones, and half a dozen organs requiring reconstruction. Complicated, messy stuff—healing that stretches the limits of what I've even studied in theory.

My Talent demands total concentration. Before the war, Elves with Talents would train under Mages to hone their unique skills. Without a Mage to teach me, and no one but myself and Mother to practice on, it's taken years to master even simple injuries like a skinned knee or a broken finger. First, I visualize each intertwining strand of his life force. Then I push and pull on each thread with the precision of a master tailor. Any mistake could be deadly. I hold my breath as I draw upon my power to mend his skull, his organs, his leg, and finally the fractures and gash in his chest. Once he's stable, I pump him full of restorative potions and slather his wounds with salves.

While he sleeps, I strip off his clothing (averting my eyes from the unpleasantries) and search for any identifying items. He'd been carrying little when he was attacked. I find no identification or papers, just a compass, a small traveler's map of the Midlands, his sword, the sheath strapped to his belt, and a pouch of coins I refrain from counting.

His body fascinates me. He's massive, at least a head taller than me, and yet still has the puppyish look of someone with a growth spurt ahead of them. His arms and shoulders are muscled, his hands callused. I notice cracked and bleeding skin in the webbing between his forefinger and thumb. His nails are bitten to the quick. He's hairy, too, hairy *everywhere*—a revelation I find particularly intriguing. As the swelling reduces, his features emerge sharp and symmetrical: a straight nose, thick eyebrows, and a wide, haughty mouth over a sharp little chin. I can't place his age. Eighteen? Twenty?

Next, I prepare the cottage, removing anything that might reveal our Elven heritage. My mother's spellbooks get shoved into a knapsack at the back of our closet. We keep a customary altar to Elowyn,

Goddess of Life, in the east window, which must also be deconstructed. I move the flowers to the kitchen table, string the seashells over my bed, and tuck the prayer slips into a napkin drawer, feeling somewhat guilty over the arrangement. My kerchief stays knotted tightly over my ears, but I recite the concealment charm every few hours as a precaution. It becomes habitual to brush the tips with my fingers, ensuring my spellwork is sound this time.

Perpetual motion over the next few days leaves little time to ponder the consequences of my decisions—something I'm avoiding at all costs. It's a technique I learned from Mother. If my mind is busy with the problem in front of me, there's no space for anything else. So I act as she does when she's troubled: fussing, double-checking, sweeping the floor just to have something to do with my hands.

Then, on the eighth morning, I see it.

A twitch. It's so subtle that at first, I'm convinced I imagined it. But then . . .

Again. His eyelids. They're fluttering.

He's about to wake up.

My stomach lurches. I back up, suddenly keen to put space between us. He doesn't move again for a long while, but I know we've turned a corner. I pace the cottage, with my stomach in knots. I wash and rewash my hands. In an abundance of caution, I find some rope and tie his ankles together and knot his wrists to the bedposts—can't have him trying to kill me after he regains consciousness. I've got my father's dagger, of course, but I swipe another knife from the kitchen and tuck it into my apron. Just in case. Then I take a seat beside him.

What feels like hours (but may have been minutes) later, his eyelids twitch again.

Then, softly, he moans, *"Eeeeaaaaarrrrhhhtttsssssssss."*

I bolt upright, heart thundering.

He moans again faintly. *"Errrrryythhhhhnnnhrrrts."*

"Sorry—I don't understand," I say. Perhaps he doesn't speak the common tongue? "You've got some strong medicine in your system."

*"Everything hurts."* His eyes open.

Slowly, he looks left to right, then up and down, appraising the rafters, the bubbling cauldron by the stove, and the narrow steps leading to my bedroom in the attic, lingering on each detail like he's memorizing it. My mind races, imagining what he might think of the house, the bedding, his bandages. Does it seem *other*? Peculiar?

Finally, his gaze finds me.

I'm hardly breathing as we lock into a staring contest that stretches on and on for eternity. Then, with a bolt of new and profound self-consciousness, I consider: *What does he think of* me?

I run a self-inventory. My hair, always fairer and finer than my mother's, is tied back into a sloppy braid underneath my kerchief. My work dress is threadbare and faded but clean. As far as I can tell, we appear to be approximately similar in terms of looks. Same brown hair, freckled skin, and sharp nose. Still, I wonder, *Can he tell what I am? Are things about to get violent?*

He clears his throat, breaking the silence. "Well . . ." His voice is deep and ragged from neglect. "Good morning."

I shiver, though the cottage is warm. "Good morning. I'm glad you're awake."

A knot bobs in his throat. "Why . . ." He coughs, hands twitching in the restraints. "Why am I tied up?"

"That's for my safety."

"For *your* safety?" he repeats, eyebrows rising.

"Yes." My voice sounds about an octave too high. "I need to be sure you're not a threat before I allow you to move freely."

"Right." A laugh rumbles out of him. "Since we're establishing present threats, how exactly did I end up in your bed?"

Does he really not remember?

"You were attacked," I explain tentatively. "I heard you screaming for help . . . and I came."

"I remember the attack," he mumbles. "I don't remember anything after."

As if recalling the fight, my Talent swells into my fingertips. I push it back down. *Not now.*

Feeling feverish, I share the story exactly as I've rehearsed it. I tell him that Mother's a Healer and I'm her apprentice, and we live in the Ironwoods to enable our foraging. All true. I tell him I got to the swamp in time to see him slay the Moragorion. Less true. But I'm hoping that the cocktail of shock, head trauma, and relief will keep him from digging further. For good measure, I add an elaborate lie about building a makeshift stretcher to drag him the half mile home—since a human girl couldn't carry him as I did. Maybe the story works, because he goes on gaping with that look I can't decipher. It's not cold, but it's not altogether warm, either.

"Was that . . ." His lips twitch, like he's choosing his words carefully. "Was that before or after you tied me to your bed?"

"It's not *my* bed," I correct him. "It's my mother's."

He smirks. "Ah. An important distinction."

I fold my arms, leveling the most menacing glare I can muster at him. "Do *not* mistake my compassion for weakness. I have a weapon, and I know how to use it."

"I'm sure you do." His smirk grows, which I can't understand.

*Isn't he scared? Should I brandish my dagger?*

"You think this is funny?" I scowl, brow knitting.

"Far from it," he says. "I just don't understand your approach. You rescue me, but now here I am, tied up and apparently in need of rescue. Your motives aren't exactly straightforward."

I shift my weight. "I'm not going to allow you to take advantage of me."

"No taking advantage allowed. Noted." He flexes his hands. "How long have I been out?"

"Eight days."

As his fingers regain mobility, they twitch toward his bandaged chest. His brow furrows like Mother's does when trying to recall a complicated recipe. I practically see the wheels in his head turn. Softly, he asks, "It was bad, wasn't it?"

"Pretty bad, yes."

Again, I can't read his expression. Horror, maybe? Shock? Awe?

"What did you call that thing?" he asks. "The monster?"

My arms prickle. "A Moragorion."

"That's what I thought. A *Moragorion*," he repeats, with an audible reverence. "I thought they were bedtime stories."

"Well, they're real. And you're lucky to be alive."

He gazes back at me, and I'm struck with a blistering sense of being perceived. It's not a good feeling. "Who *are* you?"

The question draws a lump to my throat. Because what kind of answer can I give him? Certainly not the truth. *Hello there, I'm Lyria. I'm eighteen years old, I like long walks and cinnamon rolls, and I'm pretty sure my mother thinks I'm a monster. . . .*

I counter instead. "Why does it matter?"

"You saved my life, and you won't even tell me your name?" He looks incredulous.

"I don't see how it's relevant."

For some maddening reason, he chuckles. I'm taken aback by how laughter somehow makes him even more handsome. His face folds with perfect symmetry, and the skin pinches at the corners of his eyes, like butterfly wings.

My cheeks burn. "What were you even doing in the forest, anyway? You're not from here."

"What gave it away?"

"Believing Moragorions are bedtime stories, for one."

He sighs. "No. I'm not from the Ironwoods. I . . . was looking for someone."

I wait for him to continue.

"If I tell you, will you untie me?"

"I'm not making any promises."

He studies me for a moment, like he's measuring whether I'm serious. Evidently deciding I am, he frowns. "Fine. The truth is my father is a hunter, among many other things," he finally says. "Ever since he was a boy, he dreamed about tracking down a . . . *particular* beast. But he was never successful. My younger brother, Damien, just turned sixteen. In old Dornik families, it's customary to get your portion of the inheritance at that age, and my parents are very traditional. Damien's got this *massive* ego, and he had these expectations stuck in his mind. . . ."

He shakes his head, breaking off. "Anyway, my father didn't give Damien what he thought he was going to get. And he was really royally pissed about it. So he made a big show of storming off to the mountains to find the beast and bring it back as a trophy. Y'know, to prove to my father that he's a better man or whatever."

I try to absorb this. I'm familiar with Dornak, though it's not a pleasant association—it's the coastal region where King Verdin originally ruled before the Long War. The Dornik are descendants of seafaring raiders, infamous for their bloodlust and skepticism toward magic. Considering their violent history, it tracks for Dornik traditions to involve violence. But Mother and I have only ever hunted because we were hungry. I can't wrap my head around killing for sport, or worse, spite. "What was he hunting?"

"A fyrehound."

Every muscle in my body stills. "A . . . fyrehound?" I repeat, feeling sick.

Fyrehounds are sacred to Elves. Our connection dates back thousands of years, to when warriors rode them in battle during the golden age of Evermore. It used to be customary for children to bond with a pup when they started training with a sword. But after the Long War, humans hunted the fyrehounds into extinction, a symbolic way of crushing Elven resistance. It's almost too much to hope that there might still be some fyrehounds left—survivors, like Mother and me.

"Is that why you're in the Ironwoods, then?" I ask, unable to keep the disdain out of my voice. "You're trying to beat your brother to the punch?"

"I was trying to stop him from doing something I thought he'd regret. Clearly, that plan is going great."

"Well," I say, scowling, "maybe it's the universe passing judgment."

"You're saying I deserved to be attacked?"

"I'm saying hunting for sport is immoral."

He looks exasperated. "Listen, Damien is a menace, all right? He was either going to do something terrible or get himself hurt in the process. That's what jackass little brothers do. I never wanted to be here. I thought he was way off base looking in the Ironwoods, anyway. Everything I've heard suggests the target was near Sulnik."

I fold my arms, huffing. "I'd like to meet this brother."

"Why? So you can tie him to your bed, too?"

"It's not *my* bed."

"Ah, yes. It's your *mother's* bed. Much better." He starts to chuckle, but the sound snags, and he starts hacking instead.

I rush forward, reaching for his chest. "Take it easy. You're not out of the woods yet." I edge closer. "Mind if I check your bandages?"

He coughs until his shoulders slump in surrender. "Go ahead."

As I peel back his shirt to examine him, my hands tremble. Fortunately, he's mending well. The gash through his chest still looks nasty, but the lung's rebounded. His skull fracture has closed. As I re-dress his wounds, I scan surreptitiously underneath. My magic lets me perceive his pain, sampling it like dipping my toes into hot water. His innards feel like they've been carved out with spoons. His skull feels shrunken by two sizes.

At last, I pull away. He needs to sleep before I can use my Talent on him again. I can slip nocturn into his food, but he needs to trust me enough to eat it. So I take a deep breath and offer an olive branch. "My name is Lyria. What about you?"

"I'm Finn." His eyes meet mine, and for the first time, I notice their color. It's green with hints of gold, like an oak leaf held up against the sun. Something flutters in my chest as he smiles. "It's nice to meet you, Lyria."

# 3

have a problem.

In the beginning, I took every precaution with Finn. His hands and feet stay tied to the bed. I allow him up only three times a day to attend to his needs. These trips are taken under supervision, and with a weapon at his back. He makes countless attempts at conversation, but I stonewall the camaraderie with a stoic and, hopefully, menacing persona.

My problem is that the whole stoic-and-menacing thing becomes increasingly difficult to maintain because Finn turns out to be charming.

Extremely, *annoyingly* charming.

"I'm beginning to think you've got a streak of voyeurism," he informs me one morning, three days after awakening. Finn walks ahead on his way to the outhouse, limping slightly, and I follow with a crossbow. On this, our *ninth* trip to the outhouse, I'm starting to question my resolve about the whole arrangement. "What do you mean?"

"The whole frog-marching to the privy thing. I think you get off on it."

"I get what?" I ask.

"Get off?" Finn grins over his shoulder. "Meaning you find it sexy? It *stirs* something within you?"

I try not to look as confused as I feel. "Nothing's . . . *stirring.*"

"I wouldn't judge you," Finn teases. "It's good when a lady knows what she wants."

"The only thing I want is for you to shut up."

"I'm just saying." He shrugs. "The whole arrangement is suspiciously kinky."

*Kinky?* My face flames. Though I might not be familiar with the term, his smirk makes the insinuation clear. But I refuse to reveal my ignorance. "Has anyone ever told you that you're a pain in the ass?"

"Plenty. Who told *you* to be so afraid of people?"

"My mother," I snap. "Didn't yours?"

Finn considers. "If my mother should have warned me about anything, it's small women with rope."

"And the Moragorion."

He winks. "That too."

I wait outside the privy while he finishes his business. The sun is bright overhead, and when Finn emerges, his face glistens with sweat. He keeps smiling as I steer him back to the cottage. His gait has significantly improved. I think in a few more days, he'll be ready to travel.

He watches while I retie the restraints on his sickbed. Then he asks, "Are your parents hard on you?"

I look up from my knots, surprised by the question. "Why would you think that?"

"I dunno. You're obviously independent." Finn gestures around him the best he can with his hands tied, alluding to the hanging flowers, the bottles of tinctures, the pots bubbling on the stove. "All this healing stuff is beyond me. I thought *my* parents pushed me, but based on what *you've* accomplished at this age . . ." He shrugs. "I guess I just imagined they might be hard on you, too."

I'm still for a long moment as I consider his question.

"My dad isn't in the picture," I finally admit. "He died shortly after I was born." My heart pounds as I wait for Finn's response.

"Forgive me." His entire demeanor softens in sympathy. "I didn't realize. . . ."

My shoulders jerk in something like a shrug. "I never knew him."

"That doesn't make it better," he says firmly.

"No. It doesn't." I rub a knot on my neck.

"So, it's just you and your mother?"

"Yeah. And . . . she *is* a little hard on me," I admit. I recall her expression when I asked to accompany her, my heart jerking at the memory.

Silence falls. I finish cooking and help Finn with his portion. When I settle down at the table to eat mine, he tries again. "So, no father in the picture. But your mother is a Healer, you're her apprentice, you live out here alone . . . *and*?"

I stare at him blankly. "And that's all correct."

"Come on, give me *something*," he prods. "At least a little lore!"

I roll my eyes. "What *lore*?"

"Where you're from . . . how you got here . . ."

This is dangerous terrain and *way* too close to my unshareable truths. "No."

"Please?"

"It's too long a story."

Finn jokingly tugs against his restraints. "Fortunately, you've got a captive audience."

I have to suppress a smile, but my skin prickles. I hate lying. I want so badly to be honest with someone, the confession threatens to climb out of my throat. I can't imagine how good it would feel to come clean about all of it—my Talent, my mother, her absurd paranoia and insistence on my incompetence—but the truth is dangerous.

I settle for another half-truth. "My mother had some . . . problems in her old life." Not quite a lie, but not the whole story, either.

His eyebrows rise, but he is quiet, waiting for me to go on.

"At a certain point, it wasn't safe for us to keep living in my father's hometown," I continue, choosing each word carefully. "She took me and fled. We've been living here for as long as I can remember."

"Here? In this cottage?"

I nod. "Or others like it. There are lots of empty places like this around the Ironwoods, left by families who moved when the wall went up." I shift my weight. "What about you? You're inwall?"

Finn smiles like I've made a joke, and only he knows the punchline. "My family's about as inwall as it gets."

"Did you grow up in town?"

"In the capital."

"Really? Wow." Illustrations of Crown City from books rise to memory: huge spiraling towers and gleaming cathedrals. "I've never been. Is it as beautiful as they say?"

"You get used to it."

"I guess." I fear some of the wistfulness clutching my chest has leaked into my tone, so I hurry to change the subject. "What about your family?"

"Well, there are five of us, including my parents. Plus cousins and aunts, but who counts them, right?"

I marvel at the idea of so many relatives. "What's it like having siblings?"

Finn leans back. "Well, Damien, my younger brother, he's . . . generally sort of a dick. But he's not too bad most of the time, and he's my favorite person to ride with or go hunting with. And then Sebastian, our older brother . . . he's the best of us. Everyone would agree with that, too."

"The *best of us*? What does that mean?"

He snorts softly. "In my parents' eyes or mine?"

"Whichever one matters."

"Hmm. I like your questions." He considers. "They both matter. *I'd* say it's because Sebastian knows what he's supposed to do with his life and he does it. My *parents* would say it's because he's the most responsible."

"What would Damien say?"

"He'd say *he's* the best."

I laugh. "And you? Damien's the worst, Sebastian's the best, so you're . . ."

"I'm the fun one," he says with a waggle of his brows.

"And what does that mean?" I ask, still laughing.

"What I said." He smirks. "I'm the one you'd want to have fun with."

"Is that what you tell the girls in Crown City?"

"Oh, I don't have to tell them," Finn says with a wink. "My reputation precedes me."

I roll my eyes again. "Does the arrogant, smirking thing work on them, too?"

"Depends on the girl." His eyes suddenly flash. "What about you? You've got *trouble* written all over you. What sort of mischief do you get up to in the Ironwoods?"

I sigh. Little does he know, carrying on this exact conversation is probably the most rebellious thing I've ever done. "Let's just say nobody would call me the fun one. It's only ever really been my mother and me."

"Really?" asks Finn. At my nod, he continues. "How would she describe you?"

"She'd say . . ." I take a deep breath. "I think she'd say I have a lot to learn." I draw my knees toward my chest, resting my chin on them.

"That's all? Give me something else."

*What else?* A thousand little criticisms flash through my mind. "She'd say that we're opposites. According to her, I'm too focused on the big picture. She's all about the details. She'd say I need to think before I act. And *slow down*." I swallow.

"Well, if we're focusing on critiques, *my* mother would say that I'm foolhardy," Finn counters. "My father would say I've got dog shit for brains, but he's said a lot of worse things about better people, so . . ." He shrugs. "That's taken with a grain of salt."

"Your father sounds lovely."

"He's difficult."

We finish our food, and I clean up. It's quiet while I get ready for bed, latching both locks on the doors and braiding my hair. When I climb into my bed, I still clearly hear his breathing. Every inhale, every exhale. I'm oddly attuned to the sound.

I speak to the darkness, loud enough so I know he'll hear me. "For what it's worth, I don't think you have dog shit for brains."

After a long moment, Finn answers, "For what it's worth, I'm glad you act fast."

It is a long time before either of us sleeps.

---

I try and maintain stoicism—I really do. But as the days go by, resistance to his charm begins to feel futile. I still escort him to the privy, but with my crossbow slung casually across my arms. When he's tied down, the restraints are loose. And when Finn starts to open up about his universe, I can't contain my curiosity. Questions tumble out in a landslide. *Have you ever been outside of Verdinae? Is it true they have indoor plumbing in Crown City? Do you fight with your brothers? Did you go to school with other children?*

I learn that he's traveled everywhere: the Ashlands in Sulnik, the vast deserts of Dasken, the free port cities of Sontaag, even the great painted palaces of Ursandor. He describes modern wonders that defy my imagination: hot-air balloons and mechanical toys and aqueducts that span hundreds of miles. He speaks three languages and had tutors in music, dance, mathematics, history, and literature. The more I learn, the harder it is not to feel inadequate in comparison. The adventures he's lived are the same fantasies I've escaped to. While Finn forged friendships across the Midlands, probably basking in the privilege of that exquisite upbringing, I was here. Alone. I envy the complexity of his lived experience. I envy his siblings. A chasm opens in my chest when he talks about his brothers and the mischief they got up to together. I wonder what it would have been like to grow up with siblings—to share in the capers I've read about in books.

"Have you ever been to a party?" I ask, on the heels of one such anecdote about him and his brothers, while sitting at the kitchen table.

Finn bursts out laughing, then stops abruptly. "Oh. You're serious. Uh, yes. I've been to a party. Many, actually."

By this point, I've given up the attempt to conceal my curiosity. "Where?"

"Uh . . ." He rumples his hair. "I'd say everywhere, but that makes me sound like a heathen, doesn't it?"

"What do you mean, everywhere?"

"Ballrooms, taverns, rich people's houses, poor people's houses . . . I don't discriminate when it comes to having a good time." He grins. "Why, are you jealous?"

"Very jealous," I admit.

"Let me guess—your mother's too protective to let you go to something like that."

"To say the least." I turn to go stoke the fire so that he doesn't see my tightening mouth.

"It's nice to know she cares, at least," he offers.

"That's a given, isn't it? All mothers love their children."

"Sure."

His tone makes me pause, and I look back at him over my shoulder. "You think yours doesn't?"

"I don't think she's a particularly maternal person. She loves me as well as she can." He swallows. "I think she would rather have had another Sebastian, if you catch my drift."

"No." I blink.

Finn looks like he's struggling for words. "I just mean, my mother cares more about *what* I am than *who* I am. Does that make sense?"

"Sort of." A memory of Mother flashes across my mind—one

where she's staring down at me with pure, unadulterated horror. I squeeze my eyes shut to banish it and turn away.

Finn is uncharacteristically quiet as I pick up a log and shove it into the coals. We watch as the flames consume it. Then I retake my seat.

"My mother's not the most nurturing, either," I finally offer. "Truth be told, I'm not really sure she ever *wanted* to have children. Sometimes, I wonder if she regrets it."

We lock into another one of those staring contests that seem to go on forever. Finn looks empathetic, and for the first time, I notice a flicker of pain behind his eyes, like a crack in a mask. I wonder how much of his joviality is a front. Could he be hurting as much as I am?

"Nobody deserves to feel like that," Finn says softly.

*I do.*

An old wound burns in my chest, reminding me of all that I've done. All that I *am*.

But those truths stay unspoken.

---

When the sun rises the next morning, I watch it through my attic window, just as I did on the morning Mother left. I'm filled with resolve once again, but it's not the hopeful kind. It's cold and heavy.

It's time to send Finn away. I've probably been selfish by waiting this long to call it. His wounds are little more than scars now, and his limp is almost imperceptible. I'm certain I have to let him go.

What I don't know is how to find the strength to do it.

I creep downstairs to start breakfast before he wakes. I tell myself he shouldn't leave on an empty stomach, but really I'm stalling for time. Maybe something of Mother possesses me, because I find myself cooking the same meal she always leaves me with. The eggs are sizzling when I notice the change in Finn's breathing that tells me he's awake. He stays quiet for a while, but I can feel his eyes tracking me. I pretend not to notice. It's an unexpectedly pleasant feeling.

Finally, he cuts the silence.

"What do you think your mother will say? When you tell her about me, I mean." His voice is lower than usual, still rough from sleep.

I look up, then back down at the frying pan. "I'm not sure I'm going to."

"You're not going to tell her? Why not?"

"Why should I?" I dish the eggs onto a plate and cross the room to deliver them.

"I dunno, it just seems like something that would come up." Finn shrugs. *"Hello, Mother. I hope you've had a nice trip! By the way, there's been a very handsome young man sleeping in your bed—"*

I jab his shoulder amiably with the dull end of a fork. "I'm thinking about it."

He snatches it from my hand. "Are you scared of what she'll say? Is that what's happening here? Because I can personally vouch, you've been a *very* good warden. Kept it all aboveboard. Shared no damnable information. Major points for moral fiber. You've even managed to divest me of all my secrets."

"I wasn't divesting you of your secrets."

"And why not? Again, a mystery. What an enigma you are."

I cross back to the kitchen, returning with a plate in one hand and a large carving knife in the other. Finn eyes the blade as I approach. "Is that in case I make another comment about your cooking?"

"That's for this." I cut his ropes.

Incredulously, he massages his wrists. "What did I do to deserve such an honor?"

"My mother's going to be back in three days. I've decided you should probably be gone by then."

"You're evicting me?" I must be imagining the disappointment in his voice.

"I think it's time that you moved on," I say, suddenly very focused on my eggs. "You can sleep here one more night, if you'd like, but you should leave first thing tomorrow."

"Fair enough." Finn sighs. "As much as I've enjoyed captivity, I assumed our arrangement couldn't last forever."

I search his expression. Have I offended him? That's not my intention. Even as I send him away, my whole body aches for proximity. "Where will you go?"

"Back home to Crown City. I'll tell them I didn't have any luck retrieving Damien, and if he hasn't turned up by then, I suppose I'll organize a search party."

"I hope you find him."

"I'm sure we will."

We tuck into our food. As we eat, I'm conscious of his body beside mine. His arms, now free of their restraints, are coltish. I focus on tucking my elbows to avoid brushing him accidentally. I can't tell if he's preoccupied with the same concern. After we finish, I check his bandages and try very hard not to think about his eyes on me as I work.

"You shouldn't need more of this." I finish applying the salve on his chest. "You'll have some scarring, I think. But you'll be back to full mobility."

His eyebrows rise. "I'm all better?"

"It would appear so."

Finn buttons his shirt back up. "Well then, how are we going to enjoy my newfound freedom before you kick me out of here for good?"

"What do you mean?" I ask.

"We've been cooped up for weeks," he says. "Don't you want to get out?"

I can't tell him that going out is something I wouldn't be doing even if I hadn't spent the last couple weeks watching him. "You're feeling *that* much better?" I say instead.

"You're the one who said I'm fine."

"It . . . it could be dangerous," I counter weakly.

Finn just rolls his eyes. "Come on, Lyria, *live* a little."

I let the words wash over me, my chest twisting. Isn't that exactly what I've envied? That he was living a big, beautiful life while I was stuck here, in *this* pitiful existence? I've been alive for eighteen years, but how much of that was *living*? What does that even mean? Am I brave enough to find out?

*If I am damned, it might as well be thoroughly.*

"Finn," I ask shyly, "do you know how to swim?"

---

The path winds north from the cottage, hugging the base of the mountain. We follow a trail that clings to a rocky shelf, splitting the dark forest floor. Evergreens sweep sky-high overhead. As we come around a bend, the path levels and then drops into a canyon. We scramble together toward the base, where the waterfall spills off a cliff before plummeting into the pool below. I scurry to the edge and shuck off my shoes and apron, but I keep my kerchief on. Finn catches up to me as I tug off my left sock.

"WHAT ARE YOU DOING?!" he screams over the roaring around us.

"GETTING IN!"

I peel my overdress off my shoulders, stripping down to an ivory slip. Finn quickly looks away—his cheeks flaming—and words seem to hover over his soundless lips before he turns back to me. His reaction sends sparks through me that have nothing to do with my Talent. There's a different kind of power in learning I can make him blush.

Giving him a wicked grin, I run into the pool—the river is fed by glacier runoff; I scream as the icy water hits my burning skin. Half pain, half relief.

Finn composes himself and throws off his tunic to hurry in after me. We swim fast through the neck-high water. I lead him to a part of the rocks where you can scramble up and stand beneath the driving waterfall. I go first. Finn follows, panting by the time he finally catches up to me.

"YOU DO THIS A LOT?"

"YEAH!"

We bask there together for a moment, trembling under the onslaught. My smile is uncontrollable. Standing with him under the water, I can't recall a time I've felt so happy, felt so *free*. Then—without warning—Finn reaches out and takes my hand.

His expression mirrors my joy. His grip feels familiar, like the handle of a favorite blade, or a familiar branch of a climbing tree. I could stand here forever. The moment feels rare and miraculous, like a brief glimpse of sunlight through the clouds. We wait under the torrent until I think my chest might explode. I'm the first to break away, splashing into deeper water. Better not get used to the feeling. There's no sense in pining after what you can't have.

I swim in some lazy circles, working to calm my pounding heart. Finn paddles up beside me and then seizes my ankle, tickling the bottom of my foot. I shriek and laugh, splashing away from him. We play until we're both exhausted and my feet are numb. Then we collapse together on the grassy shore.

"I can't believe you grew up like this," Finn marvels. "This forest, it's the type of place you read about in books."

My skin crawls. *And what a caveat that existence includes.* "It's nothing special," I mumble.

"Looks pretty special to me."

I can't help but notice that while he is talking about the forest, his eyes are on me.

Finn reaches up and snags a fluffy dandelion puff caught in a breeze. "I mostly grew up behind walls. My father always acted like he didn't give a damn about me or my brothers, but that didn't stop him from shrinking our world down to the size of a postage stamp. I wasn't allowed to go much farther than our front door until I was sixteen." Suddenly, he blows on the puff, sending the individual seeds scattering. "Since then . . . I've tried to be anywhere but home."

I didn't expect this confession, or how much it would resonate. My chest feels hollow, hot and cold all at once. "My mother's the same. Before I was born, she experienced some pretty terrible violence. I think those scars have never fully healed. It's like she doesn't know when it's all right to stop running."

He rolls over, bringing his face inches from mine, and my breath hitches. "Tell me something you haven't told anyone before."

I roll away, putting more distance between us. "Like what?"

"Like a secret." Finn folds his arms over his chest.

I don't know how to tell him that everything I've shared *is* a secret. "I don't have any."

"Everyone has secrets. I could go first, to get started."

"Go ahead."

"My secret is: I *hate* my father."

I study him sidelong. Finn glares up at the clouds like they're withholding answers. "Everyone loves to tell me that I look just like him. My mother says my personality is the most like his, too." His idle hand tousles his hair. "You know how terrible that is? Getting told you're just like the person you hate most in this world?"

"What makes him so bad?" I ask. "I mean, besides the murdering innocent animals and saying you have dog shit for brains."

*"Everything,"* Finn mumbles. "Just . . . everything." He rolls his head to face me again. "Anyway, that's my secret."

We appraise each other for a long moment. I know he's waiting for my answer. In the wake of what he just admitted, a half-truth feels insufficient. So I speak honestly. "I guess . . . I guess my secret is that I've never done this before."

"Done what?"

"Showed someone *this*." I gesture around us. "Due to my mother's general paranoia, we usually keep to ourselves"—I gulp—"so I haven't had a lot of chances to meet people like you. Boys, I mean."

A little smile twitches on his lips. "I haven't met anyone like you, either, Lyria."

As we lie there sunning, with the waterfall roaring around us, something swells within me. It's a revelation that makes me feel filled to the brim with golden light—weightless, like a dandelion seed drifting on the wind.

I daresay Finn is my very first friend.

# 4

I don't sleep that night.

Instead, I lie awake listening to his breathing as anxiety twists my stomach into serpentine coils. The inevitability of his departure has me plummeting into bottomless dread. Finn's arrival imploded my life, infinitely expanding the scale of my world. I can't fathom how I am supposed to shrink it again after he's gone.

After a subdued breakfast, I retrieve his sword in its scabbard from where I stashed it in the cupboard. "You'll probably also need this."

Finn lights up like a hearth. "I thought I lost that!"

"Technically, you did," I say wryly, handing it back to him. "Maybe try to hold on to it next time."

Now I don't know what to do with my hands.

Perhaps Finn is racked with the same indecision, because he pauses much longer than necessary. "Can I . . . expect to see you again?"

The question makes my heart skip, then plummet just as quickly. I toss back a joke to evade the painful truth. "Maybe the next time you try to fight a Moragorion."

Finn suddenly reaches out and tugs me against his chest. Cradling my head with one hand, he breathes heavily into my hair. *"Thank you for saving me."*

My stomach tugs, like free fall in a dream. I haven't been hugged since I was a child. I don't want to let go. Not now, not ever. How can I explain how much he means to me?

I've spent years bracing myself for the possibility that when I finally met someone my own age, the experience wouldn't live up to my expectations. How could I explain that he is even more wondrous than my dreams? I want more time with Finn. I want to go on adventures together. I want to confide in him about what I'm really scared of. . . .

I never get the chance, because that's the moment we get interrupted.

It's voices. Outside.

Horror lances my veins, freezing me in place. "Someone's here," I hiss, and we hurry to the window.

Through the mottled glass, we see three armed men approaching. Two are massive, with dark hair and beards, and the other is shorter and round, built like a boulder.

*"Mercenaries,"* Finn murmurs. "See the patches on their vests?"

I scrutinize the men more closely. Indeed, they each have a triangle sewn onto the left breast of their uniform, but I can't make out the detail from this distance.

"Those are Sulish raiders," Finn continues, in a low voice. "Sellswords. They're officially employed by the Verdish Empire, but most of them operate more like pirates."

*If they catch you, they will kill you.*

I feel like throwing up.

Finn emits a noise like a growl. "You should hide."

"What?"

"Hide. Before they make an example out of you." Our eyes meet, and Finn's hold a dark glint of desperation. "If they know you're out here alone—"

"I know," I say, cutting him off.

I'm well informed of the dangers of being found. I'm a lone female in the Ironwoods, defiantly living outside the Crown's protection even as tension rumbles through Verdinae. To the wrong pair of eyes, I look like someone with something to hide . . . someone without proper papers. The empire has agents trained to hunt down Elves with Talents, like me. One brush with one of them, and I'd end up in a prison cell, begging for my life to be ended quickly. Imperial mercenaries would be less formal. They'd treat me as spoils of war. A prize to be shared.

Mother has good reasons for training me to stay within the wardlines.

I feel sick with shame. When I ran to rescue Finn, I broke the only rule that mattered in her absence. And here are the consequences, arriving to damn me. Stepping outside the wardlines shattered every protective spell concealing our cottage. We're sitting ducks.

Terror clamps down on my throat, and my skin flames.

"I'll deal with them," Finn says firmly, grabbing my shoulders to force me to meet his gaze. When I don't move, he adds, "*Now,* Lyria. I have this under control."

I pause. My Talent churns underneath my skin, already swelling in anticipation of release. But I can't use it in front of Finn without revealing what I am.

Seeing no other choice, I obey him, scrambling into the closet. I try to steady my breathing as I watch Finn through a tiny crack in the wood. He swipes a blade from the kitchen before hurrying to the door.

My Elven ears home in on the mercenaries outside.

"There's smoke in the chimney," one of them says. "Someone's in there."

"What d'ya think?" another replies.

"I think I'm hungry."

I hear the door swing open, then measured footsteps. It's Finn. "Gentlemen," he drawls, sounding remarkably casual. "Is there something I can help you with?"

"Nice place you've got," the first voice answers. "Not a lot of folks out here these days."

"It's just me and my father," replies Finn, and I marvel at how easily he lies.

"Just you and the old man, eh? Where is he, then?"

"On a hunting trip. He should be back soon."

"Well," another man says, "with Daddy gone, I'd say the proper thing to do is offer us some hospitality."

"Of course," says Finn. "Come in, and I'll see what I can spare." My blood runs cold as they push past him, storming inside. But there's a dark curl in Finn's voice I don't recognize when he adds, "I hope you boys brought an appetite."

Someone starts to respond, but the attempt is cut short with a gurgle. I can't see clearly from my hiding place, so I don't realize what's transpired until a mercenary thuds to the floor and I see the knife buried in his neck.

Then everything happens all at once.

Finn leaves no time for reactions. His sword is out before the other two can charge, and I stop breathing entirely as Finn whirls, plunging his blade between the nearest mercenary's ribs. The man topples as Finn yanks it back with a grunt.

The third soldier is all that remains, and he raises a longsword to meet Finn's next attack, bellowing curses. Steel meets steel. As they lock into a duel, I realize that what I saw in the swamp didn't do his skill justice. Finn fights with lethal efficiency, darting and feinting to match the larger man's blows.

His movements aren't just precise. They're perfect. Every decision is quick and unyielding. There is no hesitation about what needs to be done. He could almost be dancing with the mercenary, executing choreography known only to him.

He's doing exactly what I would have done in his place. Eliminating the threat. This is the inevitability I've braced for my whole life—a fight to the death. I just never expected I'd have someone to battle alongside me.

It's over as fast as it started. When the last body drops, Finn rushes straight to the closet and yanks open the door. "Lyria! Are you all right?" As I shakily step out, apologetic explanation pours out of him. "I'm sorry that was so quick, I calculated that my greatest odds were if I struck while I could still surprise them. . . ."

Restraint is beyond me. Apparently sanity is, too, because I leap forward and crash into him. Finn's arms envelop me, his body folding against mine. We're both trembling.

I scan with my Talent to confirm he's uninjured. Then, with my face buried in the warmth of his chest, I choke out, *"Consider us even."*

Finn stays to help me burn the bodies.

We work together in silence. I stack wood for the pyre while he strips them of their weapons, then helps me haul them over. His movements are deft, his expression hard and unreadable. When it's finally over, we stamp out the flames to avoid attracting any more unwanted attention. I walk back to the porch and sit, drawing my knees to my chest.

I've seen death before. It's not a memory I care to revisit, but the cold, lancing ache of guilt is familiar. And when I close my eyes, I can still see Mother's face against the blackness, her revulsion burned there like a brand.

*Monster.*

"Lyria," Finn says gently, rousing me from my thoughts. "If I hadn't handled it, if those men had found you *alone,* they would have done the same to you, or worse. You realize that, don't you?"

"Yes," I answer dully, my throat raw. Mother has always been candid about how women and girls pay the price for men's wars. My gaze flicks sidelong. "You've done this before?"

Slowly, he nods. "More than once. Never if I didn't have to."

I feel dizzy. "Who taught you?"

"My family had swordmasters. And then I served in the military."

*Swordmasters.* Plural. I add this to the information I've gleaned. *Hunts for fyrehounds. Trained by multiple swordmasters.* And the last, most distasteful fact, which now requires clarification. "You served in the *Verdish* military?"

"Yes."

My thoughts flash to Mother's stories: the cities burned, the loved ones slaughtered, the people driven from their homeland by soldiers like him. Finn didn't just inherit that legacy. He's *continuing* it. My stomach goes leaden, weighing this revelation against a lifetime of fear.

*If they catch you, they will kill you.*

Except Finn just saved my life.

I feel numb as he collects his belongings inside a travel pack I gifted him. Before departing, Finn embraces me one final time. When he pulls away, his eyes drop to my mouth, and he leans in. For one bizarre, heart-racing moment, I think he might kiss me—but his lips press against my forehead instead.

"I won't forget you," Finn whispers.

Then he hesitates. I sense that he's waiting for something. *A declaration? An offer to return? Some kind of promise for the future?*

There are a thousand things I want to say, but they all wither and die on my lips. Because there *is* no future. Not for us. In the end, all I can manage is "Be safe."

Finn smiles. And there it is again, that flicker of pain behind his eyes. A glimpse behind the mask. "Take care of yourself, Lyria," he says softly.

I listen to his footsteps long after he's disappeared.

---

Finn's absence makes the cottage feel unbearably vacant and cold. Even the colors look dim. The next morning, I force myself through my usual routine, but every part of it feels wrong. I can't look at my sewing kit without remembering the holes I patched in his clothes. I search for my favorite chipped mug, and find it by the windowsill, next to a book Finn was reading before he left. Even the smell of him lingers, ruining everything.

Mother will be home tomorrow. I know I've got a big storm coming. There'll be hell to pay if I tell her what I've done, but I can't bring myself to care.

To cut through the loneliness, I pick up the book.

It's a volume about the Aldain dynasty, the old kings and queens of Evermore, including some accounts that terrified me as a child. My favorite chapters were about Queen Soleste, the last Elven queen. She was born in the Ironwoods as a commoner and married into the royal family before the kingdom crumbled. The fables claim that Queen Soleste worshipped Nocturn, Goddess of Death, and could kill with a glance. There's a whole section dedicated to her execution after she surrendered to King Verdin. I've never taken these stories at face value. It doesn't make sense that humans vanquished someone so powerful. If anyone knew the truth, it would be Mother, considering she served the queen until the queen's death. But Soleste exists in the same category as my father: wholly unmentionable.

I flip through the worn pages until I find the one Finn bookmarked. It's the prophecy of the Heir of Evermore—more of a song than a story, the preachy, sentimental kind that makes Mother misty-eyed. She sometimes sang it to help me fall asleep when I was little, so the lyrics are familiar.

*One day, through ash and ice and fyre, an acolyte will rise,*
*To hoist the fallen banners and to break the binding ties.*

*A hero with the gifts of Gods, rekindler of the flame,*
*Honor-sworn and duty-bound, a homeland to reclaim.*
*With starfalls of divinity at hand, and heart, and brow,*
*They'll walk two worlds and dine with Death, unconquered and unbowed.*
*When legions of our fallen kin rise up and march again,*
*The unbreakable will shatter and unyielding knees will bend.*
*And all will hear the triumph of the old kingdom restored,*
*Through pain and retribution by the Heir of Evermore.*

I slam the book shut, annoyed with myself. It was foolish to think revisiting the book might make me feel closer to Finn. It's just a painful reminder of his absence and the vast chasm between us. I've never found comfort in the prophecy as Mother does. The empire stole her past and robbed me of my future. Those aren't things you can reclaim.

I try to shove Finn and the stupid fables out of mind as I prepare for Mother's return. No doubt there will be dire consequences for my rebellion, so I compose another speech—this time, an apology.

But by dusk the next day, Mother hasn't returned.

One day of waiting rolls into two, and then three, and my apprehension grows exponentially. In all her years of travel, Mother has *never* returned late. After a week with no word or sign, I resolve to go after her. But a raven arrives in the midst of my packing, carrying a note with a word scrawled in Elven runes:

*Delayed.*

Frustration sears through me. Of course she wouldn't feel the need to explain any further. What does it matter if I wait here another day, another week, another month? What does she care?

I crumple the note and toss it into the hearth, gritting my teeth against the swell of my Talent. I can't remember the last time I was this furious. The magic is *screaming* for release. I pace the cottage, considering another trip to the waterfall to temper the liquid fire. The wardlines are shot to hell anyway—what's one more rebellion?

I'm on my way to grab my shoes when I hear the *BANG! BANG! BANG!* of a fist on the door.

I wish I could say I spring into fighting stance, ready to face the threat. But the knock catches me so off guard, I jolt with such force that I fall flat on my ass. I'm clambering back to my feet when I hear a man shout from outside:

"OPEN UP! THIS IS THE ROYAL GUARD!"

# 5

Peering out the window, I count half a dozen soldiers around the cottage.

They're mounted in a semicircle: some men, some women, all wearing gold armor that shines in the sun. There's a symbol emblazoned on their chests with the intertwining letters *VIA*. It takes me a woeful amount of racking my brain to realize they stand for *Verdish Imperial Army.* The soldier at the door is a big man with red hair. He knocks again, with the sharp cadence of someone who expects to be answered.

Fear closes my throat as I plan my next move. *Can I pretend not to be here?* My eyes dart to the hearth fire. No. There's smoke in the chimney.

Another knock. Better move quick. My hands fly to my ears, and I murmur the concealment charm at top speed. I knot my kerchief for good measure. With a deep, steadying breath, I open the door a crack.

Up close, I get a better look at the big redheaded soldier. "Good morning. I'm sorry if we startled you. My name is Edmund Roburn, and I'm captain of the Royal Guard," he says. "We're here on official business of King Rodrick and the Thorne family."

*Run.* If Mother were here, that's what she would command.

Out of all the monsters I've been taught to fear, there is none worse than King Rodrick Thorne. Everything I know about him tornadoes through me in an instant. He's a distant descendant of Verdin, and perhaps the most fanatical Verdish ruler yet. Like the Vanquisher himself, King Rodrick's lust for territorial expansion is insatiable. Equally endless is his hatred toward Elves. I'm nauseated, recalling horrors Mother described: mass executions, torture, whole Elven families ripped out of hiding to be forced into servitude or massacred.

If King Rodrick knows I exist, I'm a dead girl walking.

All this I process in an instant, gaping at Roburn and the unit behind him. The primal instinct to flee roars through me like wildfyre, but I'd never outpace them. Not with them on horseback.

*I could fight.* Maybe. I consider it—six of them, one of me. My weapons would be useless against that armor. It'd have to be my Talent, then. But I've never attempted using it on multiple beings. *Could I even draw up that much power? Even if I somehow managed it, could I live with that much blood on my hands?* They feel filthy already.

An uncomfortable amount of time has passed.

*Say something. Anything.*

"What do you want?" I finally croak. I clear my throat, then try again more firmly. "We have no business with the king."

"We're here by order of his son Prince Finneas."

My heart plummets into my shoes.

"Prince . . . Finneas?" I repeat dizzily.

*Finneas as in . . . Finn?*

"That's correct. He's ordered us to escort you to the palace."

The world pitches. Shatters. Re-forms. Fragments of the last weeks click together, sparking like flint against steel: the way Finn described his swordmasters, plural, his childhood behind walls. . . .

*Palace* walls, I correct myself.

Finn is a prince. And not just any prince.

*Finn is King Rodrick's son.*

It takes every last infinitesimal shred of my willpower to keep my Talent from exploding out of my palms. The monster in my chest claws for escape, howling like a banshee for answers, for vengeance. I sway, sweat trickling down my temples and spine, as I struggle to shove down the magic that's shrieking for release.

Roburn holds out a letter. "He asked me to deliver this."

I try to still my shaking hands as I accept. It's been sealed with wax, and the imprint is deep and precise . . . a thorned rose against crisscrossing blades. I trace my fingers over it, disbelieving.

Everyone's watching as I tear it open.

*Lyria,*

*I must begin this letter by entreating you to forgive me twice. First, forgive me for not delivering this message in person. I wanted nothing more than to accompany our guards and invite you to Crown City face-to-face, but my position dictates that I fulfill responsibilities outside my control. Since I'm not able to be there, I hope you'll put your trust in Captain Roburn. I would trust him with my life.*

*Second, forgive me for leaving without confessing my feelings or revealing my true identity. If I'd been more courageous, I would have admitted just how thoroughly you dazzled me. Now I can only pray you'll give me another chance.*

*I left the Ironwoods resigned to the probability that our paths would not cross again in this life. However, it seems providence has other plans. Upon my return to Crown City, I was met with news of a terrible plague threatening our kingdom. Up until his recent death, our royal apothecary was working diligently to develop a cure, but his efforts were fruitless. With most of our Healers dispatched to support the campaign in Sontaag, there are few continuing his work. Fewer still can be trusted to maintain the discretion we require. If word were to get out about a plague sweeping toward the capital, it would trigger mass panic. The Crown requires an apothecary with the ingenuity to outfox this disease and the character to maintain the utmost secrecy.*

*You are our perfect candidate.*

*I believe fate has brought us together in more ways than one, Lyria. Beyond my selfish desire to see your face again, it is concern for my people that compels me to beg you: Please, come to Crown City, join me in the palace, and help us defeat this horrific plague.*

*I pray to the One God Almighty that I will see you again soon. Until then, my heart is with you.*

*Yours most sincerely,*
*Finn*

I read it three times, each time memorizing a different detail. I see Finn all over the page—in the sharp slope of the *Y*'s, the cramped tilt of the script, even the dark smudges in the margins. I picture him hunched over a desk, scowling at his unruly, ink-stained hands . . . and a little shiver runs through me.

He wants me. Finn wants *me*.

Skimming again, my eye snags on three words: *You dazzled me.*

Maybe I'm not so pathetically delusional. *Can it be possible? Might he feel something close to what I do? Is there a future for us in Crown City?*

*NO, Lyria. Listen to yourself.*

There's a long stretch where all I can hear is my own pounding pulse. This is all *way* more than I can process with so many people staring at me. Perhaps sensing my confoundment, Roburn asks, "Would you perhaps prefer to speak privately?"

I blink at the captain, remembering Finn's words: *I would trust him with my life.*

Reluctantly, I widen the crack in the door.

I offer the captain tea and a chair, but he politely declines the former. When Roburn sits at the kitchen table, he looks comically large for the furniture.

"Can I ask you something sensitive?" Roburn asks as he settles.

I nod.

He swallows, uncomfortably. "Are you perhaps . . . with child?"

"Excuse me?" My cheeks burst into flames. *What the hell did Finn tell him?*

"It was only a guess!" He quickly backtracks. "Sometimes women feel shame about those situations. The prince was clear that we were to bring you to the palace and that you were to be protected—"

I cut him off, mortified. "No, I'm not pregnant. Thank you for the concern."

"Forgive me. It was only a guess."

I eye the window, considering hurling myself through it. Roburn looks like he might be pondering the same. Then it suddenly occurs to me . . . "You haven't done that for him before, have you?"

"What?"

"I mean . . ." My hands tighten into fists in front of me. Gods, I need air. "Has Finn ever sent you to fetch a girl because she ended up . . . in a situation?"

"Ah, no. Definitely not," says Roburn awkwardly. "I've never fulfilled that particular type of request on Finneas's behalf. Or his brothers', for that matter."

I turn away so that he doesn't see the turmoil in my expression.

The captain clears his throat. "It must be interesting living in the Ironwoods. I can't imagine there is much to do out here for a young woman like yourself. Do you live alone?"

I weigh my response. *How much has Finn said already?* "It's just me and my mother," I finally admit. I am hesitant to mention the plague, so I scramble for a lie. "She's . . . getting on in years. Her health is failing. She needs me here, or else she won't make it through the winter."

I'm not sure it's believable. Roburn squints as he considers my response. "Why doesn't she join us? The Crown isn't short on resources; we could make your mother very comfortable in the palace."

"She's a very proud woman," I mumble. "I'm not sure she'd accept your offer."

"Why don't we ask her?"

*Damn it.* Now he has me.

Roburn clears his throat. "Listen. I can see that you're afraid. But to be perfectly frank, if we were here to hurt you, we would have done so already."

His eyes flit to my hands, and I realize I've crumpled Finn's letter by gripping it so hard. I need to refuse quickly, or else I might not be able to. Already my heart is doing backflips. So I say forcefully, "My mother is away, and I don't know when she will be returning. I can't leave without her. Please send the prince my apologies."

The captain is quiet as we appraise each other. I see no calculation or distrust in his face, just concern and perhaps some pity. Maybe I look as lonely and desperate as I feel. "This invitation doesn't have to be permanent," he says quietly, after a while. "You've been summoned as a guest, not a prisoner. You'd be welcome to leave at your leisure."

My brow knits. "What are you saying?"

"Come with us. Report for your duties, rendezvous with Finneas, and do whatever it is he's summoned you to do. You could leave a note for your mother explaining your whereabouts, and you'd always be welcome to return and retrieve her."

"She wouldn't want that," I mumble.

The captain cocks his head. His voice drops, and his tone softens, like I'm a wounded animal. "And what is it *you* want, Lyria?"

*What do I want?*

The question is so foreign, he might as well have asked it in a different language. Cold sweeps through me as I take a long beat to consider, a thousand options bubbling up my throat. *Safety. Control. A father. To be someone different. To make Mother proud. Finn.*

But one word rises above all others.

*Freedom.*

I break Roburn's gaze, looking out toward the crimson sky. Mother was seventeen when she first left the Ironwoods. A year younger than I am now. I've sworn up and down for years that I'm ready for the real world, begging her for the opportunity to prove myself.

*Isn't this my chance?*

I imagine myself riding up to the gates of the palace, becoming a royal apothecary as she once did. I see myself working alongside the other Healers, shoulder to shoulder with the greatest minds in the Midlands, engaged in a vital mission. And I envision our reunion, with a cure in my hand . . . and the look on Mother's face as she realizes how wrong she's been about my capabilities. I could prove that I'm more than a monster. If I can pull this off—travel to Crown City, successfully conceal my identity, and find a cure—she can never again claim that I don't have what it takes to survive in the real world.

*No more wardlines.*

*No more cages.*

"All right," I say finally. "I'll do it. I'll go with you."

# 6

It's a three-day ride to Crown City.

I don't bring much: just my satchel, my dagger, some spare clothes, and an old apothecary belt I dug out of the back of a closet.

I equipped it with the six most useful potions in my arsenal: grizzlefoot for pain, nocturn for sleep, all's-cure for wounds, everhart for courage, jacksbane for strength, and silvertongue to elicit the truth.

Our first day of travel takes us to the Ironwood foothills, which is the farthest west I've ever ventured. We reach Rodrick's Wall by mid-day on the second. I've heard Mother describe the hateful landmark many times. The books say the wall took a century to build after the war. The royal family claims they raised it to protect the Hartlands from monsters, but its true purpose is clear—to keep the Elves from ever returning to our homeland. Although Elves are legally permitted to reside in outwall regions of Verdinae—often facing human prejudice and oppression—they are not allowed to enter inwall cities. The wall juts abruptly from the landscape, its edges as smooth and unnatural as a sword plunged into the earth. It's made of massive blocks of stone and rises a hundred feet tall or more, crowned with jutting spikes.

Our party rides toward a lone gate, which from a distance appears to be a small, rounded hole in the base of the structure. As we approach, I make out what I think at first are birds perched at intervals along the top of the wall until I realize my mistake and have to hold in the rising vomit.

They're not birds. They're heads.

*I shouldn't be here.*

Panic floods me, though I battle to keep it from my expression. I glance around for the reactions of the soldiers, but no one seems the slightest bit fazed. Roburn's eyes stay fixed ahead, his expression stoic as usual. I see one soldier glance up grimly but then quickly avert her eyes.

I can almost hear Mother beside me. *This is who they are. This is what they do.*

"You ever seen it before?" I turn to see the guard who spoke. He's pale with jet-black hair and acne scars. He follows my gaze to the top of the wall. "They're Elves who tried to climb the wall. Bunch of idiots, in my view. No one makes it over."

I grip the pommel until my knuckles go white.

When we near the gate, I'm terrified that they're going to stop us and interrogate me about my citizenship. But to my relief, the VIA guards just wave us through. The wall is so thick that it takes several minutes to pass through the tunnel. We do so in darkness, with the sounds of our horses' hooves echoing in cacophony. When we emerge on the opposite side, the sun is blinding. I blink, trying to regain my vision. But something's wrong. The colors look too bright. I rub my eyes, squinting . . .

No. It's not my eyes. It's the land.

Before us is the most incomprehensibly gorgeous landscape I have ever seen. Flowers blanket the rolling hills in a dazzling kaleidoscope: reds and violets and blues and yellows, plus some colors I'm not sure I've ever encountered. The roads are paved in glittering ivory stones. All around us, meadows of the brightest, purest greens ripple in the gentle breeze. Jutting off from the wall is a massive stone aqueduct, which soars overhead parallel to the main road as far as the distant horizon. Waterfalls cascade off it at intervals, feeding streams and various lakes with turquoise water.

I thought I knew what beauty looked like: the first tulips of springtime, or sunlight sparkling on water, or the fresh fall of snow. But as I gaze out over the valley, I'm met with the stark and maddening realization: Our Ironwoods sanctuary is a barren wasteland compared to this.

I'm so busy gaping that I hardly notice Roburn riding up beside me. "What do you think?"

"I mean . . ." My mouth dries out as a hurricane of emotions is running through me—none that I can express without screaming.

"I was just as speechless when I first saw the Hartlands," Roburn murmurs. "Hard to get your head around, isn't it?"

Numbly, I nod. I think I know what he means. The contrast is incomprehensible. With an ancient ache churning in my stomach, I suddenly understand perfectly why someone would risk their life to attempt the climb inside.

*This should have been our home.*

We reach the capital at midday. Crown City, Verdinae's capital, sits in a valley with white-capped mountains to the east and a lake to the west. I see hundreds of buildings, thousands, even—some crowded one on top of another. Rising from the northern hill is a many-spired palace of bone-white marble. There are structures I've read about in books but never comprehended: amphitheaters, libraries, steepled cathedrals, rambling parks. Soaring above the gleaming avenues is a complex system of aqueducts that stretches in every direction, like a compass rose.

Our party enters through the city's southeast gate and follows a sun-drenched boulevard toward the castle. As we ride through the bustling quarter, my head swivels like an owl. There is so much detail I want to memorize. Through open doors, I catch glimpses of jewel-box restaurants teeming with patrons. Vendors pepper the streets, displaying carts of fine fabrics, whimsical toys, and delicate pottery. Pedestrians mill about, stopping to gossip or peek through the windows at a shop's latest offerings.

More overwhelming than the sights is the sheer volume of life around me. There are babies shrieking, people fighting, and women laughing—more sound than I can sort through. My Talent, so finely attuned to the complexity of the forest, is blasted out of balance. The onslaught of information has my power near overflowing and aching for use. I grit my teeth when the swell manifests as a physical pain in my spine.

Toward the northern edge of the city, the road slants sharply uphill ahead of the looming castle. The horses grow slick with sweat as we ascend, and at last we arrive at the castle gates. They're pure, shimmering gold.

Roburn issues instructions as we pass through. "Someone will take your things up to your room. I'll escort you for your introductions."

My heart pounds. "Introductions?"

"Yes. You'll be presented to the Crown. That's customary."

I'm struck with the image of an ominous throne room, where Finn stands between two faceless and menacing figures—King Rodrick and his wife, Queen Davina, both figments of my nightmares. The prospect makes my Talent claw into my spine. I have to keep from doubling over.

"Is there any possibility I can speak with Finn privately first?" I ask, hoping I don't sound as desperate as I feel.

"That's *Prince* Finneas while you're inside these walls," Roburn corrects me. "You'll want to be careful with formal terms like that. Address everyone properly. And I'm not sure he's here. I can ask around while you're getting settled."

"Oh." My chest craters. It hadn't even crossed my mind that Finn might not be home to meet me. He mentioned other responsibilities in his letter, but it didn't occur to me they might be away from the palace. Of course, most people get to *leave* home regularly. I feel like a fool.

"What do I say when I meet them?" I ask.

"You say thank you. Be confident but gracious. Don't act like they're better than you but give them a very wide berth of respect," Roburn instructs in a low voice. "Queen Davina doesn't do well with sniveling, so no sob stories. But she likes to feel beloved among commoners, so she'll respond well to flattery."

I'm immeasurably grateful for this insight. "And King Rodrick?"

"Not home. He's at the front lines in Sontaag."

Relief washes through me. *"Thank Gods,"* I whisper, unthinking.

Roburn pauses. "Be careful who you trust. The politics here are ruthless. And keep your head up—some of these courtiers can smell fear." The captain pats my shoulder stiffly, broadcasting a vague paternal concern I'm unfamiliar with. "If anyone gives you trouble, come straight to me and I'll handle it."

I try to take in this advice as we're ushered up the drive. Our party dismounts in the courtyard, where a slew of staff is standing to meet us and a freckle-faced groom takes my horse.

When Roburn guides me inside, my first impression is a blur. The palace is labyrinthian. We clip through hallways and parlors and up winding stairs, moving too fast for me to gain a sense of the layout. There's just one thing about my new surroundings that's impossible to miss—the opulent, decadent, mind-boggling *wealth*.

There is not one inch that isn't gilded or painted. We pass over marble floors and under ceilings dripping with chandeliers. Some halls are bedecked with paintings, others with tapestries depicting elaborate hunting scenes or seascapes. Nothing feels cluttered or cramped. Each room is wide and expansive, and some spill into open-air courtyards. There are windows everywhere. Through some, I catch glimpses of the view; from its mountainous perch, the palace looks down on the entire resplendent valley and the city it cradles.

"The queen requested that you join her in the chapel," Roburn explains as we finally stop in front of an ornate door. "Ready?"

I smooth a hand over my kerchief, subtly checking that my ears are still covered, and nod. "As I'll ever be."

In contrast to the opulence of the palace, the chapel's beauty is subdued. Two rows of wooden pews lead up toward a marble altar. The floor is smooth stone and the walls are undecorated. The architectural centerpiece is a spectacular stained glass window. Each panel depicts a vivid figure against a backdrop of sea-green glass, which casts the room in a hazy glow. It's not an unsettling color; I'm reminded of sunlight when viewed from underwater.

Dominating the space is a lone worshipper kneeling at the altar with a fur-lined cloak sprawled behind her like magpie wings. The woman, who I assume is Queen Davina, stands at our approach.

Roburn stops a few paces short of her and bows. "Your Majesty, as requested, please allow me to present Lyria of the Ironwoods."

"Thank you, Captain Roburn," says the queen, with a cursory nod. Then her eyes dart to me. Something tells me she's awaiting it, so I jerk an attempt at a curtsy. Amusement twitches her lips.

"*Lyria*. Welcome. I'm so glad you've arrived safely. My son has told us so much about you. Please. Join me." She gestures for me to sit beside her in a pew.

I take a few tentative steps, earning a better look at her features. The queen is wearing makeup, something I've never seen close-up before. Her skin looks expertly painted. Her eyelashes are darker than natural and her cheeks flushed. Her body has the generous shape and soft lines of someone who has never done physical labor. I'm drawn to studying her hands, which are remarkably smooth and adorned with long painted nails. Something about her sloped shoulders and the dark hair piled around her neck reminds me of a bear. I find something of Finn in her mouth and the sharp set of her brows. She's beautiful. Her expression doesn't waver as I edge closer. She looks placid and benevolent—very deliberately so.

"I hope that your journey was pleasant. Is this your first time in Crown City?"

"Yes, Your Majesty," I answer, with a nervous glance back at Roburn. He's moved back toward the wall, watching impassively.

"Well, we're very glad to have you." The queen gazes up at the stained glass. "I hope you'll forgive our unusual scenery. I prefer worshipping here in the afternoons when there's no one to bother me."

"I don't mind. *Your Majesty,*" I add quickly.

She smiles. "There's no need to be overly formal. We're all equal in the eyes of the Almighty."

At the mention of the deity, I stiffen. I know little about the Verdish Church, except that their customs vary greatly from Elven ones. They don't keep with the Gods like Elowyn, Nocturn, or Rashielle, the first mothers of magic. Instead, they believe there's only one God, whom they call the Almighty, and they've used him to justify heinous, *heinous* things.

"Captain Roburn, would you please fetch Cygnus?" the queen asks.

Roburn nods and dips into a low bow before leaving the chapel. I feel like sinking into the floor. Something about being alone with the queen feels like I've swapped one cage for another.

When her gaze falls back on me, I stammer the first question that comes to mind. "W-where's Finn?" Catching my mistake, I amend: "I mean, *Prince Finneas*?"

The queen waves her hand dismissively. "Oh, whoever knows. I imagine he's off riding, or maybe in town. It's hard to keep up with Finneas. He's very free-spirited."

"Oh" is all I can say as disappointment washes over me anew. *Finn's letter claimed he was attending to responsibilities. Did he really just . . . lie?*

"I've been told we owe you a great debt," the queen says serenely. "Finneas spoke highly of your abilities. He told me you're training to be a Healer?"

"That's right."

"Where are you studying?"

"My mother teaches me."

"How charming. What's her name?"

I hesitate. *What's the danger in a name?* "Melia Fletcher," I finally tell her.

The queen's mouth twitches, but her expression is quickly replaced by another smile. "And she was traveling when you found Finneas, correct? Where was she exactly?"

I squirm a little, admitting, "I'm not quite sure, Your Majesty. That's partly why I came. My mother was traveling to investigate rumors about a plague. I think it's probable she was investigating the same one Finn alluded to in his letter."

She nods gently. "I'm sure your mother would be very proud of the courage you've shown."

I swallow, imagining Mother returning to the empty cottage and realizing what I've done. *Proud* is the last thing she'll be.

But the queen interrupts the thought. "Lyria, what I'm about to tell you is a matter that pertains to the life or death of thousands of people," she says, in a low, measured voice. "Everything I disclose in this room must be kept in utmost confidence. Only the king, my sons, and select military advisors are aware of this information. If word gets out, it would cause utter chaos across Verdinae, and we cannot risk that in these desperate times. Do you understand?"

I waver, feeling doubt creep in. It's a few seconds before I finally ask, "Why?"

*"Why?"* she echoes.

"Why did you choose me, Your Majesty?" It's the most honest question I've let myself ask, one that's troubled me since I opened

Finn's letter. "There are any number of apothecaries and Healers in the kingdom. You could have summoned anyone."

She reaches out and takes my hands. The intimacy feels bizarre, but I manage not to recoil. Her bright blue eyes search mine, completely earnest. "Because you had the courage to help a total stranger. Do you know how rare that kind of heart is? You are a very special girl, Lyria. Experience comes to everyone with time, but *character* is born." Her hands squeeze mine. "You proved yourself to Finneas, and I trust my son's judgment. In this, our direst of hours, I have faith that you'll prove yourself to me, too."

Something unlatches in my chest. As the queen's words wash over me like summer sun, they rouse some shred of self-belief that I long ago buried. Has she really just summoned me because she *believes I can do it*? Is it really so impossible that the queen sees me as I see myself . . . as someone far more capable than I've ever been given credit for?

I ask, "What exactly do you need me to do?" I feel, finally, as bold as I sound.

"For months now, the king and I have been fighting to contain a terrible plague that we believe was created as a weapon by our enemies in Ursandor," she explains, her voice dropping into a hush. "This disease is a horror like nothing our Healers have ever seen. It kills indiscriminately. We don't know how it spreads. What we *do* know is that it can wipe whole villages off the map. If it were to reach Crown City, the fallout would be catastrophic. There wouldn't be enough able-bodied to bury the dead."

"That sounds horrific."

"It is. It *will* be." Her voice wobbles. "We've *got* to stop it, or else it could kill everyone in Verdinae." For the first time, Queen Davina actually looks vulnerable. "We've managed to keep the disease from spreading by implementing a strict quarantine on the infected area. We've got hundreds of soldiers dispatched to enforce it; we're doing everything we can, but we won't be able to hold it back forever. We need a cure."

My head whirls, finally making sense of Mother's plans. If she heard about a quarantine zone where people were dying, she'd absolutely want to investigate—and the delay must be because she is still working out a cure.

*I'll beat her to it.*

My body tingles at the prospect. Can I do it? I begged my mother for an opportunity to prove myself. And here, the most spectacular of opportunities has walked through my door. I can't deny the serendipity.

"I understand." I nod to the queen. "I can travel to the village and start working immediately."

"Oh, no. That isn't possible." She withdraws her hands.

My brow furrows. "Why not?"

"As I said, we've implemented a strict quarantine. It won't be necessary for you to travel into the infected region. Our previous apothecary was working intently on developing a cure before his passing. We've been assured he was on the brink of a breakthrough. All you should need to do is dot the *i*'s and cross the *t*'s, so to speak."

A new wave of doubt washes over me. How can I cure something I can't study? But the queen's expression leaves no room for argument.

She goes on. "We'll put you up in the tower in the East Wing. There's a comfortable chamber I hope you'll find to your liking. Officially, you'll be titled the royal apothecary, and you can assist our Head Healer if he has any pressing matters he needs you to attend to. But you'll report your work on the cure directly to me. You'll have every resource at your disposal. If there's an ingredient you need, or a tool we can source for you . . . one word, and I'll see that it's done."

My chest swirls with inadequacy. Perhaps Queen Davina knows it, because she reaches out and cups my face with her palm. I shiver.

"I know that this work is a massive burden for anyone to carry. But I would not ask it of you if I didn't believe you were capable." Her eyes shine. "Nothing happens for nothing. The Almighty put you in my son's life for a reason. I believe it's because you were born to do this work."

Her confidence triggers a swell of hope. I stammer out my reply. "I—I don't think I can make any promises, but I can do my best, Your Majesty."

"That's all we ask. Thank you, Lyria. *Thank* you. Brave, clever girl." She kisses my forehead. "You are a gift from the Almighty."

A door clicks behind us, and her gaze dips. "Ah, Cygnus, here you are. There's someone I'd like you to meet."

I turn to find a tall man striding toward us. He's dressed in dark pants, boots, and a shabby white long-sleeve coat rolled up to his elbows. His jaw is stubbled, but his features are youthful—a round face, full lips, and delicate cheekbones. He can't be much older than I am, but there's something weary about his appearance, like he's exhausted by life already.

"Lyria, this is Cygnus, our Head Healer," says the queen.

I meet his gaze. I notice the peculiar color of his eyes—an intense, icy blue. Something dances in them that I can't place. Disdain? Curiosity?

"Cygnus is one of our *very* best and brightest," she continues. "Cygnus, you'll be happy to hear we've located a new apothecary to fill Ragglestaff's post. This is Lyria Fletcher—all the way from the Ironwood Mountains."

"I'm delighted to meet you, Lyria." Cygnus bows, sounding far from delighted.

"I've asked the servants to prepare Ragglestaff's old chambers," the queen says. "I was hoping you could give her a tour of the castle and help make her comfortable."

"Of course, Your Majesty." Another bow.

Then, without another word, Cygnus heads swiftly for the door.

I have to scramble to catch up. Just before exiting, I whip around and jerk another curtsy. "Thank you, Your Majesty. I won't let you down!"

She's smiling as the chapel doors swing shut.

I expect the Head Healer to stop and make a less formal introduction after we step into the hall. But he hardly even glances at me as he continues striding across the rotunda.

"There are two main sections that make up the castle," he explains in a near-monotone. "The inner part, and the outer part. The inner part is made of stone. The outer part is not. Right here, the rotunda, is the middle. If you get lost, go back here and start over."

A little annoyed, I scurry to match his pace as he heads down a wide hallway.

"This takes you to the East Wing," he continues. "Follow it all the way down and you'll hit the hospital." We pass statues, potted plants, and portraits of balding men—way too fast for me to absorb any of it. There are a million things I want to ask, but Cygnus seems about as receptive as a porcupine.

"What's your job as Head Healer, exactly?" I venture, hoping the question is inoffensive.

He tosses me an irritated glance. "I oversee all of the hospital's operations."

"Which entails what, exactly?"

"Whatever the Crown requires."

The hallway crests over an arched bridge. His stride is considerably longer—I'm getting winded trying to keep up. Finally, he stops at a set of double doors. Beyond them, I can see the hospital.

My earlier annoyance evaporates. All thoughts eddy out as I take in the sunlit chamber. It's enormous and pristine, the ivory walls so bright that they almost glow. There are dozens of rows of cots and crisp white sheets as far as the eye can see. Staff members in pale blue and gray scuttle between bedsides, some laughing amiably with patients.

All my life I've dreamed of this. A *real* hospital. Somewhere my Talent would be an asset, not a liability. Under different circumstances, I'd be euphoric. As it is, I'm awestruck. *I made it.*

Now I just need to not screw it up.

At last, he stops abruptly and turns to face me. I've been following so closely that we nearly collide. "You'll have tonight to make yourself comfortable," says Cygnus, glaring down at me. "I'll expect you to report for your first day of work tomorrow. Staff is expected to report each morning at six *sharp*. I recommend waking at five to eat. They're long days, and you'll want a big breakfast."

"Six. Big breakfast. Got it," I say, still looking around at the hospital. I don't know where to start. I gesture to the scroll hanging at the end of a nearby cot. "What are these for?"

"Those indicate the condition and care plan to keep track of who's receiving what." Cygnus's eyes narrow, like he's suddenly suspicious. "Which university did you attend?"

"Oh, I—I actually learned from my mother."

"Your *mother,*" he says, sounding intensely unamused.

"Yes."

His expression sours further. Cygnus looks like he has more thoughts on the subject, but instead he says, "I'll show you your room." We abruptly turn down a corridor and he asks, "How old are you?"

I pause. "Eighteen."

Cygnus sighs, and I can almost tell what he's thinking. *Too inexperienced. Too stupid.*

"How old are *you*?" I toss back, still hurrying to keep up with his long strides.

"Nineteen."

"Isn't that a little young to be Head Healer?"

He stops walking and rounds on me, eyes narrow. I'm suddenly aware of how much taller he is than me.

"*Listen.* I've spent the past two years building that hospital into the most efficient medical operation in the Midlands," he says in a low, tight voice like a snarl. "I am willing to dedicate any amount of force necessary to ensure that *my life's work* is not compromised by *anyone.* No matter what kind of sway they hold with the royal family."

Before I can form a response, he shoots me a disgusted look and hurries on, eventually stopping at the base of a set of stairs. "Your room is up there."

I come to a halt and glare at him. "Is there a reason you're so rude?"

This man actually *rolls his eyes* before turning to leave. But he's not getting away that easily. Not with my Talent searing through my veins.

*"Hey!"* I storm after him, right on his heels. "I asked you a question!"

Cygnus whips around. "Which I chose not to entertain."

"What's your *problem*? I haven't done anything to make you hate me."

"I don't hate you," he scoffs. "I hate that you're here. In Crown City, a Healer is someone who attended *university*. It's a title that takes years to earn. You might be the best apothecary in whatever little outwall village you grew up in, but our hospital has actual standards."

"You haven't given me a chance," I protest as shame heats my face. "You can't just decide I'm not capable." His words wouldn't sting if it weren't for their undercurrent of truth. I can hear Mother's voice in every word. My fists clench as the monster of my Talent grapples toward the surface, but I force it back down.

*Stay calm.*

"It's not about capability, it's about training. Which you lack." Cygnus leans in. "Honestly, Leenia—"

*"Lyria."*

"Right." His eyes narrow. "*Lyria.* You want my advice? If I were you, I'd eat a nice big supper, enjoy your night in the palace, and go home tomorrow morning with a story to tell. Trust me. You would be better off."

I can't believe his dismissiveness. "Why?"

"Because the Crown's favor is not the bulwark you think it is," he snaps. "Warming Finn's bed won't protect you forever. I've known him my entire life. He likes to play with his girls and then drop them. In the meantime, I'm not putting lives in danger because the prince can't keep it in his pants. *Understood?*"

He doesn't wait for my objections before turning away.

*Thank the Gods for small miracles.*

He's gone before I start to cry.

# 7

y chambers are predictably plush. After drying my tears, I take inventory: a big four-poster bed draped with pastels, a desk, an empty bookshelf, a wardrobe, a closet, and a huge marble fireplace wafting sweet-smelling pine smoke. My scant belongings have been laid on the bed. They look out of place amid the silk and velvet: too shabby and devoid of color. I notice my satchel has been cleaned and emptied . . . in other words, searched. When I start to unpack, I realize the futility.

My wardrobe is already overflowing with garments that look like they've been stitched specifically for me. Marveling, I withdraw dress after dress, each more luxurious than the last. There are outfits for all seasons: garden frocks and evening gowns, day dresses with fluffy skirts and sleeves looped with ribbons. I find a dark blue winter cloak with fur trim and six pairs of shoes, including several sparkling pairs of slippers. The closet drawers contain several new work dresses in soft, fine-woven linen, and I'm relieved to see that my uniform includes a white kerchief. When I open the bottom drawer, I encounter a heap of sheer, short, lacy undergarments . . . and quickly slam it back shut.

The best part is my washroom. It has hot running water and a claw-foot tub, something I've ardently fantasized about but never actually seen. After some experimenting, I figure out how to fill it. When I sink into the steaming water, I decide it's the single most decadent thing I've ever experienced.

After bathing, I pull on the most subdued pair of pajamas I can find and crawl into the sheets. But sleep doesn't find me. I'm too busy strategizing for the day ahead. Cygnus had a lot of Gods-damn nerve calling me unqualified, considering he's only *one* year my senior. Unless he started studying in diapers, I can't be that far behind. I may not have had a fancy royal education, but I had *Mother's* scrutiny to contend with, and I'm willing to bet that was about a hundred times stricter.

Determination roars through me. Mother told me that when she started school at the High Houses, some other students looked down on her because of her upbringing in the Ironwoods. Elves came from all over the Midlands to study at the Evermorean universities, but even back then, it was considered more sophisticated to grow up in the Hartlands. She had one strategy for overcoming their bias: *Be so good they can't dismiss you.* So that's exactly what I'll do.

And when I find the cure, no one will ever doubt me again.

---

My first night in the castle is restless torture. I jolt awake at every chime of the clock, panicking and slick with sweat. At five, I crawl out of bed and draw another bath to brace for the day ahead. I'm sure it will be a long one.

Upon my arrival at the hospital, it takes a few minutes to be directed to Cygnus's office. I find him hunched over his desk. Determined to be the bigger person, I greet him as cheerily as I can. "Good morning!"

He doesn't look up from his papers. "You're late."

I glance at the clock in annoyance. He's correct—by two minutes. At least he and Mother would get along.

"Last night, we had six wounded soldiers brought in from Karapesh in Sontaag, so I won't have time to onboard you this morning," he continues. "Anna will show you the ropes."

"Who's Anna?" I ask.

He gestures vaguely down the hall. "She's our head of staff. You can find her in the storehouse. Big woman, curly brown hair. You can't miss her."

"Is she my boss, or are you?"

"She's second-in-command. If you do something to upset Anna, you've done something to upset me. Is that clear?"

"Crystal," I return, with some bite. "Do you need any help with the soldiers? If there's any way I can assist . . ." I trail off as he finally looks up at me, and I read his expression. The acidity could wither daisies.

"Right now," he says, "the most helpful thing you can do is disappear."

I leave with my face burning.

When I track down Anna, I'm relieved to find her far more welcoming. A direct, no-nonsense woman, she reminds me of a taller version of Mother. She only asks a few questions about my competencies before launching into a straightforward explanation of the hospital's operations. "The Crown funds everything, so there's no cost for our patients. People travel from all over to get treated—that's why we're practically always full. We might see hundreds of patients in a single month."

"How have you functioned without an apothecary?"

"Oh, our medicine for patients is imported from Sulnik," she clarifies. "Your predecessor, Ragglestaff, was brought on to serve the *Crown.* Not the public. He pitched in here and there when we needed extra hands, of course. But even toward the end, he was busy with private projects."

My spirits sink a little. I'd been looking forward to the opportunity to test my skills. But of course, the cure needs to come first. Perhaps when I'm finished, I can speak with the queen about weaning the people here off their reliance on Sulish medicine.

Anna gives me a quick tour of the staging area before leading me out onto a patio. We follow a stone path down through the hospital's designated terraces, which contain rows and rows of waist-high planter boxes. The plants look wild and unkempt, but I spot a host of familiar friends, like yarrow and calendula. "Did Ragglestaff tend these?"

"Once upon a time, yes. Most of it's gone wild now. Pretty to look at, but no one here knows how to use them."

I drag my hand over a patch of yarrow. The heads have dried and gone rough. "That seems like a waste."

"Indeed. But we've been stuffed to the gills. With all that inflow from the western front, resources are spread thin." She continues down the terraced steps until we stop before a small, thatched-roof cottage. "I should warn you, the storehouse has been somewhat neglected. It's a bit of a mess."

She pushes open the door.

First, the smell hits me—chemicals and carrion. As we venture in with tentative steps, I decide she was too kind when she called this place a mess. *Cesspool* might cover it. The place looks like it's been ransacked. Rubbish and broken bottles are strewn across the floor. Several cauldrons have tipped, their contents leaking and rotting in some places. The scant equipment looks rusted beyond repair. Pinching my nose, I ask, "How long has it been like this?"

"A few months or so?" She covers her nose with her apron. "I didn't realize how bad it'd gotten. We've been under strict instructions not to touch anything."

We hurry out, gulping fresh air when the door shuts behind us.

I'm itching to start, but the tour is not over yet. Anna leads me back inside and into the hospital's main washroom, which smells heavenly in contrast. The walls are lined with shelves of glass bottles labeled in black script. This must be the imported medicine she mentioned.

I'm ready to head back to the storehouse, but before I can do so, Anna hands me a list. "Cygnus left a list of jobs he'd like you to complete."

I glance down, skimming quickly—

- *Wash laundry in hamper #8*
- *Fold bandages in hamper #3*
- *Fold sheets in hamper #4*
- *Change all chamber pots on the staging floor*
- *Scrub the laundry room floor*
- *Dust the bookshelf in the Head Healer's office*

—and look up incredulously when I finish. "These are common chores."

Anna tuts at my expression. "Everyone needs to start somewhere!"

When Anna leaves me to my work, I curse Cygnus internally. I should have known he'd try to sabotage me. He made it clear he thinks I was only hired as a glorified consort—maybe he thinks I'm some prissy nobleman's daughter who'll refuse to get dirt under her fingernails. Or maybe his aim is to make me so busy that I can't complete the work. Perhaps he thinks I'll go whining to Finn. It doesn't matter. He picked the wrong girl to underestimate. If he wants to make me his maid, I'll be the best damn maid he's ever seen.

I tackle the most distasteful task first. It takes two hours to empty the chamber pots, including the trek up and down stairs, three hours to fold laundry, and an inestimably long stint in purgatory while scrubbing the floor of the staging room. Irritation doesn't bode well for my Talent. I start sweating in the first five minutes, trying to keep it at bay, and can't stop. By midday, I'm an aching, sticky mess with shit stains on my apron. Staff members snicker behind my back.

Still, I work quickly and hard, racing the clock to return to the storehouse. I complete the stupid list a little after three, which leaves just a few hours to get started on cleaning Ragglestaff's mess. I'm so focused on my real work, it's not until Cygnus clears his throat that I realize he has been watching me.

"Oh. Hi. Sorry, I was just—" I gesture at the mess. "How did it go? With the soldiers, I mean."

"Everyone's stable." He shoves his hands in his pockets. "I was just checking to see if you're settling in."

"I am. Thanks."

"I . . . also wanted to mention our earlier conversation." Cygnus hesitates, his eyes boring holes in the floor. "I shouldn't have taken out my frustration on you."

I feel a little rush of appeasement. This is *not* an apology, but perhaps the closest I'll get to one. "You've decided not to hate me, then?" I ask.

"I've decided not to blame you."

"Very generous."

Cygnus looks up. "It's not your fault the Crown put you in a position to fail."

*Never mind. Still a prick.* "What makes you sure that I'm going to?" I grind out.

He blinks. "Because you have no idea what you're doing."

I resist the urge to fling the nearest bucket at his head. "How would *you* have any idea what I'm capable of?"

His eyes darken. "If you had a patient admitted with painful white sores, coughing up blood, what would you give them?"

The question catches me off guard. "I . . . I would examine them first."

"Sure. But any second-year medical student could tell you they had crow's cough, and they'd need draught of leatherweed."

I swallow.

He fires off another question. "If a mother were delivering a child, and she hemorrhaged, what's the first thing you'd do?"

Shame blazes through me. "I'm not sure."

"And if an infant was vomiting so violently that they were approaching dehydration, what would you give them?"

*I know this one!* "Sandal bark?"

"Wrong. Sandal bark isn't appropriate for infants. You'd stop the child's heart."

Rage swells in response to his smug expression. I don't need reminding that I have plenty to learn. My Talent claws up my spine, hissing to silence him. I have to struggle through a few calming breaths before saying, "Look, I didn't say I know everything—"

"I would settle for you knowing *anything,*" he snaps. "From here on, that's the assumption you should be working with. You know nothing and have everything to learn. *That's* your baseline."

*He sounds just like Mother.* "Do you talk to all your staff like this?"

"The rest of my staff knows how to respect authority."

"I don't respect cruelty."

Cygnus laughs mirthlessly. "It's actually indicative of your naivety that you think I'm being cruel right now."

"You are being *mean.*"

"I'm trying to help you."

"How is this helping?"

His nostrils flare. "There is a certain way things are done here. I'm warning you that you *must* learn to conform to that system, or you will draw unnecessary attention to yourself."

*Is he seriously trying to mask his disdain under the guise of protecting me?*

"What do you want me to do, then? Go back to my room and twiddle my thumbs?"

"I want you to learn when to shut up and listen," Cygnus growls. "Put your head down and *do the damn work.*"

"Fine," I snap. "In exchange, I'd like you to stop treating me like a simpleton."

Cygnus gives me a long, hard look. "You can have my respect when you've earned it, Leera."

"It's Leer—ee—uh. *Lyria!*" I shout at his retreating form.

As my first week in the castle passes, Cygnus and I sink into a stalemate.

He barely glances at me each morning when he issues the day's instructions: chamber pots, laundry, scrubbing, *repeat.* I learn the definition of loathing while marching off to complete them. The impasse takes hold as he realizes, gradually, that I'm willing to take everything he throws at me.

I scrub bloodstains from bedsheets until my fingers are raw. I crush lice eggs and wash corpses and sweep urine-soaked mats. As I work, I'm trailed by glares and whispers. Anna is the only person who will even return a *hello.* Loneliness devours me, but that's nothing new. When I catch myself pining for Finn, I smother the thought. His rejection still stings, which is mortifying. It was stupid to expect that he cared enough to be here when I arrived. My value to him is my craft. Nothing more.

I take Cygnus's advice, put my head down, and do the damn work. But I hate every second. I race through my tasks, but I complete them so thoroughly that he can't protest when I finish early. For the first time in my life, I feel grateful I was raised by such a perfectionist. There's a special satisfaction when I stroll into his office each afternoon and announce the completion of my drudgery. Then I skip off to the storehouse, where my *real* work can start.

Cleaning Ragglestaff's mess is a daunting undertaking. The more I excavate, the worse it seems. It takes hours and hours of scrubbing, wiping, and hauling Gods know how many buckets of soapy water, but toward the week's end, I have something close to a functioning workspace.

One night, I return to my chambers to find a box on the bed. My heart skips a beat when I see the royal crest on the accompanying letter, thinking that perhaps Finn has written to me, but it sinks again as I tear it open.

*Lyria,*

*I've accumulated Ragglestaff's notes for your inspection. Please cross-reference the information here with whatever else you find in the storehouse. I appreciate your attention to this vital matter.*

*With warmest regards,*
*Her Royal Majesty*
*Queen Davina*

I stifle my disappointment and examine the box. Inside is a trove of handwritten notes, diagrams, and charts. A few books are included, with notes scrawled in the margins in the same spidery script. Most of the documents are baffling. I find no reports of experiments or outcomes—Ragglestaff mostly seemed to scribble nonsense. I find some rambling thoughts about blood and the elements, and countless pages detailing symptoms. Some descriptions make me shiver: *PAIN. SO MUCH PAIN.*

I decide that the best first step is to transcribe everything into a fresh notebook. Once it's all laid out, I can decipher possible meanings. I'm in the middle of copying a diagram of a cliffcrow one afternoon when I'm startled by a crash behind me. I nearly tumble out of my chair as I whip around to meet the intruder. It's a tiny girl around my age with short, frizzy blond hair.

"Uh . . . hello!" She jerks a little wave, wincing as we both glance at the bottle she's tipped. "Sorry about that. You're Lyria, right? My name's Daisy. I heard you're new here and sort of just . . . came to say hello. Do you need help?"

"Uh, sure," I say after a moment's pause. It's been so long since anyone's spoken to me, I don't know what to make of her offer.

"How've you been settling in?" Daisy asks, glancing around the storehouse. She wears a cornflower-blue uniform, which I've come to learn means she's a nurse. She takes a nearby sponge and begins scrubbing the counters. Before I can answer her question, she adds, "I've always wondered what Ragglestaff had in here. He was so secretive. Nice man, but really kept to himself, y'know?"

"You should have seen it a week ago," I say. "So far, I've done basically nothing but clean."

"I noticed you on the staging floor yesterday!" Daisy grins. "I've never seen anyone scrub floors so enthusiastically."

"That's because Cygnus is trying to work me to death," I grumble.

"Cygnus?" She giggles.

I'm a little alarmed to see her blush. "You know him?"

"Of course! I mean, I don't interact with him much . . . but he waved to me last week in the dining hall, so he definitely knows who I am."

"He's the worst, isn't he?"

She looks puzzled. "You think so?"

"He's been hateful since the minute I got here," I confide. "You're the first person who has actually talked to me."

"I'm sure he doesn't hate you."

"Oh, yes he does." I picture his disdainful expression. "Or at least he doesn't think I have what it takes. He actually made it pretty clear he doesn't want me here at all."

"Don't listen to him. It's all bluster—probably some unhinged psychological tactic he learned at school. Ever since he came back from Belshire, he thinks he hangs the moon."

I frown, imagining younger Cygnus seated in a lecture hall. Belshire is the most prestigious school in Sontaag, where I hoped to one day complete my education if Mother would ever allow it. The fact that Cygnus got to study there while I was stuck in the Ironwoods feels like a crime against justice.

"Why is he even in charge?" I ask. "He's awful."

"Because he's a damn good Healer," Daisy says matter-of-factly. "Before Cygnus got involved with the East Wing, things were a mess. Ask anyone who was around then. Back then, the hospital just treated the royals and guests. He got in here and completely turned things around, so they promoted him right to the top. The queen *loves* him. She'll give him anything he wants. That's the reason we treat the common folk. Cygnus was the one who pushed for it."

I don't like how this information opposes the impression I've formed of the Head Healer. Something churns in my chest—guilt, maybe? I don't need Cygnus to give me reasons to like him.

"But he's so . . ." I do a rude impression of his posture.

"He's a genius. That's just how they are, I suppose." She shrugs.

As we clean, Daisy chatters on and on. I find her unnerving at first but gradually grow to appreciate her chipper attitude. I don't have to interject much and can mostly just listen. She tells me her whole life story. I learn that she loves fashion and dreamed of making gowns for noblewomen but was the only one in a big family with the grades for the Royal Nursing Academy.

"I still like it here," she says. "My sisters are all sweating in a kitchen somewhere, while I get to be in the heart of the city. How did you end up in the castle?"

I open my mouth, then shut it again. *What if she forms the same impression of me as Cygnus did?* I'm reluctant to admit I was summoned after a chance encounter with Finn. The story might trigger dangerous questions, and I don't need anyone scrutinizing his recovery too closely. But being surrounded by people while having no one to confide in feels even worse than total isolation, somehow.

In the end, I tell her almost everything. Daisy is wide-eyed as I describe healing Finn after the Moragorion—omitting, of course, the magical details—and his subsequent skirmish with the mercenaries. I describe my first encounter with the queen and explain that she's tasked me with an important classified project. To my relief, Daisy doesn't press for details about the assignment. She's much more interested in my relationship with Finn, even when I explain I haven't seen him since my arrival.

"I mean, I've heard that about Prince Finneas," Daisy admits, her cheeks turning rosy.

"What do you mean?"

"Well . . . he's got a reputation. If you know what I mean."

I don't. "What kind of a reputation?"

She swallows. "I would never say anything to disrespect the Crown, of course . . . but, y'know, the princes all have very distinct personalities. Different strengths and weaknesses. Like, Sebastian's the best scholar, and he's always been so focused. He got engaged to Prince Roman at *sixteen,* which everyone was thrilled about, because it sealed the alliance with Sulnik . . . but I don't think he ever even courted anyone else. And Damien's the best fighter, everybody knows that. King Rodrick had to ban him from tournaments because he kept accidentally killing our allies. But Finneas . . ."

"He's the fun one," I complete, with my stomach sinking. *Didn't he tell you himself?*

"Yeah. I suppose so." Daisy nods a little, looking uncomfortable. "At least, that's what I've heard from the other nurses . . . and the maids . . . and the scullery."

I can hear the subtext in her words, echoing Cygnus. *He likes to play with his girls and then drop them.* The mental picture of Finn in another girl's arms makes me nauseous.

"I'm not saying that means he's off with a girl somewhere," Daisy says quickly.

"Right." My ears burn.

"I'm serious, Lyria. The fact that he brought you all the way here means you're obviously special to him."

I think of Finn's letter. I've spent a week and a half puzzling over the meaning of the word *dazzled.*

*Forgive me for leaving without confessing my feelings,* he'd written. But *what* feelings could he mean? Gratitude for saving his life? Relief that I might be able to stop the plague?

And if I really am so special, why isn't he *here*?

"He's given me no reason to believe that," I insist. But I'm flooded with memories of the cottage. Every tactile detail is burned into my brain: the rough warmth of his hands, the hard lines of his body against mine, the smell of his skin, like sun warming rocks after rain.

Daisy looks unconvinced. "Whatever you say."

# 8

fter our conversation, I resolve to put Finn out of my mind.

What Daisy shared about his reputation has confirmed my worst suspicions. *He's not here because he doesn't care*. The most likely explanation for Finn's absence is that he's off on a lark, surrounded by beautiful women with fascinating stories about their adventurous lives.

*You didn't come here for romance,* I remind myself firmly. *You're here to do a job.*

Everything else is just noise.

The one rumination I allow myself is about Mother. It's been nearly two weeks since I left the Ironwoods, and she still hasn't come for me or sent word. I check the ravenry daily for news, but there's nothing. I wonder if she's made it home and found my note yet. Perhaps she's still trying to sort out the plague. Apprehension gnaws, but I temper it by leaning in to my work. I'm determined to complete the queen's mandate as quickly as possible.

With a clean storehouse, focusing on the cure becomes easier as I progress through transcribing Ragglestaff's chicken scratches. Like compiling a puzzle, I see his vision more clearly with each small piece I assemble. Slowly, it starts clicking together.

He called his cure the omnidraught. I assume that the name was chosen to reference the plague's varied symptoms. In one book, I find page after page with observations on subjects in quarantine. Their symptoms ranged wildly, with no discernible pattern in age or gender. It seems that unlike me, he was afforded direct access to patients, and I wonder, with an ache in my chest, if that was the reason he died.

Gradually, I uncover his theory. I'm elated when I realize that what he was trying to create is not all that fundamentally different from all's-cure—the *most* common potion in my arsenal. The ingredients are *slightly* different, but the building blocks are the same. All easy in theory. I can't wait to share the good news with the queen.

I'm in high spirits when I finish my work and head to meet Daisy for a late lunch. We've fallen into a pattern of sharing our meals, and I look forward to our conversations, which often contain colorful reports of the court gossip. Usually, the hospital is clear at this time of day. But I notice an atypical commotion as I pass through the staging area. Nurses and Healers are clustered around the front doors, where several soldiers are being dragged in on stretchers. I spot uniformed VIA, and other soldiers in black uniforms I've never seen . . .

And then a voice sounds that I'd recognize anywhere.

*"Where is she?"* it booms.

I spin around just in time to see him hurtling toward me.

Finn.

Gods help me, my knees almost buckle at the sight of him.

He's sunburned and travel-worn and smells like a horse, but otherwise Finn is unchanged: tall, impossibly handsome, and *real.* He wears a black uniform. All my careful determination to cut him out of my heart thaws in an instant. "Look at you!" Finn closes the distance and sweeps me into a crushing embrace that has every head in the hospital snapping our way.

*"You're—going—to—break—my—ribs,"* I wheeze, and he chuckles as he lowers me.

Whispers skitter around us, and I'm half aware of how improper we look. But it's hard to care when he's finally *here,* in front of me. After the last several weeks, he feels like the first solid thing I can hold on to.

"I'm so sorry I wasn't here to meet you," he says, his hands slipping into mine. "Roburn said you got here all right.... Have you been settling in? I heard they put you up in the East Tower?"

I feel every eye in the room on us as he gazes down at me, beaming. "Yes. The room is great."

*The room is great? Really?*

"And Cyg's got you at it already?"

*"Naturally."*

The cool voice sounds from behind him. Finn rounds to reveal Cygnus stalking toward us, looking predictably unamused.

"I hear you get the credit for finding her," the Head Healer drawls. "I have to commend you; it's hard to believe someone so beautiful could be a capable apothecary." The words are *almost* a compliment. But I glare back, hearing the insinuation.

Finn, however, seems unbothered. "She's really something, isn't she?" He beams, tossing an arm around the Head Healer. "Lyria, Cygy and I go *way* back. Trust me, you are in capable hands."

I have feelings about the nickname Cygy, but I hope they don't show on my face. "Is that right?"

"You won't find a better Healer in the Midlands," Finn boasts. "He's a genius—won every prize under the sun for it when we were in Belshire."

Cygnus's smile is tight. "It's my pleasure to serve."

He's a decent liar. Finn might think him indulgent and long-suffering, but my Talent tells a different story. I perceive the slight change in his scent, the subtle flex of his muscles—telltale signals of stress. Cygnus does *not* like Finn.

And I'm already certain he loathes me.

Still maintaining that placid mask, the Head Healer slides out of Finn's grip. "If you'll excuse me, I have surgery scheduled for this afternoon." He straightens his coat. "We're taking Jeredsen's leg."

All the light leaves Finn's face.

"What about the others?" he asks roughly.

"Recovering fine," says Cygnus.

"That's good, at least."

They exchange more words I don't have context for. Then, after tossing me one more disdainful glance, Cygnus mumbles about being needed elsewhere and drifts away.

When Finn swivels back toward me, his eyes are glistening. "Those are *my* men," he explains in a low voice. "We got ambushed on a mission. I've been attending to their families."

Cold washes down my spine. I feel terrible for every assumption I've made about him being off with other women. All this time, I thought he'd been cavorting, but he really has been away on important business—just as his letter said. "I'm so sorry. I had no idea."

He reaches out and seizes my hands. "We shouldn't talk about it now. But I need to hear everything I've missed. You should join us at dinner tonight."

*"Tonight?"* My stomach lurches.

"Yes. And I'll explain more."

"Where?"

"In the Great Hall. We're hosting a few guests. You should join us and meet my brothers." He gives me one of those devilish grins. "And afterward, we can talk more in private."

Logic and emotion battle within me. I should not get any closer to the royals than absolutely necessary. Proximity invites scrutiny. But the desire to be closer to Finn, physically and emotionally, is overwhelming.

"Tonight," I agree, breathless.

Finn gives me one more squeeze before gliding back to his soldiers. I feel weightless as I hurry off to tell Daisy. When I pass the Head Healer's office, I think I catch Cygnus shaking his head.

But I must have imagined it.

---

I'm grateful when Daisy offers to help me get ready. She picks out a sleek seafoam-green gown with gold trim. The sleeves are gauzy and impractical, hanging nearly to the floor. I've never shown so much collarbone, but she insists the ensemble is *faaabulous*. When she reaches for my hair, I'm hesitant to take off my kerchief. To my relief, the concealment charm holds, and Daisy chatters on as usual while arranging my hair in an updo. When she's done, she drags me to a mirror to admire her work. Though I am exposed with my ears on display, I must admit, I feel beautiful, and I might look it, too.

I'm running late by the time I hurry into the Great Hall and find the party well underway. My pulse thrums as I pause at the threshold, taking it in.

A long table splits the chamber, with fires dancing in the hearths. Dozens of courtiers mill about, sipping sparkling wine or engaged in conversation. I see a mixture of ages and skin tones and shapes, some round and some slim, each more beautifully dressed than the next. I'm flooded with gratitude toward Daisy, as my ensemble feels neither too plain nor ostentatious. With luck, I can blend into the background.

I search the hall for one familiar face and come up empty.

"Lyria, isn't it?"

"Yes?" I spin at the interruption and come face-to-face with the most glamorous woman I've ever seen. She might be sixteen or thirty-six; between the makeup and jewels and elaborate coiffure, I can't be sure. Her dress is pale blue with a fur trim that perfectly sets off her silvery hair.

"I'm Odessa Erik," she purrs, "princess of Sulnik." The way her eyes drag up my figure makes me feel like she can see through my clothes.

I squirm. "How did you know my name?"

"I make it a point to know what's happening at court," she says, flashing a tight-lipped smile. "Your appointment caused quite the stir. In Sulnik, our Healers are women of the cloth. It's not considered *proper* for a young lady to work in a hospital. I do admire Verdinae and its liberating customs. So very modern."

Oh, so it's like that.

"Feel free to stop by the East Wing sometime." I return her smirk. "I'd be happy to help with whatever ails you."

Her smile calcifies, and my Talent flares with the impulse to smack the look right off her beautiful face. Before I have the chance, we're interrupted by what sounds like a tinkling bell. I look across the room and watch Queen Davina rap her fork against her flute of sparkling wine.

"If you'll all take your seats," she says, "I'd like to get dinner started."

I pick a spot toward the end of the banquet table, as far from Odessa as possible. Another drop-dead-gorgeous woman, this one brunette, takes the one opposite. It doesn't escape me that the chairs around us remain unfilled. I still haven't found Finn among the crowd, and when the party settles, it becomes evident that he's absent.

The possibility creeps over me: *What if he's abandoned me again?*

Queen Davina makes no acknowledgment of her missing son before she cues the servants to bring our first course. This is a totally different dining experience from that of the servants' quarters. Instead of well-worn wooden plates, we're served on gold dishes that *screeeeecchhh* when I try to use my fork. The food is divine, of course—roast duck, glazed carrots, fluffy bread, steaming potatoes, and several sweet puddings spiced with nutmeg and cinnamon.

It's a desperate fight to follow the conversation. I try to sort out which guests are Verdish nobles and which are foreign dignitaries. There's plenty of fur-lined regalia from Sulnik, and a whole host of people wearing sashes bearing the royal crest of Dasken. I even spot a few guests in flowing long sleeves—probably emissaries from Ursandor. With tensions high across the Midlands, it seems all the players want a seat at the table. At first, everyone talks about the war in Sontaag, and I feel woefully uninformed as people toss around names of generals and tactics. Fortunately, the focus shifts to supply lines and shopping. Central to the discussion is the striking brunette across from me, whom I study throughout the meal.

She speaks with a thick Eastern accent that I initially find hard to follow, but her stories are so animated and raunchy that I start laughing along with the table. I can't take my eyes off her. Her red gown perfectly complements the gold sheen of her skin. Her long dark hair is worn freely over her shoulders, glistening like a moonlit river. But it's her eyes that are most alluring. They're an extraordinary shade of violet.

Someone calls her Sandria, and my stomach lurches as I finally peg her as Sandria Malek—the princess of Ursandor. This complicates my impression. Is she among the conspirators to unleash the plague? Is this charming young woman really that much of a monster?

I study her sidelong as she entertains a question from a gray-mustached courtier. But her answer is interrupted by a booming voice.

"*PRESENTING* Their Royal Highnesses, Prince Sebastian Thorne and Prince Finneas Thorne!"

Relief barrels through me as they enter, flanked by guards in their livery. I know Finn at a glance. The lean, golden-haired one must be Sebastian. The Thorne family resemblance is not subtle. They share the strong jaw and angular features. But Sebastian's face is a little softer and rounder, and as they approach, I notice that he moves differently, too. His gait is measured and graceful. Finn clomps along like a soldier.

The seat to my right is empty. When Finn plops into it, I feel instantly more relaxed. Odessa glares daggers. Sandria smirks, taking a sip of her wine. The rest of the table looks . . . bored.

"My apologies for our tardiness," says Sebastian, sliding into another empty seat, next to Sandria. "We just finished meeting with the city's interior council; there were a few logistical points with the tournament that we needed to flesh out." Sebastian smiles, and then his gaze turns to me. "You must be Lyria. I've heard so many good things."

"Likewise," I manage.

Finn fills me in on the meeting—"*Excruciatingly* boring"—before wolfing down his meal. While he's occupied with eating, I brace for more awkwardness, but Sebastian starts up a polite line of questioning about the work in the East Wing and my experiences foraging in the Ironwoods. It's immediately evident why he's so widely liked. Sebastian is simply very kind. He doesn't poke holes in my answers or scoff at my ignorance. There's no dismissal of my outwall upbringing. He seems genuinely curious about my life and interests. I decide that I enjoy his company.

The servants come to clear our plates, at which point Queen Davina rises, claps her hands, and calls for dancing. Tables are hauled away, and the orchestra starts an up-tempo song with a wicked-fast fiddle.

I am *not* prepared to dance. Mother once put it kindly when she said I've got the coordination of a newborn moose. I'm torn between retreating the way I came and slipping out through the garden doors, but to my simultaneous surprise, delight, and horror . . . Finn reaches for my hand.

I recoil reflexively. "I can't dance."

He waits, eyes searching mine. "This one's easy. I can teach you."

"In front of all these people?"

Finn's smile widens. "Forget them."

I glance toward the dance floor, where Sebastian is leading a sour-faced Odessa to the first song. He smiles and shoots a wink in our direction.

I gaze up into Finn's eyes, searching for what swirls within them. There's resolve and curiosity and hope, all intermingled . . . and I think I might stop breathing at the spark of desire that I find there, too. Suddenly, it's just me and him, back at the waterfall, lying side by side beneath the sun.

I swallow. And then I take his hand.

I've read about dancing in books. I've done it for my enjoyment, twirling in the garden or prancing on tiptoe for fun. But *this* . . . dancing with *Finn* . . . is a joy like I've never experienced. After a while, I stop thinking about the onlooking eyes. We laugh when I miss a step, and Finn just holds me closer. Eventually, my anxieties slip away. I forget about time and propriety and my feet, which should be aching; I forget about my Talent, and the cottage, and the plague. There is only the music, and his hands, and his waist against mine.

As a particularly beautiful song winds to an end, Finn brings his lips to my hair and whispers, "Would you like to go speak somewhere privately?"

I'm about to reply but get interrupted as trumpeting floods the Great Hall.

"*PRESENTING* His Royal Highness, Prince Damien Thorne!"

We both turn as the youngest Prince of Verdinae swaggers into the chamber.

*Swagger* is the only word for it. Damien is a head shorter than his brothers, with a distinct unkempt heap of dark curls. He's barrel-chested and muscled like an ox, and his stance communicates an assurance that outpaces both his siblings'. He doesn't move like a child. He moves like a man who knows how to kill and does it often.

Reaching the queen, Damien kisses his mother's outstretched hand. "Good evening, Mother. I brought you a gift."

Whispers infest the chamber. Initially, I think it's over the soldiers in black Damien has brought with him, who all look rather road-worn. But as the crowd draws back to create space, I realize his troops aren't alone: They're leading a prisoner.

The captive is in such bad condition that my brain doesn't immediately register him as a living being. He's led by a chain attached to a metal collar, with other chains binding him to the massive log he carries over his shoulders. There's a rag stuffed in his mouth, and it's clear he's been beaten. Starved, too. As the procession passes, rattling ominously, I get a closer look at his ears.

They're pointed. Just like mine.

My legs almost give out from under me.

The room has silenced. I gaze around, horrified, at the impassive faces around me. Sebastian's expression is intent but unreadable. Odessa looks downright placid, and the queen is actually smiling. Finn wears a blank mask—and I edge a step away, revolted.

"My good people of Verdinae!" Damien calls, hoisting a goblet. "Honored guests! *Welcome!* And thank you for joining us! Tonight, it's my pleasure to bring you good news from our campaign in the west against Sontaag. As I'm sure many of you know, I've come straight from the front lines. I've been working side by side with my father to advance his vision of a united Midlands and bring our western enemies to heel. I'm pleased to report that we've achieved a decisive victory in our first campaign against the so-called free cities. As of yesterday . . . we have three of the thirteen securely under our control."

Clapping erupts. I can't tear my eyes from the bloodied prisoner, who is escorted by the VIA to the now-empty dance floor and forced to his knees. They unclip the log.

"Tonight, as a gift for my dear mother, and in thanks for the responsibility you've entrusted me with, I've brought a special present for your entertainment. *This,*" Damien says, gesturing to the prisoner, "is Fergustan of Pomeradia. Up until a fortnight past, he was high magistrate of the city."

Damien is grinning now.

"You see," he continues, "Fergustan was born with a Talent for warping minds. And as all magic wielders do, he used that magic to obtain influence and exploit the innocent. While he lived in luxury, the people of his city starved. But no more."

The prisoner—Fergustan—cries out and shakes his head, but his rebuttal is muted by the gag.

I bite down, clenching my fists until blood coats my fingernails. I keep squeezing. My Talent feels like a white iron glued to my spine; it's all I can do to contain it.

"My father's mission is to abolish the scourge of magic from the Midlands. And today, I'm proud to help him forward that work."

Damien turns toward Fergustan, who tries to speak again, but it is no use.

The prince proclaims, "For Verdinae!"

I realize what's happening just in time to bury my face in Finn's chest. I hear it anyway. A whistling blade, followed by a small, wet noise . . .

Then the *thud* as Fergustan's head tumbles to the floor.

# 9

make it to the bushes before losing my dinner.

*Out. I need out.*

The last few weeks of my life come hurtling back with the contents of my stomach, just as bitter and foul in retrospect. The wall. The plague. The nightmare I'm living. I cling to a tree as my body spasms. Everything burns. I drop to my knees through the worst of it, until it's over and I'm hacking and spluttering, clawing the grass.

*"Lyria?"*

Someone's calling for me. I look back toward the castle and the terrace I sprinted through. The doors to the Great Hall cast long, flickering reflections on its marble.

I rise quickly, shoving myself to my feet, then almost collapse again as I realize what I've done.

Everything in a five-foot radius of me is dead. The grass I collapsed in looks like it's been burned to ash. The tree I braced against has turned shriveled and gray. When I reach out to touch the hedges, dust crumbles in my fingers.

I stumble back, overcome by the carnage of my Talent.

*"Lyria!"* It's Finn.

I've never been less happy to see him. My hands fly protectively to my ears, finding that the charm has reverted after my outburst. I work to calm my racing lungs, murmuring the spell under my breath as I hurry away from the crater.

"Over here!" I croak, panting, once I've managed to change my ears back.

"Are you all right?" Finn jogs closer, coming into view. "I'm so sorry. I had no idea Damien was going to do that."

My gaze drifts back toward the castle, where music has resumed in the Great Hall. Through the glowing windows, I see the party has picked back up like nothing has happened. Servants are already mopping the floor.

I feel hollow.

"Finn, I don't know what I'm doing here," I finally admit quietly.

"Sure you do," he insists. "What are you talking about? You're my guest."

I shake my head, not meeting his eye. The sound of Fergustan's head as it tumbled echoes again and again. Damien claimed the Elf was abusing his magic but didn't even let him speak. *Did Fergustan really use his Talent to harm others? Or is he just a casualty of Verdish ignorance?*

I will never know, because Fergustan didn't have a chance to defend himself.

If it had been *me* in those shackles, would Finn have done anything different?

"Could we take a walk together?" Finn offers, his voice drawing me back from my inner turmoil. "And I can try to explain?"

*Take me home,* I want to say. Instead, I mumble, "Sure."

He grasps my hand and steers me through the moonlit garden, far from the music and the patch I obliterated. My thoughts are a world away. I'm planning my escape route: the horse I'll need, the path I'll take out of Crown City . . .

Finn leads us out of the hedge maze, over a lawn, and through the swaying rose gardens. We pass between twin statues of dragons and through an ivy-covered door before arriving at a secluded lake. At the water's edge is a massive willow tree with gold blossoms decorating the sweeping branches. It's breathtaking, almost otherworldly. If I weren't so distraught, I would ask about it.

"My brothers and I used to call this place the swan garden," he explains. "We liked to hide here from our parents."

I say nothing back.

Finn sprawls out near the water's edge. It's an uncanny re-creation of our trip to the waterfall that makes my guts twist. I gingerly sit down beside him, making sure we don't touch. I wrap my arms around my shoulders and gaze at the wobbling reflection of the stars.

"Where were you?" I ask. My Talent is still fighting for control, so I am desperate for something else, *anything* else, to focus on. "What was so important that it drew you away?"

Finn looks guilty. "I got orders to ride east practically the second I got home. My job, it's . . . it's special. I can't say much about it, but it required me to go to Sulnik. I couldn't refuse."

"Sulnik?"

"We're on thin ice with them. No pun intended. Sebastian is engaged to their crown prince, which should go a long way toward mending fences. But the Sulish king hates my father, and he's closely allied with the king of Ursandor. Neither of them wants a united Midlands."

"What do you want?" All my muscles tighten, waiting for his answer.

"Peace," Finn says simply. "I want peace, and I want everyone I love to be safe."

"You call what just happened *peace*?" There's venom in my tone, and it makes Finn frown.

"Have you ever actually set foot in the Republic of Sontaag?" he asks. "Because I have, and they're a *mess*. They call themselves free cities, but there's nothing free about them. The magistrates like Fergustan live in opulence while their people starve in the slums. I'm the first to criticize my father's tactics, but when I look around Crown City, I don't see people suffering."

"Then maybe you're not looking closely enough," I snarl back. "Or maybe you just don't consider everyone *people*."

A cold, heavy space widens between us. I think back to the cottage and all the conversations we shared. We touched very little on politics, and what I've just implied might be considered treason.

"I've told you from the very beginning that I don't see eye to eye with my father," Finn says slowly, breaking the long silence. "I don't think being Elven makes someone evil. I don't think being Verdish does, either. And using magic doesn't make you a bad person any more than sitting in a chapel makes you a good one. I didn't start this war. It's bigger and older than either of us, and all we can do is our best at the role we've been given."

I feel a little relief hearing confirmation that Finn doesn't share his family's prejudices. But his words are far from satisfying. "You could change things," I argue. "If you don't agree with the war, you should advocate to end it. That's your *duty*. You're the prince!"

"I'm *a* prince," he corrects me. "One of *three*. And in case you've missed it, none of us have crowns on our heads."

"What do you mean?" I ask, confused.

"My father hasn't chosen an heir. And until he does, if I want to have any shot at *any* power to make *any* changes, I need to convince him I don't actually have dog shit for brains."

I blink. "But isn't Sebastian the heir?"

"No," he huffs. "It's supposed to be confirmed at sixteen. He's twenty-two now. When my father didn't crown him, everyone said it was going to be me, and like an *idiot*, I believed them."

All at once, his story about the fyrehound finally makes sense. "That's why Damien freaked out after his name day," I deduce, almost whispering. "It wasn't about a portion of the inheritance.... He thought he was going to be named heir."

Finn nods, looking agonized. "You see why I'm on such a short leash?"

I fall quiet, trying to process this. Anger and disgust fights against the all-too-familiar reality of a soul-crushing pursuit of parental approval. It's hard not to see fragments of myself reflected in Finn.

In the end I can't reconcile my empathy with the rage and confusion swirling within. "So, you'll do whatever he orders you to, if that means becoming king?" I finally ask.

"No! *No*," Finn says quickly. "But I need to play the long game. If I were to end up on the throne, my rule would be dedicated to ending this war. I'd swear that on my *life*, Lyria. But there's no world in which I can do that alone. To broker peace, I need the support of the noble families, the VIA, our allies abroad, not to *mention* my brothers and cousins. I need people to believe that a different future is possible. I need to convince them to believe in *me.* Because right now . . . nobody does."

His voice trembles on those last words, which makes my chest ache like there's too much emotion trapped inside it: mistrust and longing and shame, all mingled. I understand his single-minded devotion because I've lived it.

Who am I except my mother's daughter? I never questioned the cage she trapped me in. Why would Finn question his?

"Why couldn't you have told me all this sooner?" I ask. "Why not tell me who you really were at the cottage?"

He draws a deep breath. "If you'd known the truth, could you honestly tell me things would have been the same?"

I chew over my answer. "No," I admit.

"No," he repeats. "I didn't think so. And . . . I wouldn't have wanted anything to have gone differently, in terms of you and me."

His words heat my cheeks. I know I should continue to press him, but I can't help but smile a little as I say, "Except for the whole tying-you-up bit?"

"That was my favorite part, actually."

I laugh and look out toward the city. My thoughts swim for a while in the soup of revelations I'm processing—all the ways my world has wobbled, tightened, and expanded. I'm highly aware of the distance between us, and that it's our first time alone together, apart from the Ironwoods. Those stolen weeks feel like a lifetime ago.

"I told you my father has an outsize degree of influence over my life," Finn continues. "I didn't tell you about my family and all *this* because . . . I don't know. That time in the cottage, it felt special, like we were just on an island somewhere. Like none of the rest of it mattered."

Something blooms in my chest.

"I didn't just invite you here to be our apothecary," Finn says, reaching for my hand again. "I invited you here because I couldn't stop thinking about you."

My stomach lurches. There it is—the option I'm not prepared for. The words I've been *aching* to hear. Since Finn left the cottage, I've been internally at war, torn between my heart and the cooler rationale of my head. *Am I delusional? Does he feel the same way?*

*Or am I just another toy to be discarded?*

I'm steeling my courage to ask when suddenly I hear a distant crying. It's high and reedy—almost catlike, or like a small child. "What is that?"

"What's what?" Finn looks at me blankly, but I'm already clambering to my feet.

The noise emanates from the distant trees. It's farther away than I thought, probably farther than Finn's human ears can hear. I hurry toward it, peering into the darkness. There. Amid the ferns. It's the size of a small dog, with dainty paws and a pointed muzzle. A fox, a very young male one. It has a large gash along its side, and its front paw is mangled.

I crouch, extending a hand. "You're all right," I whisper. The fox sniffs my fingertips and looks up at me, and my heart swells. "What happened?"

He looks pitifully out of place—a wild thing among the perfect manicured gardens, entirely alone. That is a feeling I am far too familiar with.

Tentatively, I stroke his head, and he leans in to the touch. Finn runs up behind me. "What happened?" His footsteps slow when he catches sight of the fox.

Gingerly, I scoop the creature into my arms. "He's hurt. I need to help him."

Finn's eyes widen, and for a split second I think he might protest. But after a beat he nods. "My mom wouldn't like it. But she doesn't have to know. Should we take him to your room?"

He helps me smuggle the fox inside, reassuring me along the way.

"You're sure he'll be safe here?" I ask.

"Considering Damien hid a ten-foot python in his bathtub for years when he was a kid, a fox should be fine."

I make a nest for my new guest out of cushions and blankets, and Finn dashes down to the kitchen for some food. While Finn's gone, I slip the fox some of the nocturn to induce sleep. Then I use my Talent to heal the worst of his wounds. When I'm done, I bandage the fox's side wound for show. I don't want Finn asking questions. The front paw is an older injury, so I can't mend it completely. It still twists at an unnatural angle—and always will—but the pain should be gone.

Finn is breathless when he returns. "How's he doing?"

"Sleeping," I say as he sets down some minced meat and bread in a saucer.

"Is he tame?"

"I suppose we'll find out when he wakes up." I meet his eye. "Thank you for helping me."

"Of course." He smiles and reaches out to stroke the sleeping fox along his protruding ribs.

"For a split second I thought you might say no."

He huffs through his nose. A quick breath. "I wasn't going to stand in the way of you helping an innocent animal. If it wasn't clear, I'm not actually the worst person ever."

His eyes flit from the fox to my face. They're very intense as he asks, "What are you going to name him?"

I consider a moment. "Dante." Then I wait with a little apprehension to see if Finn will recognize it. Dante, the name of Elowyn's fyrehound in legends, who supposedly chased the moon across the sky. Mother taught me how to find him in constellations.

If Finn understands its Elven significance, he gives no sign. He just smiles, settling beside me. Our knees touch, and I shiver.

"For the record . . . I don't think you're the worst person ever," I say.

He chuckles. "I appreciate that." Then his voice lowers to a hush. "I don't want to be like my father. I know more than anyone that he's done terrible, terrible things. But I want to be different, and better. . . . I will be better. I promise. And I promise to be honest with you. I'm just asking for you to give me that chance."

I lie awake for a long while after he leaves. I can't stop seeing the horrible scene in the Great Hall: the mix of apathy and enjoyment on the faces around me while they watched. I've heard the stories; I've seen the heads on the wall. I thought I understood Verdish prejudice, in theory. However, *seeing* their hatred—*feeling* it—is different. For the first time, I realize why Mother was so afraid to let me escape our cottage.

Even with these revelations and a mounting awareness of the very real danger I'm in, I can't find it in me to go. Maybe it's foolhardy. But as I listen to the crest and fall of Dante's breathing, I'm reminded of what brought me here: the last beautiful creature I couldn't resist saving. Deep inside, I feel some small, blazing kernel of satisfaction, like I'm on the right path somehow, even if I can't see it all clearly.

I did something good today. Maybe, if I finish the omnidraught, I could do something great. Finn wants to see the world shaped differently, as I do. Maybe I could be a part of that, too.

I can't give up this life. For the first time, I have a purpose. I have friends.

I have *him*.

After a lifetime alone, the prospect of surrendering any of that outweighs all other fears.

# 10

he nocturn keeps Dante sedated until about an hour before dawn, when I get abruptly awoken by a small furry assailant pouncing onto my face. A semiconscious scramble ensues, during which I get twisted in the sheets and topple off the bed before realizing I'm not being attacked by a tiny assassin.

Dante retreats to a corner as I untangle myself, rubbing the sore spot on my tailbone where I crashed onto the stone floor. The fox sinks onto his haunches and stares at me while I stand up, rubbing the sleep from my eyes. "Well," I grumble, "good morning to you, too."

He's ripped off his bandages. When I step toward him, he growls.

"Unbelievable." I stop, frowning. "You should be thanking me! I saved your life!"

He just blinks at me suspiciously, tail flicking.

I sigh. "Hungry?"

I put my kerchief back on to fetch him some breakfast and take him out to tend to his needs. But when we start to leave, I find a letter slid under my door. It's from Finn, informing me that he's been called off again on official business and is unsure when he can return.

I read it carefully before shoving it into my pocket. I'd like to have it with me on what's sure to be a difficult day. Tonight, I'm supposed to meet with the queen and report on my progress making the omnidraught. After last night's sadistic display, I might prefer a pleasure swim in shark-infested waters.

Worse than my apprehension, though, is the memory of what I did. I *completely* lost control of my Talent, something I swore I would never do again. Covering my tracks after Finn left took the better part of last night. It's nothing short of a miracle that my lapse occurred under cover of night, and in private. I don't even want to consider the alternatives. *If I slipped like that in a room full of people . . .*

Dealing with Dante takes much longer than I anticipated, and I'm running late by the time I head to the hospital. I'm not looking forward to explaining my tardiness to Cygnus. But upon arrival, I discover his office empty. After poking around, I determine he's in surgery with one of the soldiers who was injured in the ambush with Finn. It seems he's forgotten to assign my chores in the chaos.

On the staging floor, I overhear a pair of nurses gossiping about a fire that broke out in the gardens in the wee hours of the morning. No one was hurt, and the blaze was extinguished quickly, but not before it devoured several trees. Apparently, they recovered a pipe amid the charring. There's a lively debate about who it might have belonged to. I listen with a smile, then hurry to the storehouse to prepare for my meeting with the queen.

It takes the better part of the day to compile a list of the ingredients

I need sourced to complete the omnidraught. Some, like cliffcrow feathers, I can forage myself. But there's a long list of specialized items, including unicorn hair and dragon scales, that must be sourced from illegal markets. Though I am not sure if it counts as an illegal market if the Crown's buying, considering *they* make the laws.

Fortunately, my meeting with the queen is quicker than expected. When I show her the list of ingredients, she just nods and hands it to one of her soldiers. I hoped I could convince her to let me travel to the quarantine zone for additional research, but she insists there's no need to leave the palace. Feeling a little miffed, I do my best to smile and thank her for her generosity.

The ingredients arrive with remarkable swiftness.

A sack of dragon scales appears in the storehouse within days of my request. The other items trickle in within the following week. Sourcing the flowers is the biggest challenge, because it quickly becomes apparent that whomever Davina tasked with finding them is clueless. I asked for meadowblood and dillfeather and grizzlefoot, but they deliver locoweed and toadflax and thistles. Eventually, I have to sketch and paint diagrams so that they'll stop mixing up shapes and colors.

When the correct flowers finally arrive a few days later, they're delivered in huge crates packed with ice. As I unpack, I have to chuckle at their methodology. The plants were dug up root and stem. In some cases, they even included the dirt.

I'm given much more than I need, so I set aside the surplus to replant. Daisy volunteers to help clean up Ragglestaff's old gardens, full of chatter. I even sneak Dante outside, and he runs laps around our feet as we work. Over the past few days, the little fox and I have become inseparable, and he appears to have given me his full loyalty in exchange for daily meals and lots of pets. Daisy and I salvage what we can and prepare the new plants. But after encountering the Head Gardener one sunny afternoon, I'm deflated to learn that Cygnus has to sign off on planting anything new in the medicinal terraces.

I tell Daisy at dinner, and she just rolls her eyes and tells me to go ahead and ask him. She tends to think I'm being too hard on Cygnus; I think she's biased by a crush. I have to talk to Cygnus. I return to the hospital after dinner, determined.

I catch him late, after it's cleared out. There's a serenity to the hospital after hours that I find calming. One can really appreciate the chamber's scale and symmetry when it's nothing but sleeping patients and the odd night nurse. The shadows paint everything in shades of blue, and I love how the southern windows gaze out over the twinkling city. I'm busy admiring the view when I hear the *clip-clop* of familiar footsteps. An exhausted-looking Cygnus is aimed for his office.

I hurry after him, arriving in time to see him yank a decanter off the shelf. He pops off the lid and pours out a glass before noticing me.

"Can I help you?" His voice sounds like gravel.

"Sorry." I start to retreat. "I can come back later."

"It's fine, it's fine." He waves me in. "Believe it or not, I'd actually like the company."

I cautiously enter and sit, wondering when the world turned upside down.

"Did you run out of insults?" I ask, only half joking.

He returns a faint smile. "Would you like a glass?"

"No, thank you."

He downs the liquor in a single swig. Then pours another.

"Long day?" I guess.

Cygnus sits behind his desk, letting out a lengthy exhale. "Have you ever seen something that made you rethink the profession?" he asks after a beat.

The question surprises me. Partly for its vulnerability, partly for the acknowledgment that I'm *in* the same profession—not a glorified consort.

"Yes," I say truthfully. "It was . . . it was years ago. But yes."

As the memory rises, shame spears my chest, just as white-hot as the day it happened. I can still hear the woman's voice, still feel her living flesh cool in my hands.

*Monster.*

"Afterward, I really wasn't sure if I should ever be a Healer," I say. Recalling the incident feels like scraping an old wound. I haul in a deep breath to temper my Talent.

Cygnus watches me for a moment, then sips. I'm tempted to ask him the same. But when has he ever been receptive to questions?

"Was there something you wanted?" He shifts.

"Yes, actually." I procure a short list of flowers and herbs and slide them across his desk. "I've been working on a project for the queen, and she sourced several plants for the draught I'm making. They're all mountain flowers with powerful properties. If we planted them here, we could ease off our reliance on Sulnik."

Cygnus sighs before picking up the list I've offered. He only skims it for a few seconds. "I'm not authorizing it."

"What?" My skin heats. "Why?"

"I said no." He flicks the list back toward me.

*Gods,* he reminds me of Mother.

"You don't even have to do anything!" I argue. "I just need your permission to plant them!"

"Do you even know what these are?"

"*Yes!* I've been using these plants my *entire* life!"

"I didn't ask if you knew how to use them. I asked if you knew *what* they are."

"*YES!* Grizzlefoot, meadowblood, nocturn—"

"These are *wellsprung* flowers."

I gape at him. "What?"

"*Wellsprung* flowers. That's the term you learn in healing school for plants used in traditional Elven medicine. They require different preparation methods, different growing techniques, and different tools." His eyes narrow.

"I—I didn't know." I feel sick.

"Right." He stands. "We don't grow those flowers in our medicinal gardens because our staff doesn't know how to use them, because they are forbidden. So, you can go right ahead and plant them, but you'll be simultaneously painting a sign on your forehead that says *My mother taught me how to use illegal medicine.*"

I rise as he stalks toward the door, then opens it. "If you'll excuse me, Lyria, I've had enough company for one evening."

I start to leave but pause in the hallway. "Cygnus . . ."

"Yes?"

I gaze into his eyes and find them frigid and depthless.

"Never mind."

I spend a very long night churning with mortification.

I had no idea how close I came to revealing my identity. Part of me is furious at Mother for never clarifying which parts of our potioneering could damn me, but eventually it occurs to me that she simply never knew. Mother studied potioneering centuries ago. Of course there'd be different terminology now, and divergences in the discipline. It's not like she's had access to a university since the war.

I push my resentment aside to focus on my task. In the storehouse, I start the distillation process while I make calculations. If all goes well, I should finish the omnidraught by Verdinae's biggest holiday, midsummer.

I'm deep in thought about the omnidraught as I exit the hospital on my lunch break. On a regular day, I'd be eager to eat with Daisy. But after a long morning, all I want is to curl up in my room and not move until the clock forces me. Plus, I need to check on the fox. So I head to my tower instead.

I can tell something's wrong when the door comes into view.

It's not closed.

*Dante.*

The fox is my only thought as I hurtle into the chamber. I'm not prepared for what I find: the table overturned, my mattress sliced open, the wardrobe and closet both ransacked.

And Dante is nowhere to be found.

"No, no, no . . ." I mumble, and start tearing through the wreckage.

Who could have done this? Why would they do this? Did they hurt him? Did they kill him? I feel about to combust.

Until I spot a red blur streaking past the open door.

*"Dante!"*

I sprint into the tower hall and find it empty. After a moment's indecision, I take the stairs, rounding into a long corridor. I see six doors—servant chambers. All closed. Either I left my door open, or one of the maids must have when they were cleaning my room. I grit my teeth against the flare of my surging magic and dash down the hall.

I hurry toward the central chamber of the castle, passing studies and dining halls and armories, sticking my head into every possible room, calling out for Dante when I am sure no one else can hear me. My search brings me almost all the way to the throne room, and I am rounding a corner when I hear the clanking of armor and heavy footsteps.

Thinking fast, I dash into the nearest chamber, which looks like an empty dining room. A dozen empty chairs sit around a wooden table, and a massive tapestry and curtains dominate the flanking walls.

Heart pounding, I wait for the footsteps to pass. To my horror, they only grow louder—approaching me—and I have just enough time to duck into a hollow space between a tapestry and a window before the door bursts open and a cohort streams into the room, debating at top volume.

"I don't care what the proportional response is! These were *my* men!"

Ice water plunges over me at the all-too-familiar voice.

*When did Finn return to the castle?*

The answering voice is also familiar—high, measured, and soothing. "And their attackers will be brought to justice in due course," says the queen. "But we can't go making any rash decisions."

"He raises a fair point, Your Majesty." The third speaker sounds like Roburn. "We can't ignore the fact that they attacked a royal party with banners raised. Whether or not they knew your son was among them is beside the point."

"We don't *know* if Ursandor funded them."

"Who else?" Finn snaps. "I want heads. *Heads on platters!*"

*"Finneas."* The queen's voice is dangerous. "You need to— *Ahh!*"

Her scolding vaults into a scream, followed by an explosion of expletives and scraping chairs.

"What *is* that?"

"Get it out!"

Finn's voice rises over them. "Wait! I *know* that fox!"

I leap from my hiding place. In the chaos, I'm not sure who notices as I sprint after him. Dante tears down the vaulted hallway, and I go hurtling behind at top speed.

*"Lyria!"* Finn shouts from behind.

I whip around in the briefest acknowledgment. *"We need to catch him!"*

We're both left in the dust as Dante streaks up a staircase. The steps go up and up, past column after column of dusty sunlight streaming from slitted windows. I round the landing just in time to see Dante's copper-colored figure dart through an open door. *This damn fox.* Not thinking, I charge straight after him—

And slam into something warm and hard.

Not something. Some*one.*

I stagger back, and she does the same. Blinking, I take in her appearance: black hair, tawny skin, a golden gown, and a strikingly beautiful face, crowned with a tiara.

It's the gorgeous brunette from the party. *Sandria.*

"And where," asks the princess of Ursandor, with a glance that strips me to my socks, "do you think *you're* going?"

I don't get the chance to explain. Before I can form a coherent thought, the chamber erupts into shrieking.

Behind Sandria is a cohort of girls who scatter as Dante blitzes around their ankles. Commotion erupts, chairs scraping and bustles ruffling as they clamber out of his path. Needlepoint and knitting fly everywhere. Dante aims for the next door, dodging a sofa—and I leap forward, crashing onto my forearm as I tackle him to the ground.

"Aha!" I yell triumphantly, and scramble upright with my wriggling quarry in hand.

Then I turn to meet a dozen furious glares.

Every woman in the room looks like she wants to hang me by my entrails. Some cover their noses (which is ridiculous, considering I'm holding Dante, and he most *certainly* doesn't smell).

There is only one thing to say. "I am *so . . . incredibly . . .* sorry."

Sandria saunters toward me with that singularly unreadable expression. "Is that a *fox*?"

"Yes, ma'am."

"Yes, *Your Highness*," a sour-faced lady corrects me.

"Well," says Sandria, with a dazzling smile. "He's quite the handsome little fellow, isn't he?"

I glance down at Dante, who stops squirming long enough to appraise her. Right as I'm floundering over what to say next, I'm rescued by the clatter of footsteps in the hall. Sandria turns toward the door right as Finn barrels through it, red-faced and disheveled.

*"You got him?"* he pants.

I cringe. "He's fine."

More rustling sounds from behind me, harmonizing with a chorus of giggles. I glance back and realize the ladies have all sunk into curtsies at Finn's appearance. *Should I do that?* The notion feels ridiculous.

The princess looks disarmed by his entrance, smoothing a hand over her hair. But I notice she doesn't bow, either. "Finneas. What a pleasant surprise."

"Sandria." Finn tips his head in the barest acknowledgment. "My apologies for interrupting . . . whatever this is."

Sandria shrugs. "Nothing like a little novelty to shake up the day. We don't mind some excitement, do we?"

Her ladies do not seem to share the sentiment. As their glares accumulate, I can only guess what they're thinking, and the tension turns suffocating.

I edge toward the door, desperately seeking an exit. Dante's writhing like he wants a closer look at the princess. "If you'll excuse us, I'll just get him back to my room. . . ."

"No, you should stay!" Sandria protests, with another practiced smile. "And perhaps you'll join us as well, Finneas."

"Actually, Lyria has to get back to the hospital," Finn says tightly. "They're expecting a large inflow today. Perhaps you're unaware, but a Verdish scouting party was just attacked past the border of Ursandor. We lost two soldiers; another three remain in critical condition."

"That's terrible." Sandria's expression does not match her words. "My ladies and I will have to pay them a visit and offer our condolences."

"I'm sure they'd appreciate your attention, Princess." Finn gives a stiff bow to Sandria and then holds an arm out to me. "Lyria?"

He doesn't have to ask me twice. With another muttered string of apologies, I escape with him out the open door. We descend the stairs in silence. Once we reach the landing, I can finally ask, "You think Ursandor was behind the attacks?"

His brow furrows. "Just how much of that meeting did you overhear?"

"More than I understood," I admit.

Finn glances around us, though the hallway is empty. "Can we go somewhere we can speak freely?"

I hesitate. "I can't. I need to get back to the hospital—I've been gone too long already."

"Please?" He takes an entreating step. "I don't know when I'll get ordered away again.... It could be as soon as tonight. I've been so desperate to speak with you, I feel like I'm losing my mind...."

My conviction splinters, but I still try to hold fast. "I really shouldn't," I protest. "Cygnus will be furious if I'm not back in time for my shift."

Finn laughs. "He can manage for *one* afternoon."

I can't argue with that. Even though I'm desperate to help the wounded soldiers that arrived, Cygnus still won't let me do any healing. It won't make a difference if I scrub floors today or not.

He leads me back to the garden where we escaped after the feast. In the light of day, the scenery is even more spectacular. I let Dante down to explore, and we sit together beneath the willow tree with the golden blossoms, near a duo of preening swans.

"Look," Finn says, once we're settled, "I promised you that I was going to be honest."

"I'd appreciate that very much."

He takes a deep breath. "The truth is... I don't get to be honest with people very often. So it's a little hard for me to say the right things. But I believe that I can trust you, Lyria. And I'm going to try and never lie to you."

Finn meets my gaze, and I am swept away by those eyes again. It isn't fair, actually, for a person to be this beautiful. I wonder what kind of childhood he had, buoyed by royalty and looks like those.

"We've had tensions with Ursandor as long as I've been alive," he explains, and I force myself to focus on the conversation. "During the Long War, the Ursandorns backed the Elven. Even after the accords, they harbored war criminals, and we've had analysts comb through the books on their exports and manufacturing—everything points to continued involvement."

"What do you mean by *involvement*?" I ask. "Are you talking about the plague?"

"That," Finn says, "and we think Ursandor's backing the Elven insurgency."

The world lurches. The planets might have stopped spinning.

I blink—once, twice, three times—trying to recalibrate my senses.

"I've never heard of an Elven insurgency," I mumble, losing the battle to steady my voice. Internally, I dive backward through a decade of conversations—every book I've ever read, every song I've heard recited—and come up absolutely certain Mother has never even mentioned the concept. Her dream for the restored Elven kingdom? Yes—as a theological idea. Her belief in the stupid Heir of Evermore prophecy? Copiously. But those are prayers and daydreams. The idea that there are enough Elves left after King Verdin's massacre of Evermore for an actual army is unfathomable. Let alone one backed by the second most powerful kingdom in the Midlands.

Finn's eyes flicker as he measures my reaction. "Well, it exists. And it's not an insignificant threat. For months, we've been vetting a source in Belrick, this little mountain town near the border. He claimed to have intel about insurgent Elves hiding out in the canyons. It turned out to be a trick."

Finn swallows hard, a muscle working in his throat. "We went to meet him at this rendezvous point in a canyon and got completely ambushed. Half our troops were hit before we knew what was happening."

My stomach tightens as I picture Finn under a firestorm of arrows.

*My* people ... *my* countrymen. Mother told me that the few surviving Elves were in hiding and just trying to live peacefully, but this doesn't sound like peace.

"You must have been terrified," I say.

He nods. "There was nothing I could do. We had a couple of archers, but they were the first targets. I couldn't fight back. I couldn't do *anything*." Finn's chest sharply rises and falls. "I'm sorry for unloading all of this on you. I can't usually trust anyone in court. Everyone wants something from me. It means a lot to have someone I can confide in."

I blink. Is that really the truth? Finn is surrounded by people. But he's shared so much with me—expanded my worldview so comprehensively—it's hard to imagine that this might be a lie. I search his eyes, trying to understand what's real.

"Don't apologize," I say. "It feels good to have someone actually be honest with me." I phrase it carefully to emphasize what I want. What I need. Honesty.

"What do you mean?" Finn asks.

"My mother educated me according to *her* terms. Obviously, I learned healing and how to read and everything. And I can survive in the forest. But the longer I live here, the more I realize that my mother didn't really teach me anything about the world. Anything that mattered." I flex my fingers, gazing down at my cuticles, which are bitten and raw. "I guess she never trusted me."

"That was a mistake," Finn says firmly. "You're a good person, Lyria. You deserve to know the truth about all of it."

There's a strange, hard edge to his voice. I wonder if he's thinking about his father ... whatever secrets a king keeps from his spare.

We savor the rest of the afternoon, talking and laughing by the water. For the first time, this moment with Finn feels like it did back in the cottage. Finn tells childhood stories about causing mischief with his brothers. I tell him about exploring the Ironwoods and the storybooks I like to get lost in. Dante plays by our feet, chirping at the occasional butterfly.

At some point, Finn's hand finds mine. Then his fingertips start tracing lazy circles up my forearms, and it feels so decadent I do the same to him. Before I know it, he's pulling me into his arms, drawing my head against his chest.

Twilight falls with a chill. I don't think either of us are anxious to get back to reality, so we stay until it's well and truly dark, just holding each other and watching fireflies. In the silence, I sort through my emotions, which feel raw and disjointed, like an unraveling tapestry.

I feel ashamed of my people, and their cruelty. More so, I'm ashamed of my ignorance and overwhelmed at the horror looming over us. My impression of the conflict has been muddied, but this much remains clear: I'm terrified. I don't want war. I don't want this plague. I want what I can't have: a peaceful future, with this man's arms around me.

I lean my head back against Finn's chest, struck by an extraordinary wave of appreciation for his existence. Finn will keep me safe. That truth hums unspoken between us, a single golden anchor amid this tide threatening to sweep me under. For the first time, I'm not worried about my ears, or my mother, or my Talent. I know I'm safe with him. Protected. And I will protect Finn, too.

Eventually, we untangle and force our stiff bones to rise. Dante follows our cue, uncurling with a yawn and a big stretch. Finn takes my hand and stays holding it as we walk. A pleasant, companionable silence falls. As we reenter the castle and head back to the East Wing, his touch doesn't waver—impropriety be damned. Maybe if I were shrewder, I'd pull away. But as it is I can't bring myself to do it. I'm too flooded with happiness.

Every drop of which evaporates when we turn and see Cygnus walking toward us.

No, not walking.

*Storming.*

Cygnus is a man on the warpath. "Where the *hell* have you been?"

A curse slides through my teeth. Reality crashes back over me in an instant—carrying the appalling discovery that I haven't even *thought* about the hospital.

My impulse is to run. The faster, the better.

But Finn cuts in before I get the chance. "The fox got out," he explains. "We were tracking it down."

"What *fox*?"

As if he understood the question, Dante trots up dutifully and sniffs Cygnus's feet. The Healer gives him an incredulous look and then shakes his head.

"For *six* hours?"

I start to reply, but he stampedes right over me: "You can't just take off in the middle of the day with zero explanation! You have a job to do. You have actual *responsibilities*!" His eyes catch on Finn with that last word.

Shame and fury duel within me. I'm in the wrong, and Cygnus knows it. *I* know it. But something about his condescension pushes me over the edge, taking any semblance of remorse with it. I fire back with venomous sarcasm, "*I'm sorry*, were there more chamber pots that needed cleaning?"

Cygnus recoils. "I can't *believe* how entitled you are. You've been here for *a month. A month!* Some of the nurses have been here for decades. You *don't* get to turn up your nose at their duties, and you're certainly not entitled to take off for a whole day because *you felt like it*! You are a spoiled, petulant child!"

I take a step closer, shouting, "At least I'm not a bully!"

Cygnus closes the gap. *"At least I didn't sleep my way here!"*

"That's *enough*!" Finn roars. Like a blur, he rushes forward and shoves Cygnus, *hard.*

The Head Healer stumbles, barely catching himself before he whirls to unleash his fury on the prince. "*This* is why no one respects you! Soldiers died on *your* orders, and you don't give a *rat's ass*!"

Somehow, Cygnus does not anticipate the punch.

I feel it coming: the windup, the flare in Finn's scent, the sudden heat in the air. That doesn't diminish my shock as his fist connects with Cygnus's face.

We all hear the unmistakable *crack* of bone. *His nose or his jaw?* I can't tell.

Cygnus staggers back, covering his face with his hands. Blood seeps through his fingers in seconds.

"I—" Finn makes a garbled noise, and he staggers toward Cygnus, palms raised like he's trying to help, or surrender.

But Cygnus just straightens slowly as his shoulders slump. With crimson flowing down his arms, he asks, "Is there any other way I can serve you, *Your Highness*?"

He doesn't wait for an answer. We watch together as Cygnus walks away.

# 11

I spend hours composing my apology.

The main points are:

1. I am sorry.
2. I was stupid for sneaking off with Finn.
3. He should never have resorted to violence.
4. I am sorry.

It's a good speech, but I don't get the chance to share it. Because Cygnus never shows up.

"He's on bed rest," Anna says matter-of-factly when I ask after him. "Got into a brawl and had his face bashed in. *Stupid* pastime, fighting, if you ask me."

I nod mutely, swallowing my distress. Cygnus seemed fine after the altercation. *Furious?* Yes. But unyielding, as always. Frankly, he took the hit with more stoicism than I would have expected from the erudite Healer. After all the time I've spent cursing and hating and fearing him, it's hard to fathom that such a larger-than-life figure can be leveled by a single punch.

In Cygnus's absence, there's no one to assign me stupid housekeeping chores, and my work in the storehouse proceeds at double time. Before I know it, I've completed the distillation process and can start adding the powdered ingredients. I meet with the queen again, and she commends my progress. But as the days stretch into a week, and Cygnus still doesn't reemerge, I begin to fear something is terribly wrong.

He's not my only source of anxiety.

On my way to the queen's chambers one evening, I run into Odessa with one of her ladies. She smirks at my approach. When I've stepped past but am still well within earshot, she practically purrs, "I heard someone trashed that poor girl's room. Such a shame."

Her companion giggles, "You'd *think* she could take the hint."

It takes everything in me to keep walking.

Well, that solves one mystery.

The worst part about Odessa's ire (other than the time it took to clean up the mess) is how quickly it has become groundless. Finn vanished after the incident with Cygnus. I expected him to seek me out to apologize, or at least explain what I witnessed. Instead, I got a cold shoulder so sudden and thorough that I've begun to rethink my entire perception of our relationship. In the garden, I thought that we were perfectly aligned, that he felt the same imperative pull that I did. I even dared to imagine we were dreaming of the same future. But days pass with no word, days I *know* he's spending in the castle, thanks to Daisy and the scullery rumor mill.

Finally, more than a week after the incident, Finn shows up at the hospital—with Sandria, of all people. Daisy runs straight to the storehouse to inform me, and when I hurry onto the staging floor, Finn pretends not to know me when I meet his eye.

I have never felt more confused in my life.

Heartsick, I stagger into the washroom to hide. The chamber's spacious windows provide a clear view of the ward. The smell of soap and linen is comforting. I breathe it in steadily, my mouth tight, as I watch the prince and princess stroll among the patients. Finn walks with his hands clasped behind his back, nodding and bowing politely. Sandria is more personal, holding babies, kissing hands. They look disjointed together, like game pieces from different sets.

Not that I care.

On her way to pick up a fresh batch of sheets, Anna catches me staring at Sandria. "She's a born politician, that one," she remarks. "The queen's been trying to get them together for ages."

This fact—predictably—does not ease my distress.

"You don't think Sandria's sincere?" I swivel, facing her.

Anna shrugs. "She might be. But that doesn't mean she's not campaigning. There's a reason the Ursandorns sent her to court. With all the tension and whatnot, they want someone building goodwill from the inside. She does a fine job of it."

I wonder, with a pinch of skepticism, why Ursandor would waste Sandria's time building goodwill while simultaneously unleashing a biological weapon that would brand them as monsters. What's the point of polishing their image if they're right on the brink of declaring war?

"By the way," Anna adds, just before leaving, "we're about to have some changes to the staff. Once things get shuffled, I'd like to recommend you as a Healer's apprentice. It's a longer path than traditional school, but you wouldn't have to leave the castle. And from what I've seen, you'd be fantastic."

"I— *Thank you!*" I gasp, chest swelling with elation. "That means the world, Anna! You have no idea— *Thank you!*" I'm swept up with the urge to fling my arms around the Healer and twirl her . . .

Until the implication hits.

"What do you mean, *changes to the staff*?"

---

I pause in front of the door, wondering once again if this is a mistake.

Precariously balanced in my arms is a tray with chicken soup, nut bread, assorted vegetables, and an orange that keeps threatening to roll away. I'm in the highest room in the South Tower, which I was only able to locate thanks to several helpful guards.

Deciding I'm being cowardly, I knock, balancing the tray cautiously on a knee to do so. Harrowing silence follows. During those painfully slow seconds, I fret I might have picked the wrong room. Then a weak "Come in . . ." sounds from the chamber, and I press open the door.

It's dark. The chamber has one large window, but the curtains are drawn fast, leaving only a narrow strip of light. The furniture is only faintly illuminated around the edges, but my Elven eyes adjust quickly. I spot a desk, an empty fireplace with books stacked both in and above the mantel, a saggy armchair, and a huge four-poster bed that occupies most of the limited space.

The person lying in it can only be Cygnus. As I edge toward him, tray rattling, I brace for his fury, expecting him to scream, or insult me, or both.

But Cygnus hardly moves. When I get close enough to see him clearly, I understand why. His eyes are swollen beyond recognition, outlined by ghastly purple bruises. Bandages cover half his face. As I set the tray down on the trunk at the foot of his bed, he rasps a familiar chuckle.

"To what do I owe the pleasure?"

I take a deep breath. "I came to apologize."

"You don't have to do that."

"I want to."

"I'm the one who should be sorry," Cygnus says, surprising me. "I've made your life hell. Of course you'd fight back eventually."

"No. Well, yes, it's not been great, but Finn shouldn't have hit you. I'm sorry he did."

Cygnus remains silent.

I ask tentatively, "What's the diagnosis?"

"Well, it turns out Finn's got quite the punch. He hit my orbital bone, we think. I'll have some nerve damage and, for now, a really, *really* bad headache."

My stomach lurches. I know that tone. It's the same one Mother uses to cushion terrible news.

"I'm so sorry, Cygnus."

"It's not your fault." His hands twitch, tenting over his chest. "That confrontation was a long time coming."

Without asking for permission, I sink into the armchair. "What do you mean?" I ask, partly from curiosity, partly to lure some life back into him.

I'm not sure if he'll answer. But to my surprise, Cygnus takes a deep breath and explains, "Finn and I grew up together. We're only a year or so apart in age—I'm not exactly sure, since I didn't know my mother. But we experienced everything together: first dueling lesson, first fight, first time falling in love. We used to be inseparable. In some ways, I think I know him better than anyone. He might say the same.

"When we were kids, all the titles and bullshit didn't seem to matter. He said he didn't want to be king, that he wouldn't want the attention. But people are a product of their environment, right? And he's the son of the king. You can't escape that.

"As we got older, I watched him get corroded by privilege. Finn never had any checks against his impulses—the king barely paid attention to him. I think that made him sad at first, and then he got angry and started acting out. So, when I was studying to be a Healer and starting to find my footing professionally, Finn was out chasing skirts and getting hammered and making messes for other people to pick up. He got foolhardy. He stopped *seeing* how his actions affected anybody else."

He meets my eye, and I know Cygnus is questioning if he's gone too far—shared too much. But I want him to feel at ease with me. "Go on."

He continues, gaining steam. "By the time he turned eighteen, he was out of control. That's when his father shoved him into military service. And even then, I don't think he ever sobered up to the responsibility of it. Sure, he got passed up the ranks, and he's good with a sword. But the Frumentari don't respect him. His men only follow him because they must."

"The Frumentari?" I've never heard the term.

"Our intelligence network. The ones tasked with hunting down the remaining Talents. You know those soldiers that sometimes lurk around the West Wing? The ones in the black uniforms? Finn is their captain."

I take a slow, deliberate breath, attempting to keep my voice level. "That's . . . that's what Finn does?"

"Yes," says Cygnus flatly.

All this information makes my head spin. This must be the position he referred to—the one he didn't want to say much about. *Finn is an agent of the Frumentari.* He hunts people with magic. The facts plunge through me, lancing and cold. Do I really know him at all? How badly have I misjudged him? I draw a deep breath, recalibrating. "Does he know what he did to your face?"

"Yes. He arrived before the Healers did." Cygnus smiles weakly. "I had to talk him down from jumping out the window when they told him I'd lose my sight."

*"What?"* I leap out of the chair.

He chuckles darkly. "Sit down."

"No! *No!* Cygnus, you've got the best Healers in the Midlands here!" I argue. "They've got to be able to do something. There's got to be some kind of a procedure. . . ."

"It's nerve damage. It's not reversible."

"You can't just give up!"

"I appreciate the passion, but there's nothing to be done about it. Please—sit down."

I obey shakily.

Cygnus swallows, his words sharp and unexpected. "You . . . you care a lot more than I deserve, considering what a perfect ass I've been."

"You *have* been an ass," I admit.

His lips twitch. Almost a smile. Then slowly he says, "In a few days, I'm leaving for Dasken."

"To heal?" I ask.

"To start my new life."

"Your new life?"

"There's a monastery that's offered to take me in and help me adjust," he explains. "It's an outstanding facility. The queen has already made arrangements."

Alarm rises in me. Fast. "You can't leave," I argue. "The hospital is your passion."

"Anna will take over my position."

"That doesn't mean you have to leave!" I push back. "You can still work at the hospital without your sight."

"I can't do surgery!"

"So what? Support in other ways!"

"You don't get it," he snaps. "It's not just about surgery. I don't want to be here anymore. It's less painful for me to start over somewhere new."

"That doesn't mean it's the right thing to do."

"I'm very tired, Lyria," he says softly. "Thank you for the food, but I'd like to sleep now."

It's a gentle dismissal but a dismissal nonetheless. I stand reluctantly. "Is there anything else I can get you?"

"I'm fine, thank you," he says. "And I'm sorry for what I said."

"Me too."

As I close his chamber door and start down the steps, my Talent flares—not quite painful this time, but present. Demanding.

I know what I have to do.

In the early hours of the following morning, I tiptoe back into Cygnus's chambers. The curtains are open this time, and moonlight washes the chamber a ghostly pale blue. Thanks to the nocturn I snuck into his tea after dinner, he doesn't wake at the *click* of the door, or at my gingerly approaching steps. His breathing is regular and deep.

My Talent is red-hot and pulsing with anticipation. Drawing a deep breath, I reach for the coil at the base of my spine and tug a thread—willing a strand to unspool and flow through my fingers.

When I touch Cygnus's face, I keep the contact featherlight. Nocturn should hold him, but I can't be too certain. His wounds are complex. As I graze my fingertips over his brow and cheek, I sense each of the infinite threads that comprise his life force. Some are tangled and battered, pulsing raw in the spots where the nerves had been damaged or severed. I find the fractured section of delicate bone just below his left eye, and behind it, a whole mess of swelling and bruises.

Discretion is everything. I can't mend the wound outright without risking discovery. I focus on the inner nerves around his eye, weaving my magic into his invisible tapestry. I leave the fracture, merely aligning the bone fragments to ensure minimal disfiguration.

It's complicated healing, even more detailed than what I did for Finn. Working so close to his brain makes my heart race. By the end of it, I'm panting and slick with sweat. But when I step back to admire my work, I feel confident that no one can discern what I've done. His eyes are still raccoon-like, his bandages untouched.

Nothing looks changed.

But everything is.

I linger at his side for a beat longer than necessary, watching his chest rise and fall. In sleep, Cygnus's features are more peaceful, less jaded. Overlooking the swelling and gauze, I can appreciate the slope of his nose and the gentle arc of his lips. He is almost as beautiful as Finn.

As I creep back to my room, my heart is pounding again.

This time, it has nothing to do with fear.

# 12

t's late afternoon, a fortnight after the incident, and Daisy and I are high on the rocky cliffs flanking the north side of the castle.

"Let me get this straight," Daisy shouts into the wind. "You chased the fox into a war meeting, met the princess of Ursandor, blew off work with Prince Finneas, *and* started a brawl?"

Daisy offered to accompany me to find cliffcrow feathers for the omnidraught. They are the last ingredient I need, and the queen's soldiers have yet to bring me any. I agreed, mostly so that she'd stop pestering me with questions.

I cringe. "I didn't start a brawl. It was *one* punch. And Cygnus and Finn already have a history; I just got wedged into the middle of it."

Daisy sits with Dante on the rocks far below me. I'm currently clinging like a spider between two walls of a slot canyon. I learned the method from Mother. She taught me how to look at walls of stone like riddles to be solved, finding the footholds, the finger-wide ledges, the narrow pathway forward and up. I can vividly picture her scooting up a canyon like this one, shouting encouragement for me to follow. The memory makes my chest ache.

"What I don't understand is why Cygnus was so invested," Daisy muses. "Do you think he's in love with you, too?"

"What do you mean *too*?"

"I mean in addition to the prince."

"Finn's not—"

"Whatever you want to call it." Daisy rolls her eyes. "Infatuated, interested, trying to get into your pants—"

"No." I cut her off. "Definitely not."

A massive bird lands near Daisy and caws.

She shrieks, "Is that one of them?"

"Yep." I grin. I admire the cliffcrow as he takes flight, flapping his jet-black wings. The iridescent streak down his back glints in the sun. I've made it halfway, but the slot narrows the higher I go, and my muscles are starting to cramp. I shift and brace, catching my breath.

"You good up there?"

"I'm fine!"

I pretend every muscle in my body isn't screaming. Starting again, I wriggle up to what looks like a perfect foothold. I reach up to seize it . . .

And my fingers close on a moist handful of cliffcrow shit.

"Aaaaaaugggggggghhhhhhh," I groan.

People are going to *die* if I don't make this draught. People are going to *die*. . . .

There's not another foothold. I grimace and try not to think about the squish as I reach again for the same ledge. I haul myself over a ridge and at last come face-to-face with three baby cliffcrows.

Two are sleeping. The other opens slitted eyes and lets out a tiny *peep,* widening a red diamond of a mouth to be fed. I grin in wonder at their fuzzy little figures. There's plenty of feathers in the nest, so I pick four or five. "Got it!"

Daisy cheers.

As we head back to the castle, she chats eagerly about the upcoming midsummer celebration. I stop listening when she starts speculating about the fruit tarts. There's just too much else on my mind—notably, Finn and his job in the Frumentari.

All along, I've known he's my enemy, in principle. He's the descendant of Verdin the Vanquisher. His kin slaughtered thousands of mine. But I somehow managed to convince myself Finn is separate from these crimes, or at least the ideology. When he said he has different ideas from his father and doesn't think magic makes someone evil—was that a lie? Was he just *tolerating* Verdish oppression, or actively upholding it?

And why did it take me so long to ask?

My thoughts are interrupted when Daisy yelps. She's ahead, with her back to me.

"Daisy?"

She stumbles backward, clutching her hand as the yelp vaults into a scream.

"DAISY?" Now I'm running. "What happened? What did you do?"

"I don't know! *I don't know!*" she howls. "I was grabbing onto a rock, and I got bitten. Or stung—"

"Let me look at it!"

She extends a trembling hand, revealing a swollen red lump on her pointer finger. I press my hand on it, sweeping with my Talent, but for some reason I can't sense the wound. I hiss with frustration.

"Is it poisonous?" she asks, echoing my own thoughts.

*I should know. Mother would know.* "I haven't seen a bite like this before," I admit, trying to keep my voice calm as panic floods me. "We should get you back to the East Wing as fast as possible." I rummage in my belt and tug out the grizzlefoot potion. "Take this for the pain."

Daisy downs it, wincing at the taste.

It's a long hike back, and it feels like hours later when we finally reach the castle gardens. By that point, she's staggering. Her eyes are unfocused, and her hand has nearly doubled in size, turning a nasty shade of purplish red. There's something wrong about her life energy, like rot spreading from a blemish. Halfway through the gardens, she collapses. Cursing, I scoop her up and start running.

I barrel through the hospital doors. "Help! Please! Somebody help us!"

A few nurses hurry over, eyes widening in alarm.

"Is that Daisy?"

"*Daisy!* What happened?"

I try to explain, and my voice chokes. "I think she was bitten by something . . . a spider, or some kind of snake."

"Here, lay her down."

"Get her some water—"

*"Lyria."*

The sound of my name cuts straight through the chaos. I spin, and when I see Cygnus approaching, my stomach plummets through my shoes.

I haven't seen him since I healed him, and this is about the worst possible reunion I could imagine.

*He's going to kill me.* That's my first thought.

The second: *No, he's going to fire me.*

He does neither.

"I have the antivenom in my office," Cygnus murmurs when he reaches us, lifting Daisy's swollen hand. "It's a narrow blue bottle labeled *skakabri*. You'll find it in the left cabinet, at eye level."

"Is it a snake bite?"

"Please do as I say. Time is not our friend."

I hurry and retrieve it. When I return, I find the nurses gone and Cygnus carefully making an incision. Dante has hopped onto the bed and curled up by her ankles like he's keeping vigil.

"Can you put her to sleep?"

"What?" I'm too disheveled to process Cygnus's question.

He takes the antivenom and loads a syringe. "Give her something to make her sleep, please."

"Yes . . . yes, of course." I pull the nocturn from my belt.

He injects the antivenom while I administer the nocturn. "She was stung by something called a skakabri," he explains calmly. "The Daskish call them ghost scorpions, since they burrow in desert caves. They can grow to be ten or fifteen feet long. Fortunately for Daisy, she was probably stung by a newborn. Otherwise, the venom would work much faster."

I let out a long exhale. "I can't believe I've never even heard of them."

"You won't find them in Verdinae often. The skakabri are full-blooded daemons straight from the Demeridian. Creatures that adapted to survive in the underworld instead. They have magic flowing through them."

I understand, then, why my Talent couldn't properly perceive the venom in Daisy's wound. Unlike the Moragorion, skakabri didn't originate in this world. I ponder this while Cygnus stands. "The antivenom works quickly, but it will take time for the swelling to subside, and it's going to hurt like hell in the meantime. We should keep her sedated."

I nod numbly.

Cygnus pauses. "It's not your fault, Lyria."

I look at him in surprise—*really* look at him. I haven't encountered him since the incident. His features are as hard and unreadable as usual, except for the faint violet bruises around his eyes.

My throat tightens, and I struggle for a response. I almost can't believe he's not screaming at me.

Cygnus opens his mouth, and I think he might say something else. But he shuts it again quickly. "I've got other patients. Keep an eye on her. But you did fine."

I stay at Daisy's side all night and most of the next day.

The swelling gradually reduces, just as Cygnus promised, and when she finally rouses, Daisy reports cheerfully that she can hardly feel the pain anymore. I'm beyond relieved.

"Respectfully, you look like shit," she observes, swinging her legs off the side of the bed and then standing. Daisy pauses and sniffs. "You sort of smell like it, too."

I laugh wearily, glancing down at the cliffcrow dung that's still smeared all over me.

She blinks. "I'm *fine,* Lyria. Go sleep. And bathe. Seriously."

After Daisy declines my several offers to escort her back to her room, I finally concede and trudge back to my tower with Dante.

Sleep hits me the instant my head touches the pillow. I'm out like the dead, and when I finally wake, it's to sunshine streaming through the window. I leap up, muttering a string of curses—I'm hours late for work.

I hurry to the hospital, bracing for the Head Healer's wrath. But I arrive to find his office door closed, and I don't see him or Daisy on the staging floor. When I ask around, I'm told Cygnus is busy in surgery—*thank the Gods*—and that Daisy got the day off.

So I trudge down to the storehouse alone.

There's one good thing about the ordeal—I now have all the ingredients I need to complete the omnidraught. I followed Ragglestaff's recipe to the letter. The blossoms have been distilled, I've added the dragon scales and unicorn hair, and everything has sat under the full moon as instructed. All that remains is to powder the feathers and add the Ironwood sap. Then I should be able to activate the mixture by stirring it with a pewter spoon. If it reacts like all's-cure, I'll know the draught is complete when it starts steaming and turns gold.

My mood picks up as I complete the final tasks. I'm *so* close, and the prospect of seeing Mother again soon makes my chest swell. But after I add the sap and start stirring . . .

Something's wrong.

I know it immediately. The mixture's too viscous. I keep stirring, but the mix just grows lumpier and then starts to congeal. Panic heats my neck, and I start cursing. Weeks of work crash around my shoulders in slow motion.

It's wrong. *It's all wrong.*

The stirring is futile. Eventually, I shove away from the workbench, roaring. I've got half a mind to fling my cauldron across the room. I'll have to throw the whole mixture out and start over.

*Disaster.*

I'm nauseated at the prospect of relaying my failure to Davina. Starting over will set me back weeks. How many lives will my mistake cost? Dozens? Hundreds?

*A Healer is precise,* I can hear Mother saying. *We can't afford mistakes.*

Suddenly, my whole plan to impress her feels astoundingly foolish. Why did I think I could do this? Who was I to believe I could accomplish what she couldn't? The simple fact that I haven't heard from her tells me Mother hasn't conquered the plague yet, either. She has three *hundred* years of experience over me—finest potioneer of her generation, Royal Healer to the Aldain dynasty. If she can't do it, *nobody* can.

I'm in the midst of this mental spiral when I hear footsteps approaching the storehouse. I manage to wipe my tears away just as Cygnus steps through the doorway. When I whirl to face him, there's an awkward beat. I'm sure he can tell I was crying.

"Would you take a walk with me?" he asks stiffly. He's got a satchel slung over one shoulder, and the shadows under his eyes have all but vanished.

I blink back at him. "A walk?"

"Just into the gardens. To clear our heads."

My stomach sinks. *Here it is. The lecture I've been waiting for.*

"Sure," I agree reluctantly.

I follow Cygnus out across the terraces and past the reflective pool where the castle glitters in reverse. It's after dusk now, and the chatter of frogs fills the cooling air. I don't recognize our path until we round a familiar corner, and the lake comes into view.

"I've been here with Finn," I blurt out.

Cygnus rolls his shoulders back, smirking. "I showed him this spot when we were kids," he says. "Typical of him to pass it off as his discovery."

"He didn't say he discovered it."

"No. This lake is thousands of years old." Cygnus approaches the shore and crouches, slipping his fingers under the surface.

"And are you an expert on lakes?"

"I'm an expert on this castle." With his back to me, he traces lazy circles in the water. "Do you know who built it?"

I pause. "Verdin, I assume?"

"Wrong. That's a common belief, though, since it's the story the Thornes tell—all about how Verdin raised his glorious castle after arriving in the Hartlands." An odd, caustic edge has taken over his voice. "A shining beacon to the prosperity of the empire."

I've gone very still. "Interesting fun fact."

I don't know what the hell is happening, but something is *definitely* wrong. I don't recognize this person. I almost wish Cygnus would insult me or something just to make this all feel less weird. He slowly stands and turns toward me, and when our eyes meet, I mark an intensity in his I don't recognize.

"Anna told me you were asking after me," he says quietly.

"Is that why you're acting so weird? Because you thought I was snooping?" I fold my arms. "I only cared because she said there'd be an open position."

Cygnus chuckles, which unnerves me even more. "You're good at that. The quick jabs, the evasion. When I met you, I thought you were a terrible liar, but you've really improved. I gotta give you credit—you're a quick study."

My neck prickles. "What are you talking about?"

"I misjudged you, Lyria. I really did. I thought you came to the castle for selfish reasons, but you are a thoroughly decent person."

That sounds suspiciously like a compliment. My eyes narrow. "What made you change your mind?"

"What tipped the scales for me?" Cygnus's head bobs reflectively. "That was probably when you fixed my face."

I edge back a step. "What are you talking about?"

*Play dumb, Lyria.*

"You didn't have to do that," he continues. "You had every reason to hate me. You didn't have to save Finn from the Moragorion, either, but you did."

He knows. A hundred curses pinwheel through my head.

*He knows.*

"*Finn* killed the Moragorion," I correct futilely, skin burning. I edge back another step.

"Sure. Maybe." Cygnus huffs. "But I examined his scars myself. You're telling me those wounds healed naturally?"

*Run.* The instinct bolts through me. But where is there to run *to*? If Cygnus is about to bare my secret, there is nowhere I can go in the castle for safety.

Nausea floods me, but not from fear. No, this queasiness rises from disgust toward myself, how quickly I identify what needs to be done and how readily my magic swells as need crystallizes into decision.

This is the crisis I've prepared my whole life to meet, the cold, inevitable cost of my birthright. I've always known a moment would come when I'd have to do the worst to keep my secret. I regret that it's him.

I can't run. Therefore, I can't let him live.

Cygnus steps toward me—an asinine move, considering he's

about three seconds away from death. It's like a third party has taken over my thoughts, guiding me through each grisly calculation. The Moragorion's fate is too horrible. I don't wish him pain. For all his assholery, Cygnus still dedicated his life to healing people. He's got my begrudging respect for that. So I thoughtfully consider my method of ending his life. *The jugular? The spine? His brain?*

Another step.

"Lyria, I'm not going to hurt you. . . ."

The problem is the corpse. If I shatter something inside him, that leaves a body with no understandable wound. I might as well poke a hornets' nest and pour honey on my head. Countless people saw us walk out of the East Wing together. Even if I kill him in a normal way, how much time would I buy myself before they string me up for murder? Enough to escape?

He's almost close enough to touch. My fingers close around my father's dagger.

"I just want to talk," he says. I don't need my Talent to know that's a lie.

We lunge at the same time.

I grab my dagger off my belt. Cygnus catches my wrists, stopping me just before the blade would have plunged into his neck. We wrestle for a strangled moment. He yells something I can't hear. I'm struggling too hard to get my hands on him, fighting for my life.

But he's stronger. *Impossibly* strong. I'm jolted by surprise and accompanying horror. No human should be able to fight back like this—and the struggling ends when Cygnus rips the dagger from my hand and shoves me into the tree, which parts around me. A hollow opens up inside, bigger than should be possible, and my eyes widen as the world vanishes.

# 13

brace for an impact that never comes.

Instead, I'm falling.

My brain can't catch up as the world reels around me. I see churning darkness and an intermittent light fading from view as I plummet *down, down, down,* on and on.

*Could this be the fall into the underworld?* My stomach swoops and the earth narrows around me, pinching until I feel like a cork being screwed into a bottle. I hurtle faster and faster, spinning aerial somersaults as the darkness consumes everything.

And then I slam into a wall of water.

The impact blasts my senses to oblivion. I can't tell which way I've landed. Something vital is broken. *My ribs? My pelvis?* Pain. There's so much pain.

I choke, and my lungs fill with water that burns like a flame. The current drags me—up? Down? I can't orient myself. I can't move, I can't breathe.

Then something seizes my shirt. A hand. It pulls, *hard,* and some inner voice screams: *SWIM, LYRIA. SWIM NOW OR DIE.*

I kick, and every move sends spasms of pain through me. My bones feel like rubber. But I struggle, thrashing; the blackness pitches, then all at once the world explodes around my ears as I slam through the surface.

*Air.*

I gasp the deepest breath I've ever taken.

"Hold on," someone growls.

I know that voice. I think I hate that voice.

Arms like tree trunks clamp around me. I'm being dragged. We hit pebbles—the shore. Cygnus pulls me onto rough terrain, then collapses.

I roll and vomit until hacking consumes me. When it's over, I lie still, trembling.

"Are you okay?" he pants.

It's all I can do to shake my head a millimeter. I'm sinking deep within myself, allowing the Talent to take over, to rush through my limbs and heal what's been broken. I don't know how long it takes, but the healing exhausts me. So much harder to fix things than break them. Seconds pass, filled with Cygnus's tense and shallow breathing.

"Lyria?" Cygnus drops beside me. "Lyria, talk to me."

Gradually, the pain eases. The fire in my blood recedes as the magic ebbs from my system, until finally, I can sit up and examine my surroundings.

We've fallen into an underground lake. The only light comes from a tiny shaft in the ceiling, some inestimably vast distance above. Blinking up at the opening, I'm reminded of the stained glass window in the chapel where I met Davina. It has the same greenish glow, except the light behind it shimmers and swirls. The glow is unlike sunlight, or firelight; it's something else entirely, something I only recognize because it puts form to what I have always felt flowing through my veins.

The light comes from *magic*.

The cavern is huge. You could put the whole of Rodrick's castle inside and the tallest tower still wouldn't scrape the ceiling above us. As I tear my eyes from the portal, they adjust, and the otherworldly landscape clarifies. What I initially mistook for pitch-blackness is actually a mesmerizing mixture of dark purples, blues, and greens. The stalagmites tower higher than Ironwood trees, some bedecked with pale bioluminescent fungi.

I look behind at the lake. In order to reach the portal we just fell from, we'll need to cross the lake, climb a boulder field, and then traverse a rocky cliffside. I feel exhausted just thinking about it.

*Where the hell are we?*

"Lyria? Are you all right?" Cygnus asks.

I blink, coming back to my body.

"Lyria. I need you to answer. Can you hear me?"

I pounce. "WHAT—IN—THE—ETERNAL—HELL—" I hit any part of him I can reach. Head. Shoulders. It's too dark to see clearly, so I whale aimlessly. "WAS—THAT?"

Confusion and reactive fury blast through me, and my primal self takes over—that small and scrappy part of me that's determined to stay alive. Cygnus is a threat. He's always been a threat. *He is the enemy*, that desperate inner part of me roars.

"I can explain!" Cygnus seizes my wrists. "Lyria, listen to me!"

"You tried to kill me!" I struggle, but he's so much stronger. I'm not thinking clearly enough to listen. I'm saturated with panic, terrified by his much larger body wrestling against mine, even as he's trying to calm me.

"I didn't mean to hurt you!" he shouts. "I didn't know how to explain! There wasn't another way!"

"Another way for *what*?"

"TO PROVE YOU'RE AN ELF!"

Silence.

I've stopped struggling. My body is frozen. Realizing Cygnus is still holding my wrists, I yank back, lurching away. We're both breathing hard.

None of this makes sense. How does falling through a tree prove anything? Questions assail me one after the other.

"How . . ." I struggle to make my voice function. "How long have you known?"

"I had my suspicions from the beginning," Cygnus explains quickly. "The signs were there. You cover your ears every day, you grew up outwall. When you asked about the wellsprung flowers, I was almost positive. I've only known one other person who knew how to distill grizzlefoot or meadowblood, and that was Ragglestaff. *Also* an Elf."

"Ragglestaff?" I choke. This is all too confusing.

But Cygnus is no longer looking at me. "If you could do me a favor and pull yourself together, I'm also going to need you to prove your Talent in about ten seconds."

My heart skips. He also knows about my Talent?

"Why?"

"Because I'd rather not die today."

His delivery is ashen, but there's a charged current beneath it. Cygnus is scared.

I follow his gaze, straining to make out what is approaching from the shadows. Faint clicking rises from the void—what I thought was water dripping on the rocks. But as I track Cygnus's eyeline, my stomach plummets with dread. . . .

It's not dripping. It's tiny appendages, tapping against stone.

Emerging from the darkness are dozens of giant, bone-white scorpions. Panic flames my skin as I recall what Cygnus told me about the skakabri that stung Daisy . . . that it was a juvenile version of a much larger underworld daemon. He spoke like he's had experience with them. I didn't even question where he'd gotten the antivenom or why he had it.

I guess now I know. It's because he's fought them before . . . *down here.*

A curse slides between Cygnus's teeth, and he draws a sword. My hand drops to my belt, and I'm almost overcome with panic until Cygnus hands me my dagger.

The skakabri approach quickly, some crawling up the walls, others skittering toward us across the stony ground.

"Should we go to the lake?" I ask.

"No," Cygnus shoots back instantly. "They can swim."

My head whips toward him. "How do you know?"

"They just can, okay?"

We slide almost automatically into a back-to-back stance. "Great. Absolutely *fantastic,*" I snap irritably. "Any other ideas?"

"Don't die?" Cygnus offers.

The nearest skakabri lunges, pincers snapping. I dodge, scrambling as its stinger whips around lightning fast to find me. A second is almost on top of us. I try to dodge them again, but they're too quick. The first monster's pincers snap around my leg, and I let out a shriek of agony. There is venom in their saliva—I can *feel* it. Another cry behind me punctuates my scream. Cygnus is hit, too.

The self-restraint I've been clinging to shatters. My Talent has become a beastly thing, rioting for my survival. It blasts free from the white-hot coil in my spine, expanding and burning away all trepidation as it rises. Euphoria takes over. I will survive this. Death won't win today.

I point my palms toward the daemons and unleash my power.

With the Moragorion, it was slow. That first attempt was marked by trepidation. Not this time. *This* time, the power comes roaring. There's no chance to isolate organs or pick through the invisible tapestry to pluck a precise thread. My will is simple.

*Destroy.*

The skakabri let out a horrific, high-pitched, strangled sound, and their bodies torque with a *crack* that pitches my stomach. They spasm as they crumple to the cavern floor. But there are two more behind them, with another three on their tail.

My head whips toward Cygnus, who's managed to bring down two and is dancing with a third, hacking at its legs until he leaps to dodge the stinger that slams into the earth, right where he stood seconds before. I summon another wave of power, channeling it through my back and arms and palms. Then, as a raw, animalistic sound tears from my throat, I aim it toward the next wave.

More strangled squeaking. Several explode this time, à la the Moragorion.

Exhaustion forces me to my knees.

Never have I drawn so much power at once. Stars pop into my vision, and I blink at the remaining scorpions. Two more rush toward us, scrambling down from the walls.

I hear a *thunk* and whirl toward Cygnus. He's clutching his arm as the sword clatters to his feet. The scorpion he's been fighting scuttles around to bite again.

I reach for my Talent, and it is like scraping the bottom of an empty sack. Nothing. Blood rushes to my head; I feel myself teetering on the edge of consciousness.

*NO!* that internal voice, that primal part of me, roars. Desperately, it battles to keep me awake. I claw at my power like I'm digging into frozen ground with my fingernails. That voice cries again: *IT WILL NOT END LIKE THIS.*

I lunge for Cygnus's sword.

The nearest scorpion strikes at the same moment, but I'm faster. I seize the handle and swing the sword overhead. It connects, slicing the scorpion's head off. But its tail swings, clipping my shoulder and knocking me to the cavern floor. I crash headfirst, blasting with pain upon impact.

*One more. Just one more.*

Back turned, I can hear the monster scuttling toward me. I can smell its awful stench, like carrion and metal, infecting my every labored breath. . . .

My eyes fall shut, and I brace for the blow that will take my life. My last thoughts soar to Finn. How he looked in the garden, the sunlight against his hair, his laugh, the rough feel of his hands . . .

I hear a *crack* and prepare for pain and darkness. But neither comes.

Something heavy *thuds* behind me.

Then silence.

Slowly, disbelieving, I lift my head. Cygnus stands over a fallen skakabri, a jagged rock buried in the monster's head.

His gaze meets mine. Blue fire in the darkness.

"I'm *so* sorry," he mumbles.

And then he collapses.

# 14

raw, guttural howl fills the darkness, and I don't understand at first that it's my voice. As I drag myself toward Cygnus, I'm commanding him over and over to live. Screaming that he is *not* allowed to die. Not like this. First, I need answers.

He's fallen face down. It takes all my strength to heave him over. Ripping his shirt open, I discover a deep pincer slice across his pectoral and bicep. I rip another strip of the fabric and knot a tourniquet, hard. It won't be enough. He's lost so much blood already.

I reach for my magic, but there's nothing left after that fight. The absence is like a missing limb. I can *feel* what I need to do, where the threads of his life force are withering, fading into nothingness.

Violent tremors take over my hands. I press my palms on the wound, and blood oozes around my fingers. *"Please,"* I'm begging, but to whom? The Gods? My Talent? Him? I press harder, and my vision blurs. It must hurt, because Cygnus's eyes flutter open.

*"Water,"* he rasps.

"What?"

*"Water,"* he repeats, with even more strain.

"I know, I know, you're probably thirsty. . . ."

Cygnus's eyes drift shut, and I can tell he's fighting for every breath. *"Takeussstothhhewater,"* he slurs.

I finally understand.

Wobbling upright, I seize his good arm and one leg. Then—agonizingly slow—I drag him toward the gleaming onyx surface. It's all I can do to get him knee-deep into the shallows. When we're semi-submerged, I wait, shivering.

"What now?"

No answer from Cygnus. His eyes are closed, his face expressionless.

I realize he's lost consciousness again. "NO!" I shake his shoulders, and when that fails, I slap him as hard as I can.

"Come *back*!" But he won't rouse.

I look down at the water, and a wild idea seizes me. I drop to all fours, plunge my face into the lake, and start gulping down the icy contents as fast as I can. The taste of mud and ten-thousand-year-old bat shit almost upheaves my stomach, but I clamp down on it with an iron will. *Keep going.*

Another gulp. Another. I drink until my stomach is bursting, then pull up and gasp for air.

It's working. *It worked.* I giggle in hysterical shock as warmth spreads from my stomach, like the first rays after a storm. I don't know why or how, but the river is healing me. Strength surges back into my limbs. Then, like a familiar old friend, power bubbles through my skin, pooling in my palms. For once, I welcome the heat.

I hurry toward Cygnus. His life force has faded to embers, an emaciated ghost of a soul. I place a palm on his chest and bid my Talent to flow.

It's not until it's over that I realize I'm weeping.

---

After carrying Cygnus to the shore, I wait a long time for him to stir.

When he finally does, it starts slow: a twitch in his feet, a slight shift of his torso. Then finally he groans, reaching toward the wound on his shoulder.

"I'm not sure that's done healing," I say quietly. "You'll want to be careful."

Cygnus sits up and looks over at me. Swallows. Then he says roughly, "I should have told you they were down here."

I burst out a laugh of complete disbelief. "You knew they were waiting for us?"

"Yes."

If we hadn't just cheated death, I would throttle him. As it is, I just sink my head into my hands. "All right—answers. Now. What is this place? How did the magic water just save us?"

Cygnus sighs, meeting my eye. "What do you know about the Everwell?"

My brow furrows. "Nothing?"

"Well . . ." He hauls in a deep breath. "The Everwell is believed to be the source of all magic. Legends say it was gifted to the Elves thousands of years ago by the Goddess Elowyn, and they built a temple and a series of gates to protect it.

"The entrances to the spring are guarded with spellcraft, so that only Elves with pure intentions can ever approach it. That, up there"—Cygnus gestures toward the portal we tumbled through—"is an Everwillow. To humans, it's a regular tree. But Elves used to travel back and forth between the spring and Evermore regularly. After the war, Verdin ordered all Everwillows to be chopped down, during the same time he was hunting down fyrehounds. But there is still one in the queen's garden, maybe as a trophy. Or maybe not. I'm not sure Davina or Rodrick even realize its significance."

"You said only Elves can enter?" I ask, instinctively glancing at his ears. They're rounded.

Cygnus notices the glance and brushes his earlobe self-consciously. "My mother was Elven. She was born here in the Hartlands, a few years before the Dornik invasion, and grew up during the Long War. Apparently, she had some personal grievances against the Elven royals. So she worked with Verdin selling secrets and became his most valuable spy. The information she leaked enabled the invasion of the Hartlands and eventually the fall of Evermore."

His words leave me dumbstruck.

Out of all people, Cygnus is the *last* person I would expect to share my heritage. I can't decide how I feel about it. Relieved? Angry? The idea of his mother selling Elven secrets fills me with a mix of disgust and pity for Cygnus.

"Where is your mother now?" I finally ask.

"She was killed by King Rodrick. I don't know why, but he grew suspicious of her. I was only an infant at the time, and the only thing I know about my father is that he was human. Rodrick took me in as a ward of the Crown. I assume my father is or was someone powerful, and he wanted me close enough to control."

I swallow, allowing this revelation to wash over me. "Did you . . ." I have so many questions, I'm not sure where to start. "Did you always know what you were?"

"No. I had no idea until I was sixteen. My ears look human and I have no bloodborne Talent. As far as I could tell growing up, there was no difference between me and the princes." He takes another deep breath. "As a child, I was taught to hate the Elves and everything they stood for. I truly believed Rodrick was making the world a better place. I was wholly committed to his mission and was training to be a Healer on the front lines."

Cygnus's gaze drifts toward the darkness.

"But on my sixteenth name day, Ragglestaff sat me down and told me about my mother. I was horrified. I went all the way to Belshire in Sontaag trying to escape it, like running away from *him* would change anything. But school is where I actually *met* Elves—refugees who had made a home in Sontaag—and began learning just how much I'd been misled. Verdin tried to destroy all records of Evermore, but the libraries in Sontaag and Ursandor never burned; there's thousands of years of recorded history showing humans and Elves coexisting in peace. There was never any threat of Elven domination. There was no secret council of magic wielders trying to take over the world. The story was entirely fabricated by Verdin to justify his conquest. Without Verdish imperialism, we'd still have peace in the Midlands today."

"It took you sixteen years to put that together?" I can't keep the judgment out of my voice.

"I know. Believe me, I'm ashamed." Cygnus hesitates. "But we don't know what we don't know, do we? I had no reason to question my worldview."

I think of Mother and how much she has withheld from me—an ever-lengthening list. Does she know about Everwillows? Does she know King Verdin worked with an Elf? Did she know Cygnus's mother? I feel sick.

"When I came back from school, I saw everything differently," Cygnus continues. "I couldn't look at anyone the same way. The people who raised me, people I thought were brothers and friends, they were all complicit in the empire's crimes. *I* was complicit. And I just became *so* angry *all* the time. I *still* am."

He closes his eyes and then starts shaking softly. "While I was relearning my worldview and becoming a Healer, Finn was training to be his father's perfect weapon. When I completed my schooling and returned to Crown City, I realized I no longer had anything in common with my best friend. Maybe I never did."

As this painful thought seeps through me, he goes on.

"I changed career course right away. I told the Crown I wasn't interested in the military anymore and convinced the queen to appoint me to the royal hospital instead. At that point, our facilities were almost laughably inadequate. The post was a huge step back in prestige. People thought I was insane. But I didn't care. I couldn't stomach supporting the expansion, and I was desperate to actually help people. I stayed on the Thornes' good side, and gradually, I used my influence to divert more resources to the hospital. We opened up more and more beds to the public, until it became what it is today."

I try to absorb this. "So, that's what the hospital is to you? Penance?"

"It's my chance to make the world just a little bit better," he says fiercely. "I can't undo who I was for those years. I can't get back lost time. All I can do is be better tomorrow, and the day after. I can try. That's all any of us can do."

My chest tightens against the truth in his words.

"After I came back"—Cygnus shakes his head—"I can't even describe how lonely I have been. I can't trust anyone. Even when people are kind to me, I'll be wondering deep down if they'd hate me if they found out the truth."

I'm all too familiar with the feeling.

I'm struck by the same sense I had when I found Dante in the garden: overwhelmed with empathy for someone I recognize myself in.

"All my life, there's only been one thing I could rely on to make me feel better. It might sound strange, but it's studying. That's what I do best. It's the only thing I'm *really* good at. So, when I was feeling terrible, I decided to do something about it. I dug into the royal archives and searched for anything I could find about Elven history, which was not much. I started asking questions, and subtly interviewing patients, and eventually I figured out what's *really* happening in Ursandor."

Chills rise as I recall what Finn told me in the garden. I need Cygnus's confirmation to fully believe it. "Which is what, exactly?"

"They're helping the Elves raise an army."

I squeeze my eyes shut, feeling like my skin is tightening. My ribs threaten to compress my lungs, and a dark pit has formed in my gut, an emerging black hole of dread. I think of the plague and Ragglestaff's scribbles of *PAIN. SO MUCH PAIN.* If the Elves are working with Ursandor, does that mean they are part of spreading it? Is that the price of regaining our freedom? Would the innocent become collateral damage?

Cygnus explains, "Elves have been centralizing in Ursandor for *years* now, streaming in from all over the Midlands. From Sontaag and Dasken and Sulnik. Even people like us, who've been hiding in Verdinae. They're all coming to fight for Evermore."

I feel like I'm choking on conflicting emotions. "Why . . . why is Ursandor getting involved?"

"Because Rodrick is winning," Cygnus says simply, his voice hard. "He wants to finish what Verdin started, and he's not far from achieving it. Sulnik's almost completely under his thumb. Dasken has all but surrendered their sovereignty. Sontaag is just a loose republic—all the free cities are individually wealthy, but their coordination is piss-poor. In less than a year, Verdinae's taken a *third* of their territory. They're not going to hold out much longer. And then it's just Ursandor against the rest of the Midlands."

"What are they waiting for?" I ask, still trying to make sense of this. "Why don't the Elves strike while Rodrick's attention is diverted?"

"That's the plan: attack when Verdinae is weakest. But all the stars have to align, and there's a lot of moving pieces. Mainly, they've got to find the Evermoreans first."

My knees wobble. The world pitches—

"What did you just say?"

"The Evermoreans," he repeats. "The Elves of Evermore."

"I know what it means!" I shout. "The Evermoreans are gone."

Cygnus just blinks. "The Evermoreans aren't gone," he says. "They've been under your feet this whole time."

# 15

I feel like Cygnus just punched a hole through my chest.

My legs collapse, and I pitch forward, knees slamming against the rocks. I can hardly feel it. I can't feel anything—my whole head is *roaring*—I can't breathe. *I can't breathe.*

*I can't breathe.*

My chest heaves, trying to force air into unyielding lungs.

"Lyria . . ." A hand touches my shoulder.

I yank back like a wounded animal, howling, *"Get away from me!"*

I'm not angry at Cygnus. I'm warring with every *inch* of my being to keep my Talent from obliterating him . . . and every other living thing in this cave. I feel ten thousand pounds of iron pressing down on my chest, and my vision goes completely black. On all fours, I start dry heaving, still gasping. . . .

*"Lyria . . ."* Cygnus's voice is pained, but he doesn't draw closer.

It's a long time before I can get down a real breath. Even longer before I can sit back up. Gradually, the attack eases. My trembling slows, and I find the will to draw back my infernal Talent, until it's a manageable fire under my skin.

*There are Elves under Crown City. The Evermoreans live.*

*I'm not alone.*

My throat is raw. One word is all I can manage.

"How?"

Cygnus's eyes spark, and I know he understands what I'm asking. "You know about the fyres at the end of the Long War?"

I wobble a nod.

"Well, Verdish history doesn't tell the whole story," he says.

*No shit.*

I'm too raw to retort, so I just wait for him to elaborate.

"When Verdin took control of Evermore, he made sure that every account of that battle reported zero survivors," Cygnus explains.

This was the version of history I grew up with. The fyres were the decisive end of the hundred-year Long War, when Verdin used dragons to raze the Evermorean capital. In a single day, the fyrefleet leveled an entire city. Magical fyre doesn't burn like regular fire; it melts rock into liquid and can swallow a home in an instant. It's impossible to know how many thousands of Elves were lost in the fyres. But it marked the single most horrific act of the conflict. A whole generation, an ancient dynasty . . . gone in a day. Mother won't talk about it, like so much of her life, but I recall once when she had too much wine, she described the horror of seeing ash fall from the sky and the clouds turning crimson as the fyrefleet soared over the mountains. . . .

*Wait.* I feel like an idiot as it hits me: *How could she have seen the fyres? How did she get out?*

Cygnus's next words answer my unspoken question.

"What the history books leave out is what was *under* the capital. In the cavern around the Everwell, there's an ancient city where our people once made pilgrimage to worship the Old Gods. They call it Ruin. And it was reinforced with spellcraft to protect the most sacred, well-guarded resource in the world."

The name draws only faint recollection, like something I've heard in a lullaby.

Cygnus leans in. "So, on the day of the fyres, Queen Soleste led a host of Evermoreans underground to take shelter."

"Queen Soleste was never executed?" I say. Cygnus nods. My chest seizes. "And the Evermoreans survived?"

"Some of them did, yes."

I'm burning with shame from my ignorance. Carried with it is rage toward my mother for not telling me any of it. She was *there*. She had lived through every horror Cygnus was describing. How could she think it wasn't important for me to know? If there is a secret Evermorean stronghold, why didn't she *take* me there?

"If there are Elves underground, why haven't they come to help?" I finally ask.

"Because once the Evermoreans fled to Ruin, they never returned. No one knows why."

I gaze out into the mottled darkness, trying to sort through my internal chaos. How many times can a person's paradigm be shattered? I must be approaching a record. "If there are really Elves living under Crown City, how is it possible that nobody in Verdinae knows?"

"Because King Verdin worked hard to wipe out the truth," answers Cygnus. "He couldn't destroy the Everwell, but he *could* destroy evidence that it ever existed. It's been hundreds of years since the fyres. The only people who can remember are Elves, and he's effectively eliminated their presence in the Hartlands. People believe what they're told to believe. He wanted all memory of Ruin gone, and he's nearly succeeded."

My head churns with follow-up questions about Ragglestaff and Queen Soleste and Sandria and how all the fragmented parts are connected. One rises above the rest, and I turn back to Cygnus. "Have you been there? To Ruin? Is that where we are now?"

"No," he says. "But I've tried. I came down here once, last year. I found a book at Belshire that told me about the Everwillow and realized the tree in the garden matched the description. So I went out to test it—by myself, since I'm apparently an *idiot*. Zero preparation. You can imagine what happened when I touched the trunk. It's nothing short of a miracle I hit the water feetfirst. And then obviously, I got swarmed by skakabri. They chased me back to the water, and I was able to hide in the rocks, but not before they stung me here, and here." He taps his back and thigh. "The poison worked fast. I'm still not sure how, but I managed the climb to the surface. I was half dead when I made it back. Fortunately, Ragglestaff was the one to find me. He knew what had happened at a glance because he'd tried the same thing years ago. So he treated me with antivenom, and he told me about the Goddesses' Gates."

"What gates?"

"The Everwillow portal is only the first line of defense." Cygnus points toward the void. "Down *there* is a maze, which leads to a series of portals that they called the Goddesses' Gates. Ragglestaff said there should be three of them—one for Elowyn, one for Nocturn, and one for Rashielle. If you can get through all three gates, you should be able to reach Ruin. But neither of us could make it past the skakabri."

All this feels like too much to take in. My Talent prickles under my skin as my confusion builds into despair. How much of this information does Mother know? How much has she kept from me? Why is this ten-minute conversation with Cygnus more enlightening than eighteen years with her?

Yet again, I agonize: *Why can't she just trust me?*

"What's the point of all this?" I finally ask, forcing myself to take a calming breath. "What was your grand plan in dragging me down here?"

"I thought it was obvious." He blinks. "We should work together to get through the gates."

A laugh bursts out of me. "Are you insane?"

"No?"

"Cygnus, did you miss the part where the skakabri *kicked our asses?*" I grow heated. "We need to get the hell out of here as fast as we can! There's no telling what else could be lurking down there. We are lucky to be alive!"

"People die *every day* in this war!" he pushes back. "You don't always have to watch it, but *I* do! I don't get the luxury of looking away. I've had to tell boys younger than me that they're never going to walk again. I've had to physically tear mothers away from their children because they can't accept that they're dead. Some of the things that I've seen—" He breaks off, dropping his head in his hands.

Cygnus's shoulders rise and fall through a few deep breaths before he tips his face back up. "People will *keep* dying and suffering unless someone stops the imperial machine." He jerks a hand toward the void. "Someone has to at least *try* and get through to them. There could be a whole army of Evermoreans down there waiting to fight!"

I'm watching him carefully. "Cygnus, if it were easy to get through the gates, someone would have done it already. Those gates are probably sealed by spellcraft. If they are, there's nothing we can do."

"How can you be so sure?"

"Magic doesn't have negotiable rules. You're saying the Evermoreans have been down there for, what . . . hundreds of years? And no one has been able to reach them? You and I aren't going to change that."

"So you're not even willing to try?" Cygnus snaps back. "To be clear: I don't want to die down here any more than you do. The difference between us is that I'm not convinced we will."

"Well, I *commend* your self-confidence."

"It's not myself I believe in," he counters. "It's *you,* Lyria. What you just did to the skakabri is unlike any magic I've ever even read about. If anyone can make it through the gates, it's you."

I shake my head. He's either lying or more stupid than I thought.

"Then that would be your first mistake," I say.

Cygnus exhales hard in frustration. "I don't know what your mother did to make you so self-doubting," he says. "Maybe it's just something you do to yourself. But it's not helping anyone. We have a duty to those people, Lyria. *Our* people."

My throat wobbles.

Gods-damn him.

I choose my next words very carefully. "Say that I did decide to help you get to Ruin. What, exactly, would that entail?"

"Simple. We try to get through the gates. If we get stuck, we start over."

"And if we *die*?"

"Commend our souls to Nocturn, I suppose," he says easily.

I scoff. "Your life doesn't mean much to you, does it?"

"I'm the fatherless son of a traitor." He shrugs. "My life doesn't mean much to anyone."

I scowl in disagreement. But I can sense his desperation and—reluctantly—understand it. This is personal for Cygnus.

He's not just fighting for the Evermoreans; he's fighting for *himself.* His future.

I know how it feels to long to be a part of something bigger, to ache for belonging so badly it becomes a physical pain in your chest. I know the sorrow of a stolen future.

Compassion swells as I consider all that Cygnus has endured. I'm an expert on loneliness, and it's not something I'd wish on my worst enemy. I have always had Mother. Even in the palace, I've managed to find a sense of community with Finn and Daisy, but who does Cygnus have?

"I'll help you unlock the gates," I finally say slowly. "On *one* condition."

"Yes?"

"You start telling me the truth about *everything.* And you promise to never lie to me again." My nostrils flare. "I'm done making decisions without all the information. If we're working together, then I am your partner. An *equal* partner, who is equally informed on *all* things. Is that clear?"

A knot bobs in his throat. "I can try."

"Is that a yes or a no? Because those are my conditions."

He takes a deep breath. "Fine," he says at last. "I promise not to lie to you."

"Good." I stand up. "Now, let's go see about these gates."

---

Cygnus, it turns out, came prepared for our adventure. From his satchel, he procures torches, flint and steel, writing materials, three days' worth of food, several spools of white thread, and three round bottles of a green potion I don't recognize.

"What's this?" I ask, picking one up.

"It's drakesbane."

I almost reflexively chuck the bottle in alarm. "What the hell?" My gaze snaps back to Cygnus. "Were you planning on mentioning that?"

I know of drakesbane from my mother. The liquid explodes when it makes contact with oxygen, and was used liberally by Verdin's soldiers during the Long War. It's one of the few potions she'd never teach me to make.

"I had a friend source it for me," Cygnus explains. "In case we encounter anything worse than the scorpions."

*"Worse?"* I feel dizzy. "You shouldn't be hauling that around. It's a miracle you haven't blown us up already."

Cygnus takes it back gingerly, placing the potions back into his bag.

"You didn't bring any other weapons?" I ask, holding out the torch.

He lights it. "I brought you?"

I scowl. "Very funny."

The underground lake is fed by a cold, swift-moving river flowing from the deeper part of the cave. We walk close to the bank, following its curve as we ascend into the void. We crest a ridge after several minutes, and as flames illuminate the darkness, the darkness transforms.

My breath catches.

The path before us appears to stretch on and on for miles. The walls have been carved out of the cavern itself, in the same dark, silver-veined marble that surrounds us. From this vantage point, we have a perfect bird's-eye view of the labyrinth layout. In some places, the walls look unnatural—sharp angles and perfect curves—but in others, the path follows the natural rock formations. Stalactites plunge into it, with stalagmites rising from other places, so the path looks as old as the cavern itself. It might be. There is one wide entrance, an arced gate guarded with a crowned statue. As we approach, I recognize the Goddess Elowyn, and my flesh tingles.

At the entrance, Cygnus stops to tie one end of the white thread to a boulder. He unspools the bobbin until he has a loose length of thread in one hand.

"After you," he says.

Reluctantly, I step through the gate.

The tunnel is almost wide enough to lie down sideways. The walls are oddly textured.

I hold up my torch and the uneven ridges come sharply into focus, the fire casting their shapes into flickering outlines.

"These are runes," I murmur, tracing a hand over a symbol I recognize.

"Can you read it?"

I bite my bottom lip. "Not *that* well."

Mother was adamant I should learn the Elven runes, even though the common tongue is now used widely across the Midlands. Until now, I never really saw the point. But as onerous as I found the lessons, I've always appreciated the beauty of the ancient script. I love the way the letters swirl back on themselves like coiling serpents, the tilting lines and playful dots accenting certain vowels.

As I walk ahead, the torch illuminates larger and larger sections of runes. I pick up on a few symbols I recognize: water, family, fyre, fate, and divinity. The writing goes on and on, swirling in circles until it disappears around every darkened corner.

It takes hours of trial and error, using the spools of thread to retrace our steps, but Cygnus and I follow the labyrinth until the passage finally widens and then opens up entirely. I step into a cavernous space, behind which rises an enormous pair of doors. The stone is smooth and unbroken, the carvings clean—not a single flaw mars its surface, like it was carved by the knife of the Gods themselves. I suspect it *was*. The polished stone reflects our torchlights, illuminating orbs over distortions of our puzzled faces. Midway between us and the doors stands a small pedestal with a silver chalice sitting atop it.

Cygnus approaches the chalice first. "There are runes around the base."

I catch up with him and hold up my torch to read it, squinting. It takes several long moments to put everything together.

*"'I am always in your heart, and I can never be replaced. Once gone, I go forever, but you see me in every face.'"* When I've finished reciting it, Cygnus's annoyance matches mine.

"It's a riddle?"

"I hate riddles," I mutter.

Cygnus nods. "I've always been shit at them."

I frown and examine the chalice more closely. Decorative ivy encircles the handle. I glance up at the runes carved into the stone walls. They're underlined with a similar ring of vines. The symbols stir an old mental image . . . something I almost remember. "I think it . . . wants something for the door to open," I slowly suggest.

"What do you mean?"

"Like, an offering. I don't know." I gnaw on my lower lip, scowl deepening. "But I think we're supposed to fill the chalice. With a draught, maybe? Or some other kind of liquid?"

"Maybe we could blow it up?" Cygnus suggests.

"There's a winning idea—blow up the cavern while we're in it. I see no flaws in this plan." My stomach growls to remind me that it's been hours since I've eaten. How long have we been in here?

In silent agreement, we both sink to the floor. I turn the riddle over in my head until my sit bones ache, trying to elicit any possible meaning. I come up blank.

"What do you want to do?" I eventually ask. I feel cold and exhausted and useless.

Cygnus sighs with palpable disappointment. "Well we can't go any farther until we figure out how to open the door, can we? I suppose we turn back."

This feels like a highly anticlimactic conclusion to our struggle. "That's it?"

Cygnus musses his hair. "What other choice do we have? Let's go back to the palace. We can try to work out what the answer to the riddle is there."

We look together back toward the entrance to the cave—the portal's turquoise light is little more than a pinprick from this distance. Glancing sidelong at Cygnus, I see he's wearing the same grim expression.

"Ready for a hike?"

# 16

'm getting nowhere." I drop my book onto the table with a *thud*. Somebody shushes me.

"You're supposed to be quiet in the library," says Cygnus with a scowl.

It's been nearly a fortnight since our descent into the maze. Climbing back out took the better part of a day, most of which was spent bickering over possible solutions to the riddle. I've been simmering it over since, but haven't come anywhere close to a solution.

Part of the problem is that we've been too busy. The hospital is teeming as Damien's forces make headway in southern Sontaag. We've just received news that they conquered another of the coastal cities, leaving only nine independent of imperial control. Now that Cygnus and I are allied, he's stopped wasting my time with chores. If I am not working on the omnidraught, I am helping patients. And every night, with his assistance, I sweep through the East Wing, administering my Talent to do what he can't. We have to be careful to avoid detection. I can't save everyone. But we are making a difference.

I can't say as much about the omnidraught. The queen has been asking about my progress, and I am too embarrassed to tell her about my failed first attempt. I told her I need more time to work through Ragglestaff's notes, which isn't a lie. But I doubt she'd be impressed if she knew I've attempted the recipe now *four* separate times—each ending in another round of failure. It is becoming increasingly clear that there is an ingredient missing. What that could be eludes me. I'm very close to enlisting Cygnus's help, but I don't trust him that much quite yet.

I find myself wishing I could talk to Finn, but the prince is still avoiding me. His absence aches more than the skakabri's venom. Why won't he just talk to me? I am tempted to seek him out directly, but the impulse deflates when I remember the truth about the Frumentari. According to Cygnus, his entire job is to find and hunt people like me, so why do I still miss him?

Cygnus turns the page he's examining. "The reason you're getting nowhere with *that* particular text is because it was written by an imperialist simpleton."

I push aside my thoughts of Finn and refocus on our work. "How do you know?"

"Check the colophon." He gestures toward the back of his volume. "There's information about who made it and when. The inscription should tell you whether the book was printed or copied AV or BV."

"BV?"

"Before Verdin."

I flip to the symbols, studying the curling script.

"Anything stamped AV is probably pure propaganda," Cygnus explains in a whisper soft enough for only our ears to detect. "Verdin the Vanquisher liked to reimagine events the way he'd have *preferred* them to happen and record *that* as truth. When his dragons razed Evermore, they hit the libraries first. That was deliberate. Elven knowledge: the runic language, spellcraft, wellsprung potioneering . . . it was always our most powerful asset. So Verdin went at it the hardest. Muddling the past is still their strategy today."

He reaches for one of the books stacked between us, an old leather volume with a glossy black cover. Then he flips to the colophon. "See this? Read the inscription."

*By my mother's blood and my father's name: I seal these words.*

"And the date—there." He points. "That's where the librarian has stamped the year."

*345 BV.* I try to imagine an Elven scholar roaming these halls. It's hard to fathom.

"After the war, runes and spellcraft were banned in schools," Cygnus explains. "Verdin ordered anything with explicit magical knowledge be burned. For the first hundred years or so, people resisted by passing on knowledge orally. But the Verdish caught on and criminalized that, too. I found a record of an opera singer in Westgard who performed *The Heir of Evermore* in public, and they slaughtered her with her entire family. People eventually got scared, of course. Other than what was preserved in Sontaag and Ursandor, that knowledge was essentially lost."

My teeth grind as I realize how much I've taken Mother's spellbooks for granted. I never fathomed their value.

"Aren't we wasting our time here, if every reference to the gates has already been burned?" I ask.

"You've got to read around the bullshit," says Cygnus. "Like this one—look." He slides a volume toward me.

I pick it up skeptically. "This is an encyclopedia of imperial sewage systems."

"Right. It's all the crap you have to read around. But check this out—page four hundred thirty-eight." He flips through the book eagerly, stopping at a page that contains what looks like a map of Crown City with webbing over the top. He reads aloud: *"'When erecting Crown City, the resourceful king utilized a natural system of tunnels beneath the city to divert sewage from his castle toward the designated dumping zones.'* There is a chance that could be referring to what's under the Everwillow."

"You read four hundred pages of a sewage encyclopedia to get to that?" I don't know whether to be impressed or horrified.

Cygnus looks offended. "I wanted to be thorough."

"My mother would *love* you." I sigh and shut my book. I'm pretty sure that the answers we need aren't going to be found in books—let alone books in the royal library.

"Recite it for me one last time?" Cygnus asks.

I've repeated the translated riddle so many times I have it memorized. *"'I am always in your heart, and I can never be replaced. Once gone, I go forever, but you see me in every face.'"*

Cygnus nods and starts muttering under his breath, repeating the riddle to himself. His brow is furrowed in concentration. Seeing him focused and hunched over a stack of books, I can picture him at Belshire—studious, determined, and thirsting for knowledge. *In a different world, would we have attended school together? Could we have been friends?*

"It couldn't be love, could it?" I guess, turning the riddle over in my head one more time. "I know a few recipes for love potions."

His brows rise. "Setting that terrifying notion aside, love doesn't make sense. Love doesn't leave forever. People change their minds all the time. And how do you see love in every face?"

"Well, aren't you romantic?"

"I'm not the one brewing love potions."

"I've never used one!" My face burns. "Forget it. It was a stupid idea."

Cygnus doesn't reply—just stands abruptly, looking over my shoulder, and dips into a bow. "Hello, Your Highness."

Panic stabs through me as I realize I'm half hoping and half dreading it's Finn. But when I wheel around, I'm disappointed to find it's the princess of Ursandor sauntering toward us.

I bang my knee on the table as I rise, attempting a curtsy. "Your Highness."

"Oh, come on," Sandria huffs. "Drop the formality, will you? When you call me Your Highness, I feel like a governess."

I study the princess warily as she sinks into a chair beside me. She's wearing a silver gown today with billowy sleeves and a neckline that sweeps invitingly off both her shoulders. Her corset is embroidered with layered pine trees—Ironwoods, I assume, considering their significance as the number one export of Ursandor. At the feast, I found Sandria charming. But nothing in this castle is quite as it seems. I wonder now if that charm is a well-made trap. I can't read intention in those violet eyes. *Is she someone who would unleash a plague?*

"I can't picture you as a governess," says Cygnus, casually covering the books we were reading.

"True." She purses her full lips. "I'd be *far* too corrupting to innocent minds." Sandria leans back and appraises us. "Are we working on a groundbreaking medical discovery this morning? Or have I interrupted a date?"

Cygnus almost chokes.

"It's not a date," I say very quickly, my face growing hot. *What's she playing at?*

"Really?" Her eyebrows rise, and she looks between us. "I can see it."

I think she's baiting me, and I don't like it. She can't possibly be threatened by my existence. Sitting next to Sandria makes me feel like a cuckoo among songbirds. Except maybe *she's* the cuckoo in this situation, scheming to toss me out of the nest.

"Is there something we can do for you, Princess?" asks Cygnus.

Sandria smiles. "As a matter of fact, there is. I'd like to invite Lyria to accompany me to Sebastian's name day party in Easton." She looks at me pointedly.

The invitation has me taken aback. "You want what?"

Sandria sighs, like I've caused her great inconvenience with my question.

"The Thornes are throwing a party for Prince Sebastian this weekend, and I'm inviting you to join me. I'd like you to ride in my carriage. You can bring along a friend if you'd like. You don't have any other plans, correct? I assume there's nothing else important happening around here."

I am not sure how to respond. I suspect I can't refuse a princess without attracting ire. But the idea of extended confinement with Sandria makes my skin crawl. What if her intention is to sabotage my efforts at making the cure?

"Thank you, but I don't think Cygnus can spare me at the hospital right now," I say, shooting him a pleading look.

Cygnus's eyes dance with something unfamiliar, and I swear he smiles as he says, "Actually, I think the hospital will be fine without you."

I glare back at him. *Asshole.*

"Well, then it's settled," says the princess, clapping her hands together. "Our carriage leaves at dawn, so meet us in the forecourt before then. Don't eat too big of a breakfast—the Verdish roads are *heinous*. You won't want to get sick."

I'm opening my mouth to protest as she fixes one of her radiant smiles on Cygnus.

"I hope you'll be joining the party as well?"

He clears his throat. "Unfortunately, I've got too much on my plate to take the time off. But I wish you both a terrific time, and I'll be eager to hear all about it."

Sandria looks disappointed, and I think it's the first time I've seen her express a genuine emotion. "Hmm. Well, you'll be missed."

*Does she actually* like *Cygnus?* The wonders of this castle never cease.

Quickly schooling her features back to her disarming smile, Sandria stands. "See you tomorrow, Lyria." With a wink and an expert toss of her glossy black hair, she slinks away.

I turn a glare on Cygnus, who is barely withholding laughter.

"I don't see what's so funny," I grumble, once she's out of earshot.

He just grins. "Gods, you *hate* her, don't you?"

"No! I don't hate her," I insist quickly. "She just . . . you know. She's so . . ." I gesture.

Cygnus smiles, returning to his reading. "She's lovely, once you get to know her."

I huff, crossing my arms. "Yeah? You two seem friendly."

Cygnus is suddenly quite intent on picking a piece of lint off his Healer's uniform. "Sandria's been at court since we were kids. Her parents sent her here as a political move when their conflict started with Verdinae. We practically grew up together."

For some reason, these words make a lump stick in my throat. I'm imagining Cygnus and Sandria as children with Finn and his brothers, all running around in a gleeful game of tag. Odessa is there, too, even though I know that's an anachronism. Plus, Sandria doesn't even seem friendly with the Thornes. None of that eases the longing at this daydream's core.

"Nothing ever happened," says Cygnus abruptly.

"Huh?" I ask, broken out of my thoughts.

He's clearly embarrassed. "I know what you're thinking. Just to set the record straight, we never did anything like that."

"Like what?" I ask, feigning innocence.

"Stop it. It's not funny."

I grin wickedly. "I have no idea what you're talking about."

"It's not like that!"

I laugh, raising my hands in mock surrender. "Look, whatever you and Sandria do is none of my business. But you're being awfully defensive about something that apparently never happened."

"I've got work to get back to." Cygnus sweeps to his feet and energetically gathers his books. "If you figure something out, let me know, all right? I'll keep reading in the meantime."

I start laughing again. It feels pretty damn good to have him be the one squirming for once. "Your secret is safe with me."

"There *is* no secret!"

"Whatever you say."

I can't resist grinning as he stomps away.

# 17

invite Daisy to join me in Easton. My invitation has two purposes.

One, to make up for being a bad friend—I am very aware that between the time I've spent working on the omnidraught and searching for an answer for the first gate, I haven't had much time to hang out with her.

Two, to provide a barrier between Sandria and me for the weekend. Daisy is elated to be invited. Apparently, Sebastian's name day is known to be quite the event, and all the court is expected to attend. Her agreeability helps temper some of my dread. I don't know how I am going to face Finn, who I am sure will be there. Much less Odessa or the Ursandorn princess.

I expect Sandria to be joined by a host of ladies-in-waiting, but when Daisy and I arrive at the forecourt, it's just her and two young cousins, who are apparently visiting for the weekend. The girls look about ten and share her thick black hair. All three are in traveling dresses with long, billowing sleeves and the open necklines I've come to expect from Ursandorn fashion. Sandria introduces them with their titles, and I immediately forget both names.

We board the carriage, which could easily accommodate twice as many ladies. Sandria orders the footmen to open the curtains so we get a cool cross-breeze and can see the landscape as we pass on our rumbling journey eastward.

As we travel, Daisy interrogates the princess. She wants to know everything about her life: the courtiers, the fashions, the cuisines. "Is it true that the princess of Dasken only eats green or purple food? Is Codswallow as nice as they say it is this time of year? Do you have any dresses from the West? How many?"

Sandria humors her, while I tune out the conversation. I commend Daisy's enthusiasm. Small talk is beyond me at the moment. Like the younger girls, I gaze out the window toward the verdant landscape rolling past, thinking about locks and gates. My emotions are a tangled mess, with Finn at the center.

Tonight will bring me face-to-face with him for the first time since the incident with Cygnus. I thought space would help me sort out my feelings, but I still have no idea what to expect from our reunion. He might give me the cold shoulder again. *I* might not want to speak to him at all. I keep mentally writing and rewriting speeches, but no words seem sufficient for the complexity I'm navigating.

Here are the facts I cannot escape: Finn fights for Verdinae. His father's empire seeks to obliterate Elves and magic from this world, and that very same magic is inexorably bound to my blood. Only *one* of those facts is mutable. I can't reverse the proliferation of Verdish ideology any more than I can split my Talent from my soul. The only thing I might be able to change is Finn's heart. But is that a lost cause already? He told me that he doesn't subscribe to Verdish ideology about magic and Elves. How can that be true if he's actively working for the Frumentari? The idea of Finn raising a blade toward my people should curdle any foolish feelings I've been harboring toward the prince. I don't know why it doesn't. I can't fathom why, deep down, I'm still fighting for us. With duty and blood and propriety stacked against us, is there any future to fight for?

I thought I knew him. In the Ironwoods, I saw Finn as brave and compassionate—someone who'd act fearlessly to protect me, someone who spoke openly of his hatred toward Rodrick. Somewhere between the cottage and the castle, I convinced myself we shared a disdain for imperialism, that Finn was my ally, not my enemy. But everything since has painted the opposite picture.

Despite what he claims his personal beliefs to be, he enforces his father's will without question. Rodrick dangles the heirship like a bone before a hungry dog, and that's exactly what Finn has become: Verdinae's bloodhound. Someone who would idly stand witness to harm, who has to be convinced of his power to enact change. Each time "duties" draw him away from the castle, is he really just killing on the empire's behalf? How much Elven blood is on his hands? And if he knew what I was, would he kill me? I can't picture him as a ruthless imperial soldier. When I try, the only image I can summon is of him sleeping in the cottage. Peaceful and innocent. The stranger I rescued. The boy who saved me from isolation.

There's one detail of his story I keep returning to now that I know about the Frumentari, a barbed and persistent thought. Finn said they were looking for a source in Belrick, someone with information about the Elven strongholds. Belrick isn't far from the location of the quarantine zone.

Mother never shared all the details of her work on the road. I always thought it was because she found it monotonous, working booths at market, hauling bottles of all's-cure and grizzlefoot, meeting patients in run-down outwall cottages like ours. It must be lowly work for someone of her skill set who stood shoulder to shoulder with the greatest scholars in the Midlands. She'd share stories if they were interesting and of course taught me about her history, but she was quiet about her trips.

But I've started to wonder, *Could Mother be assisting the rebellion?*

I know her heart. Her whole life is devoted to the service of others. She gives and gives until she runs empty; she can't stand to see anything in pain. If there were people in the insurgency who needed her help, any families that needed care, she'd feel duty bound to intervene. Maybe that's the great tie that binds us. When I heard Finn screaming in the forest, I couldn't stop myself from running. In a way, that's what she's been doing all her life: rescuing people who need help.

Didn't she constantly deride the empire? Didn't she pray steadfastly for the resurrection of Evermore? Endless talks about the great future I need to strive toward—one I sullenly refused to believe existed. She fits the profile of a rebel. Verdinae took everything from her. She is part of the last, most-robbed generation, the one whose lives were shattered in their youth, right at the turn of her adulthood. Mother watched her home burn. She saw her people exiled, scattered, driven to their knees. Wouldn't she seek to fight back, with her bleeding heart? Her faithful dream of Evermore arisen . . . isn't that worth fighting for?

But that also doesn't make sense. If the Elven rebellion is tied to the plague Ursandor is orchestrating, Mother would never help them.

Would she?

I'm drawn to reconsider her lack of communication since my departure. Is Mother too distracted to make contact with me? Or have I taken a step too far? What secrets does she hold?

The carriage hits a bump in the road that jolts me back to the conversation. Daisy and Sandria are discussing fashion.

"For the best silk, you've got to go to Sontaag," Sandria says. "There's this one little shop I love in Cinnamon City, and they've got a patio in the back overlooking the coast. It's *gorgeous.*"

"What about fur?" Daisy asks eagerly. "Where do you get your fur?"

"Oh, all the best fur is from Sulnik," Sandria says idly. "But nobody's buying there these days."

Now she has my attention. I scrutinize the princess's face—she looks placid as ever. An act?

"What do you mean, nobody's buying from Sulnik?" Daisy presses.

"They've closed the border." Sandria picks at her fingernails, and I wonder if she's deliberately avoiding my gaze. "As of four weeks ago, the king of Sulnik stopped all trade. Nothing's getting shipped out, but everything's getting shipped in. Apparently, the Sulish Crown is ordering weapons as fast as they can ship them. Plenty of Ursandorn merchants are making a fortune. Blacksmiths, too."

My brow furrows as I absorb this. Sulnik wouldn't pick a fight with Verdinae, even if they want to, because of their prince's engagement. So who is Sulnik arming against?

"Why? What are they preparing for?" I speak up.

Everyone looks at me.

Sandria's eyes flicker. "That's the mystery, isn't it?"

My chest tightens. Elves seem an unfathomable enemy for Sulnik. Has Verdish ideology taken root in the frigid north, as it has here?

Daisy looks terrified by something that I haven't grasped. "You don't mean . . ."

Sandria nods. I see a crack in her courtier's mask, a slip in that careful nonchalance. It conceals a very real fear. "There are some in Sulnik, the king's advisors among them, who believe that the Four Wars Prophecy is coming to pass."

Daisy emits a strange little squeak, like she's choking. I glance at her in confusion. I've got no context for any of this.

"Have they been seeing the signs?" Daisy asks breathlessly.

"The Demeridian is receding," Sandria says mildly, like she's recalling the weather. "Last fall, a plague swept through most of Sulnik and a good portion of Ursandor, killing birds by the thousands. Songbirds mostly, but some big birds, too. In Sulnik, they use icehounds to send letters. But we use ravens in Ursandor, and people certainly took note when our whole ravenry dropped dead."

At the word *plague,* my blood runs cold.

*Should I have been studying birds this whole time?*

I turn backward through memories, reviewing conversations. I can't remember either Davina or Mother mentioning an avian strain of the plague. Was the queen unaware? Did it slip her mind? Is Sandria confiding a secret I need to protect?

*Birds.* What do I know about birds?

There's avian content in Ragglestaff's notes—diagrams of

cliffcrows. Is it possible those were the birds dropping dead? Are the two plagues related at all? But if they are, why would the avian strain impact Ursandor?

"I don't understand," I say. "What's going on with the birds? What is the Four Wars Prophecy?"

Daisy explains, "*The Book of the Almighty* foretells how the world will end. It says death will paint the sky black in the last hour. Which sounds to me a lot like birds dropping dead. Combined with the river drying up, those are two clear indicators that the Four Wars are at hand. And we're already fighting Sontaag. . . ." Perhaps recalling her audience, Daisy catches herself and trails off.

Sandria's eyes are blazing. Her two cousins are watchful—perhaps intrigued by Daisy's terror, or just morbidly curious.

The princess asks Daisy the same thing I'm also speculating about. "Is your family devout?"

"My mother is. Especially since she got sick. And my nana. I don't make it to chapel much, but I try."

I don't envy Daisy for whatever fears gnaw at her. Followers of the Verdish Church have harsh ideas about saints and sinners in the end times. Considering I'm Elven *and* a magic wielder, Daisy would probably think I belong firmly in the second category, if she knew the truth.

"Well, you're better than me," Sandria drawls. "I haven't visited a temple since I was home. That's more than five years at this point."

I catch a glimmer behind the princess's eyes—a well-concealed longing. Maybe Sandria has parts of herself that she keeps tucked away, too.

Daisy looks grateful for the change in subject. "Right. You worship the Old Gods in Ursandor. How does that work? Do you pray to them all at once, or one at a time?"

I try to look uninterested in the princess's answer.

"There aren't specific rules," says Sandria mildly. "Traditionalist families typically adopt a particular deity depending on their values or occupation. A family of warriors would keep an altar to Orix, for example, because he's the God of War. A Healer like Lyria, for example"—our eyes lock—"would pray to Elowyn, Queen of the Gods and Goddess of Life."

Did she mean to suggest something? My eyes narrow. Was the suggestion innocent, the insinuation unintentional? Does Sandria do anything without intention?

"I keep an altar to Aurelis," one of the cousins interjects. I look over to see who's spoken. It's the smaller of the two. Her nose is slightly longer, her look slightly more austere. Her eyes are a bright, startling violet.

"Right, and that's why you're so gorgeous," Sandria coos, tweaking her nose.

To my relief, there are no more discussions of Gods and wars. We continue until the carriage splits from the road, and we turn for a gravel path leading up and up through the hills. At the end of a driveway, the Thornes' summer home comes into view.

The manor crouches atop a cliffside in a way that reminds me of a vulture squatting over its meal. This is splendid Hartland terrain: snow-capped mountains, a sparkling lake, and lush land teeming with critters and birds. The house is built from fine white granite, and soaring columns adorn its huge, gilded entryway.

A hundred-piece orchestra greets the guests as we arrive. Daisy is in heaven; Sandria looks like it's nothing she hasn't seen before. The place has been well-designed to facilitate airflow; the doors are flung open, and guests stream freely through the front door, across the entryway, and into the grand ballroom, which has symmetrical back windows overlooking the sparkling sea beyond. A party is sprawled across the back lawn.

A group of servants swarms the carriage to help us out and take our bags. Sandria says something about helping her cousins get settled and flits away, leaving Daisy and me to descend into the revelers. As we make our way into the heart of the celebration, I gain some sense as to why Finn felt so certain that Sebastian is his parents' favored child. The scale of the party is mind-bending. No expense can have been spared. Carnival tents spring from the lawns, plump, well-dressed children are being led around on the backs of ponies, and beyond the placid fountains, I see dozens of hot-air balloons, a menagerie, and other head-spinning delights. The sun is high, but the guests are already deep in their cups. I spot some courtiers I recognize, laughing loudly and looking punchier than usual.

It doesn't take me long to find him. Finn stands a good head taller than the sycophants clustered around him, except for the lanky blond figure at his side. Sebastian looks relaxed, at least as much as someone in the center of this scale of a celebration might be. Mingling near the Verdish princes are Odessa—looking like a fashionable goat in a double-pronged headdress—and a handsome boy who resembles her. I assume that's Prince Roman, heir of Sulnik, and Sebastian's groom-to-be. While Odessa wears the same haughty look she had during the feast, her brother looks far less icy as he smiles lovingly at Sebastian. The group laughs as Finn suddenly jumps, corkscrewing bizarrely, and then lands. Cue more laughter. I'm sure he's doing something hilarious, recounting a story or performing an impression, being the *fun one*. If he notices me, he doesn't show it.

I look away when my chest starts to ache.

"Are you hungry?" Sandria materializes at my side. "I spoke with Queen Davina. She said dinner isn't until seven but we're welcome to send for something from the kitchen."

She smells like vanilla. I'm very conscious that I've already begun sweating in the sun, but Sandria looks as unruffled as she always does. There is something so infuriatingly effortless about her. Meanwhile, my hair is rumpled from the carriage. My kerchief itches. Even in the pretty pink frock that Daisy helped me pick for the occasion, I look nowhere near as glamorous as Sandria.

The princess seizes my wrist, dragging me toward the lawn. "Come on! I want to try that hot-air balloon!"

Sandria pulls me across the sweet-smelling grass, with Daisy chasing to keep up. The pair want to ride every hot-air balloon, but in the end, we settle on three. Sandria squeals with delight every time we are lifted in the air, and Daisy clutches me in distress through each. I've never cared for heights, but it's thrilling to see the party from this angle, with guests scattered across the lawn like so many specks of pepper.

After the hot-air balloons, we tour the menagerie. It's run by a nice older man with a mustache who tells us with a wink to expect a special surprise after dinner.

We're sunburned and starving by the time the guests are called back inside. Sandria started drinking wine at our arrival and hasn't stopped, so she's much more talkative than usual. Daisy is slightly more sober but nonetheless swept up in the giddiness of the day. The princess whispers something into her ear, and they start laughing so loudly it almost sounds like screaming. Nobody else nearby minds. An inebriated atmosphere has slipped over the whole party, and plenty of others are laughing raucously.

The enthusiasm grates on my nerves as we follow the crowd up into the banquet hall. My body begins to tense at the memory of my last meal with the court. Sandria was there at the feast when the prisoner was slaughtered. How is she so relaxed now? When I look around—at the fountains of wine, and the hundreds of candles, and the opulent trimmings—I see flaunted iniquity. Spoils of the Long War.

Ursandor is supposed to be sympathetic to the cause of Evermoreans. How can Sandria revel so thoughtlessly, knowing all this bounty is stolen?

I'm not sure if Finn has seen me yet. At the royal table, he's surrounded again by young ladies and lords, orbiting the Verdish princes like a system of planets. Odessa looks stunning tonight. Her pale blue gown plunges nearly to her navel, showcasing her figure. She sits right next to Finn, her chair pushed as close as possible. I can't stop staring as she leans in to touch his forearm. Her hand rests there until somebody makes a joke and Finn jumps up in a performance of howling laughter.

I force myself to look away.

It'd be better if I could put him out of my mind entirely. But that's not possible. Even after weeks of not speaking, I'm so attuned to his presence that it actually *hurts*. Perhaps this is a strange development of my Talent, or just a physical manifestation of my unbearable longing to see him. To touch him. I'd give anything to spend another hour together in the garden, just breathing and being together. Like that day at the waterfall, when we felt like we were the only two people in the world.

I'm alone in my detachment. It's like I'm watching the party from outside of myself. When we're served dinner, it takes enormous effort to follow the conversation, and eventually I abandon the attempt entirely. Oddly enough, I find myself wishing Cygnus were here. His presence might anchor me, or at least steer the dialogue in a direction I could follow. I can't keep from continuously glancing toward the princes. I swore to myself I wasn't going to—that I'd ignore Finn entirely—but that invisible tether between us keeps turning my head. He's now deep in conversation with Prince Roman—his eyebrows bob as the prince of Sulnik says something interesting.

"Wine?"

The interruption cuts through my absent thoughts. Sandria holds out the decanter. Behind her, Daisy chats with the good-looking imperialist soldier with acne scars who traveled with me from the cottage.

"Sure."

Screw it. I already feel a million miles outside myself. Why not go a little further and try something new?

Sandria pours me a glass. I lift it to my lips, then gag as the foul taste hits me.

"It's rotten!" I say, shoving it back toward her. A bit sloshes onto my dress.

Great. One sip and I'm a sloppy drunk.

"It's not rotten." Sandria laughs. "It's excellent." She sips the bloodred drink appreciatively.

"If you say so." When she hands the glass back, I set it next to my plate. It's undisturbed for the rest of the meal.

The food makes up for the wine. Tonight's spread is decadent: whole roast peacocks, towering cakes with sparkling candles, platters overflowing with sausages, vegetables, and woven breads. We eat until we're stuffed. Then the band strikes up, and the crowd joins in a round of drinking songs with lyrics reworked to suit the occasion. When a song recounts an escapade involving Finn, Sebastian, and the Sulish royals, the whole crew roars with laughter.

I finally reach for the wine. Force a sip.

The alcohol seems to work a little. The room grows fuzzy and dark; though I hoped the drink would make me feel more present, more *human,* I fear it's done the opposite.

Davina takes the stand for an announcement. She's radiant in a long-sleeved gown of Verdish velvet. The queen waits for silence before addressing the crowd.

"Twenty-three years ago, our *beloved* Prince Sebastian turned me into a mother," her speech begins. "Anyone who knows my son can attest that a more clever, beautiful, compassionate boy has never lived. I am forever grateful to the Almighty for entrusting us with such a son. Our family has been immeasurably blessed by his goodness and light. Hopefully, one day, he will share that light with the entire kingdom."

Clapping rings through the chamber. My eyes go to Finn, whose face is hard.

"Tonight, my sweet boy, as we celebrate your golden name day, I wanted to impart a gift that's as special as you are." Davina smiles at Sebastian and stretches a hand toward the doors. "So, without further ado . . ."

The doors swing open, and the party turns as one to watch a team of soldiers march in. There's half a dozen of them working together to hoist a huge metal box. I know I'm not alone in my confusion when the hall starts accumulating whispers. At first, I think it's a coffin. My chest twists as I recall the horrors of the last feast. *What do they have planned this time?*

As the soldiers approach, I realize my mistake. They're not carrying a coffin. It's a *cage.* It's made of thick slabs of metal, and I can tell it's heavy from how much they're struggling. But I can't understand why they are carrying a cage until they're closer. And when I realize . . .

It's like I've burst into flames.

The fyrehound they've captured is juvenile. Barely more than a pup. According to the stories, full-grown fyrehounds should stand taller than a horse; the creature within the cage can't be much larger than Dante. But I'd guess he can probably breathe fyre already. The pup's size is comically mismatched with the ominous cage that it's trapped in. Through the bars, I catch glimpses of coal-black fur with snowy tufts, and big golden eyes wide with terror.

Davina resumes speaking. "Tonight, we will celebrate this special occasion—"

But then she's interrupted by an agonized howl.

Glass shatters as several guests drop their cups. Many clutch their ears, and whispers erupt. One lady starts shrieking.

Davina flounders. She's lost their attention but chooses stubbornly to continue. "In commemoration of the light that you are—" Her voice rises forcefully, but the howling drowns her out. She gets louder: *"TONIGHT YOU AND YOUR GUESTS WILL CELEBRATE THIS TREASURED NAME DAY WITH AN HONORED TRADITION—"*

"Get on with it already!" a drunken man roars.

*"SO LET THE HUNT BEGIN!"*

A cheer erupts, rising almost to the same volume as the howling.

The pain of my Talent is all that I can think about, a fire that rises to match the hound's agonized pleas. I'm far, far outside myself. I might be watching from the clouds.

I lose sight of Finn amid the shuffle of revelers. Everyone's jovial, everyone's *thrilled.* My guts feel leaden as the cage is lofted and the soldiers carry it out toward the sprawling lawn. A cacophony of scraping chairs and clattering plates follows.

"I don't know about you, but I've got no appetite for hunting," says Sandria, with an abrupt yawn. She taps one cousin on the shoulder, signaling for the pair to follow her. "Have fun without me."

I watch her go, feeling perplexed. I assumed she'd be keen to enjoy the merriment as long as it lasted. The princess strikes me as the type who'd squeeze all the revelry out of life that she can.

I'm very aware of the whooping and hollering as the princes and their cohorts hype themselves up for the hunt.

Daisy snatches my hand. Her face is alight with the same excitement as the crowd's. "Come on! Let's try to get a good spot," she says, tugging me forward.

Half of me wants to follow Sandria to our rooms. But the other half feels duty bound to witness this. So I let Daisy drag me with the throng of partygoers onto the lawn.

*Wrong. This is wrong.* The injustice blasts through me like flashes of lightning. Can I reach the fyrehound before the hunters and intercede? I know the land better. The hills in Easton are not dissimilar to the Ironwoods. I know how to cross the narrow canyons and become invisible in the labyrinth of pines. The smell of the forest and the cold east wind around me are aching reminders of the home I ran away from. The stars are spectacular, but I have no heart to appreciate them.

A crowd has gathered, and stable hands have brought up a dozen horses for Sebastian and his friends. Finn is among them, naturally. So is Damien. Everyone's grinning. Everyone's excited to be doing this.

*What in the hell am I doing here?*

I feel like I'm burning to death.

Fyrehounds are peaceful creatures. They don't hunt like normal hounds or wolves. They burrow and eat coal, and can have near-immortal lifespans. Queen Soleste's bonded hound is said to have lived for five hundred years. To see one bound in a cage like this . . . a *pup* . . .

Something inside me is breaking, rending.

Will it be Finn who deals the final blow? Could I ever touch him again after that?

I'm only distantly aware of my surroundings as Daisy chatters excitedly by my side. Then comes the countdown, when the crowd roars with one accord: "FIVE! FOUR!"

I am silent. Petrified. *Do something,* that voice inside me roars. *Save it!* But I feel rooted to the spot. Powerless.

The stars pitch around me.

"THREE! TWO! ONE!"

The cage door crashes open. The fyrehound streaks into the fading twilight, disappearing into the forest just as a great explosion of light and color erupts overhead. Fireworks.

The hunters shoot off, Finn among them. I lose sight of him within the horde. Their excitement is audible for a long while after they've disappeared.

And the fyrehound's howls soar above me, on and on.

# 18

A knock wrenches me from sleep.

It takes me a panic-filled moment to get my bearings. I'm upstairs in my chambers at Easton, where I fled after the hunt started. Many of the partygoers stayed outside to wait for the hunters' return, but I told Daisy that the wine had made me sick and I needed to retire early. I was so exhausted from the day that I fell asleep in my party dress, the corset still drawn tight.

Blearily, I look around. It's too dark to be morning. Another knock sounds, more urgently.

I throw on a robe, murmuring the charm to conceal my ears and double-knotting my kerchief to be safe. Then I hurry to answer. I don't know who to expect on the other side of the door. Odessa, here to threaten me again? Daisy, hoping to gossip? Sandria with another confusing invitation? I'm not sure I trust anyone anymore. But it's enough to jolt me awake when I wrench the door open and find the last face I expected.

*Finn.*

Something's wrong.

He's drenched in rain and reeks like a swamp. I don't smell blood on him, thank the Gods, but there's an ominous energy around him nonetheless. Something has happened to him. Something has shifted. He looks pale and more wan than I've ever seen him, except when he was half dead.

After weeks of being ignored, I'm torn between slamming the door in his face or collapsing into his arms straightaway. I have strong urges toward both. But, instead, I usher him in before I can stop myself.

As he steps past, I poke my head out the door and glance down the hall for onlookers. I don't need more trouble. But I find the hall dark and empty. After scanning with my Talent, I determine we're the only ones awake on this floor. Everything is still. Eerily silent.

I turn back to Finn with my heart pounding. He's standing stiff in the middle of the chamber, looking childishly marooned.

"I'm sorry for coming so late," he mumbles. "I just needed to talk."

Instinct and reason continue to clash as I take in his appearance. I've never seen him look this vulnerable. Most of me wants to comfort him. That's all I'd want for myself in his shoes. But my more rational side snarls to push him away, to punish him for the weeks of neglect. And for once, I let that half win.

"So, *now* you want to talk to me?"

"Lyria—" Finn starts.

"Don't."

"Don't what?"

I fold my arms, drawing back.

I thought it wasn't possible for Finn to look more distraught. But his face crumples another infinitesimal degree.

"Don't make that face. Don't *Lyria* me," I grind out. "I haven't heard from you in weeks. You didn't even acknowledge me at the party or at the hospital. You can't just pretend that I don't exist and then show up at my door because you need something."

At least he has the decency to look ashamed. Finn stares down at the floor. "I came to tell you I'm sorry," he starts to explain.

It's best not to look at him. I try glaring at the darkened window. "I think you should go."

He draws a heavy breath. "I thought we understood each other after the garden?"

"I did, too! Before you punched Cygnus! Before you ignored me for weeks!"

Do I really have to explain this to him?

Finn staggers toward me. "Lyria, I couldn't even *look* at you after what I did! I couldn't face myself! I was so ashamed, I even asked my father to send me to the front lines in Sontaag, but he refused—"

My stomach twists. "You *what*?"

"What I did to Cygnus is unforgivable—"

I cut him off. "Why would you send yourself to the front lines?"

"Because it's what I deserve."

"Why would you think that?"

"Because I'm a monster!" He sinks into a chair, looking tortured as the words tumble out. "I never meant to hurt him. Cygnus, he's . . . he used to be my best friend. I've always looked up to him, and he's always been better at everything, and since he came back from school, he's wanted nothing to do with me, and . . . I don't blame him for that. But when he said those things about you, I just saw red. Because if he hadn't forced me out of his life, he'd know what you mean to me, and how I feel about you. He'd be the person I was most excited to tell! And then what he said about my troops . . . That's my worst fear vocalized. He knows that. And I just . . . I didn't think. Because I've got dog shit for brains."

Finn clutches his head between his hands, and his voice drops, wobbling. "I could have maimed him. They thought he was going to go blind. Just because I couldn't stand hearing the truth . . . that everybody thinks I'm a joke."

I draw a very deep breath, closing my eyes. Behind my lids, I see Mother's look of revulsion and her bloody hands. I can hear her screaming, *WHAT HAVE YOU DONE?*

Shame swells through me, rising to match his. I know how it feels to make a horrible mistake.

"What you did was an accident," I say softly, lifting my eyes back to him. "A stupid one, but . . . still an accident. It didn't make me stop wanting to see you. And the last thing I'd ever want is for you to go fight in Sontaag. You're not a monster. And I don't think you're a joke, either."

Finn releases a long exhalation, his shoulders slumping. "Then . . . why are you still upset with me?"

"Because . . ." So many reasons rise, I'm scrambling to pick one.

*Because I'm your enemy. Because you're complicit in Verdinae's crimes. Because your whole life rests on a lie. Because you hunt Elves like me. Because none of that has stopped me from wanting you.*

I grit my teeth. Worse than the sweeping heat of my Talent is the ache in my chest. It feels like a cold blade is slowly being driven between my ribs. When I look at Finn, I see the person who unlocked my cage. Even after everything I have learned and everything he has done, I still see a dreamscape of an impossible future: deserts and oceans to traverse, cities to explore, children to treasure . . . a kingdom to lead back to the light.

A fantasy that's objectively absurd.

And has to end now.

I need to shove Finn away before I'm too pathetically attached to manage it. So I settle on the cruelest truth I can vocalize. "Because you're a coward." My vision blurs, and my throat goes tight. "And you're selfish."

Finn recoils like I've hit him.

I've already thrown the knife—why not twist it?

"In the Ironwoods you told me that you hate your father," I growl. "But all I've ever seen you do is *exactly* what he expects. Maybe the reason you're not respected is that everyone can see that you're still jockeying for his approval!"

Finn doesn't argue. He just stares at me, heartbroken.

"You told me in the garden that you wanted to change," I barrel on, gaining momentum. "You made me think I could trust you. Then, at the first opportunity, you just dropped me and disappeared!"

"I thought you wouldn't want to see me!" he says, defensive.

"I did *nothing* to give you that indication!" I retort. "And then tonight, when they brought out the fyrehound, what did you do? You didn't just stand by and watch the murder happen—you participated!"

"No, I didn't," Finn says softly.

"What?" I reel back.

Finn meets my eyes, and I find an unbearable heaviness in his. "We didn't kill it."

"You didn't catch it?" My spirits soar, hoping for the impossible.

"Oh, we caught it."

My breath catches.

Finn's voice falls, flat and low, as he explains. "We chased it for a couple hours. We tracked it over two rivers and got up to our knees in shit, trying to follow it through the marshes. Everyone had to get off their horses and pick up on foot. Eventually, we got it cornered, and Sebastian went in for the kill."

I try to picture the scene: the young fyrehound surrounded by hunters with swords raised.

"And?" I ask.

"And he couldn't do it," he finishes roughly.

Relief courses through me.

"My brother walked up to the hound, and he just froze. Couldn't stomach it, I guess. So the creature got away."

This I can imagine vividly: Sebastian looming over the hound, indecision etched across his handsome features. Did he tremble, as I did when I held Dante's life in my hands? Did he see the injustice of the situation?

Finn's expression doesn't match my relief.

"Is that a problem?"

"Yes, I'd call it a problem. We had dignitaries from all over the Midlands in that hunting party. Nobles from *every* major family. If they think Sebastian is a little bitch who can't handle blood, it reflects poorly on the whole royal family. We'll flounder in Sontaag if we don't have their support. Not to mention what my father will do when he finds out."

Revulsion rolls through me as I stare back at Finn. How can our priorities be so different?

"I don't think Sebastian is a 'little bitch' for showing mercy." I bitterly echo his words. "What I saw back there wasn't sport. That was boys pretending to be warriors. I applaud him for having the guts to do the decent thing."

Finn sighs. "I know how you feel about the fyrehounds—"

"It's not about how I *feel,*" I say, cutting him off. Fury courses through me, that vengeful part of my magic rising like liquid fire. "It's about right and wrong, and learning to see it!"

"I'm not saying he wasn't right to refuse," Finn pushes back. "I'm just saying there were better ways he could have approached it."

"Such as?"

"Such as calling off the hunt before it happened!" he snaps. "I sound callous. I get it. But Sebastian doesn't have the luxury of being this dense about politics! He could have de-escalated the whole thing if he'd spoken up earlier. The right moment was after my mother's speech. If he didn't want to do it, he should have called it off then! But he got halfway in and couldn't follow through, and that paints a picture our enemies can seize upon. They're going to take that moment and use it to forward the narrative that the heir doesn't have the stomach to lead. They'll say Sebastian would freeze on the battlefield. His mistake will blow back on us at every level. You have no idea how hard it was for me to watch him screw this up for himself!"

"Isn't that what you want?" I say back, my lip curling. "For Sebastian to mess it all up, so you can be king?"

"*No!* No, I want the whole thing done with!" Finn roars. "That's what no one understands! Not even *you,* apparently! I don't want to be king more than I want it to be over. The Crown, this fight, it's been my *whole* life, Lyria. My whole entire life. I didn't have a childhood. None of us did. We were all too consumed with the question of whom he'd choose. He made us competitors, not brothers!"

Finn shakes his head fiercely. "So *yes,* I wish Sebastian would just take the damn crown, and then Damien and I could get on with our lives." He watches me, breathing hard. "I am trying, Lyria. I know that I can be shortsighted. I make stupid mistakes; I don't always do the right thing. But I *want* to change! I don't want to be selfish or cowardly. I want to be more like you. I can't always see the right path ahead. That's why I *need* you. *Please,* Lyria. I'm not a villain. I need you to see that."

Finn's words rend my chest. His eyes are wide and pleading, begging for assurance. He looks as if my rejection would condemn him.

It's my turn to sink into a chair. I close my eyes. Gods, I hate how much I empathize with him. Beautiful, passionate boy.

"Please," he continues gently. "I'm sorry for what happened with Cygnus, and I'm sorry for withdrawing. If pulling away is not what you want, I won't do it again. And I'm sorry for handling all of this so poorly." He seems to struggle. "The truth is . . . I'm in new territory here. I—I didn't expect to feel the way I do about you, because . . . I haven't felt this way about anyone before. I know I've screwed this up, but . . . please. Let me make it up to you. Or at least try."

I'm shaking, drowning in the sea of all I can't express.

I understand Finn's perspective. I do. I see the child behind his soldier's veneer, the lonely soul aching to be known. I can't accept all of him—I can't forget who he is, or who he serves—but I can't make myself believe that he's a monster, either.

If I can suspend my disbelief just far enough, that impossible future slips into view. Between the blaring warnings of imminent danger, I catch glimpses of the dreamscape where we could bridge the impassable void separating us—a world where blood and birthright could be cast aside. Then all that would matter would be the gravitational pull between us, that bone-deep feeling that he was born to be mine.

Finn rises. His arms open.

It's suddenly very clear what he wants. What he *needs*. And finally, it's the same thing I do.

*It's not wise,* my more cautious self hisses.

To hell with wisdom.

I fling my arms around him.

There's a moment of hesitation, like this isn't what he expected. But then Finn's arms slip around my waist, and he buries his face in my hair. He clings to me like we're dying—like he's aiming to crush every bone in my body.

This is not something I should be enjoying. Not after tonight, not ever. Somewhere within me, that rational voice is screaming. *Finn is your enemy! He hunts Elves! He would hunt you if he knew the truth!* But hell, holding him is pure ecstasy. His body is warm and solid, the shape of him achingly familiar. After years of being alone, I crave the touch even though I know I shouldn't. Pressing my face into his chest, I breathe in his rain-soaked scent, so sweet it's almost dizzying. I'm feverish, blazing with desire, and his damp clothes present relief. I will this moment to last for infinity. That I never have to let go.

"Sebastian's not a coward," I murmur, loud enough that he can hear me while I'm still pressed against him.

"No," Finn agrees. "He's not."

It's a long time before either of us pulls away. When we finally do, Finn slips his hand into mine and leads me toward the chaise. We sit. Then, with him still gripping my hand like he's afraid of losing contact, we start talking, and stories from the last few weeks spill into the space between us.

Finn tells me about the mission he's been sent on, and I confront him about his role in the Frumentari. He admits his complex feelings about his involvement. I hear about violence from both sides, and learn about the escalatory tactics used by the extremists of the Elven resistance. The plague starts to feel like the least of the rebellion's iniquities. Finn soberly describes attacks conducted on human villages, including huge explosions of drakesbane meant to target as many civilians as possible. I listen soberly as he recounts the troops he's lost and the agony of informing their families. He asks about my life in the palace, and I tell him about the East Wing and my struggles with the omnidraught and even my irritation with Sandria. I don't mention Cygnus or the gates for obvious reasons.

After what feels like hours, Finn clears his throat. "Everyone is still filtering in from the hunt, so if I head back to my room now, there's a decent chance I'll be seen."

My eyebrows rise. Finn's never cared about impropriety before. I can hear what he's really asking.

"Well, we wouldn't want that," I murmur.

He swallows. "I should probably bathe."

We glance together toward the washroom. There's a massive stone shower . . . and no door.

Heat that has nothing to do with my magic pools in my stomach.

"I could help," I offer, feeling like a raw nerve.

Despite all my conflicting opinions of Finn, I can't deny how every part of me aches to be closer to him. I know our days are numbered, and yet I still want to understand him fully—to slink inside his skin and see the world from his perspective. I can't tell Finn how much I want him forever. I can just be with him now.

His smirk is an invitation in itself.

I follow Finn into the washroom as he tugs his damp tunic over his head in one fluid motion. He flips on a faucet, then starts unbuttoning his undershirt. Finn's eyes are sharp, watching me, as he peels off the remaining fabric covering his stomach and chest. I suck in a low breath, almost involuntarily. I've seen these parts of his body before. But here, in the darkened chamber, I feel very differently about the half-naked figure in front of me.

"You should wash, too," Finn suggests playfully.

My heart skips a beat, and there is only a second of hesitation before I respond, "Sure."

I'm reminded of our first encounter, at the waterfall, when I stripped off my overdress so thoughtlessly. That day seems so long ago, and remembering it makes me shiver. This is nothing like that. I'm the opposite of thoughtless as I reach up and carefully unbutton my dress. All Finn's attention is focused on me as I undo the buttons one by one, then shimmy out of the long dress. Now I stand in just my corset and chemise.

"It's best to be thorough," I whisper.

"I agree."

With strenuous effort, Finn forces his gaze from my chest. His eyes lock onto mine as he slowly reaches for his belt. It clicks and then hisses as he slides it off. As I stand, doe-eyed, in my underthings, I half expect him to make a quip about reciprocation—something to cut the tension of this moment. But he just stares and stares, until I understand that he's waiting for me to decide what I want.

I've already decided. I want him.

First, I reach gently for my kerchief, surreptitiously brushing my ears to check the concealment charm. It's still in place. So, heart pounding, I untie the silk and tug it off my hair, letting the brown curls tumble free.

Then my fingers drop to the strings of my corset. It takes longer than usual as I fuss with the ribbons. Finn doesn't complain. He doesn't say anything. He just watches with that wanting, hazy look until I've finished.

There's no change in his expression as I slip off the corset, but I hear the shift in his breathing. It speeds as I slide off my chemise, tugging it down my body, lower and lower, until it falls to my ankles. In total vulnerability, I gaze back at him.

The prince of Verdinae. *My* prince.

"Pretty easy to make you speechless," I murmur.

"Come here," he says roughly.

I obey.

With hands that speak of experience, Finn guides me under the shower. He picks a bottle from the shower bench, a creamy ivory soap that smells like vanilla. I'm looking up into his eyes as he pours the contents over me. It's cold but not painful as it slides down the plane of my stomach. I shiver.

He reaches for a washcloth. Finn starts on my upper back, washing in gentle circles until each area tingles. He works over my arms and hands, then down my legs, lingering at my feet. His hands seem to memorize my shape, tracing it over and over. Every touch aches. He takes his time, following the lines of my figure. Never quite slipping where I want him.

When he finishes washing me, it's my turn. I copy his movements with a sort of quiet reverence: just appreciating his form. Finn's hard-muscled body is a weapon of its own. I can see the hours in the sword yard outlined with every vein and fiber. Thick silence has overcome us. I'm wholly occupied with my work—every part of me blazing. Finn hangs his head, letting the hot water drip down his hair as I wash over the swell of his chest and the arc of his shoulders.

After we've finished, I change into a nightdress, and Finn rummages in the closet until he procures a clean pair of trousers, which are only slightly too small. Then we crawl together under the blankets.

My body finds his, and I curl into him.

He's deliciously warm. Muscled arms wrap around me, and Finn pulls me flush against him. I can't restrain my hands from creeping up to trace his chest . . . then his shoulders . . . then the hard lines of his stomach. All the parts I've woven back together. His fragile shell of skin.

It strikes me, as we lie in the darkness, that it's frightening how much I care about his well-being. The thought of harm befalling him makes me physically ill. I've been battling an outright obsession with him from the moment I dragged him back to the cottage. I'm no better than his sycophants, making him my sun.

It's quiet. Then Finn asks abruptly, in a soft voice: "Do you think I'm a bad person?"

I'm so taken aback by the question, I just lie there breathing for a while. His body is tense, awaiting my answer.

"I think we're only as good as our next choice," I finally say thickly. "That's what my mother would say."

I'm thinking of the raiders he fought, the prisoner at the feast, the fyrehound. It will take time to comb through the knots of conflicting experiences.

"Can I ask *you* something?" I say.

"Of course."

"You said that you'll be accepting if your father chooses Sebastian. But if he doesn't, why would you *want* to be king?"

His thumb idly traces the back of my neck. After a long silence, he says quietly, "You know, I'm not sure anyone's ever asked me that."

"Never?" I swallow.

"I would assume it's self-explanatory."

"I don't think so."

"Tell me more." His voice is tight.

I blow a puff of hot air. "Well, the responsibility, for one. Your life isn't just your own. And I imagine people are always watching and judging you. I wouldn't want that type of scrutiny."

"You wouldn't be scrutinized," Finn says softly. "You'd be an excellent queen."

With those words, the energy in the room hitches. Does he know how those words sound? Is he just being hypothetical—stating that I have the personality traits that would suit a ruler? Or is it more? Is he implying that I'd be an excellent queen *with* him?

I quickly dismiss this thought as preposterous and let out a nervous laugh to mask the pause.

"You'd be a great king," I tell him.

He smiles. "You're more generous than I deserve."

"It's the truth."

I close my eyes, suddenly very sleepy. With deep breaths, my pulse slows, synchronizing with his.

Finn is the first to drift off. His muscles twitch as sleep finds him, little spasms in his fingers and core. But he doesn't let go. It's hard to conceive of how recently he was a stranger. Now my feelings for him nearly overwhelm me.

*Why?* I send the thought toward Elowyn, a desperate prayer. What is the point of this tidal wave of affection? And why can't I shove it back down?

Do I just want to feel chosen? Is it the possibility of the palace, the glamour and luxury, the lighthearted life that I could pretend to enjoy?

*No.* I shove those thoughts aside. I care for Finn in spite of his world, not because of it. If anything, I long to do what he did for me—to steal him away from his cage and show him just how narrow those borders are. He would be someone else in a different environment. He'd be the boy I met in the cottage again.

I want him far away from his parents and Damien and the sycophants. I want to show him everything that's wrong about his world. I want to walk with him into the light, to protect and cherish him, and to learn to rely on him. I want everything with Finn. I care about his happiness, maybe more than my own.

And as I consider that thought, the truth finally transmutes into understanding, and twin realizations swell within me, unstoppable as the tide.

I am falling in love with Finn.

And losing him is going to break me.

We have no future in this world. My rational mind has accepted that. I can't ignore the conflicting duties of our birthrights, and all the years of vicious history between us. He will always be Verdin's descendant. I will always have magic. We are destined to inherit opposing sides of this war.

But I can't stop myself from dreaming, even now. And I can't deny what's threatening to burst out of my chest: the affection, the empathy, the burning desire to ensure his well-being.

I love him. Gods help me, I love him.

And I'm going to have to let him go.

With my head against his chest, I listen to the steady thrumming of his heart. It beats loudly against my ear, a reminder of his fragile human existence. Aging slows for Elves in their twenties. I have a few more years before Finn's mortal body will start wearing down at a faster rate. Time will betray us, as blood already has.

In all my life, Finn will never be replaced. I could live for centuries and never match what he represents to me: my bridge to the world, my rescuer, the catalyst to my freedom. He'll have a piece of my heart forever.

That's when it pours over me like a bucket of ice water overhead.

*I know the answer to the riddle.*

*It's blood.*

# 19

When I return to the palace, my first stop is Cygnus's office.

I'm prepared for a slew of questions when I present the solution I've worked out. But to my surprise, he just nods thoughtfully and says, "That makes sense. I think you might be right."

That may be the closest he's come to praise.

Between our schedules, it takes a fortnight to get plans in order. With the VIA pushing ever farther into Sontaag, nearly every bed in the hospital has been filled with soldiers or the displaced. Cygnus is needed nonstop for surgery, and I'm almost equally busy in the storehouse. I don't see much of Daisy, and Sandria hasn't sought me out again since Sebastian's party, which makes me think I must have been even poorer company than I realized. I still don't know why she invited me in the first place. But at the moment, I have more important concerns than my social life and the mystery that is the princess of Ursandor.

When I meet with the queen to report on my progress on the omnidraught, she informs me that the death count in the quarantine zone has climbed to the hundreds. And, of course, I receive no further word from Mother, which is increasingly concerning with each passing day. It's getting harder and harder to convince myself that there's no reason to be alarmed about her silence. I haven't confided to anyone my theory about her involvement in the rebellion, for obvious reasons. So the worry just gnaws at me. I'm duty bound to finish the omnidraught, so I throw myself into work to cope and avoid thinking of worst-case scenarios. Despite my desperation, progress stalls.

Nights become my consolation. After the trip to Easton, Finn starts taking his dinner in my chambers. We share stolen hours together nearly every evening, sometimes ending up in each other's arms again. But I always nudge him out the door before either of us can fall asleep. I tell him this is because of concerns about propriety, but *really* it's so that I can sneak back to the hospital to meet Cygnus. My Talent is needed more than ever. Each night, he guides me to the people most in need of my help, and I do all that I can before dawn.

Finally, Cygnus and I are given a window of opportunity in which to go back down to the gates. As of this evening, there are no patients currently in critical condition, the latest batch of the omnidraught needs to cure under the full moon, and Finn is busy meeting with his family to prepare for the midsummer tournament, so he won't notice my absence.

After a supper I can barely stomach from nerves, Cygnus and I head back to the Everwillow tree under a starlit sky.

"Ready?" he asks as we stop before it.

"Ready."

We've come more prepared for our second expedition. I have my father's dagger strapped to my belt as always, plus another three throwing blades that I swiped from the royal armory and my rucksack. Cygnus has his sword and his satchel, which is fully stocked. We brought food and water, more skakabri antivenom, more spools of thread, and a slew of small potions that I insisted we might need, including the drakesbane and the remaining ones in my personal quiver, which tinkle on my belt with every movement.

"Would you care to do the honors?" Cygnus asks.

I shoot him a glare but step forward. Glancing around to confirm there are no onlookers, I grit my teeth, take a running start, and leap into the tree.

Free fall. This time, I keep my feet beneath me. The black hole rises to swallow me, even faster this time, and I force my body to stay stiff, my toes pointed and legs locked. I strike the water like a blade, ice exploding over my skin. And this time, there is no pain, just the shock of the fall and the cold water. I'm treading water when I hear the splash of Cygnus following me. Then we paddle together for the shore.

The string is as we left it. The twisted bodies of the skakabri are untouched as well. I hold my breath, waiting for the sounds of small feet tapping against stone, but none come. We must have killed all the skakabri last time we were here. I step past the corpses with heart-pounding guilt as we head toward the first gate. I wonder how long it will take them to decompose. They don't stink yet. Are there scavengers in this inhospitable world?

We retrace our steps in silence until we reach the yawning cavern and the great polished wall. I approach the chalice and hold out my palm. I briefly consider making the cut with my Talent, but change my mind and withdraw my father's dagger. I'd like him to be part of this, in a small way. Grimacing, I make one clean slice. Blood flows. I hold my hand over the cup, watching as the crimson leaks onto the silver. Cygnus and I are quiet.

For a split second, I wonder if I've made a mistake. But then a great rumbling sounds, and the walls in front of us begin to tremble. Gravel rattles underfoot. I brace against the pedestal as the rumbling intensifies. The doors split in front of us, revealing a gaping chamber beyond.

We walk through the open gate.

Cygnus and I emerge into a cavern even more massive than the first. Giant stalactites hang from the ceiling, and the floor is littered with round pools of ankle-deep water. Dripping sounds everywhere. About a hundred paces in front of us, there is a massive elevated square block of stone with a lumpy figure on top that I at first assume is a stalagmite formed from the dripping water. But as we approach, I realize it's the figure of an Elven woman, standing with her hand outstretched toward the darkest point of the cave.

"Is that supposed to be Queen Soleste?" Cygnus asks, approaching from behind me.

I shake my head. "That's Elowyn. Goddess of Life."

"There's not a lot about the Elven Gods in the archives," Cygnus says softly. I hear the words for what they are—an invitation. Perhaps this is how I can break the tension between us, by offering him a piece of his culture he's never had access to.

"My mother taught me that in the beginning, there was just Elowyn and her sisters, Nocturn and Rashielle—life, death, and time. The three constants," I explain, tracing my finger down the smooth carving. "Elowyn fell in love with Solaris, God of the Sun, and followed him into the sky. Nocturn followed suit with the God of the

Moon, accompanying him into the underworld to rule over the darkness. The sisters reunite every dusk and dawn at the horizon line."

"What about Rashielle?" asks Cygnus.

"Rashielle grew lonely in the mortal realm, so Elowyn wove two children for her out of ivy. Those were the first Elves. All our people are their descendants."

Cygnus nods, and I can practically see him carefully taking note of every piece of new information.

"How do you know it's Elowyn and not one of her sisters?" he asks.

"She's got the crown of ivy. See?" I point toward her headpiece, a circlet of vines with a sapphire centerpiece like a sunburst. "If it were a statue of Nocturn, she'd be wearing a crescent necklace. And Rashielle's always got a big ring on, though I can't remember why."

Cygnus looks somber. "What do you think?"

"About the statue?"

"About all of it."

I take a moment to pick my words. As I was growing up, Mother never solicited my opinion on religion. She just taught me her beliefs as truth.

That seemed to be her approach with most things.

"If there really are Gods, I don't know how they could allow what happened to Evermore," I finally say. "Some people like having something to believe in, and it makes them feel better about the shit world we're living in. And I think that's lovely and all. But to me . . . I dunno. It almost makes me feel worse to imagine someone is watching this and choosing to do nothing."

"I don't like faith as a concept," Cygnus agrees. "I'd rather put my trust in what I can control."

*Shocking.*

"And that's served you well?"

He smiles faintly. "I've gotten this far, haven't I?"

Silence falls. Eventually, the rocky cave floor gives way to smaller stones. We pass over a section of soft, fine dust, descending into a narrow chute of knee-deep, muddy water. We're moving along, boots squelching, in heavy mutual silence, when Cygnus stops abruptly.

His head swivels, reminding me of a hawk. "Do you hear something?"

I stop, listening for unfamiliar sounds in the cave.

"No?"

"Down there." He points.

We stand frozen for a moment as I strain to hear what he has heard. Then, faintly, I catch it: a voice. High and distant. Howling, almost. Wailing. The sound is oddly familiar, but I am not quite sure how to place it. I take a step toward the noise. Cygnus looks transfixed.

I begin to say, "It almost sounds like—"

Cygnus gasps. "That's my mother!"

He starts running.

*"Wait!"* I bolt after him in pursuit.

The shrieking grows louder, wordless and primal, echoing off the walls. It's a raw, otherworldly cry of a terrible loss. Pure grief and rage.

"Cygnus, that's spellcraft!" I shout after him. "It's not her!"

But then I hear another sound, another voice rising, from the opposite end of the cavern.

I stop dead in my tracks.

*"Lyria!"* the voice screams. *"Lyria, I'm here! Help me, please—Lyria!"*

It's Mother.

I don't know how, but I'm certain it's her. I feel it with every humming cell in my body. She's down here. She's trapped and hurt, and she needs help. *My* help. Without another thought toward Cygnus, I take off after her voice.

With each step, the intensity of her screaming grows. I run with abandon, hurtling toward the sound.

*"LYRIA! Where are you?"*

The torch tumbles from my hand. I take another step—

And then I'm falling.

I hit the ground with a sickening *crack*.

White-hot pain erupts in my leg, and I cry out, clutching it. My stomach roils as I look down and see severed bone jutting out of my thigh. Mother's screaming goes on and on as my vision crumbles. I think I lose consciousness briefly. When I find myself again, the screaming is gone.

Instead, I hear slithering, like a hundred serpents uncoiling.

I've fallen into a pit. I can see almost nothing, except for pale shapes bobbing in the distance. The slithering intensifies. As it nears, I realize precisely what I've stumbled into: *banshees*.

My skin crawls. The daemons are skeletal and faintly humanoid. There is something feline in their movements. I count four of them: shrunken, emaciated bodies in dark cloaks. Their faces are ghostly, and when one yawns, it reveals a mouth of sharklike teeth. Their beady black eyes catch the light.

*"We've been waiting for you,"* the nearest one moans, with a voice like howling wind.

I am already reaching for my Talent, yanking on the thread as hard as I can, shooting the energy into my leg, trying to seal the flesh. But my focus is torn as they slink closer, one hissing with my mother's voice: *"Lyria, will you join ussss?"*

"GET AWAY!" I howl, pounding at my leg with my fist. I need to shove the bone back in place, but the agony is overwhelming. Stars pop at the edge of my vision. I'm fighting for consciousness. Darkness blooms, and I think I pass out again, because when I blink, the banshees are closer.

*"They dare send their acolyte,"* one murmurs in a high, reedy voice.

*"Will her blood be sweet, I wonder?"* another asks. *"It's been too long since I've tasted flesh."*

*"She'll be sweeter than the boy. A wellborn daughter, kissed by the Goddess . . ."*

"Stay back!" I scream. I send a violent wave of magic their direction, but it drifts away like mist. The banshees might as well be made of smoke and shadows. There is nothing for my Talent to seize on, nothing alive in them to manipulate. Terror consumes me.

They keep slinking forward with the curious, unhurried speed of scavengers. I start digging in my rucksack, trying to find something—anything—to fight back with. My hand wraps around the throwing knives.

I hurl the first blade at the nearest monster, and it catches her firmly in the chest. She crumples but does not stop. I have enough time to try the second knife, missing another approaching banshee, before the first reaches me, and—creeping steadily—draws forward and sinks her teeth into my calf. I scream again as a second does the same, ripping into the soft flesh of my stomach. I struggle for the dagger strapped to my belt, but I can't reach it. So I dig again into the sack, finding the third knife. I roar as I draw it out, burying it firmly into the banshee's skull latched onto my side. I manage to shake her off as the other two close in. I dig into the pack one more time . . .

And my fingers close on the drakesbane.

I smash the bottle onto the ground as hard as I can.

Emerald fyre explodes around us. The daemons shriek with inhuman fury as flames quickly catch onto their robes and swallow their figures. I'm on fyre, too. The flames gobble my skirts, spreading to my torso, and it takes every bit of my strength to *heave* sideways, rolling to extinguish the flames. My boot melts against my flesh; I can smell my skin charring. But I fight back, slapping the flames, until I can finally focus, scanning the broken bodies of the daemons, still sputtering fyre around me.

*Cygnus.* I have to reach Cygnus.

I reach down to my thigh. Grit my teeth. And slam my femur back into place.

The sound that tears out of me isn't human. It's the howl of an animal, the monster within, roaring for dominance. I don't know where I find the strength, but I force myself to my knees. Then to my feet. I stumble forward until my hands meet rock. I have reached the cliffside. Distantly, I hear another scream—unmistakably Cygnus.

There's no time to feel sorry for myself. No time for hesitation. So, fighting the nauseating agony . . .

I climb.

The cliffside is jagged marble. I fell maybe two dozen feet. I scramble as fast as I can, cursing my limp arms and the searing pain in my thigh. The agony doesn't ease, even as my magic stitches together flesh and bone faster than I've ever healed before.

The effort is draining. My physical and magical strength is plummeting, but I am determined. Grappling, I drag up one foot. Another. Finally, I crest the ridge and haul myself onto solid ground, panting.

Finding the torch I dropped, I scoop it up.

The path in front of me splits two ways. I hear Cygnus again. Steeling myself, I make a choice. I go left.

A prayer of thanks hisses out of me as I round a corner and find him straightaway. Cornered by a pair of daemons but untouched, Cygnus is kneeling, and it takes me a moment to understand what I am staring at. He holds a dagger at chest height, not in defense but pointed toward his own heart. His eyes are glazed as the banshees circle him, chanting something wordless, tuneless, and otherworldly.

"NO!"

I fling out both hands, and with a single, desperate thought, I shatter both his eardrums.

Cygnus doubles over, bellowing. I take the opportunity to strike, hurling my father's dagger at the nearest banshee. Blessedly, it connects with its target.

Whatever spell they have cast over Cygnus breaks. As I surge forward to meet another banshee, its teeth yawning open like the maw of a shark, something in Cygnus activates. Leaping up, he swings his sword and lops off the daemon's head with a single swipe. It *thuds* and rolls away.

At last, all is still. In the stunning silence, the exhaustion seizes me full force.

Darkness claws at the edges of my vision. I'm only faintly aware of Cygnus reaching for me. Then the shadows consume us, and the whole world goes black.

# 20

hen I regain consciousness, we haven't moved from our spot in the cavern.

Cygnus crouches by a crackling fire about a dozen paces away. I'm flat on my back. Something lumpy and hard props up my head. I feel with my hand and realize it's his crumpled-up tunic.

At first, I think he doesn't notice my stirring. But then he speaks, voice cutting through the shadow: "You've been out a few hours. I figured you needed to rest after all that."

I blink at our surroundings. The bodies of the banshees are gone, but the smell of death lingers.

"What happened?" I ask.

Cygnus shakes his head and lifts a finger to tap his earlobe. I spot the stream of dark, crusted blood running down from his ears, and I groan, remembering. "Your *ears*. I'm sorry."

"I can't hear anything," he says, too loudly.

I gesture for him to come over. "I'll help you."

He hesitates. "You should save your strength."

"We're not getting through this shit if you can't hear a word I say."

He still looks nervous, so I wave again, more forcefully. *"Come here."*

Reluctantly, he walks over and sits beside me so that we face each other. His eyes are sharp in the darkness, tracking every movement as I lift my hands to his temples. I keep the touch featherlight. It doesn't escape me that this is the most physical contact I have had with Cygnus, at least with both of us conscious. I'm keenly aware of the space between us: his scent, the heat, each cautious breath.

The wound is easy to isolate. The pain in his throbbing eardrums carries a distinct signature, almost like a scarlet thread in an ivory tapestry. With deep breaths, I sink into my consciousness, diving further and further until I reach the coil of imaginary thread at the base of my spine. I draw it out, letting the magic surge through my skin until the threads curl around Cygnus's severed ones. Healing and soothing.

I remove my hands as soon I finish.

Cygnus wobbles his head, like a dog trying to slough off extra water. "I'm going to have to start tallying my life debts," he mumbles. "You own my soul a few times over at this point."

I huff a weary laugh. "Monsters are my specialty, apparently."

"Any idea what those were?"

"Banshees," I say, scowling.

Cygnus falls quiet, staring at me with a strange expression I can't place. I always have such a hard time discerning what he's thinking. After a long pause, he asks quietly, "Does it hurt?"

My brow furrows. When I realize what he is referring to, I smile, shaking my head. "The actual healing? Not for me."

"I can tell that it drains you," Cygnus says. "I wasn't sure how much or what it felt like."

"I've always visualized it like a transfer of energy. I imagine if I were running out of blood and you had some way to give me a little of yours, it might feel like someone was taking your energy and putting it into me. That's what it feels like."

"How much energy is there?"

"What do you mean?"

"How deep does the well go?" he asks.

I consider the question, thinking of how I felt after healing Finn and repairing Cygnus's sight. "I'm not sure. There haven't been many situations where I've tested the limits. The skakabri brought me all the way to the edge, and it was terrifying. Usually, I use my Talent rarely. Typically smaller stuff."

Cygnus nods thoughtfully. "Did your mother teach you how to use it?"

I shake my head. "She doesn't have a bloodborne Talent."

"Really?" He looks surprised. "Then how did you learn?"

"I didn't have a choice." I shrug, flexing my hands. "The Talent manifested when I was very young. It's one of the first things I remember. I thought I was dying."

"A little dramatic, perhaps?"

"You wouldn't say so if you'd been able to feel it." I smile tightly. "When it builds under my skin, it feels like fire. Like I'm burning alive. The first time it happened I was only a little kid. And then I started to be able to *see* it—the life energy, I mean."

"I don't understand," Cygnus murmurs.

I sigh. This has always been one of the hardest parts of my Talent to accept: the fact that no one will ever be able to understand it.

"When you or I look at the world around us, we can perceive it all with our physical senses—touch, smell, et cetera. I see more. Every living thing: every bug, every blade of grass . . . it has a certain energy."

"Like an aura?"

"More like interwoven threads." I struggle to convey what I mean. "Flesh looks to me like thousands of glowing threads in a tapestry. When I'm healing people, it's like I can reach out and tug the threads."

Cygnus is quiet for a while. "After I learned that I was half Elf, I wished desperately that I'd been born with magic. I wanted something I could fight back with. I saw what Rodrick was doing, and . . . selfishly, I think . . . I wanted to be able to stop him."

"A bloodborne Talent is not a blessing," I say, sharper than I intended. "Not in this world. Trust me, it's more like a curse."

Cygnus frowns. "You can save someone's life with a thought. I wouldn't call that a curse."

I sigh, debating whether or not to elaborate.

"I can't always control it," I finally admit. "Like when I was a little girl, sometimes I'd be holding a bird, or petting a lamb, or something, and I wouldn't mean to, but . . ." I splay my hands.

I expect Cygnus to show some disgust or horror, but he looks utterly calm.

Emboldened, I continue. The whole painful truth starts to spill out of me. "When I was twelve, Mother and I met this woman in the woods while she was having a baby. There was something wrong with the delivery and she needed help. But Mother was sick with a fever and weak, and the labor just went on and on, for hours. . . ."

I squeeze my eyes shut, blocking out the images. "Mother became so desperate that she asked me to help. I tried to use my Talent, even though I was terrified. . . ."

I hang my head, the memory swallowing me whole.

Suddenly, I'm twelve years old again, with every tactile detail as vivid as the moment I lived it.

I can taste the tears streaming down my cheeks. I can hear Mother's hoarse voice, commanding me to make the incision. I can feel the warmth seeping over my fingers. Worst of all, I'm inhabited again by the human woman's pain, her physical and emotional agony as the child is drawn out of her, already lifeless.

And I can never forget the dying woman's last word—the hatred as she screams at me.

*Monster.*

"I killed them both," I admit in a soft voice. "I should have been able to save them. But I was too scared and sloppy, and I lost control." I swipe the tears away, turning so Cygnus doesn't see the display of my shame.

Softly, Cygnus says, "You were a child. Children make mistakes. You can't blame yourself."

He doesn't understand.

"My Talent isn't like other Elves' Talents," I explain. "There's something wrong with it. There's something wrong with *me*."

"I don't believe that."

"No! That's just a fact! My mother's been alive for over three hundred years, and she's never encountered magic that behaves like mine. It's not supposed to hurt. It's not supposed to feel like my skin is on fire if I get too excited or scared or sad. . . . I'm a monster."

"Listen to me." Cygnus grabs my shoulders. "Your magic is a *gift,* Lyria. It's one of the most amazing things I've ever seen. There's nothing wrong with you. You're not a monster."

"How would you know?" I laugh bitterly.

"Because I watch you!" he snaps. "I've seen how you treat people. What you did for Finn, and for Daisy, and that fox . . . I've seen you risk your life to help perfect strangers. Hell, you did it for me! You can't measure yourself by *one* mistake. You're better than that."

His words leave me speechless.

"You are a good person, Lyria," Cygnus says again finally, seeming uncomfortable with my silence. "Whether because of your Talent or in spite of it, I don't know. But you're no monster, all right?"

I look away, heat pooling in my cheeks and stomach and swelling through my chest.

"Thank you," I whisper.

"No need to thank me for facts," Cygnus grumbles. He throws me my pack. "Now, let's get on with it, shall we? I don't want to keep waiting around for something else that wants to kill us."

And just like that, the moment is gone.

---

Cygnus and I reexamine our inventory of supplies and pack up. After lighting a fresh pair of torches, we withdraw another spool of thread and set out again.

Slowly, methodically, we push through another section of the tunnels. We shuffle along in silence, following turns and retreating at dead ends. Gradually, the air turns colder, and eventually the tunnel opens up again. We step into another massive cavern, almost identical to the one where the blood chalice was waiting. There's another pedestal, with another set of runes inscribed on its cylindrical base. However, there's no chalice this time—just a small, circular groove in the stone.

I hold out my torch and sit cross-legged while I translate. Cygnus looks on, characteristically pensive.

"Here. I've got it," I say when I finish. Cygnus moves close to me to peek over my shoulder as I read aloud.

*"'One of three, and one of one, I glitter as the stars. Let all the pain be overcome by my eternal march. I am the seed of Rashielle, unyielding as the clock. I carry life within my sight, on this unshifting dock.'"*

Cygnus slumps when I finish. "Great. Another riddle."

I stand up, dusting dirt off my skirts.

"What are you doing?" Cygnus asks.

"We're not solving this here," I say. "Not tonight."

"Why?"

I raise a brow at him. "Do *you* have any bright ideas?"

"Not necessarily."

"Right," I say. "We go back, and we mull it over like we did the other time."

The last thing I feel like doing is the painful journey out of the caverns and back to the palace, but I don't see any other options.

"No," Cygnus argues. "We've got a supply of food and water. We should stay longer and try to work it out here."

"The last riddle took us weeks!" I protest. "For all we know, more monsters are going to drop out of the ceiling at any moment. We're not going to solve this here! We should get out while we still can, and regroup, like before."

"But we'll lose all our progress," Cygnus insists.

I roll my eyes. "So we'll come back! But we can't just stay down here indefinitely. People will notice that we're missing."

"Solving the riddle is the most important thing we could be doing." Cygnus's eyes flash, growing accusatory. "This is about Finn, isn't it?"

My face flames, and I snap, "No, it's not!"

Is this really another dig at my competence? Another shaming accusation?

*"Sure."*

I narrow my eyes. "If you've got a problem with me, spit it out."

"I just thought you'd feel a little more urgency given that it is your people in danger!" he snaps. "But no, you've got to get back to your boyfriend."

I shake my head fiercely. "You have no idea what you're talking about."

"Don't I? Can you honestly tell me he's *not* the reason you're at the palace?"

"You have no right to question my motivations!"

"Even when you're in bed with the enemy?"

My cheeks flush and my fists clench at my sides. I don't know what I am more angry about, his presumption or the fact that he is right. Not about the bedding, not the way he intends. But despite all our stolen time together, Finn is still the leader of the Frumentari. He would still hunt me if he knew the truth. And yet, Cygnus wasn't there in the cottage. He doesn't understand the way seeing Finn for the first time made something permanently shift in my chest. Cygnus doesn't know what it is like to be in love.

And I won't tolerate his judgment. Not now.

"Who I'm bedding is none of your business! And you can sit on your high horse and judge me, or be jealous, or *whatever*, but *you're* the one who chose to isolate yourself! *You're* the reason you're alone!" I pause, fuming, but I'm not done. "This is about staying alive, for me. As you so kindly pointed out, I'm only safe at this castle as long as I have Finn's fleeting attention. And unlike you, I don't have a lifetime of learning how to blend in!"

His nostrils flare as I continue to rant.

"So I'm choosing what's going to keep me alive," I say, "and right now, it's getting back to the palace before anyone starts asking questions. Since—in case you haven't noticed—I'm not very popular."

We appraise each other for a long moment. Two dueling forces of will in the darkness. I can sense Cygnus scanning me for weakness, evaluating me the way he would any challenging case in his hospital. I hate the calculated intelligence that's working behind his eyes. He's trying to predict my next move. I won't let him.

Cygnus grinds out, "I'm not questioning your decisions."

"Just judging them. Much better."

"You can do whatever you want with Finn," Cygnus snarls. "I don't care. All I'm interested in is whether you're committed to seeing this through."

"I *am*!" I take a deep breath, glaring at him. "If you want to stay here and wait for a monster to eat you, *be my guest*. That's your prerogative. But *I'm* going back to the castle." I snatch up my things, shoving them into my pack.

"Fine," Cygnus says, his voice dripping with sarcasm. "We can come back at your leisure. No rush. It's not like there's a war going on."

"*Good*. And when we finish these damn gates, you don't ever have to see me again. Happy?"

I turn my back on him and stomp off into the darkness.

# 21

ur trek back to the entrance is thick with tense silence. Cygnus offers no apologies, and I quickly give up hoping for them. I'm expecting darkness when we emerge from the Everwillow. But when Cygnus and I finally get ourselves over the last ridge and step through the murky blue-green portal, we are momentarily blinded.

I curse, blinking to adjust to the sun. "What time is it?"

"I don't know." Cygnus shrugs, shading his eyes.

There's something different about the atmosphere. I smell spices and roasting meat. The swan garden is as secluded as usual, but there's noise carrying from closer to the castle, the rumbling, pleasant cacophony of many voices, layered with music and laughter.

Cygnus reaches the same conclusion I do. "We've been gone more than a whole day."

It's midsummer.

I cover my face with my hands, cursing. How could we have so completely lost track of time? Then I remember: *Dante*. He's been alone since we departed. I left him some extra food, but not enough for more than a day of my absence. Remorse plunges through me as I picture the fox captive in my room, probably hungry and terrified. What's become of him?

We hurry back through a side entrance of the castle. Cygnus splits toward his tower without so much as a goodbye. I jet toward mine, trailing muddy water across the painted floors and fancy carpets. I am far past caring.

When I climb the steps to the East Wing and turn onto my landing, I'm surprised to find my door ajar. Remembering the last time my room was ransacked, I jolt. "Dante?"

When I barrel through the door, it's not just Dante I find. It's a whole group of people.

My eye sweeps the room, absorbing the faces assembled: Damien, Roburn, Anna, Daisy, and several guards I don't recognize. Finally, my gaze snags at the window, and the prince sitting by it who looks more exhausted than all the rest combined. Borderline haggard. Dante sits in his lap, perking at the sight of me.

"God *Almighty*." Daisy surges forward, nearly collapsing as she hugs me. "We were *so* worried about you!"

"What? I'm—I'm fine. . . ." I try to wriggle out of her embrace and realize with some embarrassment that she's weeping.

I can't tear my eyes away from Finn.

"Where were you?!" Daisy demands.

*Oh, you know, just exploring the ancient magical cavern underneath the castle.*

"With . . . Cygnus," I say weakly. Panic courses through me as the room stares back at me, awaiting an explanation. There's a beat where Dante leaps off Finn's lap and scrambles up my skirts and into my arms, and I use it to construct a passable lie. "I needed help collecting an ingredient for the storehouse. I asked him to come with me."

"For two days?" Damien cuts in. He meets my gaze, smirking.

"We were looking for a certain kind of . . . moonlily," I continue, beginning to sweat under the scrutiny of so many eyes. "We had to go farther than I expected. A lot farther."

Roburn's expression is concerned. The other soldiers look like they don't particularly care—Anna just looks annoyed that she's been drawn away from her duties.

I can feel Finn's stare on me like a blade against skin. When he finally speaks, it's almost a whisper. "You were with Cygnus?"

"Yes." Heat prickles up my neck as he frowns and looks away.

Is he *jealous*?

"Next time you go traipsing off for moonlilies, would it kill you to leave a note?" says Daisy, cutting over the moment. "We've been looking for you since last night!"

"I'm sorry. I had no idea anyone would notice I was gone." I wearily appreciate her concern. Though it strikes me as odd that this many people would be looking for me—two princes, the captain of the guard, the hospital's head of staff. . . .

"Well, Miss Lyria, we will leave you to get cleaned up so you can go enjoy the festivities," says Roburn, tipping his hat. "I'm very glad to know that you're safe."

The rest of the guards and Anna follow him out without giving me so much as another glance.

Damien continues that catlike smirk as he exits, looking like he caught a rat in his claws. "Yeah, we're all *thrilled* you got your moonlilies safely."

Daisy grows cheerful as the room clears. "The good news is, you've still got plenty of time to get ready for the festival!"

I can't tear my eyes away from Finn. He is still frowning, and he looks like he's not sure what to do with his hands. Finally, he executes a curt little bow I've never seen before, not meeting my eyes.

"I'll let you take it from here," he says to Daisy. To me, he adds, "Glad you're back." Then he sweeps away before I have the chance to reply.

I'm left staring at the threshold.

"We've got to get you out of these clothes," says Daisy. "Did you fall into a giant heap of dung somewhere?"

"Something like that." I feel numb. Daisy catches me staring at the door.

"He's been distraught. Just so you know," she says smugly.

"What?" I ask.

"Ohhhh, yeah." Daisy grins. "Wish you could have seen him last night. You could hear him screaming at the queen from halfway across the castle."

"Finn was . . . screaming?" My hazy mind struggles to imagine this. The only time I've seen him lose his temper is the incident with Cygnus, and that was like lightning—white-hot rage, there one second and gone the next.

Daisy rolls her eyes. "Come on, Lyria, you're not *that* dense. He's obsessed with you!"

I protest, "He's—"

"Save it," Daisy interrupts. "You're driving me crazy. Pull your head out of the sand!"

"I can't. It's . . ." My hands are shaking as I unlace my boots. Gods, even if I could tell her everything, I wouldn't know where to start. "It's complicated."

"Wait." Daisy's eyes widen. "It's Cygnus, isn't it? You were *with* Cygnus!"

"No!" I yelp, horrified.

"That's exactly what's happening!"

"No, it's not! *Definitely* not!"

"Don't be embarrassed!" Daisy nudges me with her elbow. "It's perfectly understandable. He's got that whole tortured-soul thing going on. Half the East Wing has a crush on him."

"I don't have a crush on Cygnus!" I splutter. I don't know why my face feels so hot. "I don't even *like* him! Like as a person, in general!"

Truthfully, I don't know what I feel. Everything has gotten so jumbled. I find Cygnus an exhausting and arrogant prick, but for some reason, I still want his approval. I hate his personality, but I can't say I hate *him*. Where does that put us? Friends? Allies? Just coconspirators and colleagues?

"Suuuuure," Daisy drawls. "You two were just out picking moonlilies. We all know what *that* means." She scoops up my dirty boots and deposits them in a muddy pile. "I was actually really hoping to pick some moonlilies tonight at the festival. . . ." She giggles as I peel off my socks, my face burning.

Daisy holds out a hand. "Now, give me that kerchief so I can do your hair."

My fingers fly protectively to my temples. *Damn it*. The concealment charm is long gone.

"That's all right! I need a bath first. Why don't I meet you down at the party?"

"Are you certain?" she asks. "Do you know what you're wearing?"

"I'm sure I'll find something."

Daisy looks a little miffed. "Suit yourself. But no work dresses, all right? Wear something fun! Like the pink shoes with the flowers!"

"I won't be boring," I promise, snapping the door shut behind her. As soon as the latch clicks, I spin around and slide to the floor, my skirts pooling around me. Dante bounds across the room, sniffing my ankles before darting away and curling up on my chaise.

I thump my head back against the wooden door, lamenting my slew of bad decisions. The unbearable weight of reality sinks in, and it's suddenly difficult to breathe.

I'm haunted by the look in Finn's eyes—all the hurt and confusion I saw dancing there. And the thought of so many people combing through my private space makes me feel wholly exposed, like a raw nerve. I'm working on borrowed time. How long can I keep this act up? How long until Finn discovers I'm lying to him? That I'm keeping secrets? I recall the warning Cygnus issued on my first day in the castle. *Warming Finn's bed won't protect you forever.* I feel in way over my head.

Closing my eyes conjures an image of home in the forest, and longing pierces my chest so violently I feel sick. I wish Mother were here. Life was lonely at the cottage, but it was safe. Straightforward. I never appreciated simplicity until now. I left home to prove I could manage on my own, but the longer I stay in Crown City, the more I worry Mother was right all along.

Agreeing to come here was a huge mistake. I need to course correct as soon as possible. I'll finish the omnidraught, and I'll keep my promise to Cygnus and help him unlock the gates.

Then I will go back to my cage.

Where I belong.

# 22

thought Sebastian's name day would set fair expectations for the scale of the midsummer celebration. I was wrong.

I emerge to find Crown City transformed for the holiday. It seems like banners are hanging from every window in the valley, and thousands have taken to the streets. The palace lawn has been opened to the public and transformed into a grand bazaar of wonders. White-and-gold tents punctuate the terraces, under which courtiers, servants, and commoners alike make merry. The air is hot and thick, but the sky is perfect: a robin's-egg blue and just a few cotton-ball clouds. Patriotic banners ripple above the crowd, featuring the crowned dragon of Verdinae soaring over a cerulean sea. I see stilt walkers and fire-breathers, mirror halls, billiards, and puppet shows. More marvels than I could explore in a week.

I don't know if I've ever felt less like celebrating. My thoughts are haunted by Finn and the argument I had with Cygnus.

I find Daisy sitting on a hillside, gnawing on turkey legs. "There you are!" She jumps at my approach, looking giddy. "You missed it!"

"Missed what?" I ask.

"Prince Damien!"

"Damien?" I try to hide my surprise and the instant dread I feel at just the sound of his name.

"He had to get ready for the tournament!" she squeals. "But he asked me to save a dance for him tonight! I know, I *know*, he's an ass. But no harm in picking some moonlilies, right?"

I don't know what to say. I don't trust Damien as far as I can throw him. But I don't want to spoil Daisy's excitement, so I try to smile as she leads me toward the stadium and hope it won't come up again.

We find a spot in the back. As we sit, I consider what Damien's interest in Daisy could signal. This could all be coincidence. Certainly, Daisy is a lovely girl, and friendlier than anyone I've encountered at the palace. But Damien's timing is alarming. I remember the suspicious way he looked at me in my room. Is he using her to get information? Does he somehow know about the gates?

Inside the stadium, there's a dozen or so jousters warming up, riding loops or showing off for the crowd. The grandstand is divided into sections for various families and dignitaries. Sulnik has the largest cohort. Odessa is among them, in one of her usual stuffy, elaborate Sulish frocks and a big silver headpiece, but I don't see Prince Roman—he must be participating.

I spot Sandria beneath banners of Ursandorn violet. She wears a dark, free-flowing gown and bangles on her wrists and is talking to a female knight who's practically falling off her horse to get closer. The princess plucks a handkerchief from her cleavage to hand over as a favor, and I envy the ease with which she converses—how easily she does everything. I feel like a guest at the wrong party.

Despite my better judgment, I also search for Finn, but he's not here. I wonder if he's looking for me.

*It doesn't matter,* I try to remind myself. Cygnus is right. He is my enemy, as much as I have tried to deny it.

Part of me wishes I had skipped the party and stayed back at the palace to work on the omnidraught. The sooner I figure it out, the sooner I can leave and hopefully heal from the heartbreak I've caused myself.

"That's him." Daisy points toward the ring, cutting into my internal despair. Following her sight line, I spot Damien, a rider in black on a huge palomino mare.

"Is Finneas jousting?" Daisy asks.

I fidget, still watching Damien. "I don't think so."

Having never attended a joust, I don't know what to expect. So, when the first pair lines up, lances aimed, my heart jumps up into my throat. The knights urge their horses forward, and I can't look away as they gallop closer, closer, and then smash into each other, splintering both their lances and toppling off their mounts.

"God Almighty," Daisy says, burying her face in her sleeve but peeking one eye out to look down at the stadium.

I'm aghast. "Why would anyone want to do this?"

"The glory," says Daisy. "And the gold."

"There's not enough gold in the world to make me sign up for that," I say grimly.

Glory must be Damien's motivation. When he emerges, the crowd goes wild. He rides a few laps of the stadium as his opponent trots out to meet him. I can't see under Damien's helmet, but I suspect he's wearing that same arrogant smirk I've seen on Finn.

Damien's challenger is from Sulnik. I recognize the pale blue banners and coat of arms with a howling wolf. There's a frenetic cheer when the riders lap the stadium. Even Odessa is on her feet, looking uncharacteristically enthused, and I realize it is her brother Roman under the armor. My gaze quickly moves to find Sebastian. The prince wears a mild smile, broadcasting relaxation. I suspect it's an act. If that were Finn in the ring, I'd be terrified.

I lean forward, intrigued.

Damien lines up, and I think Daisy's holding her breath. Then the riders surge forward. There's another explosion of splinters when Damien's lance finds its target, but the prince of Sulnik holds his seat. A cheer rises from the crowd, Daisy's voice among them. I suppose this is a favorable outcome. No injuries or international incident. But when Damien loops his horse around and yanks off his helmet, his fury is evident. Someone doesn't like to lose.

The competition goes on for hours. After the jousting, Damien dominates every event. I keep scanning for Finn amid the revelers, but he's nowhere to be found. Is he avoiding watching his brother? Is he avoiding me?

The sun is setting by the time the games are over, and we leave the stadium with the rest of the crowd. Dancers begin to gather. Daisy announces loudly that she's starving, so we traipse off in search of food, securing sweet pies that we carry over to eat on the main lawn. The music drifting over us is lively and distracting. I can almost forget about Cygnus and Ruin and the plague and the whole complicated mess of my life.

Almost.

"I think I am going to head back," I tell Daisy once we have finished our meal.

"Already?" She looks aghast. "Absolutely not! You have to at least enjoy one dance!"

Reluctantly, I humor her, and we stroll down to join the revelers dancing between bonfires. It takes a moment for me to settle my nerves, but eventually, we are spinning and laughing. I lose myself amid the crowd and let the fun crest and break over me. Drowning my melancholy.

This is a dance of trading partners, all whirling lines and playful spins. I'm so swept away by the music, I'm unsuspecting when a familiar body meets mine.

*Cygnus.*

I'm only with him for a moment—a quick brush—before the dance carries us apart.

At first, I think I might be mistaken. The skakabri seemed more inclined toward dancing than the Head Healer. But when the crowd shifts and I'm shuffled through a new series of partners, I catch sight of Cygnus again. He's wearing a fine black doublet I've never seen before over a white undershirt with a loose neckline. I've never noticed he has chest hair. His chiseled face is as unreadable as always, those soaring cheekbones thrown into sharper relief by the firelight. The crowd around us ripples with responses to his presence. I notice how ladies and their partners blush and crane to stare, how whispers hiss around him, as they do around me. What an oddity Cygnus must have been: the ward of the Crown, the prodigy.

I fall back into step, tracking his movements. I expect him to ignore me. *Maybe he didn't even notice we made contact.* But when the dance brings me back into Cygnus's arms, he surprises me and doesn't glide away as the steps demand. Instead, one of his dry, cool hands encircles mine. The other finds the small of my back.

"Mind if I steal you for a moment?" he murmurs, bringing his lips toward my ear. There's a crescendo in the music, and we spin away from the group.

"I think you already have," I mumble back, flushing. I should want to pull away right now, but I don't.

Some other couples have broken off toward the edge of the dance floor. My flesh prickles as he guides me toward them, still moving with the music. As we dance, Cygnus holds me at a distance, and I'm starkly aware of the space between our waists. His movements are flawless. I'm used to his self-assurance, but it's more prominent in this context. He's a strong dancer. I'd venture to call him graceful.

Damn him for being good at everything.

"I'm sorry for losing my temper," he whispers when we've drifted far enough from the crowd that I can hear him. The apology takes me by surprise.

"You don't have to do that." My neck prickles with goose bumps.

"Do what?"

"Lie to me." I swallow. "Pretend that you care."

"Does it *feel* like I'm lying?" His voice is earnest, but there's something else tacit in the press of his hand against my back. Every part of me warms, but I don't want to yield to him—not an inch.

"We're not doing this." I draw away.

"Dancing? You're very good. I've only lost a few toes."

I glower at him. "What do you want?"

"Just what I said. To apologize." He pauses. "I can, and should, be more patient. You're my equal partner. Your decisions merit my respect. I'm sorry."

Cygnus offers his hand again. This time, when he pulls me toward him, it's close enough that my chest presses against his.

"And I'm sorry about Finn," he adds, with a voice growing rough. "You should love who you want to love. I'm not aiming to get in the way of that."

"Cygnus . . ."

I can't miss the shift in his scent. The evidence of attraction. I suspect it might be on me, too.

Damn me straight to hell.

"Can you do one thing for me?" He leans in. I don't know the extent of his half-Elf senses. But if he can tell how I'm responding to his touch, I imagine he's savoring the confirmation of this limited power over me . . . the same power he seems to have over *most* women. "Don't make him any promises," he urges. "Before agreeing to anything, come to me first. Please. I love Finn. But I don't trust him, Lyria."

I can't understand why Cygnus is suddenly so forthcoming. I don't know what's changed. Maybe he just feels the same apprehension I do—the rising fear that our summer of parties and diversions is quickly drawing to a close.

"I'm not promising anyone anything," I assure him.

"Good girl."

I shiver.

With maddening ease, he guides us back toward the crowd. We fall into step with the group again, and I'm quickly spun toward a new partner, but the heat lingers. I feel it long after he's gone.

The celebration's fervor grows with nightfall. The action is cresting when I notice a group of revelers pouring down from the castle. They're moving sporadically, tumbling and jumping over one another.

They swarm the dance floor, and my eye catches the tallest among them. Finn is in a silver-and-blue doublet with dark embroidery, his hair tousled with sweat. And when his eyes find mine in the crowd, there's no stopping my feet.

*This is a mistake,* that rational voice pleads.

I resolutely ignore it.

We move together as if by gravitational design. I worry he might hesitate after all that transpired earlier, but Finn seems to be caught in the same spell that's infected my faculties. He wastes no time pulling me flush against him. His form is solid and familiar, everything I need to hold on to, all I want to touch. . . .

"You were dancing with Cygnus," he murmurs, finding my ear.

My heartbeat speeds. "Is that a problem?"

His hand tightens against my lower back, and we spin. "No." Finn draws closer to be heard over the music. "I don't own you any more than you own me. If you don't want my company, I can't prevent you from seeking his."

My face feels very warm. "It's not like that with Cygnus."

His eyes narrow, appraising me. I chose the most elegant thing in my wardrobe today—a sparkling blue gown with a corset that lends curves to my hips and pushes up my chest invitingly. Finn's gaze drops, following my figure, and my breath snags. "I don't believe you," he whispers. "He's got eyes, Lyria. We both do."

The music lilts. He takes the opportunity to spin me, and I land clumsily against his chest. Finn's arms tighten, and I can feel the swell of his bicep under my hand. I'm still not close enough. "Is there something I should know?" he asks.

I think of all the secrets between us—how much I'm longing to share them all.

"Nothing," I lie instead.

"Are you sure?"

*"Careful,"* I say, looking around the dance floor. "People are watching."

"Let them." His lips glide to my throat. My whole body quivers, though the night is warm. And when those lips rise to find mine . . . Gods-damn me, I kiss him back.

This is one of those moments when time hitches and stills, like a single thread snagged in a tapestry. Breaking the kiss, Finn pulls back, searching my eyes. "Was that . . ." His throat trembles. "Is this what you want?"

I kiss him again in response.

I'm only hazily aware of our surroundings as Finn leads me away from the crowd. We find a grove of trees, slipping into the shadows, and then he's all over me again—fiercer this time. Hungrier. The bark is rough against my back as he pushes me against a trunk, his hands gliding over my hips, my neck, over my hair.

This is beyond stupid. This is reckless. I'm supposed to be steeling my heart in preparation to leave him forever. Instead, I sink into him, pressing in with my waist, submitting to the driving sweep of his tongue, silently begging for more.

Finally, I shove him off. "We can't do this here."

"Yes, we can." His voice darkens. Finn's head drops, finding my neck again, drifting closer to my collarbone. . . .

*"People can see us,"* I hiss.

"I don't care."

"*I* care."

This makes him pause. Finn's eyes are firelit, searching mine. "Do you want me to stop?"

I hesitate.

He catches my pause, withdrawing another fraction. "I'm sorry. Should I go?"

"No. No, it's just that I should find Daisy." I look to where she was minutes earlier, but she's vacated the dance floor. I finally spot her on a bench a ways away with Damien. The pair look for all the world like they're headed the same direction as Finn and I just were.

"Daisy will be fine," Finn says, observing the same thing. His hand slithers into mine, and his lips press against my ear to entreat, "Come back to the castle with me?"

*I shouldn't.*

"Yes."

I'm not sure what his invitation suggests, but I'm keen for anything right now . . . and there's one activity in particular that I'm craving above all others. This night has bewitched me, I think. Our impending separation should logically make me want to withdraw from Finn, but my body is having the opposite reaction. If there is no future for us, shouldn't we at least steal this *one* moment? *One* night together, before I'll miss him forever?

I hear Cygnus's warning again: *Finn likes to play with his girls and then drop them.*

But what about me? What if *I* want to play, too?

I don't know if Finn feels anything akin to what I do. I might be alone in this all-consuming adoration. But for once, I want to just be young and uninhibited, as carefree as I might have been without the curse in my blood. Even if it's a lie, I want to pretend like this is something I can allow myself, something I might have seized without guilt in a more peaceful lifetime.

I feel breathless as we follow the long, lantern-lined stairs up the hill. The palace is close to empty. It seems everyone has already gone to bed or is still reveling. We pass a red-faced group of young men warbling a drinking song, a nursemaid carrying a sleeping child, and a scullery girl canoodling with a busty nurse I recognize.

Finn takes me straight to his chambers. There's barely a moment after the door shuts behind us before he's kissing me again.

I'm absorbed by the warmth and heat, the need that drives us closer and still not close enough. Magic has always heightened my emotions, and I'm burning now—burning in *every* way. I want my clothes off. I want to share that kind of vulnerability with him again. I want *him*.

With shaking hands, we undress each other. His doublet is quickly on the floor, followed by my gown. Shivering in my chemise, I guide him toward the bed. I have no idea what I'm doing, but I just need to be touching more of him. Finn is more than responsive, tracing kisses down my neck as my fingers roam over him before dropping to my corset. I tug on the laces.

His whisper tickles my ear again. "Are you sure you want to do this?"

"Yes."

And I am.

Finn starts, "Do you want . . ."

But he doesn't finish before we're interrupted by a distant *boom*.

Finn and I freeze as we hear another explosion—this one close enough to rattle the floor.

Then the screaming starts.

# 23

inn is dressing before I can react.

"Stay here!" he commands. He reaches for his sword in the same moment that a scream fills the hallway. It's a voice I recognize, and I leap up.

"That's *Daisy*!"

Another scream sounds, then a distant crash strong enough to make the floor shake. Finn blocks my path, and the terror in his eyes mirrors mine. "You need to *hide*!"

"No!" I howl, trying to shove past him. "I can't leave her!"

Finn seizes my wrists, shouting, "Lyria, *wait*!" but I break his grip and tear into the hall.

A nightmare awaits. Flickering amber light floods the scene. I see people fleeing in every direction, their shadows long and macabre. I smell smoke and blood. Ahead, a huge chunk of the staircase has been blasted away, leaving nothing but singed rubble.

I stumble forward.

Daisy's screams are coming from the chamber down the hall from Finn's. I can only assume that is Damien's room. Tearing toward it, I see the door flung open. A body is crumpled across the threshold, a Verdish guard. Running toward the doorway, I barely register his form before something swings at my head.

The sword misses me by a kiss. I lurch back as it slams into the doorframe, shattering wood and sending splinters flying in every direction.

I wheel to face my attacker. The person is male, but his face is mostly concealed by a dark green cloak. He roars as he swings for another strike.

Something yanks my arm. Finn throws me behind him, then swings to block the attacker's next swipe. Steel crashes against steel. Finn drives forward—he strikes once, twice, then cuts down his assailant with an overhead blow that slams into his neck.

The hooded figure crumples.

When Finn turns, he's unrecognizable. I've never seen this much hate in his eyes. The boy in the cottage is gone. *This* is the son of Verdinae, the descendant of Dornik pillagers, the agent of the Frumentari, the man who's been taught to end life for as long as I've been taught to save it.

"Are you hurt?" he demands, his eyes desperately scanning my body for any injuries.

"No." I'm shaking, but I manage to hold my footing.

"Are you sure?"

He reaches for me, but his wild eyes focus on something behind me, and then I'm shoved behind him again without warning. I keep from falling, but just barely, as he lunges forward to meet the next threat.

Soldiers. Two more. Plus countless others behind them. They're pouring up the carpeted stairs, some hooded in dark robes like my first attacker. I don't have time to worry about figuring out who they are. Right now, there are only two goals, which are simple: *Keep Finn alive. Help Daisy.* The world narrows to those objectives.

Finn takes down the second soldier in the time it takes me to consider. My Talent is screaming for use and the heat is hellish, almost unbearable, but with so many onlookers, I don't dare reveal myself.

He handles the third one next, but he's tiring.

And there are more. So many more. My eye snags on an assailant as they seize a fleeing courtier and cut her throat.

*Who are they?*

*"Run!"* Finn shouts, interrupting my thoughts.

We hurry together back toward Damien's chambers, but we're not fast enough. Two of the enemy soldiers catch up with us. I lose sight of Finn as someone yanks me from behind.

We both scramble. My attacker lands on top, and I'm clearly outmatched. I thrash and claw at his face as he struggles for something at his waist—a blade. His face is obscured by the hood. I'm screaming, kicking . . .

Instinct takes over. My Talent barrels to the surface, and I hear a scream that might be mine as the power explodes through my hands.

Rough and quick. That's all I can do. I *feel* the explosion, rather than see it, as I will his insides to oblivion. Hot blood and guts spill over me, and I roll over and vomit, overcome. I spit out the sick and shove the corpse off me. The soldier's cloak flops as his body rolls, and that's when I notice it.

His ears. They're tapered like mine.

*These are my people.*

There's no time for self-punishment. No time to orient myself in this tumbling landscape of enemies. The only thing I can trust is Finn, who is already rising to meet the next batch of attackers.

*How are there so many?*

I tear after him.

Then something happens that I don't understand at first. The floor seems to be moving under us. Finn seizes my arms, and we struggle to stay upright as the world wobbles around us. It's an earthquake. It must be. It takes me several confused moments to process as another blast rattles the castle.

"They've got drakesbane!" Finn shouts.

Another blast hits near us. We both lurch to avoid it, but the flames catch on my skirt. I roll and thrash as the fyre crawls up my legs, searing my calf—

Then Finn is there, smothering the flames with his boots.

"Are you hurt?" He seizes my shoulders. "LYRIA. Are you hurt?"

I shake my head even though the pain is overwhelming.

He tries to scoop me up, but we're tossed back by another blast. Finn lands on top of me, crushing me. I blink, squinting through the smoke and dust. There's something warm and sticky on my face. My fingers find my cheek and draw back covered in blood.

Finn struggles upright, and I follow.

We finally burst into Damien's chamber, vaulting over the fallen guard at the threshold. Within, the scene is harrowing. The window is shattered, glass strewn over the floor. Scattered amid the shards are easily half a dozen bodies. My gaze finds Daisy backed into a corner, gripping a fire poker like it's her lifeline against drowning. She's half dressed, as I am, and covered with blood. Shaking, dazed, petrified but unharmed. I nearly weep with relief.

I don't notice Damien at first. It's Finn who rushes toward him where he sits bare-chested amid the wreckage. He doesn't have a weapon I can see. He's crouching, doubled over with his head in his hands. Finn embraces his brother, dragging Damien upright.

I look away when I realize the younger prince is sobbing.

My stomach twists. Tonight, the world seems uncertain about just who is supposed to be my friend or my enemy. I've been so wrong about so many things since I arrived at the castle. Maybe I was wrong about Damien, too.

Daisy seems to snap out of whatever trance she's in. The poker clatters out of her hand, and she stumbles toward me. I've never seen a person so ashen.

"Are you all right?" I ask, surging toward her.

She nods vaguely. Her eyes are unfocused, and they keep darting back to Damien. "I'm . . . I'm okay."

"Are you hurt?"

"No . . . Damien . . . he . . . he . . ." She struggles for words.

"It's okay." I wrap my arms around her. She's trembling.

We both look up as the clatter of oncoming footsteps sounds from the hall. Finn and Damien sink into defensive stances, weapons drawn, and I lift my palms for the fight.

But the face that appears is familiar.

"They're here!" Roburn shouts behind him. Guards swarm the room, with Sebastian among them. The eldest prince looks older, harder somehow. He's armed with a sword and there's blood on his shirt and trousers. Strange, seeing him like this. I've never taken Sebastian for a soldier. But it makes sense that all Rodrick's sons would have learned how to kill.

Finn rushes toward the captain. "What's happening?"

"We've secured the lawn and we're sweeping the castle now."

"Where's Mother?" demands Damien.

"We're figuring that out," says the captain, his face hard.

Damien blanches, turning to his oldest brother. "You don't know?"

"We're looking," Sebastian says. "We thought she was in her chambers."

Damien exchanges a glance with Finn, and the pair waste no time trying to shove out the door. But Roburn and their older brother roadblock their attempt.

"No!" Sebastian roars. "You two stay here!"

"Like hell we will!" Damien shouts.

Roburn shoves them both in the chest. "Neither of you are to leave this room!"

"But—" Finn protests.

"*Back up.* Neither of you is going anywhere."

Damien snaps, "I COMMAND you to let us through!"

Everyone's watching this play out. Everyone's distracted. That's why, when the first arrow hits, I'm the only one attuned to the sound. I notice it before anyone else does—the whistle and *crack* of it striking the back wall—but it's not enough time to change anything.

Finn is the next to discern we're under fire. He tackles me without a moment's hesitation, shielding my body with his. Screams explode all around us. Roburn snatches Damien and pushes him out the door, roaring for his troops to follow. I throw out a flare of my Talent, trying to understand the scene beyond Damien's room.

There are archers in the trees outside the open window. Half a dozen of them. Calm and collected and sure. They must have been waiting for this moment.

I can't move with Finn atop me. He's so much larger, I can't breathe. Arrows rain down around us, and it doesn't stop. I start to fear it won't stop—until I'm actually considering striking out with my Talent. I could cut the archers down to end it. I could strike them all at once—I did it with the skakabri. But I need to draw back those dark impulses, move away from those terrifying thoughts of what the full leverage of my magic could achieve.

I have to wait for it to stop.

And finally, it does.

The onslaught ends just as suddenly as it started. The archers withdraw, leaving aching silence and the fallout as the cold knowledge of death seeps through us.

I'm gazing up through a narrow, slanted viewpoint. It's all I can manage beneath the weight of Finn's arm until he withdraws and speaks, placing gentle hands over me. He's unhurt. I am faintly aware of him asking once again if I'm safe, if I'm injured.

But my attention is elsewhere. On the one person who hasn't moved since the arrows started.

He's still standing beside the open window, gazing out at the night. There's a puzzled expression on his lovely face, and the red that blooms from his throat might be roses . . . or ribbons . . . or rubies.

It can't be anything else. I can't believe that it's anything else.

Until Sebastian's legs give out.

# 24

ET ME GET TO HIM!"

"Damien, stop—"

"HE'S MY BROTHER! I HAVE A RIGHT TO BE THERE!"

Finn looks up as Damien charges past Roburn. He's apparently exhausted the guards trying to keep him outside this small room.

"Let him," I mutter. Things can hardly get worse.

My eyes haven't moved from Sebastian, who is laid out on the floor. There's only a wisp of his life to hold on to, a narrow strand that I am gripping desperately with my Talent. Finn and Roburn carried him into this more protected antechamber. I can't figure out where the hell to start fixing him.

There are twelve arrows in his chest, in his arms, in his legs. I have to stop the bleeding in multiple places. I need *time,* but I don't have it. I've got all's-cure; I've emptied the bottle already. But all's-cure is for small cuts and injuries. Sebastian is dying. My Talent is his only chance.

Damien hurries toward us. "Did you send for Cygnus?"

"She's working on it!" Finn snaps.

"SEND FOR CYGNUS!" he roars at the nearby guard. "RUN! NOW!"

"You are making this worse!" Finn shouts, turning toward his brother.

"At least I'm not just sitting around!"

"GET OUT," Finn suddenly commands. At first, I think he's just talking to the guards, but he looks at Damien and adds, "You too. Go for a walk or something."

"Not a chance," says Damien.

"Do you want him to die?" Finn snaps. "Lyria needs to concentrate, and you're panicking. Please, Damien. Leave."

I look between the two princes in alarm. The guards hurry out the door, and Damien turns reluctantly to leave. Finally, it's only Finn and me.

I glance at Finn, who crouches at Sebastian's side, clutching his brother's hand. He's impossibly pale, with tears streaming down both cheeks. If he didn't look so agonized, I'd demand he leave as well. But what good would that do? He'd still have questions later about how Sebastian healed so quickly. *I can trust Finn, can't I?*

I am a Healer. I have someone's life in my hands. I can't afford to hide my power anymore.

"I need you to let go of Sebastian now," I command in a voice I don't recognize. "You're about to see something you may not like or understand, and I need you to sit down and stay quiet, or you risk your brother's life. Do you hear me?"

The prince's eyes widen, and I see several reactions flash there: shock, defensiveness, maybe respect.

"I'm doing everything I can," I continue. "But if you want me to save him, I need you to trust me."

We battle with glares. Finally, Finn says, "I hear you." He draws up a chair while I turn toward Sebastian's limp form.

I target the wounds that are bleeding fastest, cursing my fickle Talent. I need *time*. I need to work slowly and deliberately, visualizing each muscle and vein. Too quick, I could lose control again. And if I kill Sebastian tonight . . .

*NO.*

There is no room for fear in this moment. I recall Cygnus's wisdom: Self-doubt won't help anybody.

*You have trained for this, Lyria. You have done it before.*

As I work over Sebastian, I pray steadily to the Goddess Elowyn. I beg her to save him. Not for me, not for Finn, but for Evermore. It's clear which of Rodrick's sons would be best for the future of the Elves. Sebastian is good. Uncommonly kind. I have yet to hear an ill word spoken of him. Finn's eldest brother has what Davina clearly covets: the genuine love of his people. If anyone could lead the Hartlands to peace, it would be this gentle soul in my hands.

So I beg the Goddess to spare him. To give our exhausted kingdom this: One ruler who would try for compassion. One earnest leader, who would strike only when the moment requires it.

I start removing the arrows, one by one. Soon I'm sweating profusely, trembling head to foot. There's one good thing: My Talent isn't burning anymore. The absence is like a cool breeze, something I could have enjoyed under different circumstances. But as I'm drawing on so much of my power, exhaustion quickly outpaces relief. My legs lose feeling, and my hands start to cramp.

When Cygnus steps through the doors, my chest heaves. I have never been so relieved to see a person in my life.

"Get out!" Finn tells him immediately. He stands up in front of me, as if to shield me from view. I don't have time to think about what this means: Is he protecting my secret? Is he not scared?

"He can stay," I say. I meet Finn's gaze for a brief second. "He knows."

Finn frowns, but he doesn't protest and steps aside.

"Where are we at?" Cygnus asks calmly, stepping up beside me. He's brought a satchel of supplies, which he quickly unpacks and cleans while I explain.

I've closed half of the wounds at this point, but several others are still bleeding, the arrows untouched, and I'm nearing total exhaustion. Every time I remove an arrow, Sebastian loses a deadly amount of blood. His life force is down to a tattered thread.

"I've got six more," I say tersely. "Can you help me stabilize him?"

"Yes."

We duck our heads together, and for the first time, Cygnus and I move in sync.

We fall into an easy flow. Back and forth, his medicine with my Talent. I'm so accustomed to clashing with the Head Healer, I didn't anticipate how compassionate he'd seem in this context. He keeps interjecting with assurances.

"You're doing well," he tells me, once he notices my shaking hands. "Take deep breaths. That's great, Lyria."

He directs our approach as we work together to remove the

remaining six arrows. Cygnus doesn't just guide the process; he guides *me*. It's so much easier to work with someone else steadying me.

I finally understand it: why Daisy giggles at his mention, why Anna doesn't resent the hospital being run by a teenager.

He's *remarkable.*

As the process draws into hours, Cygnus and I are keenly aware that we're doing the impossible. Sebastian looks like a corpse already: his perfect features past recognition, his eyes violet with bruises, and his skin like sour milk. Clinging to Sebastian's life force is like grasping a thread tied to a running bull. His life is pulling toward death, but I'm pulling harder.

Death will not take Sebastian tonight.

Come what may, I will do this. I will not let him go.

With Cygnus's help, I work until Sebastian's wounds are mended. When I'm done, I feel certain that a human couldn't detect the scarring. Cygnus and I have worked nothing less than a miracle tonight, but we still haven't brought back his color. And despite our efforts addressing every visible injury, all that's keeping Sebastian alive is my Talent.

With nothing left for him to do, Cygnus sweeps up his instruments. He mumbles something about cleaning them and steps into the adjoining chamber, his footsteps crunching on the broken glass.

In Cygnus's absence, I look back at Finn. He's been quiet all night. A brooding angel. He looks equally ashen, his fine features rent with despair. But when our eyes meet, I find no hatred or disgust in them. Just concern.

I wonder if that will change when I'm done.

When Cygnus returns, his walk is slow.

"I've done all I know how to do," he admits. I hear the layered plea in his words. Everyone in this room wants the same thing: for my Talent to save Sebastian. But I'm past spent. I might have been treading water this whole time.

I gaze back at Cygnus, warring over how much to confide. Anything I say will be heard by Finn. Judging by Cygnus's face, I guess that I look like hell. I know I feel like it. My hair is plastered in clumps to my forehead; I've been alternating hot and cold sweats as I've drawn on levels of power I haven't touched since the Ironwoods.

"I'm trying," I say roughly, emphasizing every syllable. "I'm just holding him. Y'know?"

His eyes widen a little, and I can sense his alarm. He might be the only one who can see just how hard I'm fighting.

"Would it help if I sit with you?" he asks.

I nod.

He draws up a chair and scoots in close beside me. He doesn't talk more, just sits quietly with me. I use his breathing to measure my own.

*You can do this, Lyria. You have trained for this.*

I see very clearly what I need to do. This is how I reach absolution.

In all other things, I have failed. I have revealed my identity. I haven't finished the omnidraught. I haven't opened the gates to Ruin. But maybe this is the reason the Gods brought me to the castle. Maybe *this* is Elowyn's will. Sebastian is the king the people need. I can make this my purpose—saving him. Surely it is my duty. It's what I've prepared for my whole life.

I've walked with pain. I know its nature. I know where to strike against it, how to attack. This is an enemy I've clashed with before, every day. And if it's a matter of enduring pain for the good of our realm, for the *possibility* of Evermore, that I can do.

I let myself lean on Cygnus's quiet presence for a few minutes. But as with all else, this is stolen time. I quickly realize the situation's selfishness. The patients in the East Wing need Cygnus's help more than I do right now. I'm the only thing keeping him from that work. Once that awareness inhabits me, I'm too sick with guilt to appreciate his proximity any longer.

"You should go," I say, as soon as I can muster the courage.

"Is that what you want?" His eyes flash. There might be hurt there.

I nod forcefully.

Cygnus pauses. I suspect that he's about to counter with something clever, a quick strike, but he doesn't argue. Cygnus just stands up and leaves, without acknowledging Finn.

I'm left feeling oddly empty. Finn moves in to take Cygnus's chair immediately after he's gone.

"Can I help?" he asks.

I shake my head, closing my eyes. I'm battling not to get swept away by the insistent pull of Sebastian's last thread. It seems so much easier to let go.

Finn reaches for my hand. "*Please,* Lyria. Let me help."

*"Stay,"* I find myself telling him.

I open my eyes and find his green ones gazing back at me. They're alight with emotion: terror and desperation and hope. How can someone look so beautiful while suffering?

"Don't let go," I say softly. "Please."

That's all I'll give him. The only weakness I'll admit. I need Finn right now more than I need air. I need him to keep gripping my hand, to remind me there is someone anchoring me to this world. If I can just hold on to him, I can keep Sebastian tethered, too.

Together, we make it through the long night.

# 25

It takes Sebastian two full days to stabilize.

Finn is summoned by the queen around dusk on the second day. After some back-and-forth with the insistent guards, he obeys, but not before swearing to find me after attending to his duties. There's no chance for us to speak privately about what's transpired. Maybe that's fortunate. I don't know how I'd start to explain.

By the end of it, I'm a husk of myself. When I try to rise, my legs wobble traitorously beneath me.

The captain, who has remained a watchful presence since Finn left, surges forward to help. "Let me escort you to your room," Roburn offers.

"I'm fine," I mumble, forcing myself to take a few steps. "I just need to sleep."

"I insist," he says.

I catch myself on the doorframe, debating. I feel dangerously close to collapsing. "Fine."

Roburn lends me his arm. I use the dregs of my willpower to stay upright as he leads me into the hall.

It's quickly clear that trying to get back myself would have been a bad idea. I'm stumbling as the captain leads me toward my room, sheepishly grateful as he supports most of my weight.

I can't process the wreckage that we pass. There's glass and debris everywhere. Ash covers everything. People mill about, mostly servants and commoners, scrubbing blood and carrying bodies. Cleaning up.

It can't have been only days ago that we were dancing. I've aged a decade since then.

Roburn leaves me after promising to send servants with water and food. I think I thank him for the kindness, but I can't be sure. My head feels stuffed with cotton.

I should run. I should get out of the palace as soon as possible. Finn saw my Talent. He might not have reacted during a moment of crisis, but that doesn't mean he isn't preparing a cell for me now.

But there's no time for worries before I collapse into a dreamless sleep.

---

When I wake, the light beyond my window is flat and gray.

I lie in silence for a long time. I know what I've done, and yet I can't quite comprehend it. I don't regret saving Sebastian. I'm just scared. I let the terror burn through me, let it sear and kill everything. I imagine all the ways they could punish me, all the things they could do, bracing for the worst. My ears strain for the clatter of footsteps. At any moment, the Frumentari should be coming to arrest me.

But no one comes.

*What are they waiting for?*

There's one thing I know for sure: I need to get the hell out of this castle.

Finn didn't seem disgusted by my Talent. But that doesn't mean I'm safe. I am the being he was bred to hate and kill, the monster his kingdom has sworn to hunt.

Only two considerations stop me from walking straight out the palace gates this very moment. The first is Cygnus. After all we endured together while trying to get through the gates, it doesn't feel right to abandon him and our mission without saying goodbye. Surely he'll understand why I can't stay.

The second consideration is the omnidraught. As much as I'd like to run to the Ironwoods without a backward glance, duty demands that I at least pass off the work I've done. Am I in mortal danger every moment I stay in this castle? Yes. Almost certainly. But how many innocents would die if I just vanished to save my own skin?

Eventually, I get up and dress. I find Anna in the hospital, which is pandemonium in the wake of the attack.

"Hi. Glad you're up," she says. "We've got laundry coming out our asses if you feel up to it."

I nod dizzily, looking out over the wreckage.

"Do you know exactly what happened?" I ask, my throat raw.

"We're still trying to figure that out." She sounds very tired. "The attackers were a mix of Ursandorn soldiers and Elves. No one knows how they got in the city. At this point, our best guess is that they flew over the mountains somehow."

My gut twists. I picture dragons, Verdin's weapon of choice. The legends say they died after the fyres. I wonder, with rising dread, if the

Elves found out some way to resurrect the dragons. Are we resorting to all the empire's most terrible weapons? Is nothing off-limits?

But I don't have time to think about the Elves' war tactics. "Where is Cygnus?"

"He's with the queen. She moved him into the North Tower to attend to Sebastian."

Anna hurries back to her work, and I stay rooted in place. Frowning.

I can't risk meeting Cygnus in front of Queen Davina. But I don't think anyone else in this hospital would have a prayer of finishing what Ragglestaff and I started. I probably should have just trusted him from the beginning. I curse all the stupid, egotistical reasons I didn't.

I head to the storehouse alone, intending to write Cygnus a letter with instructions. But when I close the door behind me and look out at my work, the finely ground ingredients, the alchemized liquids dripping through the gleaming instruments—a rush of willfulness overcomes me. I'll try one more time. *One.* If it works, it's meant to be. If it's not . . . I'll walk away with my conscience clean.

I pull out my mortar and pestle to grind the last of the cliffcrow feathers I gathered. Then I snatch up a notebook of Ragglestaff's and lay it open before me. The main problem is the catalyst. I've already tried Ironwood sap, hydra venom, dead nettle nectar, selkie tears: all the activators I've trained with. I'm out of ideas.

I can almost hear Mother's voice. *Being a Healer means that you give until you have nothing left. Then you give more.*

*Please,* I pray to Elowyn—to any Gods who might be listening. *I've done all I can. Give me something.*

I flip through the pages, skimming nonsense I've already reviewed countless times. I turn past endless passages about pain, illegible charts mapping bloodlines, whole pages of the same phrases scrawled over and over: *GIVEN NOT BORN GIVEN NOT BORN GIVEN NOT BORN . . .*

*IT IS NOW IT IS NOW IT IS NOW IT IS NOW . . .*

*THE FOUR WILL COME THE FOUR WILL COME THE FOUR WILL COME . . .*

I turn the pages faster and faster, growing more desperate and furious. Finally, I just snatch up the whole notebook and hurl it at the wall. A page slices my finger open, and I yank my hand back, sucking the blood off my finger with a scowl.

Stupid, Gods-damn *useless* book.

Stupid, Gods-damn *useless* Talent.

I pound the cliffcrow feathers ferociously, slamming the pestle as if doing so with enough force will turn back the clock. For every person I have tried to help, I've hurt even more. Maybe I saved Sebastian's life, but how many will die because I just can't stay here and finish the job I was tasked with? I give up on praying and start cursing everything instead. Curse the Gods. Curse the Verdish. Curse Finn and his cowardice. Curse the infernal bloodborne magic that never brings me anything except pain. *So* much pain.

I stop grinding.

I'm frozen. Transfixed. And then all at once, inspiration blasts through me like lightning—just the way it did when I was knee-deep in the lake, trying to save Cygnus. Fractured pieces fly together, clicking into place: the chalice, the catalyst, my pain, my Talent coursing through my blood. . . .

Blood. Is blood the catalyst?

I dump the powdered cliffcrow feathers into the cauldron with my latest attempt at the onmidraught.

And then I unsheathe my father's dagger.

This time, I don't pray to any Gods. I pray to him.

*Let this work, Father. Please.*

I slice my palm open. Deep. Crimson blooms and trickles into the cauldron, and I reach for the stirring spoon. I'm hardly breathing as I stir once, twice, three times . . .

It starts steaming.

I almost weep with relief. I keep stirring, and the mixture transforms, alchemizing exactly how it should. The muddy mixture clarifies and turns a brilliant gold. It's exactly the same viscosity as the all's-cure Mother brews. And after fifteen clockwise turns, I know I've done it.

The omnidraught is complete.

I need to get it to someone I can trust—and suddenly I know exactly who. Quickly, I fill a small vial of blood to add to my ingredients and mark it in my notes. Then I heal my palm, hurry back to the main hospital, and track down Daisy in the laundry room. She's helping sweep up the glass from the medicine cabinets, which were smashed to bits.

"I need a favor," I say, rushing up to her.

"Okay?" She looks me up and down. "What's wrong?"

"Not here. Come with me."

Daisy doesn't protest as I lead her back to the storehouse. After shutting the door behind me, I wheel around. Then I take a deep breath and tell her everything. My Talent, my mother, the Moragorion, the plague. I share the whole story of the day Mother left and the truth about Ragglestaff. I tell her about revealing my Talent to Finn, the omnidraught, and my plan to leave. The only piece I leave out is the gates and my mission with Cygnus. That doesn't seem like my secret to tell. But the rest of the truths tumble free.

Daisy's eyes widen exponentially as I speak, but she doesn't interrupt me. And to her credit, she doesn't recoil in disgust. She just listens.

Finally, I come to my conclusion. "I need you to make sure that all of this gets to Cygnus." I gesture at my workbench, where the cauldron, the mortar and pestle, the jars of flowers and ingredients, and Ragglestaff's notes are spread. "And I need you to tell him that the final catalyst is blood. You've helped me with most of it. You know where to get more cliffcrow feathers. The Crown can source him the rest. With your help, he should be able to duplicate what I've done."

"Why don't you just tell him yourself?"

"He's with Queen Davina. My secret is out, and I've done the only job they brought me to do. If I don't leave now, I'm going to end up in a cell—or worse."

"You don't have to go," Daisy argues. "Finn could protect you."

I swallow at her words. I wish they could be true. My thoughts fly to Cygnus's mother, the spy who served Rodrick faithfully until he decided she'd exhausted her purpose.

"Maybe he could," I say thickly. "But not forever."

"He *loves* you," she counters.

I shake my head. "It doesn't matter. We're at war, and it's going to catch up with us eventually."

"But leaving now could kill you," Daisy reasons.

"I could face worse than death if I stay."

*Torture, a long and painful execution . . .* What horrors would they drag out for me?

We appraise each other for a long moment, and her small features are hard. Quietly, she says, "If you can get to the east quarter of the city, my nana knows how to get people papers."

Her eyes blaze. I swallow, working to absorb her meaning.

"You might have to wait a few weeks or months, but she can help get you out." She squeezes my hands. "I hope you can make it to safety. You're a little weird, but you've been kind to me, Lyria. I pray the Almighty goes with you."

When I pull her into one last hug, I wonder if I've been underestimating Daisy.

My last stop is my tower, where I collect my belongings and Dante. It's dark as I steal downstairs and out of the palace. The fox's little orange head peeks out from my pack, but thankfully he remains quiet. The air is thick and heavy, like it's about to rain. There's so much chaos in the wake of the attack that nobody notices one small figure weaving through the muddy scene. I find the stables deserted except for the horses that poke their heads out of their stalls, eyeing me curiously. It's not hard to find an unattended saddle.

I pick the horse I rode on the way here, a big bay mare. "You ready for another long ride?" I whisper, slipping into her stall.

We exit out through the forecourt, passing clusters of mourners. Some groups are gathered in prayer around bodies that still haven't been moved from the battle scene; some are loading debris into carts. There's a squad of VIA milling around, shouting orders. I hug the edges of the court, keeping my hood low.

No one stops me as I ride to the main gate. There's a long stretch of slowly declining hillside that leads toward the drawbridge and the outer wall. It's a three- or four-mile ride at least.

This hill was hit hard by the blasts. Parts are still burning, the embers wafting smoke as mist begins to drizzle over the whole miserable scene. I kick my mare's sides to pick up speed, driving us into a trot, which quickly builds to a canter.

We've come more than halfway down when I hear it. More hoofbeats, sounding from behind me. I whip around to find another rider galloping toward me. It's too dark to make out their face, but I instinctively spur my horse forward. We pick up into a sprint and tear on ever faster, but the horseman is hot in pursuit. Then I hear someone at the wall roar: "*CLOSE THE GATE!*"

I'm horror-stricken as the drawbridge starts rattling.

*This is it. The end of my story.*

I'm going to be apprehended, either by this rider or the soldiers at the gate. There'll be no stopping them from examining my ears. It's a short ride between here and the dungeons. Either I make it through this gate, or I'm not leaving this castle.

The drawbridge very slowly begins to rise.

With another kick, I urge my mare into a gallop. She takes the cue and doubles her speed. We're flying as fast as the wind now, hooves clattering, mud slinging as we hurtle toward the drawbridge, which creeps higher by the second. *She'll run her heart out,* I think, but the gate's closing too fast. *We're not going to make it. . . .*

There's nothing I can do except pull around hard before we crash. We loop to a stop, rounding toward my pursuer as he rides up and then vaults a dismount. His hood falls back as he runs toward me.

When I realize it's Finn, I don't know whether to laugh or cry. Something in between happens.

Has he come to kill me himself?

"Lyria!" he calls out, staggering toward me. "Thank God."

I see why I didn't recognize him. He's in that black uniform that I've seen around the palace—the dress uniform of the Frumentari.

My feet have locked into place.

"Why are you here?" I demand as he draws closer.

Finn's eyes are wide with remorse, but I notice he won't meet my gaze. "I came here to stop you."

My guts lurch. "So I'm your prisoner now?"

"No!" Finn says. "I'm trying to protect you!"

He grabs the mare's reins.

I slide out of the saddle, landing hard next to him. I sweep out with my Talent, confirming we've got an audience. The gateway is filled with guards—apprehensive, taut, awaiting a signal.

"Please, Finn," I implore him. "Just let me go. It's the best thing for both of us."

"The best thing is to stay together." He's growing desperate. "I have no intention of holding you against your will. But I beg you to be rational. I can't protect you outside these walls. Nothing has to change just because I know the truth."

"How can you say that?" I ask. "It's changed everything!"

"It doesn't have to! If you want nothing to do with me, *fine*. But I can't let you run away and get yourself killed for my deficiencies."

"That's not what I'm doing," I argue.

"Yes, it *is*! Can you really tell me you'd be safer out *there* than you are in this palace?! We are *fully* at war. There's not anywhere left in Verdinae that's safe for someone like you."

"You *are* Verdinae!" I scream. "Don't you get that?" All the rage I've been suppressing, all the reservations I've held back, come pouring out at once. "You might care about me, but what about the rest of the Elves? What about Evermore? Your family has spent *hundreds of years* killing people like me. You are Verdinae as much as *I* am magic. You've devoted your whole life to the empire. At least be a man and *own* that fact."

His face goes very flat as the color washes away. "But maybe that's why we were supposed to meet," he says softly. "So that you could show me how I'm wrong. You've already changed me. I believe you're a better person than I am, Lyria. I'm willing to see the world from your eyes."

"No!" I shake my head. "I'm not a supporting character in *your* story. I'm not some stepping stone on your way to the throne. Bringing me here was a mistake—saving *you* was a mistake. I should have never left the Ironwoods."

Finn recoils like I've slapped him. "Stop it!"

"Stop what?"

"Stop pushing me away! Stop acting like this doesn't matter."

"What doesn't matter?"

*"This."* He gestures between us. "You and me. Whatever weird force drew us together in that swamp."

"There can be nothing between us," I force through my teeth, willing truth to the words. "There is nothing between us."

"Why are you doing that? Why are you lying?" He edges forward a step. "Is this about what we did before?"

"No!"

"Are you sure? Because if I made you uncomfortable, if I pushed you too far . . ."

"You didn't push me. At all." I bury my face in my hands.

Finn closes the distance between us, taking my shoulders in his hands. "Then what's going on?"

"There is no good way for this to end! Don't you get that? I'm an Elf. You kill my people. You're going to marry Odessa, or some lady of somewhere, and I'm . . ." I choke up.

*I'm what?*

I'm going to go back to the Ironwoods to my mother? I'll find a hospital that needs my skills, where I'll pick up broken pieces of Rodrick's war until I'm as bitter as Cygnus?

"I'm not someone who belongs with a prince of Verdinae," I finish. I can't express anything else.

"Lyria, I need you to listen." Finn draws his hands to my face. He tilts it toward him, making me gaze up into his eyes. It starts to rain. "I have spent my entire life trying to feel the way that *you* make me feel. The way you look at me sometimes . . ." He breaks off; then his voice thickens. "I want to be a better man for you. I want to *do* better, for you."

I should look away, but I don't.

I know how Finn feels about me. I can sense it. I've always been able to sense it. It's just taken this long to wipe away all the layers of self-doubt. I'm not alone in this. He's in love with me, too. He knows my secret, and he still loves me.

That doesn't mean I don't have to leave him.

"*You're* not listening." I pull back. "My mind is made up."

"No, you're not listening to *me*." Finn moves to take my hands in his. "I want you exactly as you are, Lyria. I love everything about you, including the fact that you are an Elf. Including your Talent. I'm not naive about what stands between us. I'm prepared to navigate it. I'm prepared to change. I want to fight for you. For *this*."

His words are what I've been wanting to hear all this time. But now it's not enough.

Still, I can't pull away.

"Please, just let me show you one thing. And if it doesn't change your mind, you can go. But I need you to see it first."

I stare at him, trembling in the pouring rain. Every muscle in my body is screaming at me to run. But the anchor in my chest pulls harder.

"Fine." I surrender. "Show me."

# 26

inn's chambers are freezing when we return sopping wet. I let Dante out of my pack, and the fox chitters happily as he makes himself at home. The fire in the hearth has gone out, and Finn rushes forward to light it. "Sorry. The servants are all probably busy."

"No problem," I say. But I'm shivering.

He looks back over his shoulder as he starts stacking the logs. "Do you want to wash up first? I'll get the fire going, and then we can talk."

I pause, momentarily torn. Ideally, I should get this over with. Realistically, a bath sounds heavenly.

I cave. Finn's bathroom is equipped with a large bathtub with bronze dragon talons on the base. I feel numb as I peel off my clothes, then start the bath and comb out my hair. It's gotten so much longer since I arrived at the castle.

I soak in the bath until the water turns cold. I know Finn's waiting for me outside, and maybe that's why I take so long. I sense where this moment is headed, the crossroads we're approaching. He may not want to kill me, but I have to be prepared with all of the reasons I still need to leave. It's the least that I owe him. This is going to crush me; I can only assume it will destroy him.

I take my time drying. I don't skip the chance to raid the assortment of lotions and balms. I lather slowly, and once I'm dried and perfumed, I feel calmer than I have in days. I pad back out to his room with a towel wrapped around me.

Finn is snoring on top of the bed, still wearing his Frumentari uniform. There are dark circles under his eyes, and I wonder how much he's slept since the attack.

I creep gently toward him, focusing on small, quiet movements that won't disturb his sleep. I pick up a quilt from a chair and carry it over, then curl up beside him, drawing the curve of my body against the hard line of his back. When I tuck my head against his neck and focus on the thrumming, I can count his heartbeats.

Stolen time. That's all I'll ever get, it seems. Our impending severance hangs overhead like the blade of a guillotine, but I'm trying very hard not to think about it. Right now, I'm dividing my life into minutes and seconds. I want to savor the remaining ones with Finn. I am stepping into the daydream one more time, fantasizing about a world where we're together.

It's not long before I drift off, too.

I wake up to the sounds of Finn stoking the fire. I'm still in his chambers. Blearily, I study the room. It's still dark out. The firelight casts wobbling shadows over everything.

"Hey," Finn says, noticing my movement. He crosses to the bed.

My voice is thick from sleep. "Sorry. I dozed off."

"It's all right. I think we both needed that."

He hesitates. Marking the indecision, I lift my quilt and pat the spot next to me. "Come here."

The blankets rustle as Finn crawls in, and his warmth envelops me. His face is shadowed as he rests his head on the pillow, his gaze undressing me.

"It doesn't make a difference to me," Finn repeats. "I need you to know that. I'd feel exactly the same if you were a human. I love you, Lyria. Nothing else matters."

*I love you.*

Those words are all I've been aching to hear. I just can't ignore the ones that followed.

"Maybe nothing mattered in the cottage," I say, swallowing. I push down the rising swell of magic. "Maybe *here*"—I gesture between us—"nothing matters in *this* space. But I can't outrun who I am. And I'm not going to be able to hide it forever."

"But you could," Finn protests, angling up on his elbow. "You've been doing it this long! There are surgeries for your ears. No one would have to know about your magic. We could keep your secret together."

I bristle at the picture he tries to paint. I draw back slowly from him, recoiling. "So, I'd pretend to be human for the rest of my life?"

"Or not!" he amends quickly. "Maybe just for the time being? We could come forward once it's safe."

My Talent swells, the heat changing, shifting, like wildfyre. That's not love. That's putting me on a shelf. Keeping me waiting for a future that may never arrive.

"Our marriage would benefit all the Midlands," he continues. "You could change minds. We could demonstrate a better future, together."

I don't believe him. His words are too little, too late, and his confidence is fragile. I see a crack in his armor, and I hear the tremor of doubt in his speech. Finn's not sure if he can manage this politically. He's desperate to keep me—to control me? Cherish me? Protect me? I can't be sure—but he's desperate to do right by his father, too. I can see his internal debate. *Lyria or the throne? Love or my father?*

The offer *I've* been given is to either marry Finn and wait indefinitely for Rodrick to die, or fight like hell for the Crown, neither of which sounds appealing.

The gloves are off, so I go for the jugular. "What about your father? Will *he* approve of the wedding?" I let hurt leak into my voice—laying the sarcasm on thick. "Will his views be transformed after he learns the truth about his daughter-in-law?"

Finn swallows, straining the muscles in his neck. "You know I don't agree with my father's views. He's never going to accept magic, but that doesn't mean I can't."

"That would sound more convincing if it wasn't coming from the *captain of the Frumentari*."

"I should *not* have to tell you that life is complex," he retorts. "I'm not evil by default! I'm not the man my father is! This isn't heroes and villains. It's ridiculous I have to argue that!" Finn's head drops. "You saw what they did to my brother. I didn't start this fight, I'm just stuck trying to finish it. I want to believe there's a world where you and I can come out on the other side of this. But that requires playing my cards right."

I cross my arms. "Is that politics or evasion?"

"It's patience."

"You're asking me to live in the shadows."

"I'm asking you to live with me." Finn sighs, struggling. "The attack threw something into clarity for me. My parents have been pressuring me to finalize an engagement, but I've been dragging my feet and in denial about why. When Sebastian was hit . . . in that moment, I realized how much you mean to me, and how much I want to spend my life with you. I want a future together, Lyria. There is no one else I'd rather have at my side as my queen. But that requires you to stop running. We both have to fight to stay alive and stay together."

I don't know what to believe. Some of Finn's words echo dreams that I've held for myself, my deepest hopes for companionship and influence.

I want to believe him. Gods, I wish it could be that simple. I want a future with him more than I've ever wanted anything—even freedom. But there are fundamental parts of me that can't absorb his words as truth. I stare back at him for a long time.

"I told you I have something to show you." Finn rushes to his desk, yanking open the top drawer. He procures a fist-size item, then returns to the bed.

My pulse rises to a sledgehammer intensity, pounding at my temples.

"This was my grandmother's ring, and it belonged to her grandmother before that. It's been passed down through my family for generations." Finn opens the box. Inside lies a princess-cut diamond, set in a glittering band with smaller gems encircling it. When I meet his eyes, I can't breathe. "I've already spoken with my mother and she's given us her blessing. I'm going tomorrow morning to meet my father in Westgate and speak with him then." Removing the ring from the box, he moves back a bit.

"Lyria." He sinks onto one knee beside the bed.

Every voice inside my head screams to stop him. *Not here. Not now. It's not right.* But I can't bring myself to speak up. My chest is being torn in half.

"From the moment we met, you have made me reconsider everything about how I see the world," Finn says, with earnestness that makes my heart ache. "I have never met anyone as brave or compassionate. If you would do me the honor of sharing your life with me, I would never stop working to become the man you deserve. I would protect and honor you with all that I have and all that I am." His eyes burn with a thousand more declarations, an eternity of promises. His voice trembles when he asks, "Will you marry me?"

This is a moment when I wish I could make time stop. Because I can feel myself rent cleanly into two people: the girl who wants to say yes with a brimming heart, and the woman who needs to say anything else.

I'm at the fork in the road where one future has to die. I have to kill the dream now.

I do the only thing I can think of. I kiss him.

For the first instant, he's frozen. I can feel Finn's hesitation, his fingers still gripping the ring.

I pull back.

"Lyria?" he asks, searching my face.

Never before have I felt so uncertain about the world and my place in it. Never have I been so conflicted, euphoria and terror and hope and doubt all mingling in my constricted chest.

"Can I put it on?" I ask thickly.

My response is something like a maybe. But it's enough to light his face and turn the corners of his lips up. Finn slides the ring on. It's a perfect fit. I hold it up for examination, while Finn says appreciatively, "I could get used to seeing you in nothing but that."

I kiss him again in response because I can't say my true answer. I can't choose his side in this war.

So I communicate without words. With my hands, I express how much I love him and how badly I wish I could be his wife. I put all of that into my movements, because those words will have to stay unspoken. But I can give Finn the only thing I have to offer him. I can give him tonight.

I don't know whether Finn understands that I'm saying goodbye. He has yet to misread me. Maybe it's shared understanding guiding us, but when we fall back together, there's no hesitation. I'm driven by pain and desperate hopelessness, the weight of all I'm losing by losing him. Maybe Finn feels the same, because he dives into the kiss with unbridled intensity. As if he knows it will be our last night together.

I pull him back onto the bed. I can't get close enough, once again. His hands move everywhere: in my hair, down my back, testing every curve. Our breathing gets heavier. It's not enough.

"I need . . ." Finn swallows, pulling shakily away from me. "I need you to tell me to stop."

"I don't want you to stop." I kiss him more fiercely.

He returns my kiss. At first. His hands rise, tracing up my stomach, moving higher, and then he pulls back again, groaning. "*No.* We shouldn't be doing this."

"Why?"

"It's not fair to you."

*"Why?"* My hands move over his chest, then slip lower. Finding what I want.

He hisses through gritted teeth. I bring my lips to Finn's throat, finding the hollow part between his shoulder and his neck. It takes great effort for him to ask, "Have you ever? Before?"

I draw back slowly and shake my head. "Is that a problem?"

"No!" he says quickly. "No. I just . . . I want you to be sure. I don't want you do anything you're going to regret."

"Do you think we'll regret it?"

"I won't," Finn says. He's warring with something. "But it's not my first time."

"I understand that."

"And you don't care?"

I try to reassure him. "Isn't it better that one of us knows what we're doing?"

He laughs. "I suppose."

I lean in to him again. His lips find mine, and he kisses me fiercely. We move so I'm straddling him. He brushes the hair back from my face, finding my ears—outlining their pointed tips under my silken kerchief.

He pauses. "May I?"

I nod silently, and he gently pulls the scarf off. I watch him, breathing steadily, as he traces their shape. "Beautiful," Finn murmurs. Then he leans in and kisses them.

The sensation sets my body aflame. Then it's his turn to kiss a trail down my throat and over my shoulders. His hands run a line up and down my spine. "I just . . . I want this to be perfect for you," Finn says roughly, finding a breath.

"It will be," I assure him, kissing him again.

"It . . . it isn't, for most," he manages.

I'm surprised by the nervous edge in his voice. It's enough to make me pause, reaching up to take his face between my hands.

"I don't care if it's perfect," I whisper. "I just want it to be with you."

I mean it.

Those words seem to be the permission he needs. In one smooth motion, Finn flips me onto my back. I expect him to move over me. But instead he pulls away, and those callused hands encircle my ankles. Then they start sliding up my calves, then my thighs . . .

"What are you doing?" I ask, sounding breathy.

"Something I've wanted to do for a very long time."

I feel vulnerable like this, swept away by the same self-consciousness that characterized our first conversations. The shyness fades into the background as he dips his head and kisses near my ankle.

My stomach vaults. I've imagined this many ways, but not . . . this way.

His lips are soft enough to make me shiver. I reach out and drag my fingers through his dark hair. Finn pauses, craning to kiss my wrist; then he returns to my legs, with another brush on my thigh, as soft as the flap of a butterfly wing. He moves to the opposite leg, drawing lazy circles with his lips and tongue.

"Finn . . ." I say roughly.

He pauses, lips a breath from my skin. "Do you want me to stop?"

"No," I say emphatically.

"Are you sure?" He smirks, kissing me again.

"Yes." I swallow, trembling and flushed. I've decided I am going to face the fear. This is what I want. What I need to experience with Finn, even once.

"So you don't want me to stop?" Another smirk. Another kiss, higher this time.

I shake my head, whimpering. I'm flooded with conflicted emotions, apprehension mingling with desire. My Talent burns all over like wildfyre. Rising above all other emotions is the love I feel for Finn: the adamant, all-consuming devotion. I want him to have this moment with me. I want to take it. So I don't say no when Finn finally stops exactly where I want him.

I find myself repeating his name, something between a plea and a prayer.

*More.* I want more. I *need* more. I might be begging for it, but he just chuckles against me and keeps working, guiding me toward some unknown conclusion. He's relentless, pausing every so often to meet my gaze and smirk his enjoyment. Those emerald eyes track every movement I make, every twitch, every involuntary gasp. I can't hold this much pleasure and I might shatter trying to contain it.

And that's exactly what happens.

When Finn finally draws back, I'm limp and tingling. It's all I can do to breathe and breathe, watching him sit up and grin at me, my prince, this son of Verdinae, the picture of a conquering warrior. My miracle.

"How was that?" Finn asks, panting.

I just reach for him. He fulfills the silent request, drawing me close. I curl into his body, pressing against the hard lines of muscle, and lay my head on his chest. Finn's heart is pounding, keeping tempo with mine. I take a deep breath, savoring each of my singing senses.

Eventually, I sit up.

"So that was okay?" he says.

I nod my affirmation. I'm not sure I have ever loved him more than in this moment: the way he's gazing at me expectantly, searching for my approval, his measured breaths. He's wound so taut, he's almost trembling. And I understand why. He is attuned to me like no one has ever been, wholly intent on my happiness and pleasure.

It's my turn to make him speechless. As I crawl on top, he's watching me like I'm a predator and he's afraid of making any sudden movements. My hair tumbles around my face, forming a dark curtain. He helps guide my hips. As we move together, I realize Finn was wrong about at least one thing.

It is perfect.

# 27

I rouse to the sensation of lips against my hair.

"I just got new orders. I'm leaving for Westgate," Finn whispers. "I didn't want you to think I snuck out on you."

Gradually, the sleep lifts and I sink back into awareness. It's just after dawn, and we did very little sleeping. I'm naked, except for the sheets tangled over my chest. Finn's body is a warm, solid wall curled around me. He kisses my head again and withdraws.

I sit up blearily, looking around. The sky beyond the window is stained with the first crimson streaks of dawn. Finn is getting dressed on the other side of the bed.

"How long will you be gone?" I ask.

"I'll be back in three days, for the ball," Finn says.

"What ball?"

"It's just a VIA fundraiser. Initially, we were going to cancel it after the attack. But my mother decided to hold it anyway. Officially, it's to raise money for the war effort, but mostly it's just an excuse for the nobles to get together and peacock."

"Wow, your family really loves parties," I say.

Finn just grins and laces his boots. "I have to make an appearance. It's a typical thing. I'd love for you to accompany me, as my date."

I pause, highly uncertain. Will I even be here in three days? My instincts tell me I should be long gone by then. "Who will be there?"

He considers. "The major noblemen and women in Verdinae. Odessa. Sandria—she'll definitely want to show her loyalty after the attack, she's in full goodwill-gathering mode—and, uh . . . my father is going to be there, too."

I guess I'm not the only one withholding things. "King Rodrick is coming home?"

"For the night."

It's a miracle that I've made it this long without encountering the king. I take his return as a clear sign.

It's time to get the hell out of this castle.

"So, three days?" I confirm, trying to sound unperturbed. Channeling Sandria.

"Three days." Finn kisses my forehead. "Stay here as long as you like. I'll have the kitchen send up breakfast."

"Shouldn't I leave before the servants see me?" I ask, but Finn just beams.

"I'm more than allowed to sleep with my future wife."

When he leans in to kiss me goodbye, I stiffen.

I should tell him now that I have no intention of marrying him. I should end it right here, before we're any further into this mess. But when I try to form the words, I can't make my throat work.

"I'll see you soon," he says. "I love you, Lyria."

My heart feels leaden. "I love you, too."

---

I think I've figured out what I really want.

I want to hide. Run away from it all. I want to lie here in this bed, under the covers, and not face any consequences. I nearly do just that, since Finn offered me breakfast in bed and the prospect of remaining here in isolation is more than tempting, but I'm on a countdown. There's only so long I can postpone reality. I dress and slip from his chamber. To my distinct mortification, there are four guards outside Finn's door, including Roburn.

"Morning," I mumble.

"Good morning. I hope you slept well," Roburn says, his brow furrowing as I pass. I'm surprised when I hear his footsteps trailing me a few minutes later. "Lyria, could I speak with you for a moment?"

"Yes?"

Roburn catches up with me in an empty hallway, stopping a distance away. "I just wanted to confirm . . . That is to say . . ." He clears his throat. "Prince Finneas has been under my training for most of his life. I would hope that he's conducted himself with honor, but if he hasn't, if there's been any indiscretion . . . I would hope you know you have an ally at court, should you need one."

My chest warms. "I haven't been mistreated. But I appreciate it, Captain. Thank you."

As I hurry through the castle, I find the mess considerably reduced.

Servants must have been cleaning all night. Much of the debris has been cleared. There are already teams of craftsmen hanging new panels of glass. I'm not sure how I feel about the world being put back into order—not when I'm so personally undone.

My feet steer me toward the East Wing. Walking through the doors is a stark reminder of all that's happened: the overflowing beds, the nurses and Healers still rushing around. I see a pair of laborers hauling a stretcher covered with a white sheet. My stomach flips.

There's pain all around me. My Talent aches under my skin, but I push down the sensation. I've dealt with so much worse. I'm intent on my mission now, seeking a particular face among the crowd. Finn may have only delayed my departure, but at least he gave me a chance to say goodbye to Cygnus.

I don't spot Cygnus anywhere on the staging floor or in either of the overflow chambers. So I finally head for his office, but find the door closed.

I pause outside, just before turning the handle. Staring at the ring. It's still on my finger. I can't bring myself to take it off.

I push open the door.

It's dark. Cygnus is sleeping hunched over his desk. When I close the door behind me and the latch clicks, he lifts his head wearily. "Anna?"

"Just me."

"Oh." He knuckles his eyes, wiping away the sleep. "What time is it?"

"Dawn-ish."

"Very specific." He stretches, rising. "You should know that Sebastian is set to make a full recovery."

"When did you fall asleep?" I ask.

"Four-ish."

I was planning to ask Cygnus if Daisy gave him the omnidraught and my notes, but I am too distracted by the guilt that plunges through me at the sight of his exhaustion. Suddenly, I don't know what I'm doing here. I don't know how to tell him of my cowardice.

"You should rest," I finally say.

"Maybe." Cygnus looks around, pulling on his Healer's coat. Then he seems to remember that I'm here. "Did you need something?"

"No," I say quickly. "Just checking on you."

"Oh. Well, thanks," he says gruffly. "If you don't mind . . ."

I realize I'm blocking the door. "Right. Sorry." I move out of his way.

Cygnus pauses at the threshold. "You sure you're all right?"

I'm aware of him absorbing my appearance: my mussed hair, my flushed cheeks. My ears burn as I realize he can probably still smell Finn on me and the whole truth of what we've done.

It's not judgment that flares in his eyes. Not anger, either. It's something else, something softer and more pained.

I don't want to think about any of this. I need to get out of here.

"I'm fine. Don't worry about me."

I hurry away before he can ask more. On my way past the staging area, I run right into Daisy.

"Lyria!" she exclaims, wrapping me in a huge hug. "You're still here!"

Daisy's familiar smiling face momentarily calms my racing heart. I tell her all that happened, about Finn's proposal and briefly about what we shared afterward. Daisy goes from intrigued to shocked to flummoxed.

"And you said yes?"

"I didn't . . . Well, I guess I didn't really say anything either way."

*"What?"*

"It all happened really fast. . . . We were both so emotional. . . . I just didn't feel like I could give him an answer."

"But you're *going* to say yes?"

"I . . ."

For some bizarre reason, Cygnus's face pops into my mind. I shove it down as fast as I can.

"I'm not sure," I say weakly.

Daisy blinks at me. Her eyes drop to my hand, her lips tightening into a thin line. "Well, can I at least see the ring?"

I offer her my hand. "He said it belonged to one of his great-great-great-grandmothers or something."

I feel the other weight of this token from Finn, the many strings that it represents. This ring would mean a life inside the daydream. A life with Finn, but a half life, at best.

When Daisy looks at the ring, she gasps. "Lyria!" Her gaze shoots up to me. "This is the Rashielle diamond!"

"What?"

"This ring belonged to *Queen Elora,* Lyria. As in the wife of *Verdin the Vanquisher*. It's been passed down to queens of Verdinae ever since."

I glance down at the ring. "Really?"

"I think?"

"This is priceless." She clutches her chest. "Lyria, this ring is worth more than my whole life! Do you have any idea how much you could sell it for? Or—forget that—it belongs in a museum! In an *art* gallery!"

Something she said snags my attention. "Did you say *Rashielle*? Like the Goddess?"

"Yes, *exactly* the same." She giggles. "This is one of three jewels in the sister set. They were worn by Verdin's wife and his daughters. Supposedly spoils of the war."

"What set? How do you know this?"

"The sister set," she repeats, huffing. "The most famous jewels in the Midlands? There's three of them—the biggest jewels in the world. They're named after the Elven Goddesses: Elowyn, Rashielle, and Nocturn."

It's strange hearing the familiar names on her lips.

"The Rashielle diamond goes with the Elowyn sapphire on the king's crown and the Nocturn ruby on that necklace Queen Davina's always wearing. They're the three most valuable stones in the whole world. I can't *believe* Finneas gave this to you and you didn't even say yes."

I've stopped listening.

I'm imagining Elowyn and her sisters, Nocturn and Rashielle. I recall the way my mother starts her prayers with a triangle gesture for the sisters: Keeper of Life, Keeper of Death, and Keeper of Time. The words of the poem from the second gate twist over in my mind:

*One of three, and one of one,*
*I glitter as the stars.*
*Let all the pain be overcome by my eternal march.*
*I am the seed of Rashielle,*
*Unyielding as the clock.*
*I carry life within my sight,*
*On this unshifting dock.*

I feel a rush of urgency. "I'm so sorry, but I've got to go."

"What?"

"I just realized there's something I have to do."

My pulse is roaring in my ears as I dash straight back to Cygnus's office. I'm reminded of the queen's words on the day I arrived at the castle—*Nothing happens for nothing.* Gods, how true that is. Perhaps there really is some divine plan behind the nightmare we've been living.

For once, Cygnus is the one to jolt when I wrench open the door.

"The second riddle. I solved it," I say, panting. "It's the ring."

# 28

y nightfall, we're on our way.

I know the reason for the heavy silence that sinks over us as we work our way back toward the gates. This expedition isn't like the others. I'm not eager and excited. It's duty that keeps me putting one foot in front of the other.

One last task. One last chance to prove myself before I go home.

Cygnus seems thoroughly displeased with me. His expression turned dark when I showed him the ring. I didn't tell him the whole story of how I got it, but he seemed to put together the pieces on his own. He hasn't mentioned it, and I'm wondering if he ever will, when he abruptly cuts the silence.

"Do you love him?"

"What?"

"That would make this a lot easier for me. If you could tell me that you do."

"Yes. I love him." I blink back at Cygnus, trying to understand his perplexing expression. "Why do you care? What's it to you?"

"Just—" Cygnus breaks off. "Never mind."

I cover the ring, folding my arms. "I'm not marrying him. Not that it's any of your business. I'm finishing this, and then I'm getting out."

"Where will you go?" Cygnus asks.

"Home."

"The Ironwoods?"

I try to picture a home, my mother waiting for me in our tiny little cottage. But after all I have been through, the image feels far less like a home than it once did. "I'll figure something out."

"What about the ring?"

I glance down at it. "I haven't decided."

Truth is, I'm trying very hard not to think about it at all.

It takes several hours of solemn trekking to get back to the room with the pedestal. When we finally arrive, I hand over the ring to Cygnus.

"You don't want to do the honors?" he asks.

"I did the blood," I answer. "This one's all you."

Cygnus approaches the stone table and carefully lays the ring in the divot. Then he steps back and widens his stance, waiting. I do the same.

Nothing happens for a moment, and I wonder if I somehow misinterpreted the clue. But then the floor begins to shake, and the cave rumbles around us as the great stone doors part.

Light floods my vision.

I yelp, shading my eyes, as the entrance widens and the light pours out over us. When the rumbling stops, I remove my hand, blinking frantically to adjust my vision. Then the confusion sets in, as I cannot make sense of what I see.

We appear to be standing in the midst of a wasteland. The ground beneath us is white and gray, as is the sky that yawns above us, defying logic. There are no clouds, but no sun, either. The immense light seems to radiate from nothing at all; it is a part of this space with no clear origin, like the air and earth.

Cygnus and I walk tentatively forward, and the ground crunches beneath my feet. It cracks and peels in huge flakes, like the riverbeds in the Ironwoods at the end of a long, dry summer. Ahead lies a lake. Beyond it, a ridge of mountains, the same pale bluish gray. And faintly outlined against the water, so still that I nearly miss it, a figure stands on the lake.

"What do you think it is?" Cygnus asks quietly. "Another statue?"

"I have no idea."

We exchange glances. There is nothing else to say. It is clear which direction we need to move.

Forward.

He takes the lead, and I follow trepidatiously. I grip my father's dagger, savoring the warmth of the metal. My fingers trace the rose on its handle, the ridges that are as familiar to me as the calluses on my own hands.

As we approach the lake, the figure on the water stands still. Eerily so. Cygnus and I come to the water's edge, and I hesitate. I still can't make out a face, only dark robes, limp hair, and a slumped, clouded countenance.

"What now?" I ask.

Cygnus offers, "Swim, I guess?"

I try to stick a toe into the water. Only it isn't water at all—or at least, it doesn't have the appropriate properties—because my foot doesn't break through the surface. It hits something solid instead. Confused, I try again and meet the same result.

Beside me, Cygnus has a similar experience. He turns to me, puzzled, and suggests, "I think . . . I think we're supposed to walk on it."

Ominous energy hangs over this place. When I gaze down into the water, I don't see my reflection; the water glows from within, swirling in the same way the Everwillow portal did, the same way I imagine my magic swirls in me now.

I look back toward the figure, who still hasn't moved. Feeling deeply apprehensive, I counter with: "What if it's a trap?"

"Hasn't this whole thing been a trap?" he grunts.

"Fair enough."

I follow Cygnus a dozen or so paces onto the water.

As we approach the figure, their features gradually come into view until I am certain the person I am looking at is female—and she is not made of stone. She is very real. Hair drapes in oily sheets around a haggard face. She is Elven; her ears are prominent, sticking out from the strands of hair that cling to her like seaweed. She wears dark robes and is pale, deathly pale, her pallor more resembling that of a corpse than a living being. She stands about my height, so thin she looks skeletal. Her green eyes are deathlessly cruel.

Cygnus's voice cracks. "Lyria, I think that's . . ."

*"Me."*

She's a daemonic version of myself. Not older, per se, but unleashed, unbridled. Someone I might have become without my mother's guidance. A physical manifestation of the monster within.

Cygnus looks toward me in utter confusion. "No, I was going to say *me*."

I blink, looking back at the figure. She is unchanged, watching us with those cold, austere eyes that seem to look out of a cadaver into the world of the living.

"I think we're seeing what the spell wants us to see, Cygnus."

This is powerful magic. Ancient spellcraft. I stand trembling as I behold this twisted version of myself, both knowing and not knowing that she's an illusion. I see what the magic wants me to see. The spellcraft wants me to fear myself. It wants me to doubt.

I can't let it win.

Before I can gather my senses, the daemon Lyria comes alive, startling me. She gestures for me to follow her and then begins walking toward the mountains. Her robes trail over the water.

"We're being told to follow," offers Cygnus.

I take a long breath. Everything in me wants to turn around, but today I'm choosing courage.

"Then by all means." I step ahead.

The figure leads us over the lake for what feels like ten or twenty minutes, until we spot something looming in the distance. Two gates. Or archways, really. They are carved from gray marble, perhaps the same stone that forms the jagged mountain peaks in front of us.

The nightmare version of myself stops when she is between them, then turns around slowly. She holds out her hands, palms upward, indicating both directions.

"Which one?" Cygnus grunts.

"Right?"

"Everybody probably chooses right."

I could pummel him. "Left, then?"

We approach the left archway, but the figure steps into our path, shaking her head. Again, she holds out two hands—in opposite directions.

"I think she—or *they*—want us to split up," I murmur.

"I think you're right," says Cygnus.

We glance at each other. I can read the reluctance in his eyes, mirroring mine.

"This might be the end," he admits.

I nod. I can feel it, too. We've come to the end of the line.

The final gate.

I look at Cygnus, and an odd weight presses down on my throat. I'm not sure I can untangle all the complex feelings I have toward him right now—all the *many* varied things I've felt toward him since we met. I don't know what the future holds, but I'm grateful to have known him.

I step toward the gateway on the right. Words scroll up and over the crumbling ruins, and I translate at record speed:

*"'I enter at the breaking point, my price revealed within; some truths are only found in time, seen solely at the end.'"*

As I approach, I see that the entry point shimmers with iridescent mist. Distorted rainbows fracture against the swirls as oil spills over the murky water. I reach out to touch the mist. It isn't solid like the lake water, but it is freezing cold. I look sidelong at Cygnus. He watches me. So does the bone-chilling figure.

Old energy hangs over this place, an odd tension in the atmosphere that seems to harmonize with my Talent, like the echo of an old song. If something is to be found in here, something needs to be yielded as well.

"Here goes nothing," I say, sounding much braver than I feel. Then I step into the mist.

The lake is gone.

The light is gone.

The first step into the void brings a plunging darkness, like plummeting into ice water. The next step brings me to solid ground—stone. Darkness and warmth spread out around me, vague and indiscernible, like waking up from a dream. Then, all at once, my surroundings snap into focus, and I know precisely where I am.

Terror stabs through my heart. I'm *back* in the Great Hall. On the dais, where the queen was sitting right before they took Fergustan's head.

Seated on the throne is King Rodrick.

I can place him without knowing him. The cruelty on his face is unmistakable. I've never seen a person like this—someone who wears an evil aura around them like a cloak. There's no mercy in those darting eyes, no paternal love. He's looking down at Finn, who looks different since I saw him last. He is wearing the same outfit I found him in after fighting the Moragorion. The one I repaired by firelight with my mother's sewing kit. He wears his sword on his hip, and he still has the travel pack I gave him slung over a shoulder. It swings as he argues animatedly with his father.

I stand still, waiting for Finn to take notice of me just a hairbreadth away from his father's throne. But he is oblivious, almost shouting in his tirade. It appears I am only an observer in this world.

As the shock settles, I finally start listening. And I realize I'm not in the present at all—I'm watching Finn on the day he returned from the Ironwoods.

"She's not a warrior," Finn says. "She's not a killer. Father, I'm telling you, she could barely put her shoes on the right feet."

"It's a risk," King Rodrick counters. "I can believe she won you over, but that doesn't mean she won't be a liability."

"But imagine if it *works,*" Finn argues. "Imagine the symbol she'd become. We won't have a hard time controlling her. As far as I could tell, Melia barely lets her leave the house, like an eighteen-year-old toddler. She'll be so dazzled by court that she'll fall down and worship us. I guarantee it."

"And what makes you so sure?"

Finn laughs. "If there's one thing I can do, it's manipulate women."

King Rodrick frowns. "If her magic is what you say it is, how do you expect to keep that under control?"

"She's insecure," Finn says simply. "I've never met someone so grotesquely starved for affection. A little honey, a little praise, and she'll be eating out of our hands. I'm telling you—she hasn't got a clue about the insurrection. If we can't get Melia to finish the omnidraught, her daughter is the next best thing."

The king drums his fingers against his throne. "And how do you propose we persuade this girl to help us? Ask her nicely?"

"Yes." Finn shrugs. "She's got a good heart. Leverage that softness against her. Coercion didn't work with Ragglestaff, anyway."

"And you're willing to take the responsibility? You'll manage it?"

"Yes. I'll handle it," Finn says dismissively. "Once we get her out of the Ironwoods, she won't know where to run. And if she becomes a problem, I'll kill her myself."

I've stopped breathing. I'm no longer sure that what I'm seeing is real. It can't be. This monster speaking so cruelly can't be the prince I have fallen in love with. It must be some illusion—another trick of magic.

I don't want to watch any more, but I can't stop the nightmare from continuing. The king considers. "It would be simpler to kill her now."

Finn frowns, and there is a flash of distress on his features, but it is gone as quickly as it appeared.

"I will respect your decision either way, Father," Finn says, slowly and carefully—each word deliberate. "But it is my heartfelt opinion that killing her now would be a tremendous mistake. She fell straight into our laps. We won't get another chance like this."

King Rodrick rubs a hand over his chin, hauling in a deep breath. "Fine. I'll agree to it."

Finn looks elated.

"Under one condition," Rodrick amends.

"Yes?"

"I don't want you handling her."

"But I'm the one—"

"You are already too close to this," King Rodrick says firmly. "And frankly, I don't trust you in any scenario with a skirt. As you've said, Sulnik's hanging by a thread. You need to think about the optics of moving her into the castle. How would Sandria respond?"

"She wouldn't care."

"And Odessa?"

Finn grinds his teeth. "Odessa and Sandria want the crown. They're not pining after me. Both girls have lovers—they're not subtle about it."

"That doesn't mean you can show blatant disrespect and not expect consequences." Rodrick crosses his legs. "That's your problem, Finneas; you can't look farther than what's smacking you in the face. A king is deliberate. A king makes sacrifices for the greater good. And a king honors his duty to the throne, and the Crown, and his people. Not his prick."

Finn shoves his hands in his pockets, scowling. "Fine. Have Sebastian take over, then. I would respectfully remind you that you promised whoever found the heir would be named your successor."

King Rodrick smiles, brows rising. "I thought you weren't sure she's the one."

A muscle twitches in Finn's jaw. "If she is, I don't want Sebastian taking the credit."

King Rodrick huffs a mirthless little laugh. "Fair enough." He leans farther back. "Your mother can take point."

"And what am I supposed to do when she gets here? Ignore her? If the whole point is to get her on our side, I don't think throwing her to the wolves is ideal."

"For now, I want you back east. Keep trying to find Melia. She's going to raise unholy hell when the rebels find out her daughter is missing."

"And then?"

"And then do what you need to do to keep her happy. But don't sleep with her. The last thing we need is another bastard."

Finn just laughs. "You won't have to worry about that."

I don't hear any more.

Between the shock and the magic roaring through my blood, I didn't realize that my lungs are burning. But as I gasp, trying to fill them with air, it feels like swallowing earth instead.

I stagger back, panic rising. My world is crumbling at the edges again. I choke, stars popping in my vision, blood roaring in my ears. I am slipping away from life; I can feel it. But there is no great beckoning light, only darkness. And the monster inside me, the inconceivable power, diminishes to a ghost, a flicker of itself.

I can't remember what there is to live for. I can hardly remember my name. There is only pain, worse than the worst of my ravaging magic.

*Betrayal.*

I don't know if I can trust what I've seen. I don't know who I am, or if this is real, if it's falsehood, if it's some projection of the spell. I don't know the way forward. I only know that I love him. *I love him.*

And if what I just saw is real . . .

*No.* I can't accept it. Not yet.

When the darkness comes to claim me, I fight against it with all that I'm worth. I refuse to yield. But the harder I fight, the more weight presses down on me. Death looms like the end of time; death is an inevitability. . . .

Death is . . .

Death is something heavy slamming into my chest.

*Ouch.*

Death is painful.

Is it *supposed* to be this painful?

It slams again, more forcefully.

*Stop.*

Another crushing blow. It feels like my ribs are about to break.

*Again. Again.* Even harder.

Now I am angry. This isn't a peaceful release into the void; this *hurts.*

*STOP!* I want to scream, but my voice is gone. There is no air, no light, just the heavy thing beating me again and again. Something stirs, deep in the untouchable core of my spirit—a creature I once knew.

Then, all at once, the world floods back into focus. Sound, pain, touch, scent—they return to me in glorious clarity.

I open my eyes, and Cygnus is kissing me.

The scene is so bizarre that for a split second, I wonder if I'm dead.

Don't people's memories flash in front of them as they're passing? Is it possible my brain is extending itself even further, crafting a full-blown hallucination?

His mouth is hot. His scent is everywhere—pine and sweat and something else, an earthy smell like rocks after rain. Then Cygnus's lips pull away, and that *thing* rams into my chest again....

I roll over and vomit.

*"Thank the Gods,"* Cygnus gasps.

I choke as putrid, salty water erupts from my chest. Gagging and spluttering, I hack up wave after wave of the awful stuff until thick saliva coats my throat and my lungs feel incinerated. My guts feel raw; my chest aches tremendously where Cygnus pounded it again and again.

"You were gone," he says weakly. His voice is thick. I've never heard the Healer sound so shaken. Furious? Yes. Desperate? Certainly. But to my shock (and maybe horror?), Cygnus truly sounds like he is about to cry.

*"What just happened?"* I wheeze.

It is dark again, but not pitch-black like it was in the cave. We are partially submerged in warm, smelly, very much *not* solid water, which would barely rise to my ankles if I stood up. Very faint amber light flickers against the onyx surface. My gown and hair are soaked.

"Well, when I walked through the gate, I saw something. Something terrible," Cygnus says, with a hard edge to his tone that I've never heard before. "I think it was designed to scare us or maybe just kill us, because after a while, I realized I couldn't breathe. But I didn't know how to stop what I was seeing, and I couldn't look away."

"What did it show you?" I ask quickly.

"It doesn't matter."

I swallow, tasting salt and metal. I'm burning with curiosity, but I don't want to share what I saw any more than he does.

"Was it real, do you think?" I ask tentatively.

"I think what I saw was real," Cygnus says, looking down.

My stomach plunges. "You do?"

"I . . . I don't know. I can't be sure. Either it was real, or worse than a nightmare."

That's how I would describe what I saw, too.

*It can't have been real.* I refuse to believe it.

"The banshees tricked us," I remind him, feeling dizzy. "Those creepy people we heard? That wasn't real, either. This is all just spellcraft."

*It has to be.*

Cygnus meets my eyes. I can tell he doesn't believe me.

"How did you get out of it?" I ask.

"I guess I . . ." He forces a heavy breath. "It doesn't matter."

"No! Tell me!"

"It's stupid."

"It saved our lives!"

He sighs, exasperated. "I thought about you, okay?"

I reel back. "Huh?"

He looks furious with himself for mentioning it. "I told you it was stupid."

"No, I just don't understand."

Cygnus squeezes his temples. "I realized I wasn't breathing and I was thinking all these bad things and then I thought about you and how you were going to need my help . . ." He shakes his head. "I dunno. I guess it just snapped me out of it."

I feel like a frog has crawled up my throat. I have an odd impulse to hug him, but Cygnus folds his arms over his body and starts talking again very quickly, blocking the chance.

"Anyway, when I came to, I realized I was lying face down in the water. And you were next to me in the same position."

I start hacking again, my whole body convulsing with the effort. When it's over, I drop my head between my knees, shaking.

"Thank you," I finally say, when I've found my voice again. I tip my face to gaze at Cygnus, but he's staring away, toward something in the distance.

"We did it," he murmurs, almost to himself. "We *actually* did it."

I follow his gaze over the lake and across the darkness. The mountains are gone. Instead, there sits a glittering city.

And when Cygnus looks back at me, I realize it's the first time I've seen him beam.

"Welcome to Ruin."

# 29

hen I tip my head back and look upward, I see no end to the blackness, just yawning emptiness, a dizzying void that seems to go on forever. It might be an infinite sky above us, devoid of stars.

This is no natural cave. No ordinary sky. This is spellcraft, as old as the world itself, handiwork of the Gods.

The city before us is massive. It sprawls over what seems like miles, with buildings on buildings, spindly towers, bridges and ropes crisscrossing over layers upon layers of civilization. Thousands of lights flicker in the windows, in dim shades of amber and gold, and reflect off the lake's surface.

Cygnus and I follow the lights, like illuminated pinpricks on a walking path, wading through the shallows toward the beach's pebbly shore, which splits a pair of craggy bluffs. My eyes are ahead: on the city, and in particular the massive onyx structure that juts twice as high as the next-tallest building. It can only be Queen Soleste's castle.

"What do we do when we get there?" Cygnus asks.

"Find food."

I feel like garbage. My clothes are in tatters, and I don't dare touch the tangles that have replaced my hair. Not the most inviting condition in which to make friends.

"We've got to get dry," says Cygnus, reading my mind.

"And find water," I add. "Water first." My throat is ragged.

Slowly, we walk toward the city. The closer we draw toward the Elven kingdom, the more something seems off in the air. Our path meanders over uneven terrain, and it's all I can do to keep my feet beneath me. Silence falls—spooky silence—the overwhelming kind. Buildings perch on the sloping hills like dark birds, their beady orange eyes marking our approach with disdain.

When we reach the first dwellings scattered along the outskirts, I'm surprised: These are more hovels than homes. The buildings are short and square, hewn from stone and metal. The streets are deserted. There's no sun to tell time by. I see no children at play, no one traversing the narrow streets as they do in Crown City. The only animals I spot are scrawny, white-tailed rats. All lies eerily still.

As we approach the city's heart, the condition of the city doesn't improve. Everything is harsh and austere . . . joyless. There's nothing of Verdinae's charm. The closer I look, the more I see: walls spiderwebbed with cracks, dwellings without roofs, bricks and rags and other rubbish strewn through the streets or clustered near doorsteps.

Dread fills me, my worst fears confirmed. There may have been Elves here at one point, but they are gone now. Cygnus's dream of rallying an Elven army to take back Evermore is just that, a dream.

I glance over at him. His expression is determinedly blank, but I can feel his disappointment. I find myself tempted to reach for his hand to comfort him, but I stop myself.

But as we near what seems to be the city's central plaza, Cygnus and I finally hear some commotion.

There are voices and milling footsteps, plus the hissing sounds of a working stove. My heartbeat quickens.

That's when we start to notice signs of life: a shutter closing, a cough, the low voices of families talking inside their homes. Someone pushes a cart past, too quickly to notice our bedraggled figures. The noise grows. We turn into the main square to find a market, with hundreds of people bustling around open-air booths and vendors. Music wafts from somewhere nearby.

I look over at Cygnus, unable to stop my spreading grin. When he smiles back, I once again have the odd urge to hug him—which drives my heart rate higher still.

Everywhere I look, I see tapered ears. There are some girls wearing kerchiefs like mine but tied back so the points of their ears are shown prominently. The fashion is different than in Verdinae; there are more subdued colors and less extravagant fabrics, but the silhouettes are more daring. Everyone's bodies are freer. The women and men wear their hair long and flowing, and I spot far more beards than in Verdinae. There's a bonfire toward the middle of the square, and I see a pair of young girls sitting beside it, tossing a rippling sphere of fire back and forth the way human children might play with a ball. I gape at them, awestruck.

I could spend hours people-watching, but I need water. We both need *help*. Our journey through the lake left me exhausted past dignity.

Not thinking too much, I home in on a woman at a nearby booth.

"Excuse me. Could you help us?" My voice emerges an octave lower than normal, raspy and thick. "My friend and I, we just . . ." I swallow, not sure how to describe what we've just been through. "We've just arrived. Please, if you have any water . . ."

The woman's brow furrows in confusion. A spread of trinkets and buttons lie scattered on the table before her. She is old, her face a web of wrinkles between long, tapered ears. I wonder how many hundreds of years she has lived, how much she has seen.

"Just arrived?" she repeats, looking dazed. Her eyes shoot between Cygnus and me, her gaze snagging on his ears. She gasps, and plain horror washes over her features. "Is he *human*?"

My head swivels. "No! Well, half—"

"My mother is Elven," Cygnus explains, stepping forward. "We've just come through the gate."

She points a bony finger at him. "You're lying! No one comes in or out of Ruin! You must be one of the queen's tricks!"

*No one goes out?* I think, but I don't have time to focus on her words.

"No, he's my friend!" I try to amend quickly. "He's one of us—"

But the old woman just starts shrieking, "*Spies!* SPIES! *HEEELP!*"

Cygnus curses. The screams have caught the attention of dozens of onlookers. They don't mob us all at once, but they close in slowly as Cygnus and I wheel around, looking for somewhere to run.

"No, please!" I stagger backward. "You misunderstand!"

The woman continues screaming, "HEEEEELLLLP!"

"Please, we don't want any trouble," I plead, lifting my hands in surrender. There is no will left in me to fight, not after all we've endured and conquered. The last thing I want to do is hurt anyone else. As the Elves surround us, shouting and hurling accusations, my relief sours into confusion.

These are my people.

*My* people.

And I can't let them hurt Cygnus.

When two big male Elves grab him, I lunge.

"Let him *go*!" I try to yank the nearest one's arm. He shakes me off like I weigh nothing, growling, "He's *human*!" like that's a crime in itself.

"NO!" Cygnus shouts. "I'm half-Elven! I came through the Everwillow! Please—"

Someone grabs *my* arms, and I see red.

"Get OFF me!" I howl at the Elf who grabbed me. I kick back, aiming for his sensitive bits, but he twists to avoid it, lifting me clean off the ground, so I'm left thrashing like a child. It's the second time I've been matched for strength in a fight, and my ego doesn't take well to defeat. "LET ME GO!"

*"Wait!"* cries Cygnus. "There's been a misunderstanding—"

A voice cuts straight through the chaos. *"ENOUGH!"*

It sounded from behind me. I thrash harder, trying to turn and face it, but the man who grabbed me has my arms pinned. I hear soft footsteps, then shuffling, the sounds of a parting crowd.

I smell her first.

Cinnamon and soil and warm bread.

And I can't stop the rush of tears as I choke out, *"Mother!"*

She flings the hood of her cloak back as she draws forward. "Let her go. They're with me."

Cygnus and I get released at once.

She looks different, and it's not just the light. Instead of her usual garb, she's dressed entirely in black. Her dark eyes look different as they sweep over me—harder, somehow. And her hair isn't piled into its crown of braids; it's wild and long, disheveled.

Her eyes are solely focused on me, but I can't read her expression. I'm torn between screaming at her and begging for forgiveness, but Mother doesn't give me a chance to speak.

"Follow me," she says. Her gaze flits over to Cygnus. "You too."

Without waiting for a response, she turns and hurries through the crowd. Cygnus and I exchange a glance before we silently follow.

Mother leads us to another area of the city that looks identical to the first few streets we passed through—abandoned, with worn homes on the brink of destruction. She finally stops in front of a run-down building, pulls out a rusted key from her pocket, and turns the lock with a *click*.

"Why did everyone listen to you?" I ask as she creaks the door open. "How did you find us?"

"Get inside first," she says. "Then we'll talk."

Cygnus and I follow her inside, up two flights of stairs, and into a tiny apartment. When she shuts the door behind us, Mother fastens three locks. Then she traces runes in the air with her fingertips, murmuring incantations of safety and concealment. I've seen Mother express many things—anger, disappointment, annoyance—but I have never once seen her afraid. Right now, she looks terrified.

I look around at the space, which is about half the size of our cottage. It's far more run-down and grimy than any home we've stayed in together. But as I scrutinize my surroundings, I can see Mother's touch—the flowers strung across the ceiling, the spellbooks on the narrow shelf, the altar in the corner with a golden figure of Elowyn. Mother lives here. Or at least she did, once.

Cygnus and I stand awkwardly near the doorway as Mother finishes her spellwork. When she's done, I expect her to yell at me. I expect her to tell me what a disappointment I've been. I expect her to list all the things I've done wrong in her absence.

What I don't expect is the hug.

Her arms fling around me so tightly, I almost yelp. I'm so taken aback, I stand stiffly in her grasp for a moment, before slowly raising my arms to return the gesture. Tears sting my eyes as I inhale her familiar scent. I don't know how long the embrace lasts. But when it's over, she points to the chairs and instructs us to sit.

"We have a lot to catch up on," she starts. "And I'm assuming you probably have many questions. But first I need to know how you got here and who knows that you've come."

I try to speak. But the words clog in my throat. Overwhelmed, I glance at Cygnus.

"We started trying to find Ruin a few weeks ago," he starts, eyeing me for permission to continue. I jerk a nod, and I'm relieved as he takes over, recounting our entire struggle through the gates.

When he finishes, Mother's eyes flash to me. "And how did you get to Crown City?"

I've been dreading this moment. I find my voice and do my best to explain. Again, I'm expecting rage and disappointment. But Mother just listens silently, nodding, with her lips pressed tight. When I tell her about my work on the omnidraught, I also brace for Cygnus's reaction. I expect him to sneer at my mistakes or to scoff at the arrogance of accepting such a critical assignment. But he listens with a calm expression that mirrors hers, and both of their eyebrows rise in astonishment when I conclude that I've finished it.

"How is that possible? Have you tested it on patients?"

I shake my head. "No. I just worked from Ragglestaff's notes, because the queen said it was too dangerous for me to travel to the quarantine zone. But that's where you were, right? How did you get here?"

Her face wavers with a whole series of emotions I can't name. "I never made it to the quarantine zone," she admits thickly. "I got apprehended on the road by the Frumentari. I managed to fight my way out of it, but I was injured in the process." Mother peels down the neck of her tunic, revealing a nasty scar that plunges from her collarbone across her chest. "And then I couldn't travel for weeks. I hunkered down at an inn near the border, but by that point, the area was crawling with soldiers looking for me. I needed to contact you, but I couldn't reveal anything about my location without risk of the letter getting intercepted."

I try to process this. It's hard to imagine so many soldiers pursuing my mother—peaceful, dutiful, studious Melia. It's even harder to imagine her *fighting* her way out of something.

"And then I got word from our spies that you'd been taken by the empire."

"You have *spies*?" I repeat numbly. "How?"

Mother draws a deep breath. "Because I help lead the rebels. I have for almost nineteen years now."

When I glance at Cygnus, he looks as confounded as I am.

"Once I found out you'd been taken by the Verdish, I was desperate to reach you. As soon as I gained the strength, I rallied a unit to extract you. But on our way to the Hartlands, we got apprehended again. This time by Queen Soleste's soldiers. I expected them to kill me immediately, but instead they just locked me away. I learned from the other prisoners that Soleste has been absent traveling; I assume she was waiting to kill me herself when she returned. Before she could get the chance, I got in touch with some old rebel contacts. They helped me escape, and we've been trying to find a way to get you back since."

I feel my Talent begin to boil. "And why would Soleste want to kill you?"

"Many reasons." Mother looks down at her hands. "I've known Soleste since we were girls together. She wasn't born into royalty. She was just a commoner from the Ironwoods, like me, but with a very *uncommon* Talent."

"A siphon." I nod. I know that much from the legends.

"Yes," says Mother. "She can draw magic out of anything with a touch, including other bloodborne Talents. She can steal portions of other people's power without them even realizing, and she has never had any qualms about doing so. By the time she was your age, she was already the most formidable Elven wielder in history. Among her stolen Talents was the ability to control minds. Including mine."

The pain that crosses her face threatens to rip out my heart.

"But the magic wasn't enough for Soleste," Mother continues softly. "Her ambition was insatiable. So, eventually, she set her sights on the Crown and secured a marriage to Prince Amos—Evermore's presumed heir at the time."

Cygnus and I exchange looks.

"Is Amos the Heir of Evermore?" I ask eagerly. "Is he still alive?"

"No." She shakes her head, and my spirits sink. "After he married her, Amos became a shell of himself. He wouldn't leave his chambers or speak to almost anyone. He finally passed about two decades ago, but most people thought he was dead long before that. You have to understand the kind of power she wields. When you're in front of her, Soleste can make you forget who you are, what you care about, every person you've ever loved. That's what she did to him, and it's what she did to me."

"For how long?" asks Cygnus.

"A little under three hundred years," Mother says. "I served her through the duration of the Long War. I was at her side during the fyres, and when she led the last of the Evermoreans underground, before she turned the Hartlands over to King Verdin."

I'm trying to visualize the horror Mother experienced. I simply can't comprehend it.

"But why?" Cygnus asks. "Why would she do any of it?"

"I don't know." Mother bites her lip. "I have never been able to understand her decisions. Soleste is the *reason* we lost the Long War, on so many levels. She destroyed the mind of our king, only wielding her power when it was convenient. She never joined our warriors riding onto the battlefield. When she led the Evermoreans underground, we thought Ruin was going to be a temporary sanctuary to rebuild our strength. Instead, she sealed every gate with magic except the one in her castle. She and her lackeys can come and go as they please, but the rest of us have been trapped underground ever since. You two are the first to open one of those gates."

Cygnus and I exchange another look. I imagine he's as astonished as I am.

"But how did you get out?" I ask.

Mother's hands have started to shake. She clasps them tightly. "Do you remember the stories I told you about Faeries and name day gifts?"

I swallow. "Yes?"

I'm very still as I wait for her to continue.

"Before King Amos died, Soleste became pregnant. And when the baby was born, Soleste allowed the Faeries to visit Ruin for the name day ceremony. However, instead of bestowing a gift, the Faerie queen proclaimed that she'd seen a vision: that the child would manifest a Talent that would one day rival Soleste's."

Heat is rising through my blood.

"The only thing Soleste *ever* feared was the Heir of Evermore," Mother continues. "The prophecy says that the heir will be granted the power of Gods—the kind of power it would take to rival a siphon. And yet, before the whole court of Ruin, the Faerie queen declared that the heir had arrived and she was none other than Soleste's newborn child. The instant the Faerie queen spoke the words, Soleste struck her down with a thought. And not just her."

Mother has gone very pale. "Soleste slaughtered *every single person* in that room. Except for me . . . and her daughter."

The words sound as though I'm very far away.

"I don't know why she spared us. It makes no logical sense," she continues. "After all these years, my only guess is there is a part of Soleste that can feel love, and that part of her . . . couldn't bring herself to do it. At least not in that moment. Soleste stormed away, and I remember just clutching the baby, looking out at the carnage, and that's when I felt it. The tight hold she'd had over my mind, all those years I hadn't been able to disobey—it just shattered."

Her eyes fill with tears. "The child was in mortal danger. Soleste would eventually change her mind about sparing her. I knew it was just a matter of time. And I think, somehow, my desire to protect her baby overrode her magic. So I carried the child into the queen's chambers, and the last unsealed path out of Ruin, and just . . . walked out. I smuggled her out of Crown City and carried her over the wall."

Blood pounds against my temples. The air in this room is suddenly too thick to breathe.

"The only way to keep the child safe was to hide her. If Soleste had any hint of her whereabouts, she would have stopped at nothing to find her. And if the child herself knew what she was, and Soleste managed to get her hands on her, she'd be able to see it in her daughter's mind.

"There is so much I've been forced to keep from you," Mother explains. "*So* much I have wanted to tell you. But I hope you can understand now why it had to be done. And that I only did any of it because I love you. You are my daughter, Lyria. No matter your blood."

"No," I say, as something fundamental within me fissures. "Stop. *Don't*."

"Lyria," she says with a foreign softness. Everything about her is foreign now.

*"No."*

I know what comes next. But it shatters me anyway.

"The child was you. You're the Heir of Evermore."

# 30

very thought in my head falls silent.

I stand up, but I'm not sure I'm in control of my body anymore.

"I know how difficult all this is to process," Mother says quickly, "but you don't have to rush into anything. There's a Mage here in Ruin—a teacher, who is prepared to help you master your power. You can take time to train. You don't have to join the rebellion right away; this can happen on your timetable."

I can't get a breath in. I'm so confused and distraught, I can't even look at her anymore.

*Kidnapper. Liar. Manipulator. Fraud.*

I'm tempted to throw something at her head.

I don't know this woman. I don't understand her. I don't know what I've been fighting for.

*I need to get out.*

I stumble to the door and start yanking open the locks.

"Stop, Lyria!" Mother shoots to her feet. "You can't leave here! It's not safe!"

I ignore her, fling open the door, and run.

I don't know my way through the streets. I can just focus in one direction: Toward the lake. Toward the water. Soon I hear Cygnus's footsteps behind me. My Talent marks his desperation, his fear, but none of that trumps this raw betrayal roaring through me, the maelstrom threatening to swallow me whole. I don't look back as I hurtle to the city's edge and the black-pebbled bank of the lake. I dive in and let the water rush over me.

And then I can finally scream.

I let my Talent burn and burn. I let myself feel all that I have warred to suppress: the rage and the terror, the confusion and bottomless, infinite pain. I let it rise and flood through me, until I become the agony. Then I send the energy blast out of me and through the pressing blackness. The water absorbs it all. My screams, my pain, my Talent, I yield it all to the lake. When I'm aching for air, I kick back to the surface. Then I submerge again, and again. Over and over, until the worst of the fury has seeped out of me, and there's just that raw, swirling vortex within. The mother-size hole in my heart.

Slowly, shakily, I drift back to myself. It's a long time before I let myself float to the surface, where I roll onto my back and gaze up at the darkness. Cygnus waits on the shore. I'm hazily aware of his distant figure, sitting with his knees tucked to his chest.

I don't know why he followed. Surely my usefulness has expired.

When I finally wade back to the shore, he asks roughly, "Are you all right?"

"No," I say simply. The truth. "I have no idea what's real anymore. I don't even know who she is. Everything I knew—" My throat closes, and I cut myself off.

There's no noise for a moment, except our heartbeats and the lapping waves.

Cygnus breathes steadily. "Lyria, your mother had good reasons for concealing your identity. She didn't do it to hurt you."

"She shouldn't have concealed it from *me*!"

I feel like a fool.

Swallowing hard, I gaze back at Cygnus, recalling his expression when my mother announced me as the Heir of Evermore. He seemed unfazed by the news. Stoic as ever. Cold rushes over me, and my skin prickles.

"You knew," I whisper.

"What?" Cygnus maintains the mask; his expression doesn't flicker. But he pales, just the tiniest degree.

"You knew about the prophecy," I say more firmly. "And somehow, you've known all along it was me, haven't you?"

There's a shift in his scent—everything I need to confirm my belief. The vortex churns ever deeper, ever faster, and I shut my eyes.

He's already hurrying to explain. "I didn't *know*. I just had a theory."

"From where? How?"

"Ragglestaff told me about the prophecy. He said it describes someone with a Gods-given Talent. Based on what I learned about you while we worked through the gates, and what I've heard about Queen Soleste . . ."

Betrayal rolls through me. "You agreed we were going to be honest with each other!"

"It was just a theory! What would telling you have accomplished?"

"You wouldn't have *lied*!"

I need to get away from him. More pressingly, I need to get away from *her*. She is not my mother, and this is not my home. Everything in this Gods-forsaken place has been tricks and riddles. There's nothing straightforward here, nothing real.

There is only one person I want to talk to right now.

I start charging back the way we came.

"Where are you going to go?" Cygnus shoots up from where he was sitting and follows me.

"Back to the palace," I say. "I need to talk to Finn."

Cygnus recoils. "And ask him what? If it's true? How would he possibly know?"

"I don't know." My chest lurches—a tug of that invisible cord between us. "I just need to speak with him."

I shove away the rising thoughts of what I saw in the archway. It wasn't real. It can't be. I was tricked by the banshees before; I must have been tricked again.

Either way, I need to find out.

"Wait! Listen to me, Lyria!" Cygnus surges into the water after me, seizing my arm. "I won't tell you not to go. That's your choice to make. But *please,* be careful. Don't put your faith in anyone you shouldn't."

I shake him off. "I already did."

---

It is a surprisingly short swim back to Nocturn's gate, and I retrace the long path to the entrance. The sun is close to the horizon when I make it back out of the Everwillow.

Quick calculations tell me that my three days are up; Finn should be back at the castle, here to fundraise at the military ball. My plan is to grab him beforehand, but as I near the castle, it's clear the festivities have already started. All traces of the attack have vanished and the halls have been elaborately decorated. The forecourt teems with carriages, and I can already hear music drifting from the Great Hall. I curse my timing.

New plan: Change. Go to the ball. Find Finn there.

I hasten to my room. Dante chirps excitedly at my arrival, zooming in circles and vaulting over the furniture. I enlisted Daisy to watch him in my absence, and I'm relieved to see that he seems to be in much better shape than I am. Gods, it's good to see him.

I beeline straight for the washroom and tub. It's not until I emerge, drying my hair, that I notice the ball gown laid out on my bed, a note on top of it.

*For my future bride.*
*With my whole heart forever,*
*Finn*

My heart lurches.

*This* is the real Finn. The thoughtful boy who loves me. Not that warped nightmare from the cave. All this time, I've been holding myself back from him, and for what? Duty? To whom? I feel like I'm sleepwalking as I slip into the dress and fasten the bodice. It's a bright, patriotic shade of Verdinae blue.

When I arrive in the ballroom, I find it similarly bedecked. There are blue banners hanging from the ceiling and victory laurels strung over chairs. The guests parade about in their finery. I recognize Odessa in an ivory gown, whispering something in a nearby courtier's ear. I spot Sandria in a spectacular charcoal gown with billowing sleeves in the midst of a throng of admirers. She catches my eye as I make my way toward the front of the ballroom, and I swear there's almost something disapproving in the purse of her lips.

The Thornes sit at the high table. Scanning, I take in Queen Davina, as glamorous as usual in a velvet-trimmed gown with the Nocturn ruby at her throat; Sebastian, with Roman beside him, laughing as the Sulish prince whispers some clandestine commentary; Damien, looking bored; Finn, clean-shaven and wearing a navy tunic I've never seen before; and in the midst of them . . .

King Rodrick the Ruthless. The nightmare in the flesh.

He looks exactly as he did in the vision I was shown in the archway: like an older version of his second son. But there's nothing of what I love about Finn in his father's face; the smile lines, his tan skin, the sweet slope of his nose are all absent. Rodrick has the same sharp features, but with none of the sunshine.

As if I've drawn him to me with my thoughts, Finn stands, catching sight of me. And Gods-damn him, he is *beaming.* My emotions are distorted by the confusion of all I saw.

*What was real? What were lies?*

As always, my magic makes itself known, with swelling pressure and pain. The monster paces its cage, growing ravenous; it can smell blood in the water.

As my prince steps away from the high table and approaches, I force deep breaths and command the monster to be tame, for the moment.

*I could be wrong. I must be wrong.*

"You look incredible," Finn says.

"I need to talk to you," I murmur, drawing my lips toward his ear. "Privately."

Finn reaches for my hand. "Me too! I have so much to fill you in on. But first, there's someone you need to meet."

He starts leading me toward the high table, and I balk.

"Wait, Finn. I—"

But he just beams back at me, bending to kiss my hair. "Don't be nervous. Everything is working out perfectly for us. You'll see." The spot where his lips touched me burns.

We're hurrying toward the high table before I can register what is happening.

*Stay calm, Lyria.* Magic has turned my blood molten as my worst fears swirl through me. But much of it subsides as I gaze up at Finn. He looks the same way he did on our last night together when he held out Rashielle's ring to me: adoring, full of hope, ready to take on the world together.

King Rodrick stands as we approach. "Here she is!" he says, spreading his arms and moving toward me. "The lady of the hour!" I stiffen, prepared for an attack. But King Rodrick enfolds me in a hug. When the king's head is bent near mine, he whispers, "Well done, Lyria."

He pulls away, and I look to Finn for answers. The prince just beams.

Queen Davina taps a slender knife against her goblet. The *ding-ding-ding* draws the room to rapt attention, and the orchestra stops. "Distinguished guests, if we can please have your attention—"

"What's going on?" I ask Finn, apprehension rising.

He leans in to whisper, "I think you might have ended the war." Finn squeezes my hand again, but his smile wanes as his fingers probe mine. "Lyria, where's your ring?"

King Rodrick addresses the court. "As you're all aware, my beautiful wife and I have spent many years scouring the Midlands for a suitable bride for our second son, Finneas. It brings me *indescribable* pleasure to finally announce that we have found that match."

As the king gestures to me, applause roars through the crowd. Usually, this much attention would make me ill, but I'm overcome with relief that this whole mess is just to announce our engagement, which I never even agreed to. Embarrassing, yes, but at least nobody's losing a head.

King Rodrick continues. "We intended to forge an alliance that would strengthen the realm, a match that would serve the broader goals of our good kingdom as we look toward a united future. I hoped that my son would find someone who could help us build a better world, a *holier* one, where all men may live in peace and not fear the ravaging influence of magic. And who better to serve the interests of Verdinae than one of our own?"

The king smirks at me, and there's something of Damien behind his eyes. Something dangerous. My blood thickens and heats; the monster snarls.

"As many of you know, Lyria joined the ranks of our hospital staff in the spring. As the royal apothecary, she has made herself utterly indispensable in the fight against our enemies at home and abroad. She has gone above and beyond the call of duty in protecting these lands. Miss Dareborn, if you please . . ."

I follow the king's gaze, and I'm surprised to see Daisy entering the room. She's wearing a lovely pink ball gown and her hair is swept into a glamorous updo. In her arms, she's carrying a tray covered with a bright blue velvet cloth.

"Today marks a historic occasion for Verdinae," the king proclaims. "A day of *progress*. Because after months of tireless labor, Lyria has successfully created a cure for the vilest of all plagues on our good kingdom: magic itself."

On cue, Daisy sweeps off the velvet draping, revealing dozens of gleaming bottles of pale golden liquid. The omnidraught.

The recipe I worked on for months.

The one I *taught her to make*. She must be holding three or four batches of it.

What's happening?

King Rodrick continues, "My forefather's vision was to unite the Midlands under one banner. The Vanquisher sought a world of true equality, where none would suffer from the corruptive influence of magic. Today, I can say with assurance that no one citizen has done more to further that cause than Lyria. History will remember this as the day the war was won. And it's all thanks to our *beloved* daughter of Verdinae and my son's future bride."

My chest craters.

"With one sip of her creation—the omnidraught—those born with the affliction of a so-called Talent will no longer have to suffer. Through the dissemination of this draught, we can at last achieve justice and equality throughout the realm."

I'm praying to Rashielle to make time stop. I'm praying to wake up from this nightmare.

Everything I saw in the archway is true.

There is no plague.

There is no cure.

There is only this—King Rodrick's long-standing plan to obliterate magic forever. And I've played straight into his hands. This was always Finn's goal: to manipulate and betray me.

All my worst fears are true.

Applause smashes through the ballroom, and I finally tear my eyes away from Rodrick, forcing myself to look at Finn instead. That smile hasn't wavered. He's gazing steadily at his father, basking in his approval.

*LOOK AT ME,* I want to howl at him. *DO SOMETHING.*

But he does nothing, *says* nothing, as his father triumphantly concludes, "The era of magic in the Midlands is over. It's time for a new age to begin. With this tool in our arsenal, I have no doubt: We will win this war."

Applause fills the ballroom. When Finn squeezes my hand, I want to lurch away from him, but I am frozen by all my emotions.

King Rodrick leans in to kiss my forehead, and the cheering rises to a fever pitch. I'm falling, catapulting, plunging downward forever.

What a fool they've made of me. What a sniveling, wretched mess. Every foul way that Finn described me strikes me in succession, like so many slaps to the face.

*Insecure. Hasn't got a clue. Grotesquely starved for affection.*

King Rodrick's lips feel like acid against my skin. When he draws back, I gaze up into his eyes: this man who is more monster than human, the embodiment of everything I despise. A bully. A bigot. A dictator peddling lies. Then my eyes drift to his crown. The gold gleams beneath the chandeliers, bringing the faint metalwork into relief. The sides are etched with swirling runes. Not with ships, or dragons, or roses—the design isn't Verdish, or even Dornik.

It's Evermorean. Ivy and willow branches.

I could kill him.

The impulse sweeps through me, borne by fury. First, it's hypothetical. Then, very quickly, it becomes real. Maybe I should kill him. Right here, right now.

I remember— Oh Gods. My name day. Queen Soleste. My mother. Nausea curdles in my gut, my knees almost buckling. I'm exactly like her, aren't I?

*NO.* I refuse the thought with the same force I use to shove my Talent back into submission. My whole body starts shaking, and I don't know whether it's from disgust or fury or fear. Certainly it's fear that has glued my feet to the floor. As applause continues around me, panic clamps an iron fist on my throat.

But fear has frozen this kingdom since King Verdin, and here I am, playing my part. I am enraged at my participation in this stupid game. The dragons have been dead for hundreds of years. Why are the ashes still smoldering?

When I look over the crowd, I see cowards. Sycophants. People who draw close to the Crown to share in the spoils but don't question the laws that keep this land bound. I hate that I'm bowing to this. I hate that I'm part of this.

Something in me snaps.

I snatch Elowyn's crown off Rodrick's head.

It takes most of the room a few seconds to understand what is happening. I don't understand it myself. Something possesses me. The monster? Myself? I'm not waiting to find out. With the crown in one hand and my skirts in the other, I run, catapulting off the dais and through the crowd before any of the royal family can react.

Shouts rise behind me. I think I hear Odessa's shrill screams. I'm halfway to the door when King Rodrick bellows, "Seize her!"

Something grasps my skirts, and I feel the sudden yank and hear the rip of a huge chunk of fabric. I wheel around and lock eyes with Damien. He's snatched a bit of my dress, and his other hand is already reaching to grab me.

I react on primal instinct. My hand splays and power surges.

Damien howls as every bone in his outstretched hand shatters.

Screams erupt as the surrounding courtiers process what has transpired. I catch sight of Finn over his brother's shoulder, his face awash with undiluted horror. At any other moment, that look might be enough to break my heart.

Right now? There's nothing left to shatter.

I surge toward the doors.

A few guards try to block my path, but I clear the doors and dash to the hallway before they can catch me. My magic is hot and thick against my skin, buoyed by the zinging pleasure of release. As I run, I'm plunging into the depths of my power, drawing up cords of it as fast as I can.

I need to make it to the tree. I need to get back to Ruin. I have no plan after that. I hear soldiers behind me and try to ignore the clattering sound. My muscles ache, and my lungs scream at me as I push myself *faster,* willing myself to *fly* across the palace's marble floors toward the beckoning East Wing.

No one in the hospital knows what's happening as I blitz past. All they see is a girl in a ball gown, running like her Gods-damn life depends on it toward the east terrace. I know every twist and turn of the staging floor by heart, and I manage to shake off my pursuers as I cut down the hallway toward the storeroom, before diving through the exterior door of Cygnus's office. Then I hit the gardens, grass beneath my feet, and pick up speed with the sky over me.

I know I've almost made it when the gates of the swan garden come into view. But my stomach drops into my shoes as I rush within and find an entire squad of soldiers waiting. Roburn stands among them.

*They know about Ruin.*

*But how?*

Stopping, I find another wall of people running at me from the opposite direction; this one is fronted by Finn, with Queen Davina beside him, her skirts billowing and coiffure askew.

I'm surrounded.

*"Stay back!"* I shriek.

Finn cues the party to halt. "Wait! Just *wait*! Let me speak to her!" I can see his mind racing, trying to figure out how to spin this, how to smooth it all over.

The running stops, but the guards still creep in closer. As the closest one edges almost to a sword's length away, I scream again, "Get *away* from me! I'm warning you!"

"Lyria, please," Finn says, looking wide-eyed, devastated. "It's not what you think."

"Lyria, there's no need to panic." Queen Davina speaks up. "This is all just a big misunderstanding. Why don't we go back to the castle and talk?"

I ignore her. My gaze is locked onto Finn. "Just let me leave," I beg him. "Let me go, and I won't hurt anyone else. I don't *want* to hurt anyone. Just let me walk away."

Finn tries taking a step. "Can we just—"

He doesn't get to finish. A guard charges me. My Talent flares before I can process a single conscious thought. With no time for precision, I lash out instinctively. My intention might have been to cut off his air supply, but the magic is a riptide in this maelstrom of terror, and

I have no control, no spatial awareness, no way to stop it. The soldier's neck snaps.

He tumbles like a rag doll. Dead.

"STOP!" I shriek as others press ever closer. Tears rise, and I'm begging, "Don't make me do this, *please*!"

The guards hesitate. Nobody wants to be next.

Abruptly, the queen lunges—but not toward me. Silver flashes in the golden light, and for a moment, I can't understand what I'm seeing. Queen Davina has a knife in her hand, but it's not my throat she's poised to slit.

It's Finn's.

When the prince's eyes meet mine, they're a mirror of my shock.

Queen Davina snarls, "Surrender or he dies."

No one moves. No one dares to.

"Hand over the crown," she demands. "Surrender now, or I swear to the Almighty God, I *will* do it, Lyria."

I can't fathom what I'm seeing. She can't be serious . . . can she? The queen *looks* serious. Or perhaps closer to crazed, as she grips her son's arm with one hand like a hawk's talons holding its prey and uses the other hand to threaten him with the blade.

"He's your *son*!" I plead.

"I have other sons."

"Mother," Finn entreats, "please, you don't have to do this. Just let her go—"

Queen Davina snarls, "You *know* what she is."

As I stare into the queen's eyes, I find in them absolute resolution. Behind it swirls hatred. Zero hesitation. Zero shame. I can't understand why, but she is prepared to kill Finn rather than let me go. She would actually allow him to die.

I should allow him to die.

But I can't.

The invisible bond between us buckles but does not break. And in the same moment that I watch Finn accept his impending death, I realize it would shatter my soul.

I drop the crown.

Then I hold out my wrists in surrender.

*"No!"* Finn shouts as Queen Davina releases him. "Mother, let her go. We had an agreement! You promised!"

The guards surround me. I expect to be tied up, but as the largest man grabs my hands, another one wheels back and punches me square in the face. The force would send me crashing backward if not for the guard who grabs me from behind. The next blow hits my stomach, and I whimper, folding.

"STOP! DON'T HURT HER!" Finn is screaming at the top of his lungs, but the words are ignored. I catch a sidelong glimpse of the prince as someone yanks me up and the guards start dragging me back toward the castle. Finn fights desperately to reach me against the four or five guards trying to restrain him. "DON'T YOU DARE TOUCH HER! *LYRIA!"*

His screams fade as they lead me away.

# 31

y chamber makes an effective cell. The door bolts from the outside, and the window opens up to a sheer two-hundred-foot drop. I add this to today's long list of discoveries of my own stupidity. This was always a cell. It was naivety that made me see it as anything less.

After a full sweep to confirm there's no way out, I crawl on top of my bed and curl into the fetal position. Then I start sobbing. Once the tears come, they can't be tempered. The past few months slam into me full force: every mistake, every betrayal, every dead end on this ridiculous fool's errand. I don't know what my next move is. I don't know how I'm going to get out, or if I ever will. I've never longed for the Ironwoods more. In my heart, I travel there: I smell the cedar and clay, I hear wind rustling in the aspens, I feel the warm earth underneath me. I should never have left home.

My pity party gets interrupted by a knock at the door. I clamber to my feet and wipe the tears away fast as the door swings open.

"Are you all right?" Finn rushes toward me.

I back toward the wall as he approaches, keeping my distance. "Get out."

"Lyria, I am *so* sorry—"

"Why are you here?"

Finn stops abruptly, taking notice of my retreat. He looks confused. "So that we can figure out a plan. We've got to figure out how to defuse the situation before it's unsalvageable."

I'm actually speechless, torn between hysterical laughter and tears. "Look around you! What's left to defuse?!"

His determined expression doesn't change. "We can figure something out."

The hysterical laughter wins out. "Finn, I just *murdered* someone! The whole world knows I've got a Talent. You really think we're coming back from this?"

He shakes his head. "I'll find a way to get us out of Verdinae. We could hide in the Phantom Isles, or charter a ship and head south—"

"I DON'T WANT TO GO ANYWHERE WITH YOU!"

Finn's eyes widen at my sudden outburst, and he swallows. "Because of . . ."

*"All of it!"* I shout. "You lied to me about everything! You *used* me! You—" And then my body betrays me; shaking morphs into sobs. I abruptly turn away from him, covering my face as it flames with humiliation.

"I wanted to tell you the truth from the beginning," Finn implores. "I tried to convince my parents that it would be better to just come clean about our plans, but they were convinced you'd refuse to help us if you knew what the the omnidraught was really for."

"They were *exactly* right!"

"I'm sorry! I just thought—"

"What? You thought I wouldn't mind being manipulated? Or maybe you thought I'd be so thrilled that you chose me, I'd overlook the fact that you're a piece of shit?"

"I THOUGHT THAT WE COULD BE TOGETHER!" Finn roars. He grinds his palms against his forehead, and I wonder if he's about to start crying, too. "The omnidraught was supposed to mean that we could have it all! We could end the war, and take the throne together. We could craft a new world. We could bring the Elves out of the shadows—"

"By killing our magic?"

"By making everyone equal!"

I take a step back. "Can you even hear yourself right now?"

"You're really telling me your life wouldn't have been better if you weren't born with a Talent?" Finn challenges.

His words fall like hot rain. Of course I can't. Normalcy is my daydream. It's the fantasy I've fallen asleep to a thousand times: the world where my Talent never manifested, and we never needed to stay hidden in the Ironwoods, the world where Mother clipped my ears and raised me inwall instead.

In that world, I could have had a childhood. I could have a future. I could have him.

Marking my hesitation, Finn reaches into his tunic and withdraws a small vial of golden liquid. The sight of the omnidraught makes my stomach turn, but I'm not sure he notices my discomfort. Finn holds it out to me. "If you drink this tonight, I guarantee that everything else will be forgiven. What happened in the garden won't matter. We'll just say you were panicking, and overwhelmed. . . ."

"I *was*."

"Right. My parents would be willing to overlook it. I know they would."

"Why, because I'm the Heir of Evermore?"

Now it's Finn's turn to be floored. He snaps his mouth shut, but the expression of shock remains. "I need you to understand, it was never my intention to hurt you. All I ever wanted—"

*"Stop."* I snarl the word with so much venom I hardly recognize my own voice. "Stop talking."

His eyes widen, questioning.

"I know what you're doing," I continue. "And you think it's going to work because it has worked. Because I was naive and clueless and so fucking in love with you." My eyes burn. "You have been telling me who you are this entire time. Everyone has been telling me, and I was just the last person to believe it because for some reason, I thought there was something in you worth saving."

"Lyria—"

"NO. That is not working on me!" I shout. "I know what you really think."

He reels back, his brow furrowing. "What are you talking about?"

"What was it you called me? 'Grotesquely starved for affection'?"

Finn shakes his head furiously. "No, I would never say that! Lyria, you've got it all wrong. I—"

"I saw it! Okay? I saw it with magic! So you can keep lying to me and digging yourself a deeper hole, or you can just tell me the Gods-damn truth for once. If you're even capable of that."

His shoulders slump in surrender. And finally, finally, it all tumbles out. "The truth is . . . the plague was a hoax. We planted the rumor as a tactic to lure Elven apothecaries out of hiding. My father has been working toward achieving the omnidraught for decades. Ragglestaff was one in a line of potioneers we've employed."

"There was no fyrehound," I say slowly.

Finn shakes his head, his eyes dropping to the floor. "When Damien and my father argued about the heirship, he did storm off to go hunting. But not for a fyrehound. He was trying to find the Heir of Evermore."

"And?" I ask quietly.

Finn exhales. Then he lifts his gaze back to me. "And . . . I think I found her instead."

We appraise each other in silence for a long time.

"Why didn't you just kill me?" I ask.

He blinks. "Because I fell in love with you."

I have to look away. "And yet you still sold me out to your father."

"I—" His face crumples. "That is the single greatest regret of my life."

"What were you thinking?"

"I convinced myself it would be selfish to leave you in the Ironwoods. I told myself I had a duty to the Crown, and to my family . . . and that if we didn't intervene, the next time I'd see you would be on a battlefield. So I proposed that I could persuade you instead. But after you got here, it didn't take me long to realize what a terrible thing I'd done. And then I was at war with myself constantly. Half of me thought I should stay as far away from you as possible so that I wouldn't inflict any more damage. But the other half . . . just . . . couldn't. I wasn't strong enough. And I'm sorry for that. I will always be sorry that I was too weak to stay out of your life."

"How much of it was real?" I ask softly.

"All of it," Finn answers immediately. "All my feelings were real. They still are."

The words are an arrow straight through my heart. Poisoned by everything that might have been.

He steps toward me, as if to offer an embrace. "Lyria—"

"No." I pull back, retreating against the wall. "Don't."

I will never let him touch me again.

Finn draws a ragged breath. Whatever he plans to say next, I am positive that I don't want to hear it. The haze has lifted. It's not a hero or liberator or prince standing in front of me. It's King Rodrick's son.

And right now he looks just like his father.

"You need to leave," I say, in the same unfamiliar, venomous voice.

"Wait—"

"NOW!"

Finn doesn't move. But I'm done asking.

I surge forward and shove his chest, hard, screaming, "I said get OUT!"

Finn's never felt the full extent of my strength before, and fear flashes across his face as he crashes back into the door. I feel like a wild thing.

And he's still not leaving.

So I summon the foulest thing I can think of to push him away. The truth. And I look Finn straight in the eyes as I spit out the words: "I should have left you for dead."

His eyes are sunken with sorrow as he finally heads out the door.

I'm caged again.

I sit in the tower for a very long time, while the sun sets and the room gets much colder. The next interruption comes when I hear the guard bark from the hall, "Five minutes."

"Go away!" I say, ready for another fight if it's Finn on the other side of that door.

But it's not Finn. Instead, it's the last person I expected to see.

The princess of Ursandor steps into the chamber.

Sandria and I stare at each other for a long moment as the door swings shut behind her. "Wow," she says. "You look like *shit*."

"What are you doing here?" I ask.

"Charity work." Sandria sweeps past me, moving in to examine the windowsill. She checks it, then switches to investigating the doorframe while I rub tears furiously from my eyes. She looks like she's appraising a country inn rather than someone's cell. "You should probably start packing, by the way."

"What?" I ask.

"I said, you should start packing. Y'know? Clothes? Books? More of those kerchiefs you're so keen on?" she says. I watch in confusion as she picks up a book, frowns, and chucks it onto the bed. "You're fleeing to Ruin, yes?"

*She knows about Ruin?*

"I . . ." I make a choked noise.

Sandria drawls, "You're not the only one at court with secrets, Lyria." She leans back against a wall to evaluate me. "They say you're the Heir of Evermore. Are you aware of that?"

My stomach roils.

"As of . . . very recently, yes," I admit, feeling stupid. All at once, the ulterior motive of her invitation to Sebastian's name day is painfully obvious. Did Sandria know then? Was she testing me?

Is every so-called friend in this palace an utter fraud?

The princess cocks her head. "And . . . ?"

"And what?"

"And what do you think? Are you up for it?"

I draw a long breath. "Honestly? I don't know."

Her smile thins. "What a stirring battle cry."

Irritation rushes through me. "Well, I'm *so* sorry to disappoint you," I say sarcastically. "I haven't had much time to think about it! In case you haven't noticed, I'm in a bit of a complicated situation."

"None of this is that complicated." Sandria's eyes harden. "Don't let them delude you into thinking it is. They *want* you scared. They *want* you questioning yourself. It's the only way they win. If you play their game, they will destroy everything you love while you're twisting yourself into knots. Don't let them."

I gaze back at her, heart pounding.

"Can you do that?" she demands. "Can you trust yourself?"

The truth is all I can manage. "I can try."

She sighs. "*Gods,* you better muster more conviction than that. If we're winning this war, it's together. I can't afford for you to be scared. No one can."

I steady myself.

"Now, I need you to listen very carefully and follow my instructions," says Sandria. "I'm going to get you out of here, but all holy hell is going to break loose the second I do. You're only going to have a few minutes to get to safety, and during that time you can*not* hold back. Do you understand me?"

I nod.

She flicks her glossy hair over her shoulder. "The Verdish are prepared to kill you before letting you leave. Every fight from now until you reach Ruin will be a fight to the death. This is not the time for squeamishness and mercy. I need you to look me in the eyes and tell me that if I give you a chance to run, you're going to *use* it."

I swallow and nod. "I understand." This is not a chance I'll get again.

"Tell me that you're willing to fight," she demands.

"I'm willing to fight."

"Tell me you're willing to *kill.*"

"I—I'm willing to kill."

Though my voice shakes, I force myself to believe it. I've done it before. I can do it again. For my people, for my future, for our freedom, for *Evermore,* I will fight. And I won't hold back. This isn't a fable of heroes and villains. This is war—the wretched in-between.

Sandria searches my expression and finally nods in approval. "Good. Now get your things."

I retrieve the satchel I arrived with, then glance around the chamber for Dante, find him snoozing on the bed, and scoop him into my arms. For once, he holds still as I hug him close to my chest, breathing in the smell of his fur.

"That's it?"

I nod. "It's all I need."

"If you run, will the fox follow?"

"Yes." I hope.

Sandria looks like she wants to argue but ultimately shrugs. "Just one more thing." She rummages in her skirts and, to my astonishment, withdraws Elowyn's crown. "You're going to need this."

I blink down at it, overflowing with questions. The only one I can manage is "How?"

Sandria smirks. "I have my methods."

I gape as I take it. Stealing the crown off the king's head was an impulse, and I am not sure why Sandria went through the trouble of stealing it again for me. But as I've learned, every move she makes has a purpose. If she wants me to take it with me, then it must be important.

"I don't understand," I say. "Why are you helping me?"

She answers without hesitation. "For Ursandor." Then Sandria gives me another one of her blistering once-overs. "I hope you're all they think you are. Because if you live to make me regret this, I will kill you myself. Is that understood?"

I nod numbly. I'm about to ask her the plan when Sandria wheels around.

"Get behind me," she orders.

I step back, confused, as the princess of Ursandor sinks into a fighting stance with her hands outstretched. Her palms aim for the door.

I know that stance. Because I've used it. But I still almost can't believe what I'm seeing when flames explode from her hands.

The raw force of her magic nearly knocks me to the ground. These violet flames are hotter than any natural fire—this is wildfyre, magic flames. Is Sandria a half-Elf, an Elf with docked ears, or a Talented human?

My jaw drops.

I do not have time to fully comprehend what I've just witnessed—and how it potentially shatters everything I thought I knew about Talents—before Sandria's head snaps back toward me, and she bellows, "GO!"

I obey, leaping through the open door and past the guards, who have been knocked off their feet.

As I hightail it down the stairs, I hear Sandria screaming.

"*HELP! HEEEEELLLLP!* She attacked me, she's getting away!"

And as I sprint from the tower, with my heart swelling with affection toward the princess of Ursandor, I vow that she will not regret her faith in me.

# 32

dash as far as the central staircase before I hear oncoming steps.

As I turn into the hallway, still gripping Dante against my chest, I encounter eight VIA soldiers with swords drawn.

My vow to Sandria rings through me. This time, the monster in my chest does not hesitate.

I extend a hand, palm open, and the air fills with the sound of sixteen snapping femurs.

Groans erupt as the soldiers crumple. The impulse only took a fraction of my power. My magic surges, blazing hot, ready to meet whatever lies before me. I dash ahead, vaulting over the injured VIA.

I tear toward the hospital. I'm approaching a corner when I crash into someone also racing at top speed, and we both topple to the ground. Dante scrambles out of my arms on my way down, yelping. I stagger upright, whirling to meet the enemy, and stop dead in my tracks when I realize it's Cygnus.

He's wild-eyed and sopping wet, covered in mud. His sword is sheathed at his hip, and he's panting, like he just ran all the way back from Ruin.

"Cygnus."

I'm so shocked, that's all I can say. His name. Like it's a revelation. Like it's a prayer.

"I—I came back for you," he wheezes. "I couldn't let you face them alone."

We stare at each other, breathing hard, and it occurs to me quite abruptly that I have perhaps never seen Cygnus clearly. Not all of him.

But there's no time to make sense of those thoughts.

I grab his hand. And then we're running together.

Dante becomes a blur of copper at our ankles. Together, we clear the open doors, coming onto a balcony . . .

And find a wall of armed paramilitary waiting.

These aren't guards or VIA. They wear black tunics and gray boots, a uniform I recognize instantly.

They're agents of the Frumentari.

Cygnus takes the offensive. His sword rises to meet the nearest Frumentari's blade with an earsplitting crash. I've already gathered a cord of my power to prepare for this moment, and as the agent nearest to me swings for my right side, I dodge and shoot the magic toward her sword-bearing arm.

Her humerus snaps clean in half.

The Frumentari screams, clutching her arm. But to her credit, she doesn't drop her sword—just transfers it to the other hand. Her companion, the third agent, lunges in another attack in the same instant. Some never-before-heard animalistic noise rises out of me as I drop to dodge, seizing an ankle of each agent in either hand and then *blasting* magic with all the strength I can muster.

Flesh, bone, and sinew explode between my fingers.

Both agents fall.

I clamber to my feet, preparing to deliver another blow. The third agent doesn't rise, but the second agent is already staggering up, trying to gain ground on her remaining good foot. Her sword is too far away to reach, and she looks white-eyed, sweating, *frantic*. I'm sure I look the same. I don't know how much blood has splattered over me. I feel clumps of it drying in patches on my face and my neck.

*"Surrender!"* I scream, but she just shouts something I can't understand, her free arm swinging.

I don't see her dagger until it shoots into my thigh.

I scream. Pathetic, humiliating, and weak as it is, I shriek as I involuntarily crumple. From the placement and surge of blood, I know immediately that she struck my femoral artery. This is not a fresh-faced agent. This is a trained killer who knew exactly where she needed to strike.

A growl sounds, and there's a blur of orange fur as Dante launches himself at her.

But it's followed by a whimper as the agent knocks him aside, lunging to grab her sword. My eyes shoot to meet hers and I find them dancing with pleasure.

"You're going to die for that," I snarl.

A vow.

Her sword arcs again over me, and I try to summon my magic. But all my power is surging toward my own wound, and I swear time slows down as her blade drops toward my exposed neck. I brace for the blow . . .

That never comes.

Because Cygnus lops off her arm with a single swipe.

At last, the Frumentari falls and does not rise.

I've got my own problems, though. I'm bleeding out. My whole body shakes as Cygnus crouches beside me. He grips my upper thigh with both hands, squeezing around the dagger still embedded in my flesh.

"Pull it out," I beg.

"That will just make it worse," Cygnus murmurs, utterly calm. "You need to clamp the artery."

"I *can't*," I sob. I can't function through the pain. My magic is everywhere and nowhere. I try grasping for threads, but there's only fire—fire and agony.

Cygnus is beside me, still calm, issuing instructions—even as I can hear more guards charging up the stairs toward the balcony—but I can't find a thread to hold on to. I can't fix this.

"Lyria, I can't do this for you. You need to focus and *clamp the artery*." He takes my hand, pressing my palm against the wound. Blood blooms over my fingers; I'm in a puddle of it now. "*Now*, Lyria. Do it now. *Clamp the artery!*"

I plunge further and further into myself. Somewhere, buried in the pain, there's a monster howling, a soaring timbre that is somehow familiar. I feel pressure release. It's Cygnus's hands lifting as he's dragged off me, and I realize that the guards have arrived.

We're surrounded.

It's too late.

*NO.*

That internal voice stirs.

This time I recognize the speaker.

*My* voice. Not a beast or a daemon.

A beautiful, glittery creature. The same one who delivered Finn from the swamp, who pulled Sebastian back from death's clutches with a single thread, who restored Cygnus's sight and opened the gates to Ruin.

This is not pain or surrender. This is power, unflinching. And that voice swells like a thousand wildfyres: *LIVE, LYRIA*.

I clamp the artery. I yank out the blade.

And my Talent latches onto a thread.

When I open my eyes, I see Cygnus being held between two guards. They're holding him down as a third soldier in a VIA uniform hits him over and over. Hands close around my arms, and I cry out as I'm yanked to my feet.

*IT WILL NOT END LIKE THIS.*

"She's here!" someone shouts. "Hurry, bring it over!"

More hands restrain my shoulders. I jerk around, spine torquing, and the world wheels. The tiled roof of the palace balcony rolls overhead, and then I'm shoved to my knees by the two men who've captured me.

A gloved hand seizes my jaw, prying it open until I hear a *pop.*

"You've got it?" the guard holding my arms calls out. "*Here*, Roburn! Hurry!"

At the sound of Roburn's name, time lurches. I don't want to believe it. I *can't* believe it.

But as I blink against my fading vision, I can clearly see his approach. His face is grave, his gaze heavy. And in Roburn's hands: the omnidraught.

"NO!" Cygnus howls. There's a *crack* and another punch that cuts off his complaints. I want to scream, too, as Roburn slowly steps toward me. The bottle glints in the light from the torches that line the walls of the balcony.

Someone grabs my hair, yanking it back to force my face up. Moisture streaks down my cheeks. Blood? Tears? I'm not sure.

There's one thing I know. Something I have never seen clearly until this moment: I don't want them to take my Talent. I don't want to lose it. I can't. At long last, the truth plunges through me:

*There is nothing wrong with my magic. There is nothing wrong with me.*

*Please,* I want to beg Roburn. *Don't.* But the soldiers are gripping so tight, my jaw feels like it might snap.

"It shouldn't be done like this," Roburn says quietly.

"Our orders—"

"It's not right," Roburn argues.

"*Do it,* Captain," the soldier says forcefully. "Or I will."

I wish I could scream my agreement with Roburn. None of this is right. I'm burning with indignation, with rage and shame, clinging to my last thread of life. In this state, I might have one more strike in me. But no more. Not enough.

Roburn sighs heavily as he carefully uncaps the bottle. When his eyes lock with mine, I can only hope he can see the plea written there. The captain pauses.

Then hurls the potion into the soldier's face.

I'm showered with liquid and broken glass, but the ploy works. The soldier drops my arms, and with my hands free, I swing up, smashing my fist into his jaw.

Roburn's sword sings as he draws it, and he whirls to block the next soldier who rushes me.

I roll to avoid getting trampled, seeking Cygnus. We're making it out of this together. One of the guards drops his arms, surging to join the fight against Roburn. The monster in me doesn't hesitate. With two hands, I blast power straight at the guard, shattering both his legs. He lets out a terrible grunt, and he tumbles.

The monster purrs. Spiteful.

I lock eyes with the other guard—the one still holding Cygnus.

He drops him. Surrenders.

I grab Cygnus, yanking him toward the stairs. I spare just one backward glance, and my guts twist at the wall of guards and Frumentari streaming after us.

Roburn plants himself between us and them, his longsword rising. One man against an army.

And when he turns to watch our escape, I see everything unspoken in his eyes. Duty and honor, what's wrong and what's right, and the silent command, echoing Sandria's.

*Make this sacrifice worth it.*

I tear my eyes away, charging with Cygnus toward freedom.

My magic flings out behind me and latches onto the familiar trace of Roburn's life energy.

I'm still tracking—still hoping—when his life force winks out.

But Cygnus and I can't stop. Can't slow. Dante stays close to our feet as we push forward, limping and staggering. We stomp over rosebushes and stumble through hedges, hands locked, as the castle and its beautiful lies recede behind us . . .

Until we reach the distant lake where the Everwillow looms.

# EPILOGUE

I rise in the darkness.

There's never enough light in Ruin. That's the first thing I learned about our new home. No sun means no way of anchoring my days, so the hours blur past mindlessly. I've been sleeping late and retiring early, telling myself I'm adjusting.

But deep down, I know what—and who—I'm avoiding.

Dante scratches at the door while I'm lacing my boots. Sharing a roof has been an adjustment for everyone, but between him, Cygnus, and me, the fox is thriving the most in our new home. The one thing Ruin has plenty of is rats, and over the last couple of months, he's hunted enough to fill out his ribs. Without work to fill my days, there's time for infinite games of fetch, chin scratches, and trips to the lake, which has become our favorite place.

Word about our arrival spread quickly. Soleste knows that I'm hiding in Ruin, and she has her guards on the lookout for me in the common places. The Elven people just know that Lyria Fletcher, the former consort of Prince Finneas Thorne, is responsible for creating the omnidraught. So I'm lying low.

When Cygnus and I returned, Melia welcomed us back with open arms, at least figuratively. She put us up in this miserable shack of an apartment and connected Cygnus with the rebels. He sees her much more than I do now at meetings held in secret hideouts like this one. So far, I've declined to join them. I've declined to do much of anything.

Melia knows I'm broken. But she doesn't know how to fix it.

Not when she did so much of the breaking.

I tiptoe into the kitchen and find it empty. Not surprising. Cygnus and I have been drifting around each other like two ghosts, avoiding run-ins by keeping opposite schedules. If I hear his key in the door, I shut myself in my room. He leaves before I wake up. Peace is kept.

Mother wants me to present myself to the Mage and begin my magical training. But doing anything she wants feels like acceptance of her betrayal.

I was right about one thing: Melia *loves* Cygnus. He can do no wrong in her eyes. Maybe that's part of why I give him such a wide berth. Something about watching the two of them together, thick as thieves, makes me nauseous. And I'm more than a little irritated when she starts dropping not-so-subtle hints that I should rekindle our friendship, or at least stop pretending to be asleep when he's in the room.

It's taken a long time to work up the nerve. If I learned anything this summer, it's that postponing hard conversations makes everything hurt worse. So, after a meager breakfast, Dante and I wander together toward the lake.

I gaze out at Ruin as I walk through the streets, keeping a cloak drawn tight around me. The shape of the city is still unfamiliar. When Queen Soleste is in residence in her castle, a light is lit in the highest window to signal her presence. I've seen it flickering a few times. I can only guess what she's doing—maybe traveling around the Midlands. My instinct is to get out of Ruin as fast as I can, but Mother says I need to train first. Verdinae is openly at war with Sontaag and Ursandor. Just as the rebels hoped, the dual fronts are weakening the empire at an astonishing speed.

These kinds of reports are some of the only lengthy interactions Melia and I share. Everything else—Finn, the prophecy, my birth mother—is unmentionable.

I find Cygnus alone. He's formed a habit of walking along the water's edge each morning, so I know where to look. But it takes a while to spot him, perched on a rock as large as a house. He's got his back to Ruin, his face turned toward the void.

I climb up and sit cross-legged beside him. I shiver as we look out over the city together.

There's no good way to cut the silence, so I just blurt it out. "I'm sorry for avoiding you."

"Is that what's been happening?" Cygnus looks at me sidelong.

We share smiles. Neither reaches our eyes.

"I imagine you're wondering why," I continue.

"I have some guesses."

"Such as?"

"Well . . ." He swallows. "I imagine you're dealing with a lot of complex emotions."

"Correct." My throat tightens.

"And I imagine that anything in relation to me would be the least of those concerns."

"Not the least of them, no."

His eyes meet mine, and I'm reminded of how striking I found them on the day that we met. Like cold fire. I wonder if he's been thinking like I have, turning back through what we experienced together, trying to make sense of the moments between us that felt much more weighted than they should have. Our dance at midsummer. When he breathed life back into me at the lake. When he came back for me.

"Cygnus . . ." I start. "I just need to know something."

"Anything."

My heart is thundering. "Why didn't you tell me when you realized I was the heir?"

Cygnus is quiet for a very long moment. "I thought I was wrong. I hoped I might be. The prophecy calls for someone who's walked in two worlds. Someone with a Gods-given gift. I thought . . ." He shakes his head. "This is going to sound *so* stupid. I *know*. But I thought it might be me. At least, I wanted it to be me."

I'm not sure what I expected to hear, but this was not it. "But you don't have a Talent."

"Right." He cringes. "I said it was stupid."

"I don't understand."

Cygnus sighs, struggling to explain. "You have to realize how lost I was. When I found out about who I really am, I became *so* angry and hurt, and just lonely. I wanted all that pain to mean something. So, when Ragglestaff told me about this prophecy, and it sounded like it was describing someone half-Elven, I guess I just started to daydream.

The heir was supposed to have a Gods-given Talent, and I thought maybe they'd give me one if I did something to earn it. Like the first wielders. That's why I went looking for Ruin and even tried the gates by myself. I thought I could be a hero. I *wanted* to be."

There's so much longing and regret in his face, I almost want to reach out for him. But I keep my arms tight around me.

"And then you showed up," he continues. "That's part of why I acted the way I did. First, I resented you because of Finn. And then the more I got to know you, and started to put two and two together about your Talent, the clearer it became that it wasn't going to be me. It was you."

He pauses. It's quiet as I stare back at him, long and hard. Cygnus's features are different in the darkness. The lines are harsher, the highlights more pronounced. He looks beautiful and terrible, and I hate how the tremor in his lips makes my chest ache.

I can't look at him. So I force myself to turn back to the water and the dim reflections glittering on it like the corpses of stars.

"I wouldn't be here if it wasn't for you," I start, my voice growing thick. "Not in Ruin, and not with the living. I owe you a life debt several times over, and I won't forget that. If there's ever a moment that you desperately need me, I will be there. But before we went through the gates, you promised me the truth. About *everything*. And you lied."

"I know," he says softly, defeated.

I let my magic burn and burn, and I don't fight it.

"Every person that I have *ever* loved has betrayed me," I continue, my voice growing ragged. "And I can't let you close to me knowing you would do the same."

"I wouldn't—"

"You *did*." I take a heavy breath.

"What do you want?"

"I want you to stay away from me. We can go on sharing the apartment; we can keep up appearances. Melia doesn't have to know. I don't want our shit to affect the rebellion. If we have to work together, we can both be adults about it. But for all other intents and purposes: I don't know you. I don't *want* to know you. You can be my ally, and my partner, and my roommate, but you are *not* my friend, Cygnus. You will never be that again."

The speech comes out exactly as I've rehearsed it. Word for word. But it's a painful victory as I watch each daggered word fall and see the spark behind his eyes diminish with it. There is no room for confusion. I have made myself clear. And when Cygnus rises, I can feel it in the air: He will honor what I've asked of him. I won't receive that longing look again.

I know it's what I need. I just don't know why it's so painful.

"I understand."

That's all he says. And when Cygnus walks away, I don't watch him go.

My eyes remain glued to the darkness, and I let the sound of his retreating footsteps burn away the last embers of my childish hopes. I feel as old as the lake or the ruined city or magic itself.

I am alone. I must always be alone.

I don't shrink from that understanding. I know the purpose of my power now, and I'm not afraid. For the first time in my life, I'm not resentful, either. Nothing happens for nothing. I was born for a glorious purpose, and my inglorious burden is the price.

I know what I need to do.

The Mage resides in a lonely little house on the west side of the city. Melia has given me directions. I find it perched high above the others, the last pale block of stones before the sloping cliffs give way to darkness. It takes ages to ascend the switchbacks. I'm sweating and aching and tired to my bones by the end, but my magic blazes more fiercely than ever. Almost like it knows what comes next. The monster is coiled and trembling with anticipation, but it awaits my command.

I reach the door and knock.

When it finally creaks open, an ancient face is revealed. There's something familiar in the lattice of fine lines that forms his smile. Mischief glints in those silver eyes.

"I've waited a very long time for you, Lyria," he says.

I drop to my knees, and my Talent flares in my palms as I plead with him:

"Teach me."

# ACKNOWLEDGMENTS

Writing this book with the team at Hyperion has been nothing short of my wildest dream come true. First and foremost, thank you to my magical publishing fairy godmothers, Holly Rice and Candice Snow, who made this experience delightful. I've never seen anyone else as excited to get a work email as I've been the last six months! I grinned and giggled through every meeting, and your insight elevated this story immeasurably. Another warm thank-you belongs to the spectacular copyedit and publicity teams that worked on and championed the book.

I also couldn't have navigated this process without my amazing agent, Abigail Frank, whose wisdom, capability, and general awesomeness are highly appreciated.

It's important that I acknowledge the teachers who shaped my development, both as a writer and as a human being—Laura Hamilton, Mayela Hodgen, Cherise Bacalski, and Brooke Gregg. A heartfelt thanks goes to my mentors in the Miss Utah community, especially Amy Rasmussen, Jessica Adams, and Katrina Stephens. A special appreciation belongs to Shurooq Al Jewari, who inspires me endlessly with her intellect, drive, and compassion.

I'd never be able to list every friend who cheered me on through this journey, but I'm especially grateful for Keena, Linda, Jackie, Cami, Jena, Whitney, Austri, Olivia, Magalie, Maura, Chelsea, and Giada for your excitement about this book. A special thank-you to Julia and Courtney, without whom this story would not be the same.

Thank you to the Forst family, particularly George and Jenny, who hosted and fueled the creation of this book with Coke Zero, mashed potatoes, and endless encouragement. And of course, a special thanks to Chris, for being my anchor, my personal consultant, and Roburn's greatest advocate. I wouldn't have wanted to ride this roller coaster with anyone else!

To my big, beautiful family: Thank you for inspiring me to shoot for the stars. Reaching this lifelong dream required a massive team effort, and everything I do is to make you proud!

Finally, dear reader, I'd like to thank you. Without the support of my audience, especially online, I would never have gotten the opportunity to tell Lyria's story. I am so grateful for every person who has taken the time to watch, share, and engage with my work. I will forever be grateful.

Traveler's Map
Midlands
Dornak
Sontaag
Crown City
Rattlerik
Aster
Westgate
Farr West
Cyan Sea
Verdinae
Disputed Territory
Southgard
Belshire
Dallsport
Southern Wastes
Southern Sea